DYNASTY CODES

ORIGIN CURSE

DYNASTY CODES

ORIGIN CURSE

SARAH CAELAN

Dynasty Codes 1: Origin Curse
by Sarah Caelan

Paperback ISBN: 978-1-7644815-1-9
eBook ISBN: 978-1-7644815-3-3

First edition: March 2023
Second edition: October 2023
This edition: February 2026

A catalogue record for this book is available from the National Library of Australia

Editors: Kristy Martin, Jason Martin, and Chloe Cran
Cover Art: Florianne Briffaut
Cover Format: Donika Mishineva
Character Artwork: Florianne Briffaut
Map Artwork: Giulia Calligola. <lunarmorriganarts.com>
Typeset: Kristine Joy Magno

Author's Note

Unless mentioned otherwise, all full names in this book are written with the family name first and then the person's given name. In some cases where a person is introduced with just a single name, it is their given name.

And I write in British English. Which, yes, means I've used all the single inverted commas and littered 'u's and 's's throughout. They're delicious. Try them.

If you like global mythology and pirates and girls who can turn into dragons, this one's for you.

Come walk through The Wilds with me. Only, this series is on a much grander, global scale, so I hope you've brought good boots and your favourite snack.

To the dreamers.

That thing you wanna do?
Go do it.

After all: why not?

(Just don't hurt or kill someone. That's not nice.)

The Dynasty Codes

Magic is disappearing.

Gone are the days when mages wandered the globe and spirits crossed over from the world beyond. No longer do people deal out curses, receive wishes, or buy items imbued with magic, and the legendary creatures that inspired popular folk tales have been so rarely sighted for generations that they've slipped into myth.

Instead, the final dregs of magic linger on the cusp between worlds, noticed only by the few with connections to both the spirit world and the land of the living. There, the veil between worlds tore and the laws of this dying magic transformed when a curse placed on a noble family in the east unravelled the fragile and unspoken dynasty codes over the globe, forcing the world into a new age.

Where magic will belong in that new age depends on the actions of just a few.

ICE
NORTH
North
North West
North East
East
THE
UNKNOWN
BEYOND
East to South
East South East
South East to East

NDS
ACREIN
ECLA
TAIHEYŌ OCEAN
HIZEN
SHON WA
CENTRAL SEA
SOUTHERN OCEAN
WALL OF ICE

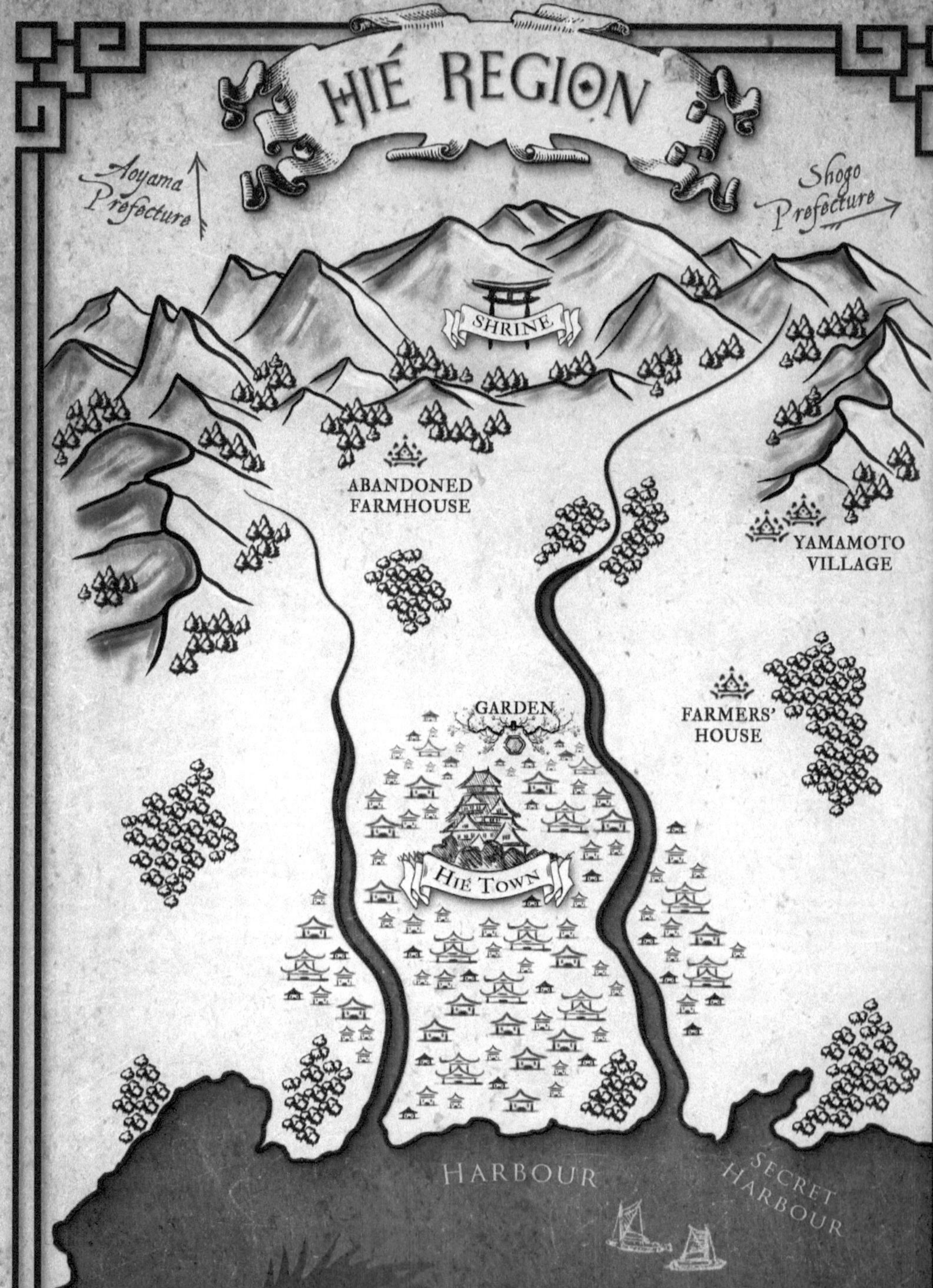
HIÉ REGION
Aoyama Prefecture
Shogo Prefecture
SHRINE
ABANDONED FARMHOUSE
YAMAMOTO VILLAGE
GARDEN
FARMERS' HOUSE
HIÉ TOWN
HARBOUR
SECRET HARBOUR

Contents

Prologue

Centuries ago—before westerners set foot in the far eastern countries, battling open seas in great wooden vessels for adventure and trade to make their fortune in uncharted lands— the far east of the map marked the edge of the world. At this edge, a small country named Hizen is left yet untouched by the expanding west.

Hizen, ruled over by the military power of warlords, was led by the shōgun and split into domains guarded like kingdoms by powerful families and their ruling household member, the *daimyō*. For centuries, these families fought to expand their territory, creating a feudal era of civil war that kept the country locked in a state of tension, creating a country with a dominant ruling class of warriors—the *samurai*—noble and strict to their code of honour, loyal to their daimyō and avowed to protect their domain. But should threat ever come from beyond the lands of Hizen, by the power of the shōgun, these warring states would unite under a single banner to protect their country, putting aside their grievances with the neighbouring domains to keep the land safe.

On the southern coast of Hizen, an ancient warring family rules a large domain called Hié, headed by a powerful matriarchal line that has gone back for generations. This family, being close to the shōgun and as trusted members of the Hizen court, was given great trust and position in the Hizen nobility, awarded a rich region with good natural defence. With the Taiheiyō Ocean to the south and east and a mountain region with rich forest to the north, the Hié region thrived, rich in crops and trade, with people living in peace in towns, villages, and on farms, crafting items of great quality and skill for livelihood and trade. And from her castle home in the centre of Hié's main town, Hié's reigning warlord, Lady Ii Asumi, defends her land and her people to keep this thriving life, working closely with the shōgun in the neighbouring region of Shogo to the north to bring an age of peace across all of Hizen.

But her family line hid a secret—a curse that would bring her family's hard-earned position and peace toppling down on itself, and with it, the destruction of the prosperous region of Hié.

1

The Castle of the Dragon Daimyō

Night shrouded the *tenshu* keep of the Hié castle compound, and Ii Yoshiko flinched as wooden floorboards creakcd under muffled footsteps in the corridors outside her sleeping quarters. Her heart thudded, and her fingers stopped tying her indigo-dyed *haori* as Yoshiko paused to listen to the quick steps shuffling towards her room. Her eyes flicked to the window. The light of dawn wasn't yet bleeding into the sky—daylight was still a way off. She frowned.

This sound didn't match the footsteps of her maid, Haruki, who padded confidently down the *tenshu's* wooden passageways, and no-one else should be coming towards her chambers at this time. The hour before dawn was for training. Yoshiko's mother, daimyō Ii Asumi, the ruling warlord of Hié, had insisted her daughter learn to fight and defend herself from a young age, and now Yoshiko was nearing adulthood, Asumi expected Yoshiko to rise for dawn training on her own, without prompting from castle staff. So Haruki wouldn't be coming here yet, nor anyone else.

Yoshiko crouched, reaching instinctively in the dark for the short *tanto* blade she kept by her futon, and watched where the moonlight faintly hit the sliding paper door to her room. She tucked her long, straight black hair behind her ear and over her shoulder, out of the way, narrowing her dark eyes and listening.

Footsteps paused outside her door. Yoshiko slipped across the tatami floor and waited beside the door, blade ready, out of view of whoever entered.

The door slid in its frame, and a young woman peered into Yoshiko's room, the moonlight hitting the woman's features and making her look like a *yōkai* spirit from folk tales. Yoshiko, her breath held, watched the intruder from the corner of her eye.

The woman bent at the waist to bow and stepped into Yoshiko's bedchambers. Concerned, Yoshiko launched across the space between them, grabbed the woman's shoulder, spun her to face her, and bared her *tanto* blade as a warning.

'Who are you?' Yoshiko growled, feeling uneasy at the intrusion of her private rooms but trying to look firm. She didn't like violence, but she knew the defence of the Hié castle and its ruling family was crucial for the safety of the domain and the people her family protected.

The young woman let out a squeak as the tip of Yoshiko's blade stopped a finger's length from her small, pale nose. She clutched the sleeve of her light indigo kimono—the colour worn by everyone employed in the Hié castle compound. A maid. Yoshiko raised her eyebrows but awaited the young woman's answer, returning her gaze to the woman's wide eyes.

'S-Suki. I'm Suki. I was employed to work as your handmaid from today.' The maid bowed her head as much as she dared with a blade in front of her face and scrunched her eyes shut.

Yoshiko paused, thinking, choosing her words carefully. 'I've not heard of this. Who sent you?'

The young woman looked at the blade helplessly, then back to the warlord's daughter. 'Councilman Chinen, my lady,' she stammered. 'He said to come for you before training.'

Seeing the fear and honesty in Suki's eyes, Yoshiko let out a sigh and lowered her *tanto*, still not ready to sheath it. Her long hair had fallen in the way again, so she tucked it behind her ear and straightened her back, watching the maid through tired, black eyes. Chinen *was* her training tutor, but this seemed wrong. 'Chinen never sends maids—especially for training. I'm expected to rise by myself.'

Yoshiko watched the maid's helpless expression deepen, searching for an answer she didn't have.

She seems innocent enough, Yoshiko wondered. *Perhaps Chinen did send her.* But she remained alert for further movement in the corridor, unable to know for sure.

Yoshiko's mother, Ii Asumi, was a renowned warrior and Hié's proud daimyō. She was a woman of adventure and success, her strong ways and skill in battle earning her admiration across the whole country of Hizen—even among the shōgun and daimyō of other regions. This wild and proud woman had married a calm man of study and the arts, adoring her consort more than anything else in their world. She'd not even been disappointed when their only child, Yoshiko, had taken more after her father, Hitoshi, in likes and nature, both preferring politics and the arts to fighting—though Yoshiko did enjoy archery, in which she could combine zen and peace with form and aim. The daimyō doted upon her peaceful family and embraced the calm of the times she could spend with them at leisure when not caught up in her busy governing life, enjoying time in the gardens or kneeling to enjoy green tea and sweets while listening to her husband and daughter chat excitedly about their learnings, art, and philosophies. Asumi still insisted Yoshiko train, and while Yoshiko had no liking for battle, she found the alertness it had given her, mixed with her unusually good hearing, useful, particularly at times like now when she had to be alert to potential intruders to keep her domain safe.

'Suki, does my mother know you've been employed recently? She's warier than me. I don't want you hurt because someone's made a mistake and we've not expected you.' Yoshiko sheathed her *tanto* and looked with concern at the young woman.

The maid's face paled further, and she stared without an answer.

'Welcome to the keep of the dragon daimyō.' Yoshiko gave a small smile, relieved Chinen hadn't sent the girl to her mother. Wondering what he was thinking, Yoshiko resolved to head to the training grounds immediately to find out more. Yoshiko rested her blade on a simple wooden table in a corner of her room, breathing slowly to relax her instincts and reassure herself. *There's no danger; it's just a mistake.*

Here, in the castle of the dragon daimyō Ii Asumi, the line of cursed warlords reigned strictly, ensuring their care for their region and fierce reputation kept Hié running smoothly and well-protected against potential attack from neighbouring regions. Yoshiko's mother had great responsibility from the shōgun to watch over this region of Hizen and look after its people, and the Ii family had ruled this region for generations, almost as long as the curse ran through their bloodline. Yoshiko didn't know too much about the curse yet—her mother said she'd tell the full story when Yoshiko came of age. All Yoshiko knew now was that something had happened in the age of magic, several generations ago, and her ancestor had been cursed with a consuming power—one that gave them advantages of strength, but at a great cost.

The curse started small, at a young age, with things like enhanced senses, increased speed, stamina, strength. This all sounded like a dream come true for Asumi, Yoshiko's mother, who was a famed warlord and made great use of these traits, but it all came with a price. One of those was hearing too much and losing sleep over any little sound. Asumi, even after decades of living like this, still suffered little sleep. Yoshiko was also starting to realise what her growing powers meant, and the pain of them, too.

Her senses had heightened like her mother had said they would, and her strength and speed had grown, too. At this early stage of development, it brought overwhelm and overstimulation among busy and noisy places as her senses adjusted, and clumsiness when dealing with her growing but awkward strength and speed. A day didn't go by when the family curse didn't cause Yoshiko some minor inconvenience, and she couldn't imagine what it would be like in later stages of development.

Even now, had Yoshiko truly been startled by the stranger entering her private room—perhaps woken by Suki—her shock and attempts to defend herself mixed with her adjustment to the growing curse could have badly hurt the girl. Yoshiko cringed at the thought.

Yoshiko turned to face Suki with a smile on her face, trying to make amends and show her true, calm nature. 'I look forward to the future of our acquaintance,' she greeted the maid politely. 'Where is my usual maid, Haruki? Is she still coming?'

Haruki had served as Yoshiko's primary handmaid for three years. A cheerful and chatty girl, in a castle with strict expectations, Haruki had been a wave of freedom Yoshiko had eagerly sought. The two girls were almost joined at the hip, Haruki telling Yoshiko of everything outside the palace, singing folk songs and telling traditional folk stories and even bringing Yoshiko simple flowers, teas, and sweets she'd found in Hié town. Yoshiko had loved and embraced every little thing Haruki had brought. Haruki hadn't just been her handmaid; she'd been her closest—and only—friend.

Suki's face went blank at Yoshiko's question, and she bowed nervously. 'I'm sorry, but I don't know that person.'

Yoshiko looked over the maid again, her brow creasing as much as her stomach knotted to hear this. Her senses raised another alarm. If the maid had been hired to work in Yoshiko's rooms, she must have met, or even been instructed by, Haruki. There was no way she wouldn't know her. Yoshiko watched Suki for any tell-tale signs there was still a threat. The young woman was the picture of innocence—a fresh, round, bright face, dressed well, her dark hair twisted smartly with a simple, decorated pin behind her head and her *obi* tied impeccably. But then, you couldn't tell just by appearance.

Deciding not to worry until she could learn more, and waiting to see if Haruki came in later in the day, Yoshiko directed Suki in helping her finish preparing for her morning training, asking Suki to help tie her *hakama*. As she finished dressing, Yoshiko thought about why Suki didn't know Haruki. Perhaps she was trained externally in a samurai family's household and gifted to the noble family? Besides, for now, Chinen would be expecting her at sunup. With Suki here, Yoshiko would have more than enough time to get there, surprise the old instructor, and find out why he'd sent Suki to collect her when he of all people knew the risks of sending unknown people into the noble family's bed chambers when they'd all be on high alert, blades beside their futon, ready for a sudden attack.

* * *

A hint of molten orange-pink highlighted the horizon and washed a warm, pale light over the castle grounds. Situated on layers of folk-made stone platforms with sheer rock faces leading to a folk-made moat for defence, the castle grounds contained many traditional dark-wood buildings with gently curving roofs and ornate gables with large, overhanging eaves for residence, political meetings, administration, defence, and storage. Along with the multitude of buildings, the grounds boasted several gardens, all towered over by the main *tenshu* keep—a white, five-storey castle with sloping green tile roofs for each layer and highly-ornate gables, large and small—that sat on the highest, inner circle of the grounds. At this time in the morning, the castle compound was still quiet, and Yoshiko, in her training *hakama* and a simple *kimono*, darted down the stone steps leading from the *tenshu* on the top platform to one of the training areas on the level below, dodging workers as she ran.

'*Sensei!*' she called out cheerfully as a familiar silhouette caught her eye across a stone-walled courtyard.

An older samurai—councilman Chinen—turned to watch Yoshiko run across the training courtyard, training *katana* in hand. A look of surprise flashed across the man's weathered face, but his expression soon cleared to beam at Yoshiko as she arrived.

'Lady Yoshiko, you're early,' he said.

Chinen was a leader of Asumi's samurai in Hié, having joined the ranks as a young man. Since then, his skills, knowledge, and easy-going nature had helped him climb the rankings, becoming a trusted military advisor of Hié. Because of that, he'd been asked by Yoshiko's grandmother, the previous daimyō, to train young Asumi—his recognised skills and energy were just what the old daimyō thought her wild daughter would need to settle down. Now, it was Yoshiko's turn for training, and she enjoyed these moments in the morning, despite the early hour. Chinen was always kind, humorous, and energetic—if a little strict—and he trained her well. If she must learn how to fight, she wanted someone she liked to teach her.

Often, Yoshiko felt people treated her differently because of her position. She didn't want that. On trips into the main town, she'd peered about her and admired the way the people joked and talked together. Upon re-entering the palace, she realised how much people guarded themselves around her. Haruki hadn't done that; the young maid easily adapted to chat with Yoshiko. Chinen had learned to do the same, and Yoshiko thought him to be relaxing further in his old age, becoming even easier to speak with.

She decided to push him. 'Yes, I was disturbed early by *someone's* clumsy new hire,' Yoshiko said, watching the man's leathery face for a reaction.

He hummed. 'There is always the opportunity for testing. It's dangerous to pick up habits.' Chinen looked at her seriously and then nodded. Yoshiko rose a brow and waited for whatever he'd say next, but Chinen moved on. 'Well, let's begin. You can watch the sunrise from your place in the dirt when I sweep the floor with you!' He sank into a strong, deep stance and gripped the hilt of his katana, face serious as he watched her, but black eyes glinting and crinkling lightly at the corners as Yoshiko saw he held back a smile.

Yoshiko scoffed and tossed her *haori* to the side, feeling the chill of the spring air prick her bare neck and lower arms. 'Have at it, old man,' were her famous last words before she parried the first hard and unrelenting hit of a tirade of incoming attacks, which set the tone for the rest of her lesson—sure enough, she wound up on the floor more often than she liked.

By the end of the training, Yoshiko had, of her own accord, flopped down into the dirt. Her muscles ached, she could barely stand, and several new blows stung her body. She stretched her legs out in front and rested back on her hands, staring at the pale morning sky. It was still cold, but it was soothing after Chinen's tough training.

'What's this? The dragon daimyō's daughter is going soft?' Chinen teased, plonking himself down beside her and crossing his legs, looking up at the sky, too.

'Wasn't I always?' Yoshiko glanced over at the older man, noticing he, too, didn't seem as energetic now as he usually would. His indigo-tunic-covered chest was heaving, and his dark brown eyes looked tired, with darkening shadows circling under his eyes.

When did he get so many wrinkles? Yoshiko wondered as she stared, then chastised herself for being rude. She looked away and back to the sky.

Chinen asked about the rest of her day, and Yoshiko casually responded about wanting to go into the gardens.

'You'll take Suki with you?' Chinen asked, a hint of worry in his voice.

'Yes, it should be fine.'

The older man seemed to relax, and Yoshiko wondered whether he'd been concerned—perhaps he'd realised his mistake in sending the unknown maid into her sleeping chambers in the morning. Either way, Yoshiko smiled at him.

'How about yourself? Mother has governance. Will you be there?'

Chinen shook his head and pulled himself to his feet, brushing down his dark *hakama*. 'I will be out of the palace so I will, unfortunately, miss the governance.'

Yoshiko nodded, understanding. And when the old samurai dismissed her from the morning's training, she grinned and grew excited for her day ahead, the pains of her morning beating washing away. She leapt up, excited, waving to the old samurai as she ran back up to the keep to have Suki help her prepare for her day of leisure in the gardens. She had an important gift to prepare, and she wanted to take as long as she could in making it perfect.

* * *

Later that morning, dressed formally in a yellow silk kimono that Suki had chosen for Yoshiko while she was training, the daimyō's daughter hopped onto the stone steps outside the castle once again and took a deep breath. When she'd trained earlier, the morning still had spring's early chill. Now, the sun's heat brought energy to the land, and it hummed with life. The recent rain brought green vitality to Hié, and as she looked down at the different levels of the castle grounds and the town beyond that, droplets of water glinted like jewels as the morning sun lit up the wet leaves of trees, the dark, sloping roof tiles of buildings, and the streams and ponds in the gardens below—her destination. She thought of her father. This was a perfect view for one of his spontaneous poems, and he loved poems about life and nature best.

Keeping to the stone path to avoid soaking her *zori*, accompanied by a quiet Suki close behind her, Yoshiko strolled down to the palace's eastern gardens on one of the lower levels of the castle compound. With small steps, limited by her kimono—and mumbling to herself about the impracticality of it as opposed to her favoured clothing of choice, the *hakama* trousers—Yoshiko negotiated the stone steps down to the next platform, past the one- and two-storey governmental buildings, towards the large gateway in the stone walls surrounding the second level compound, and down the low, wide stone steps into the lower levels and sprawling gardens below. There, Yoshiko crossed a small, red bridge that arched over a stream that fed several of the ponds around the garden. She paused at the crest of the bridge to observe a tiny terrapin pull itself past a giant, lazy, orange koi carp. Yoshiko smiled as the koi dashed away suddenly, leaving the terrapin to battle the ripples left in the koi's wake. Yoshiko watched the tiny creature a little longer before looking up and flashing a wide grin at Suki, who was equally enchanted.

'Every year,' Yoshiko started, 'I'm amazed at how tiny they start, and how they grow to be as big as, if not bigger than, the koi!'

Suki looked at Yoshiko, who could tell the woman was wondering what to say to nobility. Eventually, Suki responded with a simple, polite remark that left Yoshiko once more comparing her to Haruki and feeling rude for even thinking it. *Every person is different*, she chastised herself.

But what would Haruki have said? She'd have laughed when she saw it, large brown eyes flashing brightly, and called the koi 'rude' and crouched to watch. Yoshiko turned away as she smiled at the thought, wondering where her friend was and whether she was well. Should Yoshiko send someone to check, or send a simple flower or sweet to wish her good health? She thought of the flowers she'd come here for—Haruki had wanted to see them with her. Perhaps she should pick one and send a messenger with it.

A sound from down a garden path made Yoshiko's ears twitch, and she pulled herself from her thoughts to squint at a figure picking its way towards them. It was Chinen.

'Sensei, it's a surprise to see you again. I thought you'd be away.' She greeted him with a smile and a bow, and he returned the same.

Chinen's worn and scarred old warrior face looked kindly upon Suki beside her, and he asked to escort Yoshiko a little way through the gardens alone. When Suki bowed and dropped back, walking behind, his face became serious.

Yoshiko looked back at Suki and sighed, turning to ask her teacher whether he knew of Haruki and where she might be. She was unusually late without sending a message. Yoshiko was worried, and she frowned, looking down at her feet as she strolled beside her teacher down a small garden path.

'Your mother's head maid never arrived this morning, either,' he replied, his voice gruff, Yoshiko sensing concern.

'Does she know why?' Yoshiko asked, surprised. Asumi was strict with the goings-on inside her palace. Not long ago, they'd been living in a warring world, with generations of feuds between the different regions of the country, and Asumi had grown up knowing to protect her lands from these feudal neighbours, working hard to create alliances for a breath of peace. Even now,

Asumi walked a delicate balance of peace and war. Even those you chose as palace staff were critical to the running of the domain.

Chinen shook his head and looked up at the light spring sky. 'She seems disturbed by it. Like you, she chose those closest to her carefully. It's unusual for your mother's staff to fail to let her know they couldn't come in.'

'Where is Mother now?'

'She hasn't left her dōjō this morning.'

'Still? I thought she had governance?' Yoshiko looked up the tall folk-made stone platforms towards the keep and the grand, wooden governance hall beside it.

Chinen nodded and pursed his lips. 'It was like old times when she trained with burning eyes and a desire to prove something.' When Chinen trained Asumi, she was young and wild and felt the need to show her strength, as if to prove her place. Yoshiko heard it had given Chinen quite a hard time. 'Something is upsetting her, so she's doing what she knows—fighting until Hitoshi's calm ways console her. Your father needs to return soon. Only he is good at helping the daimyō relax and share what's on her mind; though her love for you may encourage her to calm, I wonder if she still thinks you too young to bear her concerns. And she doesn't talk to me like she used to. No, only Hitoshi can help now.'

His old face seemed weathered, and Yoshiko felt sympathy for the old man. He'd been with her family for a long time, and it was clear Chinen was worried.

'Father's not due back yet. He was staying behind in Shogo a little longer after the peace talks with the shōgun to see a visiting poet and philosopher.'

Yoshiko thought of how her father had left several days ago to attend regular political talks with the shōgun and other political leaders in the domain to the north, Shogo, as a representative for her mother. Hitoshi had been excited to learn a well-known poet and philosopher was staying in that region as a guest for a couple of months, and her father had spoken of meeting him for a while. Yoshiko had wished to go with him, to see more of the country beyond Hié, but she hadn't been allowed to accompany him this time. *Maybe next time*, she hoped each time she thought of it. She'd ask him when he returned.

Once again, Chinen shook his head, slowly this time, and closed his eyes. 'Lady Asumi received a message late last night. He returns.'

Yoshiko's heart leapt. 'Shouldn't Mother be pleased? She always gets excited when he returns.' Her face dropped when she saw her tutor's expression darken.

'The messenger arrived with two arrows in his back. He barely made it to the palace. It's a bad sign for Hitoshi's journey. The daimyō is rightly concerned. We had to persuade her not to ride out to fetch your father herself. If not for her guardian holding back her horse and warning her the archer might still be out there and trying to draw her out, she'd be long gone.' Chinen sighed, his haggard face making him look older than ever. Then he looked up at the sky and hummed deeply to himself. 'I just hope it doesn't spell war.'

Yoshiko was trying to process it all when a young samurai not too much older than herself in a dark indigo kimono and black *hakama* ran down the path to meet them, holding his *katana* close to his side. He bowed. When he stood, Yoshiko's eyes widened; surely he was too beautiful to be a samurai, she wondered. He was more elegant than powerful, with clear, creamy skin that would make any noble woman envious. She didn't remember seeing a guard like this around the compound. Hair just longer than his shoulders was pulled back into a short ponytail at the back of his head, and a full, slightly wavy fringe swept across the side of his sculpted, youthful face. He tucked it behind his ear as he addressed them.

'My lady …' It was customary for him to address her first, and his cheeks flushed as his soft brown eyes briefly met hers. He immediately tore them away to address his commander. 'Sir, Captain Daiki says the escort is ready for the journey. Awaiting you.' He bowed once more and waited for further orders.

Yoshiko spoke out before Chinen could, looking at the older man. 'You're leaving?'

At a time her mother was regressing to her wild, warrior days, her father's return was unsafe, war could be brewing, and her maid had mysteriously disappeared, Yoshiko wished her calming teacher would stay.

Chinen merely bowed and apologised. 'I must go and show my face in my holdings on the western border, show them our military still holds those parts. Your mother has agreed to it. We can't risk the Aoyama domain to the west thinking it's safe to raid—they push enough as it is. The days of civil war aren't yet behind us, as much as the shōgun tries to bring peace amongst the regions. If war is coming, the western border needs to hold.'

The young warrior stood as still as a tree during the encounter. Yoshiko glanced back at him, watching his eyes widen once more as he realised she was looking at him. He tried to look nonchalantly past her as if he were merely a part of the scenery. Yoshiko smiled at him and watched his face flush again. Old Chinen grinned too, a twinkle in his eyes.

'Ikeda, tell Daiki I'll be making my way once I finish saying my goodbyes to the lady Yoshiko. We can come back to see her again.'

Ikeda bowed and dashed off almost too thankfully.

'Did I do something wrong?' Yoshiko teased, smile widening. She was never one for stiff interactions. It made the palace lonely. Her mind flashed back to Haruki, who had always made Yoshiko feel at ease.

'He's just a young man facing the beautiful child of the powerful dragon daimyō and a renowned philosopher and artist. Some might find it awe-inspiring.'

Yoshiko fidgeted and allowed her eyes to wander to a little duck that swam past, thankful for a reason to distract herself. She didn't like being thought of that way—as someone who made people uncomfortable or nervous.

Chinen laughed at her sullenness, his eyes crinkling almost shut. Then, he turned and bowed. 'I must take my leave. My lady, I wish I could stay for Hitoshi's safe return. As it is, it's a long journey to the western border to ensure my holdings are well.'

'I understand. Safe journey.' Yoshiko didn't know what else to say. Something felt as if it had dropped heavily into her stomach, like a warning against him leaving.

The old guard bowed again and left. As she watched him stride in the direction Ikeda had darted off, she heard the shuffling of Suki approaching from behind. The maid said nothing, merely waiting at a distance she felt appropriate. Yoshiko sighed. Haruki would have bound up to her, talking about the sun, the ducks, or light gossip of something she had somehow overheard about the attractive young guard. Where was her light and energy now at the time things seemed most confusing?

War? It was almost too much to think about.

Taking a deep breath, trying to re-energise herself and ignore the things she couldn't solve for now, Yoshiko brushed her hands down her yellow kimono and thought of why she'd come down to the gardens today. She'd come to paint the blue flowers for her father. And, though he might be due to arrive soon, she would still paint them for him—it would be an excellent distraction for her now buzzing mind, which was unable to stop thinking about all that Chinen had revealed. Besides, Yoshiko was still eager to show her father the ink paintings. If there was anything she and he could talk for hours about, it was artwork. Decided, she smiled at Suki and beckoned the maid deeper into the lush green of the compound's eastern gardens, embracing the cool breeze that rustled the leaves and the soft, constant buzzing of the cicadas that fluttered amongst the trees.

2

Omens

Yoshiko shuffled deeper into the castle gardens, down winding paths and past neat bushes and ponds, reaching a bed of blue flowers and crouching to admire them closer, breathing in their light, sweet scent. They were spectacular—small, with five sky-blue petals blending to white in the centre. She remembered the year before when father had tried making them into tea, creating a light blue infusion with a sweet, delicate taste. Yoshiko chuckled and wondered whether she should try making that tea again, turning to ask what Suki thought only to see Suki staring wide-eyed in awe at the blue flowers.

'They're beautiful, aren't they?' Yoshiko poked a drop of water from an indigo petal.

'I've never seen anything like them before,' Suki admitted, her prim face softening. 'They're *blue*.'

'They're my favourites. Mother brought their seeds back from a trip to another region, wanting to plant them in the garden to surprise my father. They only flower once a year. It's one of our favourite times.'

She looked back at Suki, wondering whether she was talking too much, before continuing.

'He was meant to see them with me. We'd planned to sit with tea and a snack together, paint or write, or just watch the world go by. Blue flowers are so unusual; it feels like a fantasy.'

Suki agreed. 'I heard the lord Hitoshi is away for a political trip?'

'Yes,' Yoshiko said slowly, once again thinking about what Chinen had said a moment ago.

'Is that why you brought the paints?' Suki held out the wooden box, head tilted to one side, lips pulling slightly into a soft smile.

Yoshiko smiled. Maybe Suki would be a wonderful addition to the palace, and perhaps she and Haruki would get along. 'You're right. I wanted to paint them so he could see them.' Then, to make sure they could keep talking, she pushed Suki a little more. 'Where do you think I should sit to get the best view?'

Suki looked about, her lovely face becoming serious. She crouched further to Yoshiko's left and narrowed her eyes to focus on the view before looking round-eyed again at Yoshiko. 'How about here? You can see that tree behind them.'

Yoshiko agreed and asked Suki to help her set up her inks and cushion where Suki had suggested. She felt her father would appreciate Suki's choice. Upon hearing the news her father would be away for so long, Yoshiko had been sad she'd miss this opportunity with him, though she knew he had to attend the talks. When she'd expressed her disappointment to her mother over tea together one day, her mother had laughed pleasantly and suggested that Yoshiko paint them for him. That way, he could look at three of his favourite things at the same time—nature, paintings, and something made by his beloved daughter. Yoshiko loved the idea; it was as expected of her mother, one of the wisest people Yoshiko knew.

So here she was, kneeling on a cushion outside, idly chewing the end of her ink brush and wondering where to begin. What should she show her father about these flowers? He knew what they looked like—he'd inked and written about them many times before—so how would Yoshiko show him her representation of them instead?

A flower dipped with a pearl of water on it. A thought came to her. She wanted to show him how, even with yesterday's heavy rains, these flowers had used that energy to grow more beautiful than before. Yoshiko wondered whether her inking skills could capture the water droplets, too, and she tentatively looked back at Suki for a moment, wondering whether the young girl would get bored standing there for long. She seemed content, fiddling with the blue sleeve of her kimono again and looking around, so Yoshiko turned back and tried to focus. But, as she lifted her brush and took a meditative breath before making the first, careful stroke of indigo on light brown rice paper, a gust of wind blew up. It rushed through the flowers and knocked an inkpot over.

Suki made a strangled cry of disappointment and hurried to pick it up, calling to Yoshiko to ask if anything had spilt on her.

Yoshiko barely noticed her questions. She remained still, listening. Something she couldn't quite identify stirred on the wind—a sound she thought she should know rang at the edge of her hearing range. Her brush remained frozen in her hand, and a patch of indigo ink bled where it had dropped onto the yellow of her kimono. It went unnoticed as the sound came closer and Yoshiko's sensitive cursed hearing picked up on the noise. Hooves crashed on the main road through the town from the north-eastern road towards the castle compound, and her father's escort blared their horn to sound their arrival.

*　*　*

'Come on!' Yoshiko cried out to Suki, who fell behind and looked panicked at the idea of running, trying to make more leg room in her kimono. Even after such a short distance down the curving paths of the castle gardens, the young maid's neat hair strayed from its place, and she awkwardly shuffled in her *zori*.

Yoshiko was having the same problem. So she chose the easiest—and most ungraceful—option: kicking off her *zori* and pulling her kimono from her ankles to her knees, giving more room to run. She wished she'd worn her *hakama* after all.

Hearing the horn again, and the crash of hooves closer in the town, Yoshiko sped up and dashed out of the gardens, forgetting her poor maid who dropped behind, desperately trying to keep up with her reckless charge. People all over the compound stopped to listen, the sound of the horses crashing closer and within the hearing range of the average person. Heart beating wildly, Yoshiko grinned and darted around the corner of the same castle level towards the stables and the *karamété-mon* gate that protected the rear, northern entrance of the castle compounds.

She saw her father's banners—a simple black circle to represent the sun and a curled-up, indigo dragon (the Ii family's symbol) on white cloth—as a group of horses, samurai, and diplomats clattered over the bridge and through the *karamété-mon* entrance, slowing to a stop as castle workers and stable boys rushed to meet them. Yoshiko eagerly scanned for her father's gorgeous, black mare amongst the snorting, panting throng of horses being gently walked around the stone entryway to cool down after their journey. Her mother had given Hitoshi the mare for their union anniversary celebrations a couple of years ago, and Yoshiko would recognise the beautiful horse and its ebony shine anywhere. But the mare wasn't there. Yoshiko stalled. Now she looked closer, the group seemed too small. Her father's two guardians, who went almost everywhere with him, were missing too. She frowned and tried to think. Perhaps they'd arrived earlier, before the main group, to surprise her and her mother? He'd done that before, the energetic and light-hearted man that he was.

Thinking this was the case, Yoshiko turned on her heels and bound up the stone steps of the next two levels of castle compound platforms, up to the top level into the white, layered *tenshu* keep.

'Mother!'

Yoshiko slowed to a walk when she met her mother in the keep hallways. The dragon daimyō Asumi walked elegantly down the inner wooden stairways, but the pink flushing of her mother's face and the frown in her shapely brow told Yoshiko that Asumi was holding back. She didn't want to walk elegantly. Just like Yoshiko, Asumi would probably rather kick off her beautiful shoes and swap the tight, formal kimono for *hakama*; then, she could bound down the steps to her husband. Yoshiko's lips tugged with amusement. She knew it was what her mother wanted to do.

Asumi, though a wild child in her youth and a military power's pride now, always put on her best clothes when her husband returned from being away or if they spent any time together. Today, her mother was wearing a long-sleeved kimono her father had commissioned, and it suited her beautifully. Asumi's favourite dark indigo colour was decorated with little white and silver moon rabbits, dragons, clouds, and flowers that looked like they were blowing on the wind. It was a work of art. Enhancing the look, Asumi's long, sleek, black hair had been twisted and pinned behind her head with silver and blue hairpins.

Every inch a leader, Yoshiko thought with admiration.

The two women entered the throne room and took their seats on a tatami mat dais at the head of the large, wooden hall. Yoshiko glanced at the painted wooden frames that made up the walls and ceilings, with scenes of nature and folk tales decorating the room, before turning her gaze to the sliding paper door opposite the dais. The returning group would have to enter formally after a political visit, so to greet them, Asumi knelt on an ornate cushion, with Yoshiko kneeling on her cushion beside her to the left. Yoshiko heard a light panting and twisted to look around at Suki, frantic to make herself look presentable as she knelt in a corner at the back of the dais behind Yoshiko, there if needed. Yoshiko caught Suki's eyes and smiled apologetically for leaving the other woman behind. She'd try to make it up to her another time—it had been rude. Then, she continued to try to analyse her mother.

Her mother, who had supposedly spent all morning training her emotions out in the dōjō, was now here, looking pristine, hands resting lightly in her lap, fingers faintly brushing over the silk fabric of the edge of her long sleeves. There was something strange in Asumi's eyes Yoshiko couldn't place—a wariness—but nothing that would cause her to act like she did this morning. Yoshiko wondered if the horn announcing her father's return had reassured her mother. Asumi's hearing was as good as hers, if not better. It was that side of the family she got the enhanced abilities from, after all. Her mother must have heard the horn and realised he'd be home and safe, then rushed to get ready.

Now, people were filing into the hall, kneeling on the wooden floors to greet the daimyō's husband and returning samurai and diplomats. The edges of the room were lined with people from the council, diplomats, and castle staff. Usually, Yoshiko would be trying to take sneak-peeks at who was there, but today, she couldn't take her eyes off her mother. Asumi's breath had become sharp, and her whole body stiffened, fingers gripping the edge of her sleeves.

Something's wrong.

When the returning riders entered the room, her father wasn't one of them. Instead, samurai entered with their eyes to the floor. One stepped slowly through the throng, his hands held out in front of him with her father's katana resting in his palms. Sweat beaded down the man's sun-kissed face, his jaw was locked, and his movements were tense. Yoshiko could hear his fragile breath as if he were trying to hold it and couldn't. He ambled as if hoping never to reach the dais where the daimyō knelt, waiting to receive her husband's katana.

Just his katana? He's not here?

When the man reached the dais, he gently lay the sword in front of Yoshiko's mother and fell to his knees to bow so low his forehead touched the wooden floor. He didn't move. Not even a twitch of a finger.

'How did it happen?'

Her mother's voice cut low and controlled through the silent room. No-one dared move. No-one dared speak. No-one dared even breathe. Not even Yoshiko, whose mind had faltered. She stared at her father's sword lying before them.

The man apologised endlessly before he answered her mother. With his forehead pressed against the floor, he recounted a tale of being attacked on the mountain pass as they returned from Shogo. Enemies must have lain in waiting, he told them, for they attacked at night, like evil spirits, killing those who were awake or guarding the tents. Then, they disappeared. When the other troops awoke, the attackers had long gone, and their comrades were discovered dead. The daimyō's husband was nowhere to be found, gone from his tent, though a bloodstain made them fear the worst. Immediately, they tried to follow tracks that led away, hoping to find him. They failed.

Throughout his story, Yoshiko felt weighted down. A loud ringing noise pulsed through her ears until it became difficult to hear, and a painful, burning pressure filled her head. The world loomed in on her in a hot blackness when she forced herself to stand, almost swaying, breath caught, staring at the man on the floor. The whole room looked at her. Usually, she'd feel embarrassed and want to hide from so many eyes on her. But today, her focus was her mother, who seemed frozen, staring at her beloved husband's katana.

Time stopped as Yoshiko watched her mother, seeing only blank eyes. Life as the daimyō was a political game. One misstep here, even with the news of her dead husband, could alter the balance of the domain. There were rules. Someone could use it as a weakness and take the power for their own. Yoshiko had to get her mother somewhere she could think, but interrupting now would harm her mother's reputation and honour.

Before Yoshiko could act, hovering between the decision of kneeling again or interrupting, Asumi opened her mouth, and the hall held its breath. Silence swallowed the room. Finally, the daimyō spoke, her words calculated.

'I thank you for bearing such grave news to me. You all have suffered and lost many comrades in this tragic incident.'

Here, Asumi looked at the small returning group, all on their knees and bowing low once more on the floor. It was a much smaller group than had left for the northern region, Yoshiko noticed.

Stone-faced, the daimyō continued, choosing her words carefully. 'Please, name those we lost. We should honour them and deliver the heartbreaking news to their families.' Asumi signalled for a scribe.

Names of guards, samurai, councilmembers, and diplomats were listed. A sob came from an elderly man in the corner, whose son had been named one of the fallen. Yoshiko's heart tugged. She knew that man and his son. Her father had recommended the son join him on the talks in Shogo due to his promising political skills. Yoshiko sympathised with the man—what a tragedy that such a good opportunity for the son had resulted in his death.

As the names were listed, the silence left the room like a spell being lifted. Murmuring, gasps, sobs, cries of disbelief, and apologies, while hushed, were deafening to Yoshiko's sensitive ears. An emptiness spread through her body, and she tried to hold back the anguish that made her eyes sting with tears and her throat burn. She knew she couldn't react now. Like her mother, both had to be seen strong in front of their people at such a time. Political unrest balanced on how her mother handled this. The kidnap and murder of the daimyō's husband, a man known well around the domain and surrounding regions, was a dangerous move, even in feudal times.

Isn't this meant to be a time of peace? she thought.

Chinen's warning of the risk of war whispered into Yoshiko's mind, and the emptiness grew inside her. The feudal times had lasted hundreds of years, but in the last couple of generations, with the hard work of her mother and grandmother, there had been signs of the regions being more able to work together under the new shōgunate. At least, the regions around Hié, closest to the home of the shōgun in Shogo, had seemed civil. Was that temporary? Were the feudal times not a thing of the past?

Taking another look at Asumi's posture and lack of reaction made Yoshiko feel danger. Senses deep within her sounded alarm bells, and all remains of tears froze. Realising she was still standing, she forced herself to bow to her mother, acknowledging her mother's loss. The room bowed with her. Something stung behind her as if someone in the room was glaring at them and wishing them ill. She tried to catch her mother's eyes to communicate some sort of plan or reason to leave, but Asumi's eyes were elsewhere. They had to battle it through.

* * *

'They killed him,' Asumi whispered once they'd finally escaped the throne room and the watchful eyes of others.

They were in her mother's tearoom—just the two of them—on the ground floor of the *tenshu*, where open sliding doors looked over a small, private garden kept exclusively for the daimyō and her family. Today, the sliding doors were closed for privacy, and

Yoshiko glanced sadly at the doors, wishing for the stability and zen that looking out at that small garden gave. Instead, they knelt in silence on the tatami with cups of hot *genmaicha* on a low *kotatsu* table between them. Yoshiko looked at her mother—Asumi was inspecting something she clutched in her hands, but Yoshiko couldn't see what it was.

Some sort of paper, she thought, by the sound of it.

'They killed him,' Asumi said again, a little louder this time, turning the paper over in her hands, where Yoshiko could now see it.

'Do you really think Shogo would attack them? They've been kind to us since you were a child. The shōgun, Lord Kazuhito, is like an uncle to you. He wouldn't attack us.'

'Not Kazuhito. It was *them*. They lied.'

Yoshiko sighed, wondering who *them* was, and looked at her mother through numbed eyes, certain her mother was confused, baffled by the shock.

'But Mama …' She only called Asumi this when they were alone. She reached her hand out across the *kotatsu* to offer her hand. Asumi didn't seem to notice. Yoshiko kept it there for her anyway and sought her mother's eyes. 'He said they were attacked.'

Asumi shook her head slowly, and her narrow black eyes met Yoshiko's with a dark look unlike anything she'd seen before on her mother's face.

'He was lying.' Asumi brought her arms up to the table and put the paper down, pulling down her sleeves instinctively to cover her hands, then picking up her tea in both hands and taking a sip. Yoshiko pulled her arm back and listened. 'There are cues when people are lying. It didn't make sense only certain people were killed—those who had been either close to Hitoshi and me, or those unwaveringly loyal to Hié.'

She gestured to the paper on the table with a hand.

'I received this from Hitoshi a few days ago, by messenger. It contains a warning of some members of his party. When the messenger came last night to tell us Hitoshi was returning early, I knew he was wary. They killed him, Yoshiko. Someone on the council has betrayed us. They were the only ones who know Hitoshi's change of plans.'

Both women looked at Hitoshi's katana, lying on the tatami in his favourite seating place, where he could easily look out onto the garden when the sliding doors were opened. Asumi had placed it there when they had entered the tearoom, a symbol of his presence. Yoshiko stared at it, miserable, unable to feel or think anything.

Either way, he's gone, she mourned. *He'll never sit in that spot again.*

They sat in silence. When Asumi finally spoke again, she was calculated. She spoke quietly—so quietly only Yoshiko with her heightened hearing from the family curse could hear—and Yoshiko knew it was so no prying ears should they be outside the room would hear.

'We must pretend we don't know. It will put us in danger. We must go into mourning, as expected, and show no sign of mistrust. We must be careful and find out who on the council is our enemy, and anyone with them. Show no sign of weakness—they will grab onto that and pull until they find a reason or a way to kill us too.

'My lovely daughter, go nowhere without your most trusted guards. Go nowhere without your blades. Go nowhere without your full mind and senses ready. If anything seems out of the ordinary, you must tell me instantly. There's an enemy in the castle.'

At that moment, Yoshiko understood a little more of what peace had meant to their region and why it was so important to bring an end to the feudal era, as Asumi was helping the shōgun do. How strange it had changed so suddenly. She wondered about mentioning that morning's incident with Suki. Or Haruki going missing. Or whether those were the sorts of things her mother meant at all.

Before she could decide whether either matter counted, a small sob erupted from her mother's lips, and Asumi's shoulders slumped, shaking with tears. Yoshiko leapt up and tumbled to her mother's side, holding her close. The woman who always seemed so strong and assured, untouchable, bold, felt small and frail.

Resting her mother's head on her shoulder, Yoshiko held Asumi close as the daimyō wept silently, afraid of letting anyone else hear her cries. And, as Yoshiko's shoulder soaked with tears, the bitter weeping of her mother bringing a sting to her eyes too, Yoshiko tried to hold her tears back, trying to comfort her heartbroken mother, who had lost the gentle life partner she'd loved with all her soul.

3

When Safety Becomes the Cage

That night, in the privacy of her bedchambers and the comfort of her futon, Yoshiko had yet to sleep for mourning her father's death when she heard someone climbing the outer *tenshu* walls to her bedroom. Her heart lurched. After her father's death and her mother's warning, Yoshiko's mind leapt to the next logical thing—whoever had organised her father's death had now sent someone after her. She grabbed her *tanto* knife, ripped herself from the warm embrace of her futon, and hid in the shadows beside the window. If anyone came in, her blade would meet them.

She slowed her breath.

A soft exhale, quiet even for her sharp hearing, came from outside. Her blood tingled. Then, her eyes caught a flash of black hair whip in with the wind, and a low mutter came from whoever hid beyond.

'Did we not teach you better than to hide beside the window? It's the most obvious place to catch someone climbing through.'

'Mother?' Yoshiko watched, stunned, as Asumi appeared, crouching in the window's wooden frame. The daimyō's hair was wild and windswept, and her face was pale, making her black eyes look darker than ever. Dragon daimyō Asumi seemed unearthly and wild tonight, like the Yōkai ghost women in Hizen folk tales.

A small smile freed itself on Asumi's face when she saw the look of surprise and horror on her daughter's face. Then, she looked behind, out of the window, and gestured for Yoshiko to fall silent.

Yoshiko did.

Finally, 'Quickly, gather your most essential things. Get dressed into something practical, pack spares, your most-used weapons, and your comb.'

'Where are we going?'

'Hurry. I'll explain later.'

Yoshiko opened her mouth to ask another question but saw the dark look in her mother's narrowed eyes. She'd rarely seen her mother like this. Then Yoshiko noticed the shadows under her mother's eyes. It looked like Asumi had already spent most of the night outside.

While her mother peered outside, Yoshiko swiftly changed into a light indigo wrap tunic and mid-indigo *hakama*. She pulled on sturdy shoes and a thick *haori*, tied her hair back, and gathered her basic belongings as instructed. Finally, she tied her *katana* to her *hakama*.

'Tie it well to keep your hands free,' Asumi hissed as she crouched in the window, looking back into the room. A gust of wind whipped her hair into her face again. Asumi didn't even flinch.

Yoshiko tied her pack across her body and nodded to her mother. Asumi began climbing back down the wall. When Yoshiko reached the window and looked down, the wind picked up again. She gulped. Here on one of the top floors of the *tenshu*, it was a long way down to the platform the keep stood on, and there were few handholds.

How is she doing that?

Yoshiko stared incredulously at Asumi, who was descending with little effort. When Asumi noticed her daughter wasn't following, she looked up, an eyebrow raised.

'How am I supposed to follow you? I've not made it a habit to climb up and down the keep before!' Yoshiko hissed, leaning out of the window and looking down at her mother. The cold night wind picked up in their hair, sending shivers down Yoshiko's back.

'To your right.' Asumi indicated with her head and continued climbing.

A rope. While Yoshiko had been getting ready, Asumi must have prepared a rope for her daughter to climb down. Yet, when Yoshiko peered into the darkness below, away from the dim light of the lantern in her room, she could see Asumi wasn't using one.

Yoshiko closed her eyes and readied herself. Then, taking a deep breath, she heaved herself through the window, pulling her *hakama* out of the way so she didn't trip and plummet to the platform below. She clasped the rope and planted her feet firmly on the wall, daring to lean back. Yoshiko swallowed nervously, wondering whether the next layer down's sloped tile roof would catch her if she fell, or whether she'd slide right down it to the ground.

'Quicker,' Asumi hissed from below, jolting Yoshiko from her worries.

Yoshiko rushed to follow, trying not to think about plummeting to her death.

* * *

Yoshiko lowered herself down the keep's white wall and across the jutting, sloped green tile eaves of the layer below before hauling herself down the next layer. The Hié *tenshu* was five floors high—from the outside, with an extra floor going below the ground that you wouldn't see from looking at the building— and with her sleeping rooms on one of the top floors, she'd have to scale down multiple levels of wall and gables. Her face scrunched tight when she thought she heard one of the tiles slip in its place under the weight of the rope. Nothing fell. She dared not look down, not even at her mother, until she was well over the next layers of sloping eaves and onto hard ground, where she finally felt safe to pause. But Yoshiko had barely landed with her feet firmly on the stone before her mother grabbed her hand and pulled her away.

'What about the rope?' Yoshiko muttered to her mother as they crouched low at a corner to take stock of their surroundings.

'Leave it. It will be obvious we escaped somehow. By the time it's found, we'll be long gone. If we go back for it, they might spot us.'

'Gone where? Spotted by who?' Yoshiko still couldn't understand why they were leaving. Surely now, of all times, the people needed to see their leaders acting rationally and strong. She couldn't understand her mother's thought processes. 'Earlier, you said we'd stay. Why are we leaving?'

Her mother didn't answer her. She pulled a simple *kanzashi* hairpin from inside her jacket and used it to twist her hair up, out of the way. 'We're heading to the bridge.'

Asumi's palace, a white, five-tiered *tenshu* keep with black features and green-slated layered roofs, sat in the corner of a stone, square-shaped, folk-made platform. To create a courtyard with it, three long, single-floor white buildings with the same dark-slate roofs had joined the main building. The platform itself was a sharp stone wall of several metres. It rested on two further layered platforms that formed the main palace grounds, with steps between each platform that Yoshiko and Asumi would now have to navigate to escape. On the bottom, larger base platform were stables and beautiful gardens and walkways that Yoshiko had spent her time earlier that day to paint the flowers for her father. On that same level, a large courtyard dedicated to arrivals was guarded by an *oté-mon* gateway that led to a painted green bridge that spanned the great width of a moat that protected the castle compound and separated it from the main Hié town.

Once they'd navigated the steps to the lower platform, Asumi and Yoshiko would need to cross this moat to leave. The thing that protected them had become the trap. The bridge was well-guarded by samurai in a watchtower and had regular patrols, both monitoring those who entered and left the compound and keeping watch on the upper town for raids. Along with having to find a way to cross this bridge, only one set of steps led from the court of the top platform level they crouched in now to the second and third levels towards the lower grounds and the bridge below. If they didn't time it right, a patrol would catch them on the steps.

Asumi tugged at her daughter's *haori* sleeve and darted off, keeping low as she ran along the edge of a courtyard building towards the steps that led down to the second level. Yoshiko followed, heart in her throat. What if a maid came out to run a duty and saw them? Yoshiko felt sick. Every smallest sound rang like a warning, and her heart sounded worse. It pounded loudly, almost to the point Yoshiko thought the rest of the compound would hear it and find them. How could she escape like this? With her blood feeling like thick honey and her body sluggish. She'd trained since she was a child to be agile and should have handled something like this. But, when it came to it, she disappointed herself.

A rattling cough from around the corner made both women halt in their places. Yoshiko looked about for a place to hide, finding nothing. Her heart roared. Instead, her mother reached up, grasped the dark overhanging tiled roof, and pulled herself up without a sound. Yoshiko watched, bewildered at the ease of her mother's movements, yet followed. Her *hakama* fabric got caught underneath her knee as she pulled herself up, and she flailed sideways. Asumi caught her, a talon-like grip holding Yoshiko to the roof. Yoshiko winced at the feel of it. No wonder her mother had been able to climb up and down the walls.

A pair of guards trudged through the archway and into the courtyard. If they'd been standing there at the wrong time, Yoshiko realised, it would have all been over. She glanced at her mother's face from the corner of her eye, and though it was dark, she could see her mother's face well. It was pale, showing the same concern.

'Come,' Asumi said when the guards had long passed. She leapt from the roof, *hakama* billowing beneath her. She landed softly and tucked herself into a roll to break her fall. Then, Asumi looked back up, beckoning for her daughter to follow.

This, at least, Yoshiko felt she could do. Compared with climbing down several layers of the keep's wall, the low buildings seemed small. She checked her pack was tight on her back, held her blade handle close in her left hand, and deftly dropped to the floor below, rolling with more trouble with the pack tied around her shoulders. As she stood, Yoshiko realised how much more she liked to be calmly reading with her father in one of the garden huts, overlooking the stream and clutching in her hands a hot cup of *genmaicha*. She didn't think she had the same energy as her mother, who now seemed quite at home leaping about the compound, despite the circumstances.

Yoshiko had often heard stories of what the young Asumi had been like before meeting the poet Hitoshi. Now, Yoshiko felt she was finally able to see it for herself.

The two women peered through the gateway to make sure no-one else would march through. Almost instantly, before Yoshiko could figure out whether it was safe, Asumi ran down the steps to the second level of the castle compound where the administrative and governmental buildings were located, along with a small garden of seasonal trees. Trying to trust her mother, Yoshiko closed her eyes, took a breath, then followed, dashing through the carved stone gateway before slipping down the stone steps after Asumi.

At the bottom of the wide, shallow steps, the two women darted into the shadows of trees to the side. From the cover of the trees, they scanned the second level of the compound, watching guards on the lower levels. Usually so lively during the day, the silence at night felt eerie to Yoshiko.

'Are there more guards than usual?' Yoshiko whispered to her mother, who leaned against a tree to look past it.

Asumi looked back at her, face beautiful with the flush of their escape on her cheeks. Her lips parted as if she was going to speak, and she paused, turning to look down onto the next platform at the entrance again. 'Yes,' she muttered. 'You noticed. They will be expecting our escape.'

'Why?' Yoshiko couldn't understand it. Her father was dead, and they should be in mourning with the rest of the region. Her father had been well-loved. Yoshiko still couldn't understand why someone would want to kill him, and why people would expect them to escape their castle because of it. As far as Yoshiko knew, no-one knew she and her mother suspected anyone of killing him.

'Later,' Asumi muttered. It was a promise. 'Let's go.'

Yoshiko's breath caught in her throat when Asumi dived forward, running through a courtyard and a large stone gate before descending the last, long set of stone steps that led down to the final level, along the long edge of the garden towards the bridge. Yoshiko rushed to keep up, watching her mother's every move. As the two women ran closer to the bridge, Yoshiko wondered what her mother would do with the guards supposedly keeping them in.

Is Mother just going to barge past and fight her way through?

But Asumi didn't have her sword or spear to fight them head-on, and judging by her mother's light attire, she just had her knives. Yoshiko wasn't armed enough to deal with fully armed guards, either. She ran her hand subconsciously through her tied-back hair to ease her nerves and then raced to keep up.

4

A Historical Place

Fortunately for Yoshiko's racing heart, Asumi stopped before the bridge and hid in the shadows of the main palace gardens that Yoshiko had been in only that morning. They peered through the darkness at the bridge that separated the castle grounds from the main town of Hié. Below the bridge, the deep, folk-made moat with tall, sloping stone platform walls created a steep drop into a dark, watery abyss, and in the moat … who knew what lurked in there, though Yoshiko had heard all the rumours.

People claimed spirits and monsters lurked to feed on attackers who dared try to raid the castle. Yoshiko wondered if it was just koi, terrapins, frogs, and ducks. That's all she had ever seen there. And she doubted they'd live in the same waters as a mystical monster.

Beyond the moat was the upper region of the main town of Hié and a road to the main street. There, in the daytime, high-end food houses and market stalls lined a bustling street—only those that could afford to trade on the town's highest-costing land by the castle. This stretched for two blocks in one line, beyond which it petered into more casual stalls. Networking out beyond this and to the side were citizen homes, starting with the more high-end, and blending into commoner homes. Yoshiko had walked the first couple of streets with her parents, with Chinen, and with her guards. She'd loved it and wished she could have gone further and seen the other stalls the citizens ran and walked down through the town to the port and seen the fishing boats. She'd wanted to go beyond the town; to see the farms and rice fields, to see what her people got up to and talk to them, but she'd not been allowed. The only times she'd gone beyond the castle was to the forest in the north, where noble families met to hunt with their bows.

Life was restricted as the daimyō's daughter, and she'd not been able to venture out as she wished. Now, she'd be leaving the palace and finally stepping into the world without her guards. With the castle behind her and the town ahead, it hit the warlord's daughter that this might be the last she saw of her home, the place both she and her mother had grown up. Yoshiko looked at her mother, wondering whether she had the same nostalgia.

Her mother's face was unreadable, focused.

Mama's probably left the castle many times before, Yoshiko thought. *It's not a change for her.* She recalled the tales of her mother's warrior life before she met the young philosopher who would become her husband and Yoshiko's father.

Of course, they'd never see him again.

Tears stung Yoshiko's eyes again, soon halted at the sight of her mother creeping over the stone wall.

'Mother, what are you doing?' Yoshiko rushed forward to look, hoping her mother hadn't gone mad. *Is she expecting us to commit family suicide in the moat? This isn't the time for some tragic story ending!*

Yoshiko leant over the wall, swallowing back down her heart, to look for her mother in the ink-blackness of the moat at night. Her eyes were wide with fear, heart drumming and mouth dry, and she waited to hear for the splash of her mother's entry in the water. No splash came.

'What are *you* doing?' Asumi hissed from beside her, making Yoshiko jump as she saw Asumi clinging onto the edge of the wall like a spider. 'Come on.'

Not for the first, nor the last, time that night, Yoshiko stared in bewilderment at her mother. Asumi was digging her feet and fingers into the small dents and cracks in the stone wall, climbing along the edge of the platform that led to the moat. Climbing the moats was meant to be impossible, or anyone could invade. But then she thought of her mother's strange, inhuman abilities thanks to the curse and doubted other humans could do the same.

Once more, Yoshiko's heart threatened to seep through her body as she scrambled over the wall to follow her mother. There was barely room for grip, and one wrong move meant a plummet into the icy depths below, a potential monster, and risk of being heard and shot at with arrows by a guard defending the castle. Yoshiko's fingers burned as she gripped the small crevices with all her might, edging her way diagonally down the wall, slowly nearing the bridge. Her mother kept just on the edge of her sight, and Yoshiko felt relieved the curse meant she could see in the dark and watch how her mother was clambering along the wall so well. Asumi moved with strangely well-practised precision, and once more, Yoshiko wondered how much of a habit she had of climbing in and out of the compound. Her mother's face was as clear and determined as ever, almost peaceful, as if this were a mere walk in the gardens. But Yoshiko's muscles ached and shook, her fingers grazed and clutched the stone, and sweat trickled down her face and neck, making her itchy as it slithered over her skin.

Then her fingers met something damp and slippery, and her fear spiked. Yoshiko wasn't quick enough to grab for another hold and dropped down the steep, stone wall towards the moat. Clenching her eyes just as much as she clenched her fingers, trying to find a new grip, Yoshiko bit her lip to prevent screaming out with the pain of digging her fingers into the wall, the stone burning through her fingertips.

Terrified she'd fall in the moat and ruin their escape, Yoshiko somehow managed to open her eyes and grab at a large stone.

She missed.

A claw-like grip grabbed at her wrist, and Yoshiko's fall jolted to a stop, pulling on her shoulder painfully. When she looked up, her mother hung from the wall with one hand, catching her daughter with the other. Asumi nodded and kept a hawk-like grip on her daughter's wrist until Yoshiko had managed to secure herself on the wall once more. Yoshiko's fingers throbbed with pain, and she could feel the heat of blood. Knowing the only way to fix her injured fingers was to escape to somewhere safe, she followed her mother again, determined to ignore the terrified drumming of her heart and the pain in her fingers and shoulder as she clutched the stone walls for dear life.

Their climb grew darker in the shadow of the bridge. No moonlight shone there, and Yoshiko relied on her extended sight and senses alone. Her mother continued with no problem, hands and feet expertly finding impossible holds. Almost moving by feel, Yoshiko lightly bumped into her mother, who had stopped suddenly underneath the bridge. They weren't low yet. Yoshiko imagined it would only take a few steps upwards before hitting her head on the bridge above. So why had they stopped? Wouldn't they need to climb lower to swim across the moat and climb up the other side?

Footsteps on the stone path from the castle down to the gate and bridge tapped at the edge of Yoshiko's hearing, and both women looked at each other in the shadow of the bridge, just close enough to see one another in the darkness. Someone cleared their throat above, and more footsteps, someone in heavy armour, stomped to meet the newcomer on the path.

'*Sir?*'

Yoshiko imagined it was a guard speaking, greeting whoever had come from the castle.

'They've escaped. Don't let anyone leave the castle tonight. If you see them, don't let them through, and send someone to get me.' The voice sounded strained, anxious, but Yoshiko couldn't recognise it. Her mother frowned too, concentrating, clinging to the stone wall to listen to the conversation above.

'Who, sir?'

'The daimyō *and Lady Yoshiko,'* the strained voice said. *'They've gone.'*

A cluttering as more feet stomped above, and new voices joined in. *'What? What's happened? Are they safe?'*

Yoshiko's arms shook, and she wished the messenger would leave so her mother would move again. She wasn't certain her stinging fingers could hold on much longer. She squeezed her eyes shut.

'Just don't let them leave. Send out a hunt to find them!' The messenger sounded frustrated, and Yoshiko could hear their scuffing shoes on the stone as they turned and padded back up the stone path towards the palace, leaving the guards mumbling to one another, confused, at the main gate. Then, a loud creaking and a heavy thud as the main *oté-mon* doors shut, and a second thud as a heavy wooden beam was put in place to lock it. There'd be no-one entering or leaving that gate tonight, and the guards, grumbling in confusion to one another about keeping the daimyō in and wondering whether she was well, sent news to the barracks and the watchtowers in the castle grounds to send out a hunt to find their warlord and her daughter and bring them home to what they thought was safety. And when it finally fell quiet again above, Asumi nodded to Yoshiko and crept along the side of the wall again, leaving Yoshiko wondering whether it was much further to go before she could put her feet on safe ground again, rather than clinging on with her injured hands.

'We're here,' Asumi said mere moments later, to Yoshiko's relief, voice barely audible.

Yoshiko blinked and looked around in the darkness. *Where? We're just hanging on for our lives on the side of the wall, still under the bridge.* She could barely call that anything to be proud of. They'd have to be much further away from the palace by sunrise to call it a successful escape. Or was her mother planning to clutch here, bodies aching and straining, until things quietened down? There was never a time there were no guards at any of the castle entrances, and the gate door had been shut now, for who knew how long.

Yoshiko turned back to her mother to question her plans, but Asumi had disappeared. Again, Yoshiko's heart stopped, and she waited to hear the splash of her mother's body hitting the water. Even just the sound of scraping on the stone would give her some clue as to where her mother had gone. But she wasn't anywhere. Yoshiko searched desperately, straining her eyes in the darkness, listening out for any sound at all. In her frantic searching, her bleeding fingers nearly lost their grip on the wall. She grasped the wall harder than ever and clenched her eyes and teeth to keep herself from plummeting into the moat.

'Keep calm, Yoshi.'

That was her mother's voice. It had floated from somewhere inside the rock.

'Follow my voice. Be careful.'

Yoshiko wondered how her mother's voice had merged into the wall and whether people could absorb through stone—there were stranger things in folk tales. She clenched her eyes more and willed herself into the rock, pushing her body against it, achieving nothing.

There was a moment of awkward silence.

'No, move to where I was—a bit more to your right. Careful; the stone falls away into nothing. It's safe, but take care you don't fall.'

Embarrassed, her cheeks burning, Yoshiko found her way to a doorway in the stone. Her mother was waiting for her, out of the way. When Yoshiko was in the entranceway, her feet firmly on a stone floor, Asumi yanked her inside, edged past her, and pushed a heavy door over the mouth of the tunnel. Blackness enveloped them. Not even Yoshiko's eyes could see in this. A flame licked out of nowhere, and a stone corridor became visible. Yoshiko looked over to see a lantern in her mother's hand.

'You haven't been carrying that around with you, have you?' She couldn't remember seeing her mother carrying anything.

'See there.' Asumi indicated with her dark eyes.

Yoshiko saw lanterns resting against the side of the passageway, easy to find if you knew they were there. But how had her mother lit the lantern?

The two women looked back at the closed-off door.

'It's crafted and painted to look like stone,' Asumi explained after seeing Yoshiko's confused expression. 'Unless you know to look for it, your eyes will pass by it, expecting it just to be part of the wall.'

Yoshiko's eyebrows rose in surprise, and she looked again, leaning closer to the door to try to see the extent of the crafting skills.

Asumi turned and started walking down the passageway, deeper into the stone under the palace. Yoshiko rushed to follow before the disappearing lantern swallowed the light behind it, trying to ignore the pain of her scratched fingers.

'You can't see it from the bridge, so it doesn't matter from there. From certain angles on the other side of the moat, you can, so it had to be carefully crafted to be unnoticeable. An ancestor created it. My grandmother and mother showed it to me before I married your father, telling me to keep it secret even from him unless absolute need came to use it.' Her mother's voice trailed off, and Yoshiko noticed sadness creeping back into it.

Yoshiko saw her mother's posture change. Asumi, who usually held herself so tall and strong, looked small now. The wild look to her hair, with strands poking out from the quick updo she'd pinned, looked more 'messy' than 'war-like'. Yoshiko felt the silence that followed weigh too heavily on them, and her nerves picked up.

'So it's a secret tunnel?' she asked, hopeful yet feeling foolish at the same time. All the best stories had secret tunnels.

She heard a small chuckle slip through Asumi's lips, unable to see the warm smile she knew would flash upon her mother's face. Even so, Yoshiko was thankful for the slight ease of emotions that laughter had given. Knowing it might be safer now, Yoshiko asked if she could ask the questions she'd been burning to ask earlier.

'Yes, it's safe to talk now.' Asumi glanced around and continued, 'This tunnel runs deep under the castle grounds and the moat, into a network of other tunnels and chambers that run below the main town. I'll show you more of it and the multiple entrances we'll be using later, once we've rested. It's a safe place we can use for now. No-one will be down here, and no-one outside of the tunnels will hear us or even notice any sign we're here at all.'

Yoshiko tried to organise her questions into some logical order. She suddenly wanted to ask more about the secret passageways and why they were built, how big they were, and what they were used for, but the most important question of the evening was about her father's murder. The chill of the dark, stone tunnel shivered down her back, and she pulled the ribbon from her hair to let it fall loose around her shoulders for even a tiny bit more warmth. Even with a thick *haori*, the stone tunnel felt cold, yet her mother was walking with just a light jacket.

'Mama, why are we running? Who is after us? I know you think someone in the castle killed Papa, but wouldn't it give away that we knew if we left? Couldn't we have left normally, saying we were heading to a shrine? And wouldn't it let down the people? We should be there for them.' Yoshiko reached up to play with a strand of her hair while she asked, but stopped when the wounds on her fingertips flashed pain through her arms.

Asumi paused for a moment on a stairwell that led downwards, probably deeper than even the moat, and looked up at her daughter. The two women's eyes met, and Yoshiko saw the extent of the fear, pain, and worry in her mother's night-black eyes. Her mother's face looked haunted. The woman Yoshiko knew to be fearless, powerful, confident—the dragon daimyō—had never seemed so afraid. Then, Asumi had turned her back again and padded down the steps.

'That did trouble me,' Asumi admitted. 'But the reality of someone coming after us next was too great. We can't look after our people if we're dead.'

Yoshiko gasped and trotted down the steps a little quicker to catch up to her mother. 'Do you really think they'd have killed us too?' It didn't seem real, somehow.

'Little dragon,' Asumi sighed, calling Yoshiko by her childhood nickname. 'They killed your father—a well-loved, peaceful man— in his own camp, on a peaceful mission. Whoever it was had no fear of doing that, no fear for the skills of his guards, so it must have been someone with enough influence in the castle to have support from people equally strong and skilled to fight. Hitoshi was surrounded by powerful warriors who would—and did— die to protect him. Somehow, the enemy succeeded. Then, they thought us weak because we're women and thought they could kill us, too. In our castle, surrounded by guards and maids, we are no safer than your father surrounded by his guards. And they think we will be easy prey. I did not hesitate to think they would come after us.'

Asumi stopped again, tugging at her long sleeves and looking at the lantern before continuing with a low thought, barely a whisper.

'In fact, they already did.'

Yoshiko froze, a chill coursing through her, and she stared at the back of her mother's head, breath catching. Her mother remained still and silent for a moment, letting it sink in.

'Did you notice how quiet the palace was this evening?' Asumi asked, letting the question weigh heavily but not waiting for a response. 'How there were fewer people in the rooms and hallways before bed? I felt they were setting things up. People who are usually there weren't there. I wanted to rule and guide our people, but I knew then we had no choice, that we had to live and fight another day. I was worried I wouldn't make it back to your chambers in time. You have no idea how relieved I was I got to you first.'

Yoshiko's mouth felt dry; her voice cracked as she spoke. 'It's really that bad?'

Asumi nodded slowly and moved again, striding along a tunnel with purpose. 'You heard them on the bridge—they stopped our leaving; the council is acting. Someone with great control over the council has won them all. Our only hope to help our domain is to escape now and find out who it is and stop them.'

Yoshiko shuddered and followed, stunned, staring into the darkness beyond and wondering when it was going to lead somewhere or whether it would go on forever until they fell into the sea.

As they walked, Yoshiko thought back to her own experiences that evening, trying to figure out what she missed. Maids had tended the daimyō and Yoshiko at dinner as normal, but the silence and mourning had made more of an impact on her at the time. Then, she thought back to the corridors—where people would usually shuffle past in the hallways, there was less shuffling. Where she would usually see people going about their duties, it was as if everyone had already gone home. Then, as she'd lain in bed trying not to let anyone hear her weep, there hadn't been anyone passing her chambers on their usual evening patrols to hear her weep anyway. The palace had been silent. What she'd thought had been the hush of mourning, Asumi had spotted as something sinister.

'How did I miss that?' she whispered, chastising herself, hugging her arms around her for comfort.

'It's the unknown of danger,' Asumi said. 'You don't know it until you've lived it. It's always like this in feudal times. But I've tried to shield you from it, to make our domain safe for you and our people. I want you to be able to rule in peace when I'm gone—without the fear of other regions coming in and taking our land and our people. But now, it's come from the inside.'

Yoshiko's blood felt like it had frozen at the realisation of how much power these people had. To make the daimyō and her family feel so helpless and alone in their own keep, to make that safe place feel like an isolated cage that left them with no option but to run. For all the training they'd made sure she'd had, she'd failed to notice the signs when it was necessary. Yet her mother had noticed. Her mother was more powerful than these people believed. If it hadn't been for Asumi making that decision, Yoshiko now realised that neither of them would have woken to the next dawn.

5

A Family Heritage

They turned another dark corner in the tunnels under the palace, and a chill spiked at Yoshiko's spine. 'What is this place?' she asked, turning her attention to the dark, stone walls, feeling her curiosity get the better of her. She didn't want to talk about death or betrayal anymore.

They'd passed through a maze of tunnels and small stone chambers, like her mother had mentioned, and entered an underground cavern. It was huge—big enough to fit the town square, Yoshiko thought. When her mother first guided Yoshiko out of the tunnels, the colossal space enveloped in darkness felt overwhelming—almost threatening. Yet, as her sensitive eyes adjusted, she saw towering, curved walls slope to a high vault in the ceiling far above them. The caverns themselves were simple carved walls with stone buildings creating basic shelters for whoever would come down here, but the ceiling was something she'd never forget. Star-shaped holes dotted the stone roof in a way the light of the coming dawn was starting to seep through, taking the edge off the unrelenting darkness of being underground. Yoshiko wondered which part of Hié town was above them and whether she'd be able to see the star cut-outs in the ground if she were to stand up there.

It was incredible—like a town hidden beneath the main city, with this great cavern as a central place. Yoshiko wondered whether there had ever been a need for people to live in these underground tunnels and chambers and gather in this great hall. It looked fit for the purpose.

'Our ancestors built it in the height of the feudal era, a couple of hundred years ago. In case of attack, tunnels and entrances all over town led people down here. With the people out of the way, the samurai could fight with less worry. It's not been used since. It was their solution to looking after their folk in dark times, I guess.' Asumi shrugged as she spun around with the lantern to look about them.

'You don't agree?'

Asumi looked at her daughter with a faint smile, then led them in a slow walk around the main chamber so Yoshiko could see more. 'I think it's a waste. When you have something, you should ensure to use it.' She gestured vaguely about her and continued, 'This has sat beneath us for generations, unused and forgotten. Think of the potential it has. Yet, I was sworn by my mother to keep it secret from all except you—and even you, I was only allowed to tell on your coming-of-age day. Imagine what we could do to this place if we could make something of it.'

Yoshiko looked at her mother's daydreaming face and wondered what sorts of things she pictured when she looked at the stone walls. The two women walked in quiet company—imagining what could become of this place—until it felt their legs would crash to the floor. Neither spoke; neither needed to. And when the fatigue of staying up all night outweighed their shattered emotions and adrenaline from the escape, Asumi walked arm-in-arm with her daughter to a place she said she'd come earlier that night, a small stone hut on the edge of the cavern.

'You brought supplies?' Yoshiko looked at neatly organised futons and blankets and simple eating utensils and wondered how they got down here. 'How many trips did you take?' Her words slurred and mumbled. The simple futon itself seemed more interesting than how it got here, though Yoshiko wondered how her mother had wrestled with it climbing down the castle moat walls to reach the entrance. Her mother had said there were other entrances from all around the town. Had Asumi used one of those to bring these supplies in?

Wanting to immediately pull the futon out and collapse into it, Yoshiko looked at her stinging and bloody hands and searched for something to wash them. She didn't want to bloody the bedding.

'Three,' Asumi replied simply, crouching beside some of the supplies and digging out a *hyoutan* bottle. She gestured for Yoshiko to crouch beside her.

With the fatigue of the day catching up with her, Yoshiko lowered herself to the ground beside her mother and held out her hands, wincing as the cool water washed over the heat of her wounds. She hissed at the pain and clenched her teeth together, shaking the water from her hands before pulling at a futon and laying it out, hurrying inside it and then watching her mother for signs of tiredness.

Vision blurring and eyes struggling to remain open any longer, Yoshiko managed one more thing before she collapsed to the oblivion, wrapped like an insect in her covers and futon. 'Three? You're something else, Mama.'

* * *

Yoshiko didn't see the world above for a few days after their escape. Asumi, ever careful of her daughter's safety, asked Yoshiko to stay below until she could figure out the state of the castle above. So each day, Asumi slipped above to spy on the castle and hear some sort of news, and Yoshiko waited around in the caverns, exploring and trying to discover more. Her mother had brought news that the council had arranged a hunt for them—extending beyond the main town to the outer villages of Hié, claiming the daimyō and Yoshiko had gone missing, kidnapped by those who killed the daimyō's late husband—and told the region it was of utmost importance they were reunited at the palace. It wasn't long before the streets filled with guards, pulling over market stalls and barging into buildings to find them, showing it was more of a hunt than a rescue mission. When Yoshiko learned of this later, she realised how lifesaving Asumi's plan to hide out in the caverns had been. Had they escaped above, there would have been nowhere they could have hidden without being dragged back to the palace for whatever fate the traitors had planned for them.

And while they hid in the caverns, waiting for the search to quieten, Yoshiko continued to explore and learned a great deal from her mother. The women walked through the passageways that unfurled underground between chambers and the main caverns, of which, Yoshiko discovered, there were a few. With only their lantern flames to let them see clearly and their keen eyes to get a feel of what lay beyond the light, the idea of the spirits of those who'd been here before them made Yoshiko's skin crawl. And, with so much darkness beyond them hiding massive, empty places, it was creepy. With her mother's instructions for bravery, and remembering her father's endless curiosity and interest in how the world worked, Yoshiko found some peace. She breathed, focused on how amazing a creation it was, wondered at how and when it had been built, and talked with her mother. As they walked, her mother told her about the past, of the rulers that came before them—including those who ordered the build of these caverns—and of wars, their family history, and the gifts and unique heritage of their family line. So many things

Yoshiko was never meant to know until she came of age. Asumi told her now.

'Our heritage is rare,' Asumi began. 'It follows our matriarchal line—down the line of daimyōs. That, in itself, is not rare. What passes through each line is.'

Yoshiko met her mother's eyes, which looked as if a dark shadow was spreading beneath them. Yoshiko wondered whether her mother was sleeping well, or whether her pale skin just looked paler in this light. Both women had shrugged on thick jackets and huddled them closely as they walked. The caverns were cold, so they spent most of their time moving.

'Many generations ago, in the age the spirits walked between this world and theirs' freely, our ancestor was cursed. You've probably heard of folktales where humans were blessed or—more commonly—condemned by the spirits. Once, a heartbroken and vengeful woman was turned into a dragon, fated to hunt down the man who broke her heart, only for both to suffer. You know the story of *Kiyohimé*.

'Well, a woman in our line was cursed as such, to transform into a dragon and her descendants with her. I don't know why. That much is lost. It gave her strength and power, abilities only the dragons could have, including transformation, if strong enough. But each time she transformed, she became more and more like a dragon. Each time, her human body paid the price until, eventually, it consumed her, and when she turned into a dragon, she could no longer be human again.

'They say that's when they go crazy. Humans trapped inside the body of a dragon, they hunt down whatever is closest to what made them that way, then live until they die of some unnaturally old age or are killed.'

'But—' Yoshiko didn't understand why this was a curse or why it had anything to do with revenge. 'Aren't dragons peaceful creatures; spirits of water, blessing, and good fortune?' This didn't match what she knew of dragons, though, it was true, she'd read the folk tale of the unfortunate Kiyohimé, who had turned into a dragon and breathed fire on the man who had betrayed her. She'd never believed it, thinking it just a story. Everyone knew dragons were water and air spirits and couldn't breathe fire.

'The dragon spirits, yes. But those cursed to become one become the opposite. They became creatures of earth and fire, and they sought strength. For everything, there is an opposite. Almost as if dragon spirits are pure and natural, and the cursed dragons are imitations—blasphemous to the name of the spirits and cruel— and thus are opposites.'

Yoshiko still didn't get it. Surely it was down to the cursed person as to how they acted?

Asumi continued anyway. 'The curse travelled down our family line. A great-grandmother in our line decided the next generation should not know of the heritage until they came of age, to give them a chance of a longer lifespan. After all, if you didn't know about your powers, you wouldn't try to use them. The later in life you used them, the longer it would take for the full curse to take hold.'

At this point, Asumi pulled up her long sleeve and nodded at Yoshiko to look. Navy and silver scales dappled her mother's fair skin, and Yoshiko had to look twice to believe what she was seeing.

'Is that on your *arm*?' She couldn't believe it.

Scales?

Asumi nodded. 'They came gradually, and I've since stopped using my powers, to slow the change.'

Well, now Yoshiko knew why her mother always wore long sleeves and habitually pulled at them, trying to be sure they were pulled down low enough to hide her scales.

'Is it anywhere else?' Yoshiko wondered how Asumi would hide it if it appeared on her neck or face.

'A few places.' Asumi sounded embarrassed, as if she'd never spoken about it before. 'My back, shoulder, leg. It's worse in places closest to your core, I think. I can't remember what my mother or grandmother looked like. They both wore a lot of layers, though that wasn't abnormal in those times. Those ridiculous ten-layer kimonos nobility had to wear back then—'

'Did Father know?' Yoshiko interrupted eagerly, wondering what her peaceful, world-loving father would have thought and seeking her mother's face for a reaction, wishing to know more. With the way the scales caught the light, she thought he'd have loved it. Her wild, warrior mother only looked more so with the effects of the curse. It was like something out of a story.

Yoshiko bet her father had written about it.

Asumi blushed again. 'Of course. He was always so good about it.'

Though Yoshiko waited for her to finish, Asumi didn't say much more. Yoshiko's heart dropped a little. If her father was here, he'd have laughed and given Asumi a nudge, carrying on the story for her with grand gestures and a bright, smiling face and lively voice.

'Well, now I know how you could climb those walls!' Yoshiko teased her mother when they finally arrived back where they'd stored their belongings and took pots to make tea, trying to keep the mood light. 'Why doesn't anyone know? Surely, it's something we could use for the better and help our people, use it as a blessing, not a curse?'

Her mother chuckled. 'Just like your father.'

Yoshiko slowed pouring the water into the pot to watch how her mother lit the fire. But Asumi used stones, like everyone else. Yoshiko felt disappointed.

'People used to know. The cursed ancestor found a way to use it for good, and the power of the dragon was known through the country and celebrated. Stories say the cursed daimyō and her husband of that age governed the Hié region together before a war came from the north-west, the daimyō of that region seeking our good port location. The enemy destroyed our ancestor's husband and many others. The daimyō stood up with her powers against the enemy force, bringing Hié, and even the country, peace. The shōgun himself thanked her, and I think that's why our family is close to the shōguns even now.

'Because of that, it was changed. For a few generations, it was thought of as a blessing to protect our people. Then, someone from a distant region found out about the dragon line and came to attack, trying to convince people our family curse was a dangerous one, with warnings of the story of Kiyohimé's fall to try to turn people against our family. He brought a huge army and held our region under siege. For a long time, the ancestors held out. They began digging underground, with the daimyō of the time's dragon powers to burn quickly through the rock, to create a tunnel to go and call for help and bring supplies.

'They managed to get help and survive the siege. After the region was rebuilt, they continued digging to create these underground caverns, realising how much it had saved them in battle.

'Since then, it has been thought if one enemy had tried to come for the power, then others would. It became something kept only within the family. And, after a couple of generations, the power was forgotten. It became a myth to the people beyond those in our family—not even the people of Hié, those we use our powers to protect, remember. Now, with Hitoshi gone, only you and I know.'

They sat for a while, neither stirring, both lost in their thoughts and staring into their green tea. Then, while Yoshiko was inspecting the damage to her hands and washing them with fire-heated water to keep them clean and help them heal, her mother spoke out again.

Asumi looked at the ceiling and said there was something else she had almost forgotten. She stood, lit a lantern, and gestured for Yoshiko to follow her to the centre of the room.

'I used to sneak down here sometimes. I discovered *this*.'

Yoshiko tried to imagine her mother sneaking out of the palace and into the dark caverns alone. She shivered at the thought of this great emptiness, alone.

At the centre of the courtyard in the cavern, directly below the star-cut-out dome, was a large pulley. Asumi tugged failingly at it with one hand before passing Yoshiko the lantern so she could use both. Yoshiko watched with her head cocked to one side, holding the lantern out for her mother to see.

'What does that do?'

'You'll see in a moment,' Asumi grunted as she pulled hard, leveraging her body weight against a lever that hadn't been touched for what must have been decades.

'Good job you're a dragon,' Yoshiko said, a smile flashing across her face.

Asumi looked almost shocked until she saw the grin on Yoshiko's face grow bigger. Then her lips curled upwards for just a moment, and a glint flashed across her mother's eyes.

'Indeed!'

The lever finally gave way, and the pair heard several loud, dull clunking noises echoing through the cavern. Yoshiko felt her ears twitch at the sounds of rocks moving and more levers shifting. She couldn't even identify which direction all the sounds came from. She looked to her mother, panicked.

'What's going on?' It sounded like a cave-in. Had her mother gone mad, after all? Was she trying to bury them under a town of rock?

Then, the crunching and grinding came to a halt, and Asumi gestured upwards. When Yoshiko looked up, she saw the sparks of daylight peeking through the cutaways in the roof and trails of light bouncing around the room. It looked like stars were falling from the night sky. When she followed the streams of light down the stone dome roof, Yoshiko saw the small streams of light hit panels that had moved out from the walls and bounce in other directions. The cavern lit up with bigger streams of daylight. The small, stone huts became visible in the inky darkness, and soon the cavern was washed in breathtaking, soft light.

'I call them "star streams"'. Asumi explained, still looking at the light above. 'Silver mirrors are placed around the cavern. The light from the cut-outs in the roof hits the mirrors and is bounced in a different direction. It creates light where there is none. Only the larger courtyards have this. It was meant to create gathering places for people to interact and get a moment of light when they hid from a siege. A place they could bathe in the light from above, rather than live the unknown length of war in darkness with only fire to see by.'

Yoshiko's heart lurched—she'd never seen or heard of anything so magical. True to the name, they looked like streams of stars. Ribbons of light hung everywhere and showed her buildings she never expected to see in the caverns—little stone and wooden huts and outbuildings. When she glanced at a hut close by, she realised it even mimicked design elements they'd normally use in Hié buildings above. Even for places to hide from war, it had to feel like Hié.

'So clever,' was all she could manage, stunned.

'I'm sure this idea could be built upon more.' Asumi followed Yoshiko's gaze around the room and smiled. Her eyes then returned to the mechanisms poking out from the walls. What she said next came out as if she were in a distant dream, lost in thought. 'I've heard they don't get enough light in some countries, from those I've met while on my travels overseas, and the people are sad and unhealthy in the dark months. Maybe this would help.'

Yoshiko stared at her mother. She knew Asumi was bright—she'd seen her in the governing halls, after all, solving problems of the country and the local alliances. But how did Asumi know what it was like in other countries? All the neighbouring regions had similar weather patterns, roughly, as Hié—with rain and sun in a fair, equal measure that made the fields thrive and the rivers glisten. But other countries beyond their neighbours? Did that mean her mother had crossed the ocean? Watching her mother smiling up at the star streams, Yoshiko realised she didn't know much about Asumi or the true history of her family and Hié, after all.

6

Training a Dragon

After that first time, they opened the star streams every day. Yoshiko gazed at the ribbons of light that bounced about the caverns, wondering where the specks of dust that floated in them came from and why nobody above realised there was anything down here if the star cut-outs were visible in the ground up there.

For the first few days, they waited for the hunt to calm down, occupying themselves with Asumi showing Yoshiko the cold, dark caverns and explaining more of their family history. One afternoon, Asumi slipped out of one of the cavern entrances to learn about the hunt and returned with news that the next time she went up, she'd take Yoshiko into Hié town with her to join her in finding out what had happened in the castle. Yoshiko had hardly believed it.

'I can go to town?' She had grabbed her mother's arm in excitement.

Asumi looked amused. 'It won't be a friendly trip to look around, like the last time you went.'

Yoshiko thought back to the last time she'd been in town, escorted by her guards and tutor and limited in where she could go. Rarely was she allowed into the town, and she often daydreamed about being able to walk about and see people's daily lives. That's why she'd adored Haruki so much. She brought exciting tales of ordinary life, described the town in beautiful colours, brought songs and stories from the townsfolk and hand-made treats from small local stores. Yoshiko had always wanted to join Haruki and walk together in the streets, chatting and laughing and exploring. But she'd never been able to, and now she wondered whether Haruki was well and whether she'd see her again at all. Was she back in the castle, wondering where Yoshiko was?

'What will we do?' Yoshiko figured any opportunity to go into town would be enough. Perhaps she could persuade her mother to let her meet Haruki.

Asumi looked her daughter over and raised an eyebrow. Yoshiko felt scrutinised. 'You'll see. You performed well in your training at the palace, but your practical skills were lacking when we escaped. If we're to be sneaking around the town and finding out what's gone on at the castle, you'll need to improve.'

Yoshiko was about to interject with a reminder she'd never expected to have snuck out of her own home but knew it would be pointless to say to the warrior power that was the dragon daimyō. She shut her mouth immediately. Her mother was incredibly strict in anything related to training.

'You need to be able to remain unseen, even to a ninja, and move even beyond their skills,' Asumi continued.

Yoshiko's mouth dropped open. The ninja were notorious figures of the night—a covert group of highly-trained, stealthy fighters that was said to have unique heritages of hidden powers. There was no way she could beat them for skill and stealth. If her father was here, she'd have turned to plead him to reason with her mother—that there was no way she could or wanted to become like a ninja. He'd have chuckled and encouraged her instead, which was all she needed, really—friendly encouragement—but he wasn't there and wouldn't be ever again. She sighed, feeling dejected at the impossible wall put in front of her.

'You have the curse of our family—a dragon's enhancements will help you,' said Asumi, as if able to read the thoughts from Yoshiko's face. 'You just need to know how to use it to your advantage. From now on, I'll teach you what you would have learned when you came of age. Be prepared—misuse it, or use it too often, and the curse will show its true nature.'

'Can I learn to fly?'

Asumi chuckled. 'I'm not sure about that one. It's a lovely dream. I've heard tales of people in our family who could transform, though their curse escalated so quickly they suffered for it …' Asumi fidgeted with her sleeve. 'Worth the risk, I wonder.' Her mother snapped back to attention. 'Come, I will train you myself. It seems Chinen got too soft in his older age.'

Whether Chinen *had* gone soft in his older age, Yoshiko would never know. But that day, Asumi trained Yoshiko harder than she'd ever trained before, pushing Yoshiko beyond her limits to combine her senses with physical movements. It wasn't that it was too physically demanding, though it was, but that her mother was making her use what she'd never used before—forcing her muscles to work harder and more efficiently and her ears to strain to pick up sounds like the soft shift of fabric pulling and suggesting someone was raising their arm to attack from behind her.

'Your ears can open up a new world of sight beyond what you know. You can't see behind you, but you *can* hear behind you. Use that to open up your vision from all angles.' Asumi crept up from behind her and pushed her foot into the back of Yoshiko's knees, twisting Yoshiko off balance and dealing the final blow by tugging on the back collar of Yoshiko's kimono, pulling her crashing to the ground with a gasp as the air was pushed from her lungs.

Yoshiko swept herself up, careful not to tread on her *hakama*, and coughed, raising her guard again and watching her mother carefully. Her mother's beautiful face was still, expressionless, but

Yoshiko could see a stern fire in her dark eyes as she stood tall, watching her daughter for a reaction.

Well, Yoshiko thought, knowing her mother expected diligence. *She won't get one.*

Instead, she waited, and a small smile pulled on the corners of her mother's lips. The two women watched each other, and Yoshiko calmed her breath, wondering what her mother would do next. The instant Yoshiko blinked, her mother was gone.

How—

Yoshiko didn't get to finish her thought. Her feet were swept from beneath her and her upper body pulled backwards, bringing her crashing to the ground again. This time, Yoshiko threw out her arms to each side to break her fall by hitting the stone with her forearms and bringing her chin to her chest so the impact on her back was lessened and she didn't crack her head. The second her forearms hit the floor, she saw her mother standing over her and decided to roll to the side, sweep herself up onto one knee, and bring her arms back up to guard her face—a wise decision when her mother's instep met her guard in the place Yoshiko's face had been.

Yoshiko glared from behind her guard as she pulled herself the rest of the way up. 'Mother, are you *trying* to kill me?'

'And I'll succeed if you don't use your ears as I told you. Listen to what's going on around you. Then, you won't find yourself caught out on the floor, trying to keep up.'

Yoshiko slowly breathed out and watched her mother carefully, this time refusing to let her out of her sight. But, once again, her mother was too fast, and the pattern of being caught out and winding up on the floor continued, but each time, Yoshiko got used to listening out for the sounds around her. She started hearing the pull of fabric to her side, the sound of a light step on stone, and the quiet intake of breath as her mother prepared for an attack, but it didn't mean she could predict what attack was coming. All she could do at this stage was figure out where it was coming from and try to meet it, using this new-found advantage to try to move and block whatever she then saw coming her way.

She still ended up on the floor, she still ended up winded or wincing from the pain of a missed strike, but at least each time she was getting closer, and she even earned a small smile from Asumi one time she did manage to block and the reassurance that, with time, she'd get there.

But the warm feeling from that reassurance didn't last long when her mother pulled her into the next round of training to work on her next skill, with only a small tea break to rest. The moment the last drop of tea slid down Yoshiko's throat, Asumi hoisted her up from where Yoshiko knelt and guided her to a dark cavern with no star streams for light.

'What are we doing here?' Yoshiko asked, impatient. She wasn't fond of the dark. With no light from the moon or a flame lamp to give even a hint of warm glow, this cavern's darkness weighed on her and suffocated her. She turned to where she thought her mother was standing but couldn't feel her presence. Yoshiko panicked. 'Mother?'

A soft sound of fabric brushing to her other side made her jump, and Yoshiko remembered her mother's lesson from a moment ago— to use the gift of heightened hearing from the curse to give herself an extra sight. But here, in the dark, that only made her fear rise.

Is she going to continue the lesson here? Anxiety fired through her body in anticipation of an attack coming out of nowhere in the dark. Would she have to hear and defend her mother's attacks here to prove her point? Yoshiko rose her arms in an anxious guard.

'You're not ready for that yet.' Asumi's voice came out of the darkness, and Yoshiko found herself once again wondering how her mother could read her mind. 'Here, you're going to overcome your fear of the dark and learn to extend your sight to see better.'

Yoshiko blinked, wondering how her mother knew of her fear of the dark. She'd thought she'd tried to hide it and had insisted her father—the only one beside Haruki who knew—not tell her mother.

Her mother continued. 'You did well on our escape of the palace, using your gifted sight to follow me, especially on the wall. But now, you'll learn to see even in true darkness. See that path?'

Yoshiko heard her mother's arm rise by the light sound of the fabric of her kimono dropping, but she couldn't see the path. She shook her head.

'Oh,' was all her mother said, and Yoshiko's heart dropped at the disappointed syllable. 'Well, you're going to run along it. You're to get quicker at moving, and running in the dark tunnels and caverns will develop your speed, agility, and vision all at once. By the time you spot a wall, you'll have to dodge it. Do it until you can see the walls and easily run through the tunnels.'

Yoshiko tried to protest, but Asumi cut her off. And when Yoshiko asked what she'd do if she got lost and couldn't find her way back to the cavern they were staying in, she heard her mother chuckle. 'Perfect time to explore and get used to this place, then.' Yoshiko heard her mother turn, shoes tapping against the stone. Then, a comment was tossed over her mother's shoulders: 'You'll need to learn how to navigate this place alone. I won't always be with you, and I need you to run errands alone. Run through these tunnels, get faster, more agile, and work on your vision. Meet me back in the main cavern.' Her mother's soft footsteps faded.

'But I can't see a single thing,' she muttered.

Tempted to follow Asumi to find her way out, Yoshiko remained where she stood, until a small voice in her head pushed her on, determined to show her mother she could do it. If she could do this, she could be of help to her mother; they could find their way back home and leave this place and the dark forever.

So she pushed on blindly, forcing one foot in front of the other into the deep dark of the tunnel, starting with her hands brushing the wall to guide her as she walked slowly, then getting frustrated with herself and forcing herself into a run. Each time she failed to see a wall and crashed into it, she winced and growled at herself, imagining a look of disappointment on her mother's pale, beautiful face. So each time, she tried again, trying to run faster, looking out for a looming shape of a wall in the darkness, straining her eyes and instead stumbling over a crack in the floor and hitting the ground hard. Yoshiko tried to block out the sound of even the blood pumping through her ears as she panicked at not knowing which way was up, trying to calm her breathing, reassuring herself that if she could start to see better in the dark, she wouldn't be as afraid. So she pushed on, forcing herself to run faster, dodge faster, and ignore the pain as her body scraped against the walls or when she tripped and fell. And by the end of it, she wasn't sure which session had bashed and bruised her more—being attacked and thrown to the ground by her mother, or her own clumsiness from running in the dark. But eventually, after running for what felt like hours, with her panic rising again when she thought she'd be lost in these tunnels forever until she died of injury, starvation, or thirst, Yoshiko saw a faint light glowing ahead and grinned with relief, pushing her exhausted legs on until she collapsed, gasping for breath, onto the cavern floor at her mother's feet. Yoshiko gazed up at the star streams with reverence, noticing how, after being in those dark tunnels for so long without a flame to guide her, they looked brighter than ever.

'Well done,' Asumi said simply, crouching down beside her daughter and resting a gentle hand on Yoshiko's head. 'I wondered whether you'd need me to come find you.'

Yoshiko looked into her mother's face, wondering what emotion she'd find there, worrying it would be disappointment at not being able to meet her expectations or to even make her mother entertain the thought of coming to find her. But instead, she saw warmth, and a faint, proud smile lit up her mother's face and crinkled the corners of her eyes. Yoshiko smiled too, and the pain from all the times she crashed into things didn't feel quite so bad anymore as the feeling of receiving praise from the woman she looked up to and felt she'd never be able to reach eclipsed all else. She let herself slump to the floor on her back, arms thrown out, feeling the cold stone soothe her aching, overheated body through her sweat-soaked kimono, and laughed.

'I don't know how you do it, Mama. You do all this and look like it's a stroll in the gardens, and look at me—one day of training with you, and I probably look like I've been through a war, mostly from my own doing!'

Asumi lowered herself to sit beside Yoshiko, pulling her *hakama* out of the way and crossing her legs, leaning back and looking up at the star streams. Yoshiko looked up from where she lay on the floor and admired the way the light from the star streams made her mother's face glow.

'Well, I've got twenty years on you,' Asumi said, face thoughtful. Then, she looked down at Yoshiko, meeting her gaze, and a wicked grin flashed across her face. 'Still, another few decades training like you did today, and you might just catch up!'

Yoshiko glared up at her mother, wondering what kind of monster Asumi was beneath her elegant appearance. She knew her mother was a famed warlord, but she was starting to think she was closer to being an *akuma* demon than anything else and half expected flames to erupt from her mother's body the next time they trained. Yoshiko rested her cheek against the stone floor and reflected on what she'd learnt, wondering whether Chinen had been soft on her all along. She squeezed her eyes shut, refusing to think about it—it wouldn't change anything.

'Quickly change,' Asumi's voice came from further away. Yoshiko hadn't even heard her move. 'It's nearly nightfall. We leave for the town when darkness falls.'

When Yoshiko managed to push herself from the floor, Asumi was nowhere to be seen.

* * *

The town! Yoshiko was excited. When she lived in the palace, she dreamed of going into the town and walking about as a citizen might. Haruki brought wonderful stories of laughing children darting about your legs, men and women chatting as they went about their daily chores, and businesses bustling with activities. Yoshiko desperately wanted to see the shopfront of the mochi store Haruki had said was run by the tallest women she'd ever seen. Even if it would be dark when she and her mother slipped from their hiding place, and no customers or produce would be in sight, she hoped she'd at least be able to see the buildings and the shop signs.

'Will we have to go out of the entrance on the side of the wall again?' Yoshiko asked her mother, staring at her still-recovering grazed hands and not liking the idea of hanging off a steep stone wall again.

Asumi shook her head as she tugged on a pair of navy *jikatabi* shoes. 'Remember I said there were entrances to the caverns all around Hié town? The caverns lie under the city, so there are plenty of entrances to use. Today, we'll use one that comes out in an alleyway by one of the town's main streets.'

Asumi brushed down her *hakama* and stood, ready, observing Yoshiko. Then, she nodded and led them to a different tunnel. As they walked, Yoshiko thought this would be a much easier entrance than the door hidden on the side of the moat wall of the castle, and was bewildered as to why they'd not thought to hide a normal entrance somewhere in the castle instead, rather than making their people climb down a wall.

As they padded through the dark tunnels, Asumi leading with a lantern, Yoshiko looked about and tried to memorise the route. She thought she'd go crazy if she were to navigate these tunnels alone. If she could learn this one, she might just use it for all her future trips in and out of this place.

'Careful,' her mother hissed from ahead of her in the stone passageway as Yoshiko stumbled over her own feet.

Though Yoshiko's body had felt it would never move after her training earlier, now she felt as if she could soar. The excitement buzzed in her body, and when she could smell the air seeping through the cracks in the door ahead of them, she darted past her mother and ran through the twisting darkness.

'Wait!' Asumi's voice was short and sharp, and Yoshiko's heart and face froze, both feeling like they'd been caught mid-jump. 'We don't know what could be out there. We have to be cautious.' She caught up with Yoshiko and sent her a stern sideways look in the orange glow of the lantern. 'Remember, follow my instructions closely. It could be a matter of life or death.'

So Yoshiko bowed her head, reeled in her soaring heart, and slipped out of the door as a shadow of her mother.

Just as her mother had said, the entrance led out to an alleyway. When Yoshiko turned to watch her mother shut the cavern door to try to memorise where it was, the heavy door shut into a wall and blended into the white and black wooden building.

'It looks like a part of the house,' Yoshiko muttered, stepping closer and looking for the seams of the door, unable to find them even with her face held close to it. 'Which bit is the handle? How do you open it?'

Asumi showed her a wooden panel that raised slightly, and a soft thud suggested a hatch had been lifted. Then, Asumi pushed it back down again, once again making the door look a part of the wall. Yoshiko was impressed.

'Does the owner of the building know about this?' she asked, eagerness rising once again.

Asumi shook her head and then gestured for silence. Yoshiko gulped. She'd ask questions later.

The dark alleyway led out onto a small street with closed shops on either side, their awnings shut and produce packed away while the people of Hié slept. Yoshiko peered about in the hopes of seeing clues of what was sold here, squinting in the darkness to read the dark ink-painted signs on the wooden panels above the awnings and doorways. Her mother hissed at her from ahead to hurry.

'Remember what I said. You must follow my every order and keep up. From here, we go quicker. Remember your training.'

That was all Asumi said before she dived into a run, twisting through small, backstreet alleyways of Hié's sprawling streets, confusing Yoshiko's sense of direction. Yoshiko tried to look around and remember where they were going without getting distracted by the new sights, but Hié was a largely populated town with small bustling streets, winding pathways, and steep hills separating different parts of the town, with only those in the upper ring, closest to the castle at the centre of town, able to afford the larger, wider plots of land. It would take her many trips to learn.

Yoshiko tried to keep up with her mother, pushing her hearing, vision, and agility to the edge like she was expected to, but with her eyes boggling at new sights and her muscles still aching from training, it was a challenge. And out here in the open, away from the safety of the caverns, Yoshiko feared that someone might be watching them or following from a distance they couldn't detect, ready to attack them and take them back to those who had betrayed them. Yet despite the spike of fear, she felt more alive than ever; with the air buffeting about Yoshiko as she ran, she wondered whether air had ever felt that fresh. Its cool feel against her warm skin felt refreshing, and she drank it in as if it were her first day on earth and she'd never experienced it before. And, though this was a mission to be taken seriously, with orders ready to come from her mother any moment, she couldn't stop the grin from spreading across her face.

The direction Asumi took them on led them downhill, and Yoshiko knew that meant they were heading away from the centre of Hié, away from the palace, down to the port. This way, steep hills led in levels down to the harbour. Yoshiko glanced to her side to see the buildings change from close-knit shop establishments with sleeping areas above them to small homes with low walls and small gardens around them before turning once again into establishments: fish shops and inns and, in one open area between streets, an empty marketplace, where Yoshiko imagined an open-top fish market would fill the area with lively trade when the people of Hié awoke. Here, away from the centre of town, the air was cool and fresh and smelt of the sea. In the centre of town, the air felt closer and smelt of wood smoke, with incense from the multiple shrines, and of the large public gardens that punctuated the different zones of Hié.

The two women scrambled up onto the roof of an inn at the first sign of someone moving on a street beside it—a cough and a shuffling footstep. From there, Asumi led the way across the sloping tiled rooftops, leaping over alleyways and creeping past windows where the people of Hié slept. Then, she turned, stopping their descent, taking them on a slight incline back up the hill towards another residential area.

Where is she taking us? Yoshiko wondered as she looked around, trying to identify the smell of the place and figure out if they'd been here already. She didn't recognise it—her nose picked up scents of clay, not salt and fish, like the place with the open-top market.

As they leapt from building to building, Yoshiko wondered where in the town Haruki lived, and whether she lived in a building like these or in one of the buildings up the hill, closer to the castle. Yoshiko resolved that if she ever came into Hié alone, she'd try to find Haruki. She remembered her light scent and knew the name of the place Haruki lived; with both of those, Yoshiko thought she might be able to figure out where her friend was.

A signal from her mother tore her back to the present. She caught up to her mother, who had finally stopped and crouched on the edge of a roof. Yoshiko ducked so she could hear what her mother would say, trying to still her heavy breathing.

'One last thing. Drop down that side of that building when you're certain there's no-one about. Don't move until it's safe.'

Yoshiko looked to where her mother pointed and nodded. When she turned back, her mother had gone. Looking about her, Yoshiko tried to figure out where Asumi had disappeared to. Once again, it would remain a mystery. When Asumi had said they needed to be better than a ninja, she'd meant it. Trying to follow her mother's lead, Yoshiko turned and leapt across an alleyway, ducking immediately and checking her surroundings to be sure no-one could see. Would ninjas be hiding amongst the other roofs, watching her now? Her heart leapt into her throat at the thought. She took a few deep breaths and tried to recall what her mother had said earlier about using her senses and extending them further. No movement, no sounds beyond those of the people living in the nearby houses. Yoshiko crept across the roof towards the building on the corner her mother had pointed to. It was small, almost blending into the buildings around it. What could be so important they'd sneak out here tonight for it?

Nothing stirred; it was almost too quiet. Immediately, Yoshiko wished her mother was there to reassure her. Deciding it was safe, Yoshiko carefully dropped from the roof and crouched on the ground, hiding in the shadows of the wall. A shuffling sound came from a nearby building, setting Yoshiko's heart beating too quickly again.

Another sound pulsed down nearby streets: footsteps in the distance, two pairs, probably guards. Yoshiko wondered where her mother was. What was the next step? How long would she have to crouch here before she was found? The marching got closer and sounded like they'd turned a corner. There'd be only two options now, if she could remember the layout of this street from standing on the roof: they'd march on, or they'd turn down this street. She wondered which it would be.

The marching continued on the next street over. Yoshiko willed herself into the wall and leant back as far as she could.

Mother!

Someone hissed lightly from beside her and made her blood feel like it had evaporated through her skin. Freezing, Yoshiko dared move only her eyes. She saw a hand emerging from the wall. This made her look twice. Turning her head, Yoshiko watched the hand gesturing.

There was a pause. 'Now, find your way back to the caves.' Her mother's quiet voice came out of nowhere, floating beyond the hand in the wall. Unsure, Yoshiko lingered. 'I thought I told you to follow orders immediately?' Asumi hissed.

Yoshiko spun and leapt onto the rooftop, lying flat against the tiles and holding her breath. The marching turned and stomped down the street where Yoshiko had just been sitting. Yoshiko let free her breath and frowned. What had the point of this been? She'd not done or seen anything.

Deflated, she looked around and tried to remember the route they'd come by. It had felt like her mother had taken her all over this part of the lower town, and all the streets seemed to look the same, even from up here on the rooftops. She looked down at the streets below and tried to remember what they'd done. They'd stopped on the corner of that rooftop, and there was the place she'd been daydreaming about finding Haruki, and there—she recognised that *tanuki* statue by that building. Yoshiko took a slow step and then dropped from the rooftop, jogging towards the *tanuki* statue she remembered. From there, she recalled they'd come downhill from the centre of the town, and slightly to the side, so she'd have to run back uphill and could figure out the rest from there. She squinted up into the darkness and saw the ghostly white of the five-layered *tenshu* keep in the castle grounds rising above Hié town. Home. She wouldn't be returning there yet, but if she kept aiming that way, she'd be able to find her way back up the hill and towards the caverns.

With the castle in mind, she returned to the tunnels.

* * *

'Mother? Where did you disappear to?'

'Here, clearly,' her mother was kneeling on a cushion and sipping hot *genmaicha*. In front of her were two steaming bowls. Yoshiko edged closer and peered inside, feeling her mother's eyes watching her. Sweet adzuki bean soup with a flame-toasted rice mochi in each one. Yoshiko's eyes boggled at the sight. But her questions came first.

'I thought you'd—'

'I told you to be better than the shadows, did I not?' There was almost a look of pride on her mother's face, as if Asumi was pleased she'd surprised Yoshiko. 'You just need practice. I hope tonight helped you see how you could grow.'

Yoshiko's mood dropped. So tonight had been a test? Once again that night, Yoshiko wondered whether that was what she wanted.

'Where did you get the sack?' Yoshiko dared to ask, trying to change the conversation, though not sure her mother would give her a clear answer. Her stomach gave an inelegant gurgle as she smelled the tea and the sweet adzuki.

'Tonight, when we went out.'

'Is that where you went? I was worried! How did you get it?'

'In time, I'll show you. When you're used to moving around the town.'

Yoshiko sighed, dropped to her knees on the stone floor, and watched the flames, not knowing what else to expect for that evening. A shuffling from beside her made her look back at her mother, who was watching her and pushing the bowl of hot adzuki dessert across the floor towards her. Then, her mother took her own bowl and sat with a happy expression on her face, looking only at the food. Seeing this, Yoshiko couldn't help but smile. So what if her mother had been testing her tonight?

She reached for her bowl and looked back up at her mother, who was now distracted, hot bowl in one hand and chopsticks in her mouth, eyes staring into space. Yoshiko grasped her own bowl in her hands, gasping at the heat of it and wondering how her mother was holding onto hers so easily. Instead, she clutched the bowl with her sleeve and smiled at her mother's peaceful face—it was the first time Yoshiko had seen Asumi like that since they'd escaped. Asumi must have noticed her daughter looking, because she caught Yoshiko's gaze and spoke. 'Enjoy it while you can. We won't be able to enjoy food like this much anymore. But you earned a treat. Eat while it's hot.'

Yoshiko marvelled at her mother's polarised personality—fierce, determined warlord who loved sweets. While she wasn't as soft and easygoing as Hitoshi, whose parenting was much more consistent and open, Yoshiko realised that, in her own way, her mother was trying to show she cared—giving her the skills she needed to survive and encouragement in the form of the thing they both loved: treats.

7

The Man and the Shadow

The red-haired man scuffed his *zori* on the dry muddy track and gazed thoughtfully at the town. It had been a while since he'd last come to the main town of Hié, and something had changed. He could feel it. He glared for a moment into the long shadows as the sun rose behind him. The town was too quiet, even for early dawn. Usually, people would be making their way down the streets to the harbour to help the fishingfolk bring in the morning catch, and families would be pulling out the awning to open shop. Today, it was still silent.

He felt a chill rush down his spine, and something made him look up behind him. The red-haired man gaped. A flash of shadow flickered past his vision, and he swore he saw an older woman sprint by on the rooftops.

In the blink of an eye, she was gone, and he stared in the direction he'd thought she'd run. Towards the castle in the centre of the town.

The man rubbed a hand through his hair, thinking only the *yōkai* spirits of this country's folktales could run that fast. And then he swore. Guards had crashed around the corner, running in the same direction the woman had flashed past in, and collided with the man, pushing him to the ground. They ran on, not even offering to help the man back up, not even looking his way.

That had changed, too. Some of the samurai were a bit up themselves, but if they were in the wrong and crashed into someone, they'd always act with honour and help.

The man sat in the shadowed streets, the rising sun yet to light the pathways, and wiped his face with the back of his sleeve, glaring at the guards' backs.

Since when did guards chase *yōkai* women, and in full armour, too?

'Fuck it.' He'd do what he needed and then leave. He'd heard too many stories of things happening in the main town these days. Nothing here was special enough to risk getting involved in anything dangerous. Not again. He'd run away from all that.

The countryside was better, anyway.

The red-haired man picked himself up and brushed the dirt from his dark green kimono and grimaced. *Just what the fuck is happening now?*

8

The Farm

Weeks passed. Yoshiko grew used to sleeping on a thin futon on the cold, stone floor, and her eyes adjusted to the darkness. She could run through the tunnels during her training without crashing into walls and tripping on the floor and could even strain her ears to hear her mother's attacks from all around her, even starting to identify the different sounds that gave hints that an arm or a leg might be moving. She still couldn't tell what attack was coming, but at least she could tell which height it came from, which helped her prepare to meet the attack.

The caverns didn't feel quite so cold or creepy, but Yoshiko couldn't say she enjoyed being here—she missed the sun, she missed the gardens, she missed Haruki and the other people who lived and worked in the palace—but she enjoyed the time she spent with her mother.

Back in the castle, her mother had been busy with her role as daimyō, so she hadn't had time to splurge on her daughter and husband. But Yoshiko treasured the moments they could spend together dearly, moments like drinking tea and chatting in one of the ground-floor level rooms of the castle, the outer paper window-doors open so they could see part of a private garden. Yoshiko loved to speak to her parents about her learning and of culture and politics, and whether they'd let her visit other regions, see the shōgun and other daimyō, one day.

She smiled sadly at those days past, never to return, and was thankful that she still at least had her mother, and though it wasn't ideal time together—hiding in a network of caverns underneath Hié—she wanted to make the most of it and learn as much as she could.

Asumi was militant in her daughter's training and her organisation of tasks. After that first trip into town, both she and Yoshiko would regularly take trips back there to complete missions that Asumi organised that would help them, eventually, return to the keep. The plan, as Yoshiko knew it, would be to gather information about what was happening in the castle and to collect names of those who could have betrayed them. Once they had those names and some idea of what to do, they could take that to the region to the north, Shogo, where her father had been for a political meeting before he died, and take a request to the shōgun for help. Yoshiko wondered why they didn't just go to the shōgun now. She was sure Kazuhito would easily listen to Asumi about what had happened, but it seemed her mother wanted to try something herself, first.

So they took on disguises—dressing in simple kimono, Asumi applying powder to their faces, showing Yoshiko how to do it, claiming it could make subtle changes to their face shape—to go into the town in the day and hear the region's news through the people or guards, taking their time in shops and cafes, asking subtle questions and eavesdropping. Yoshiko loved this best, going out in disguise and getting to see the town in the day and be amongst the people of Hié. Even though she knew she was on a mission, and it would be life-threatening if she was found, it energised her to be among the throng of Hién people going about their day, weaving through the crowds, watching them talk and laugh and work, hoping to one day be able to walk freely among them.

'I need you to gather supplies and listen for the news in the town,' her mother said to her one day as she tied her *katana* to her *hakama*.

Over the weeks, her mother had been limiting herself to going up to the guard barracks and castle grounds where she spied on the administrators, giving Yoshiko the daily tasks. Not that Yoshiko minded—she loved going to town best—but each time her mother went up to the castle grounds, Yoshiko worried one day her mother would fail to return. Yoshiko tried to push that thought from her mind and smiled, nodding to her mother and taking note of the things Asumi needed. While she was in town, she was to collect a few food items and listen to the locals for any useful information that would help them find out what was going on, bring down the traitor, and return to the castle. Each day, she and her mother would discuss what they'd learnt and write a list of names of those they suspected. Her mother would then spy on each person to see if she could learn more and whittle down their list. So when Yoshiko padded in the darkness through the tunnels of the caverns that led up to the entrance in the building in the main town alleyway, she hoped she could learn something new today that would help them.

She pushed the door open a crack and listened. No-one was outside. Relieved, Yoshiko dashed through and shut the heavy door behind her, pushing down the panel. This was the entrance she used most. There was another she knew on the edge of Hié town that she used when she was heading to the outskirts, hidden in a nook in a stone wall of a public garden, but this one was the most convenient. Yoshiko stepped into the now-familiar street beyond the alleyway and kept her head down, shuffling among the buzzing crowd towards one of the shops she frequented to get their supplies.

The town of Hié was much friendlier and brighter in the day. Shopfronts that were dark and shrouded in shadows at night were bright and full of colourful produce. Dark-haired people of Hié mingled in colourful kimono and called gleefully to one another, with children weaving between the crowds to play and chase one another, round cheeks flushed with joy. Women and men with bamboo-woven baskets picked through the marketplaces for fresh, locally grown food, and others ran stores selling freshly caught fish or homemade crafts, bantering with their regular customers. Yoshiko even caught sight of a small old lady, likely in her eightieth years, dashing up and down the narrow steps in her store to collect items for the customers, selling them with a big smile on her face and a friendly pat on their arms.

Smiling nervously to herself, Yoshiko ducked under the cloth awning of the shop next door to that old lady's and subconsciously touched her face, hoping the disguise would hold. Her mother had cut her hair, giving her a full fringe that came down to her eyebrows, and powdered Yoshiko's face. Despite this, Yoshiko felt nervous someone would recognise her, though she'd never met anyone in town before leaving the castle. She still felt a paranoia that a guard or a politician would cross her in the street or in a shop and sound an alarm.

The shopkeeper called out to Yoshiko in a friendly voice and told her she'd be with her in a moment. Until then, Yoshiko waited, eying up the produce, eyes hovering over a block of sweet *imo youkan*, wondering whether she could afford some in her small budget to take home to her mother. Asumi had been pale lately and pushing herself too much. Knowing her mother adored sweets of all kinds, she wished she could buy something to cheer Asumi up.

'*Harumatsuri* was cancelled?' the shopkeeper said, her voice shocked as she passed her other customer their change. 'But the festivals are never cancelled. Even in bad weather, they're just postponed. Are you sure they didn't give another date?'

The other customer, an elderly gentleman in a grey kimono, nodded, his weathered face pulled into a frown. 'My daughter works at the castle. She says the search for the daimyō and her daughter must be the reason.'

Yoshiko shrank back.

The shopkeeper sighed. 'The sooner they're found, the better. The guards are getting worse in their hunt. Only this week I've had them raid my shop twice! As if whoever kidnapped the daimyō would be hiding here. They're long gone.'

The elderly man nodded, and the shopkeeper thanked him for coming before turning her attention to Yoshiko. Noticing the look on Yoshiko's face, the woman's face fell into a kind smile. 'Don't worry about it, dear. There's only so much the guards can do. It'll be fine once the castle is returned to normal.'

Yoshiko nodded and made her purchase, high spirits brought down and heart in her stomach. If the guards hadn't stopped hunting for them in Hié, then they suspected they'd still be there. Her senses on high alert, and the paranoid feeling of being watched returned, she quickly pushed through the crowds and returned to the caverns as soon as she could, wanting to return to the safety of the quiet stone walls, for once anxious about being in the crowds.

That night, when Asumi returned late, Yoshiko heated some water to make a simple tea and told her mother what she'd heard. Asumi seemed distracted, replying only with short responses and distant gazes. When Yoshiko tried to bring her mother's attention back to what she was saying, the daimyō looked sad, and Yoshiko wondered whether her mother was thinking of Hitoshi—she'd been up at the political halls today, a place her father regularly went to help with the running of Hizen.

They still rarely discussed her father. Yoshiko wanted to speak about him—to peacefully discuss their loss and their joyful memories of him. She longed to joke about her father's quick wit and recite the poetry he wrote, or discuss the time he used haiku to subtly insult the over-confident and rude general who insisted Asumi marry another man and begin a harem.

Instead, Asumi wore her grief in silence and alone, and Yoshiko was forced to do the same. She recited Hitoshi's words in her head and tried to find patterns in the stone walls or constellations in the star-cut ceiling and wondered what he'd see in them. Her mother was wise and powerful and beautiful and kind, but she wasn't a philosopher, artist, or a deep thinker, and for that, Yoshiko felt alone. Her thoughts about the world and life didn't interest the practical Asumi so much as they did her father, and not being able to even speak to her mother about that loss made Yoshiko's heart ache.

But this wasn't all that worried Yoshiko. As the weeks continued and spring turned to summer, signalling they'd been in the caverns for a few whole moon cycles, Asumi became more absent—physically and emotionally. She was out often, rarely spoke with or even looked at Yoshiko anymore, and sometimes came home covered with blood. Yoshiko didn't know whether it was her mother's blood or someone else's, but she didn't want to ask. The dark looks on her mother's beautiful face got darker, and Asumi seemed increasingly obsessed with something around the castle. Asumi would spy at the castle or the guard towers and be away for many hours, not reporting what she learned.

Hadn't we agreed to discuss our plans? Yoshiko wondered as she lay in her futon one night, waiting for Asumi to return. *To write the names of those we suspect on a list? Aren't we meant to be finding out how to return to the keep together?*

But Asumi closed off more and went days at a time barely speaking to or looking at Yoshiko. Yoshiko increasingly worried about her mother's health, anxious that Asumi was becoming careless. With so little sleep and these strange obsessions, Yoshiko knew her mother could make a mistake. Even someone as great as the dragon daimyō could. If only her mother would speak to her, reassure her.

On those nights alone in the caverns, Yoshiko had nightmares about her mother falling into some trap and tried to figure out how she could approach it with her. What would her father say or do? His calm manner and quick intellect ensured he always knew the best way to deal with a situation and could calm his wife down like no-one else could. His charming grin would catch Asumi off guard, and then he'd speak calmly and take her on a walk. Yoshiko looked about the cavern and wondered how she could help, listing ideas in her head. Could they visit a garden at night? She could bring back a treat for her mother. How could she talk to her mother and convince her to slow down? That it was okay to ask for help? That it was time to go to the shogun?

So she thought of it each time she was alone on her missions, whether gathering information or collecting supplies, dashing through the main town's streets, or out into the surrounding countryside, rice farms, and forests. One day, Yoshiko ran beyond the town and down the dirt tracks that passed the rice fields and the vegetable farms. She was becoming familiar with Hié's territory and found herself thinking she'd have loved to have come here more before they were forced from the keep. *Surely, a future daimyō needs to know her empire*, she thought as a small, wooden house zipped past in the dimming twilight.

Yoshiko's mission was on the edge of the town, so she jogged past country homes, inhaling the scent that wafted through windows as people cooked their evening meal. Her stomach gurgled as Yoshiko passed. They'd been keeping their rations well, which meant small, bare meals. It was a far cry from what they ate at the castle, and it gave her more reason to think about the state of her domain—what did citizens eat daily? She wanted to know.

As Yoshiko ran past the houses, she thought of Haruki and all the things she'd told her about living the daily life of the folk of the region, wishing to share with her friend her own experiences from being able to walk in disguise amongst the people of Hié and the winding, bustling streets. It had been months since she'd seen her friend, and with her mother out often and having to be alone most of the time in the caverns, Yoshiko wished she could at least see and speak with Haruki once. She'd snuck to see her one day while her mother thought she was on a mission, using her new knowledge of the town to figure out where her friend lived. She'd sent messengers there before but never been herself. This time, she'd wanted to find out what was wrong—why her friend hadn't come in that fateful day—and to give her friend some clue that she, Yoshiko, was safe now. *I bet she's worried,* she'd thought, as she'd leapt over the rooftops to near where her friend lived. Haruki hadn't been there, and more concerningly, there had been no sign of someone being there for weeks.

The scenery that flashed past her melted into the night—dark, low shapes of the rice fields, the water shining in the moonlight. The fresh ocean air carried well at night. Yoshiko had come to realise the air was fresher in the country, away from the town. She loved it. Yoshiko took a deep breath and felt like closing her eyes, stretching out her arms, and drinking in large gulps of pure air. At times like this, she wished she could fly.

She threw out her arms for a moment as she ran, feeling the cool night air stream past her and the resistance on her arms. Grinning, Yoshiko imagined what it would be like to be in the sky rather than on the ground. Ever since her mother had told her some women in the family had been able to transform—

though it sped up the effects of the curse—Yoshiko had spent time at night visualising what it would be like to turn into a dragon: large, powerful muscles, sleek scales that shone like water slipping over jade, a mane that always looked as if it were flowing and twisting in a permanent stream of wind. She imagined twisting and turning in the night sky, dancing among the stars with wind currents ebbing around her long, large, serpentine body as she swam in the air. What would the view look like from up there? What would the ground look like from so high up? She tried to imagine it, remembering the time she'd visited the tallest temple in Hié for New Year's Day once with her mother and father. The empire spread out like a map below her, the fields like fabric stitched together and the ocean stretching further than she imagined it could. How she wished she could see that view again, this time from the sky, and even fly over the ocean to see never-ending, glinting blue.

'One day,' she told herself, as if willing it to happen and not giving it any other choice. She pulled her arms back in and pushed herself onwards. The farmers would be waiting.

In the many weeks they'd been hiding, they'd slowly managed to gather a few people they could trust to go to for resources, though they still disguised themselves. They'd found a friendly farmer couple after Yoshiko had hunted in the forest behind their farm. They'd offered to help her by selling fruits and vegetables cheaply, and they gave her eggs, too. Asumi had found a seamstress to fix their clothes (which had become worn from hard training and had needed replacing once already). Asumi had also given Yoshiko her father's sword, one of the only things they had left in memory of Hitoshi since leaving the palace with only the necessities, and taught her to use it, and Yoshiko had swallowed back tears at the gesture, knowing how much both of them missed him but still wouldn't speak of it. Mostly, since Asumi's behaviours had changed, Yoshiko was only given supply jobs like hunting in the forests on the edge of the outer town. She caught small prey, mostly squirrels, birds, maybe a baby boar or rabbit. Other nights, she went fishing, using her keen eyes and reflexes to fish with knives, a dagger, or a net the farmer had made for her.

'You'll probably need it,' was all he had said.

She stopped running as she neared the farm and smoothed her worn, navy *haori* and simple green kimono, pulling it back into shape from where it had ruffled from her running, and twisted her long, thick, black hair back, pinning it with a simple *kanzashi* pin. As she walked up the path to the farmhouse, Yoshiko felt comforted by the hens' quiet clucking and the glow of a hearth inside the farmhouse. A dog huffed and then bounded out, barking, when it noticed her approach. Upon recognising her smell, his bark subsided and became a pleased yelp. He started running in circles around her, following her with a wagging tail. The door slid open before Yoshiko could even knock, and an old woman stood in the entrance with crinkling eyes and a beaming smile. The dog nudged his head against Yoshiko's legs as she stopped to bow.

'Kaori! We knew it was you. Mochi always acts the friendliest towards you!'

Yoshiko grinned, bowing in greeting as they called the name she'd given them, worried about giving her real one. The old woman said this every week. Apparently, Mochi acted extra friendly around Yoshiko. She wondered whether she felt more like an animal to him with the dragon curse.

'Hana, thank you for taking care of me.' Yoshiko slipped off her worn shoes and bowed again as she entered the house.

'Not at all. It must be so difficult—working every day to get the money to help your family. So hard. I wish you could live more freely, like someone your age should.'

Hana's usual chatting began, and Yoshiko easily listened to the old woman natter excitedly. She felt comforted by it. At this point, her husband padded into the room.

'Hana, are you pestering young Kaori again?' His face was just as kind and just as crinkled when he smiled. He was as sun-kissed and wrinkled as a nut, but his bright, keen eyes made him look years younger than he was. Hana chuckled, and Yoshiko listened to the old couple chatter about life in the past week, happily sipping a simple vegetable broth they'd given her.

Yoshiko had learned much since she left the castle—she felt it was more than she could ever have learned from inside. Interacting with real people, hearing them talk freely, and wishing she could have had that simple, normal interaction too. She tried to listen as much as she could to make up for lost time. People of the town spoke about everything that was going on, even those in the farms. In some ways, she wished they'd never go back to the palace and hoped they could start living an ordinary life. Couldn't they just run away and be free?

Throughout their chatting, the old man fidgeted as he knelt and spoke gruffly. He was worried about something, Yoshiko noticed.

'And there's the issue of young girls—' Hana said, glancing at her husband. They both looked concerned. 'You need to be extra careful, Kaori. They say people are going missing, particularly young girls.'

The old couple looked at her with worry. 'Will you be safe to get home?' the old man asked her. She recognised the gruffness in his voice now.

She nodded and said she'd get home as quickly as she could and hide if she saw anyone else on the road. They nodded. And for the rest of the evening, they chatted about the weather, the harvest, and the giant daikon they'd grown that week and put it in her basket as an extra treat, along with homemade rice cakes. 'We thought you wouldn't get enough treats.' The old man winked. 'Enjoy it warm with something nice, like sweet red beans or crisped nori.'

Yoshiko felt like she'd drool and hid her face from the obviousness of it. The old farmers laughed, teasing that it was okay to look forward to good food. But tears stung her eyes. She knew what life could be like outside the castle and how the simple folk of the country relied on basic food and didn't eat as well as she had in the keep. Yet they still found it in their hearts to give and share when they had the slightest luxury. They always shared a warm and simple meal with her when she came, and always slipped an extra vegetable into her basket. The kindness of people, she learned—true kindness—was hard to bear. It made her cry. She thought she'd never find this true kindness in the castle, where people operated out of duty, except, perhaps, people like Chinen and Haruki. The old woman reached over the table and placed her hand on Yoshiko's, smiling as the tears dripped down Yoshiko's face when she failed to stop them.

'It's okay to cry, and it's okay to show your feelings,' the old man said.

Yoshiko looked at their calm faces and soaked up the view as if she'd never see it again. She tried to smile. Then, they all agreed it would be a good time for her to leave if she was going to get home safely and have any rest that evening. The old man rested a heavy, calloused hand on her shoulder and grinned, but his eyes were grave.

'You're doing a good job, kid. Don't give up.'

The door slid shut, and Yoshiko left. She couldn't wait to show her mother the rice cakes and ask if they could cook sweet adzuki beans to go with it. She remembered how she'd sit with her parents in their leisure room, kneeling on soft, silk cushions with cups of high-quality matcha tea on the *kotatsu* table. Her father would tease that her mother could never eat too many sweets, and they'd eat beautiful, decorated treats from artisans all over the country. Her mother loved sweets, both the high-quality, beautifully decorated ones and the simple ones she requested her maids buy in town. In winter, the family favourite was the hot sweet imo potato, roasted in hot stone ovens to be naturally sweeter. Yoshiko had always thought the simple ones to be best. Tears sprouted once more at the memory, and she imagined the smile on her mother's face as she handed her the hand-made rice cakes from the farmers.

They'd share them, and Yoshiko would share her worries with her mother—how she was worried Asumi was becoming reckless, how they needed to travel to Shogo to get help from the shōgun Kazuhito, and how she wanted her mother to take a break, even for a day, before she got ill. Sharing sweets was the perfect time to share her feelings, and she needed her mother to know how worried she was for her—before something went wrong.

9
Hunted

The old couple had been kind about Yoshiko's tears, but she wanted to be calm when she approached her mother, asking Asumi to stop her recklessness and whether they could plan their next steps together. If she cried, her mother might see it as a sign of weakness. Asumi needed her to be strong and determined to move forward so they could return home. Now Yoshiko had met the town's people and seen how they lived, she wanted to learn as much as she could and how to lead best. To do that, they needed to regain the castle and get rid of those who scared the people with their power-hunger, curfews, and house raids.

She held the basket closer as she reached the town, becoming more alert to signs of people. That people were disappearing worried her. Something made the hair on Yoshiko's neck stand on end, so she tried to run quicker again. Something was tugging at her—an urgency or some sense of danger. Would dawn come early? Were guards close and she'd not heard them while thinking about her mother? She couldn't tell what was setting her on edge, but her heart tugged. Something felt dangerous, as if there were a trap. Yoshiko slowed before she arrived at one of the hidden entrances to the caverns—this one on the edge of the main Hié town and the closest one to the road towards the farm—and rested against the walls of a building. She expanded her senses, trying to watch out for guards or signs of danger. Instead of danger, though, it was all too empty.

Thinking it was panic over everything from earlier, she dashed to where the entrance hid behind a stone wall. A giant wall circled a public garden that grew beautiful plum trees—*Suki would love this place in spring*, she thought—and Yoshiko couldn't wait for them to bloom to enjoy with her mother, even at night. The colours would glow in the moonlight, and a blanket of blossoms would rest over the ground, providing beautiful beds of pink, white, and purple.

Spurred on by yet another thing to share with her mother, Yoshiko slipped into a gap between two fake walls. Just like the moat, a hidden door lay between the walls, and she could just about squeeze through the gap before the heavy trap door closed after her. The darkness swallowed her for a moment, but she lit a flame lantern that rested on the floor by her right foot, in an alcove she'd learned was in every entrance. The light bounced around her, and she dashed down the steps that led to the cavern she and her mother had been staying in.

Jogging to the central dome, Yoshiko slowed to greet her mother with a smile. She wiped her face on her sleeve to hide any stubborn tear trails on her face.

'Mama, I've returned!' Yoshiko called out, rushing forward to place the lantern in a rest and the basket beside it. 'And I have a surprise.'

She was greeted with silence and darkness.

'Mama?'

Asumi had been due back before her today. Yoshiko had travelled the furthest, and Asumi was meant to be waiting for her. *She's still out?* Yoshiko frowned, knowing her mother had been gathering information, but Asumi hadn't told her from where or what she wanted to find out. She'd been more secretive, not even telling Yoshiko where she was going.

Yoshiko padded back to the lantern and the basket and picked it up. It was heavy. She tucked it into a nook in a stone hut they used for storing their belongings. Then, concerned her mother hadn't yet returned, Yoshiko wondered what to do.

That uneasy feeling was back, and Yoshiko's heart froze. She strained to listen for any sound, every smell, and for her eyes to see all. Why hadn't Yoshiko asked her mother where she would be going? She'd have had some clue as to which entrance she'd use, then. This place was so vast and full of tunnels you could miss someone from a different route. She thought of the entrance she knew was near the castle, by the moat, and headed there. It would be the best place to begin.

As far as she ran, she heard no sound other than the sound of her own feet pounding on the stone. The place was too quiet, as if anticipating something. She felt as if the whole town—above and in the caverns—was holding its breath, and it nearly made her lose her breath with fright. It couldn't be an earthshift, could it? Things always went silent then. Would they be safe underground? Is that why her mother wasn't here? But surely her mother would have told her that the underground wouldn't be safe in an earthshift?

She tried to keep her nerves under control—this wasn't the time to panic.

'Fear is your worst enemy,' her father would always say when she was scared. 'It can turn your brain and your body against you and be more of a danger than the thing that scares you. Breathe, calm your mind, and take back control.'

So she took deep, deliberate breaths. The caverns' musty air filled her lungs, and she tried to process the smells that came with it. She searched for the smell of her mother, finding a couple of trails that raised her hopes. But those scent trails just led her to places they'd been recently, empty of anything but memory. She growled. There wasn't any sign of Asumi having returned to the caverns this night.

Yoshiko slumped onto the stone ground back at the main cavern. If her mother was hurt or forced into hiding, it'd be in the area she was working in. She knew her mother would return as soon as she could, so should Yoshiko just wait? Yoshiko shook her head at this. Something tugged at her, saying she should look. Chinen had always told her in training that if your instincts were telling you something, you should listen. Yoshiko rested her cheek on her fist and stared at the ground. Where could she look? The only reason her mother wouldn't come back is if she thought it wasn't safe. Even if she was hurt, she'd do her best to return. It was safer to hide and recover in the caverns than in the town, and Yoshiko could help her. So it had to be that her mother thought she was being watched. If she was, she couldn't come back to the caverns, as their hiding place would be found. And she couldn't hide in the town—the watcher could just grab her.

Yoshiko startled. What if her mother had been found?

Then, she remembered her mother showing her a place in the outskirts where they could go if they thought they were being followed: a derelict farmhouse in the forest on the mountainside. It was far enough away that only those with dragon blood could run high-speed for that long, and difficult terrain would exhaust anyone following on foot. There were also plenty of places to dive and weave and hide to lose their hunters, and people on horseback would struggle through the tight trees. If Asumi thought it was too dangerous to go to the caverns, she'd go there and try to lose her pursuers on the way.

Yoshiko leapt up and grabbed what she needed from their stash, then ran through the tunnels that let out closest to that forest towards the north-west and rushed after her mother, dread flushing through her that her mother's life could be in danger.

* * *

Yoshiko's lungs felt like they'd explode. She'd never run this far this hard before, but she couldn't stop. Slowing down would open her senses to follow her mother's trail better, but fear kept her going. What was it her father had said about fear before? Right now, it didn't matter. Instead, she saw the forest rise ahead on the foot of the mountain in the distance and kept her eyes rigidly on her goal. She pushed herself harder, grimacing.

Eventually, the forest loomed ahead of her, climbing the mountain like a giant wall of trees. Usually, she'd be impressed. Yoshiko loved looking at this giant forest. Sometimes, she wondered why she and her mother didn't live there, among the trees like the little forest *kodama* spirits she'd heard about in stories.

'Because of bears,' Asumi had said. It wasn't worth the risk.

Even so, Yoshiko often thought the forest would be a better— and healthier—place to hide. They'd live amongst the warmth of the bark, feeling the fresh air and hearing the leaves rustle as a lullaby. It was nothing like the stale air and heartless stone of the caverns, which felt dark and lonely. But she understood. She thought, deep down, that Asumi couldn't bear to be too far from the castle.

Even so, *One day*, Yoshiko thought every time she saw the forest, *I'll sleep here one day—even just one night.*

This time, Yoshiko thought nothing of it. She'd found her mother's scent—it was deep and warm, and she could pick it up against other smells with ease by now. Her mother had run this way, she knew it, and she'd been fast. Leaves and branches were crushed, but it looked like too much damage to just be her mother. Yoshiko slowed for a moment to crouch and look closer. Heavier, larger boots had also stomped here. So her mother *had* been chased. But, if her mother was faster, and these boots looked like they'd travelled slower and heavier, how could they have kept up with the escaping woman? She inspected the crushed ground closer and saw tiny prints. Of course, dogs. So that's how they managed to keep tracking her. Yoshiko froze. Dogs could find them, even track them to the cavern entrances if they picked up the trails. What if the hunters discovered the entrances?

Yoshiko bit her lip. If she hadn't hunted the caverns, maybe she would have been able to catch up with her mother before the dogs could catch up. She dashed after the tracks, hoping she could still make it and help draw the dogs and the hunters off.

As she got closer to the derelict farmhouse, the tracks spread more. Her mother had tried to shake off her attackers, but by this point, perhaps it was obvious where she was heading. Would Asumi have turned off course and hidden elsewhere? But the tracks of the men and dogs didn't stop, either, steadily following her mother the entire way. Yoshiko's heart leapt, and she knew she should have crawled on the floor to pick up as many signs as she could, but her anxiety drove her back into a run.

She skidded on leaves as she caught a smell—her mother, definitely—but something was wrong. There was a dark smell, rancid and metallic, with something smoky mixed in. Her throat caught and, unable to breathe, Yoshiko ran directly for the farmhouse. *Please don't be her*, she begged, gasping for air as she tumbled through the trees. Tears streaked down her face before she even knew what she'd find. She stumbled and caught herself on branches, gashes catching on her skin. Her mother would have killed the men who hunted her, she knew. Asumi was a powerful warrior; she could have killed them all. She had the dragon curse, too, so she was stronger. Surely, at moments like this, she'd risk the curse and use all her might?

Believing nothing else, Yoshiko ignored the burning pillars of smoke ahead and the way the air rippled with a strange shimmer and dived forward. Her soul oozed out of her with the stress of what she'd find. Every second it took to reach the farmhouse felt like she'd burst from her body. Legs screamed, lungs screamed more—smoke now mixing with the stress of running so hard—and Yoshiko nearly did scream out with the effort. She lunged through the smoke surrounding the farmhouse, into its courtyard, and saw it more wrecked than ever. Scorch marks sizzled and smoked with small embers of white fire; the dusty ground was a confusion of tracks, prints, and skids as if bodies had fought hard here, fallen, and been thrown. Yet, despite the evidence that so many people had fought and fallen here, only one remained.

Yoshiko swayed, rooted to the spot. She knew that body, those clothes, that hair that now lay messy, spread across the dust and fanned across the face. She knew the pale skin, covered in dirt and blood.

'Mama?'

One sandal was lost, and the one that remained was dusty and marred on Asumi's pale foot, twisted at an unnatural angle. She remembered those shoes: she remembered picking them out for her mother happily, only recently, when they replaced their clothing. They should have lasted her much longer. Now, stained with dust and blood with the skeleton of a leaf clinging onto it, the one that remained made Yoshiko choke.

Finally, she dared to step closer. Wishful thinking made her hope there was a chance her mother was hanging on. She must be—she was so strong and clever. There must have been a way for her to win. Yoshiko's legs dragged beneath her with the strain of running. Her leg twinged, but she shuffled on. She didn't even think to look about for the people who'd hunted her mother. Only her mother mattered. Heart dead, Yoshiko almost thought she'd let the enemy catch her. Did things even matter anymore if Asumi was dead? She'd be alone.

Yoshiko fell to her knees beside her mother and reached out to touch her. Yoshiko's reaching arms shook—she could even see it—and as her fingers brushed Asumi's delicate chin, Yoshiko drew her hand back with a cry. It was scorching. Taking a deep breath, Yoshiko reached again. She was cursed with dragon blood too; she could handle a few burns. Wanting to see her mother's face, she struggled to move the hair out of the way. An unfamiliar noise escaped Yoshiko's throat—something between a moan and a bawl. Asumi's face, or what of it Yoshiko could see past the blood, once the most beautiful thing that Yoshiko loved, was marred with determination, suffering, and a gouge from an animal's teeth or claws—the dogs. There was no hope Asumi could have survived.

Yoshiko slumped, falling face-first into her mother's shoulder, pushing Asumi fully onto her back. She screamed into her mother's stomach, scaring even herself with the animalistic cry that escaped. Her body shook, and she knew that if her mother was alive, she'd have felt this and given her a sign.

But Asumi didn't move, and her burning body was growing cold. Asumi had been left too damaged. There had been no grace or honour—no quick death. She'd been beaten, broken, damaged. Bones were fractured and crushed and showed obvious signs of disfigurement all over, and her skin was lacerated, bruised, and burned. Joined by dog attacks, and punctured and gashed where weapons had got her, the soldiers who had killed her mother had been dishonourable. No respect for their warlord. She'd been killed with a vile energy that made Yoshiko lose what little contents were in her stomach to the floor beside her mother.

No-one should die like this.

10

The Forest Shrine

At some point, the sounds of the forest had returned. The previous silence had made Yoshiko's hair stand on end, but now, the buzzing of summer life, the rustling of the wind brushing the trees, and the birdsong created a juxtaposition to the scene before her. Yoshiko pulled herself to her feet and stretched out the burning in her legs before pacing the battlefield.

There was no further threat, from what she could see, but Yoshiko scolded herself for not having checked. She could have been in danger the entire time she was mourning her mother. But after a thorough search around the ruins and the trees, Yoshiko found no-one. She was alone.

The gushing of the wind in the leaves pulled her gaze upwards, and Yoshiko saw the sky still rippled from smoke. She frowned up at it. *It really doesn't look like smoke,* Yoshiko thought, seeing the multitude of colours with an unnatural shimmering undulating across what almost looked like a tear.

That's impossible; the sky doesn't just tear.

But the more she walked around the area looking at the sky, the more she thought she saw different colours weaving amongst the smoke, almost as if the sky was weaving itself together.

Trying to stop herself from seeing unreal things and instead focus on her problem, Yoshiko returned to the ruins to assess the damage. Deep dents showed where dogs slid across the mud, the ground scuffed with dried blood and tufts of fur. Scuffs and stomps showed soldiers skidding, ducking, jumping. Yoshiko also saw smaller prints and dips, showing where her mother had been pushed back or attacked or run to avoid being hit. Yoshiko frowned—her mother's prints only had one shoe. So she had lost her other shoe before the fight. Perhaps while running. Yoshiko hunted the floor, looking for a closer idea of how her mother had held off her attackers. She could see that Asumi had managed to injure more of the soldiers who'd come after her and killed several of the dogs. But Asumi had taken torrents of abuse in return. Yoshiko found many areas where Asumi was thrown or knocked to the floor, her blood resting in the mud with strands of her hair.

Yoshiko felt angry at herself. If her mother had managed to hold them off this long, perhaps—had Yoshiko been quicker—she'd have been able to help her. If only she'd left the caves earlier.

No. Father always said it didn't do to dwell on the past—you can't change it no matter how you try.

She returned her gaze to the mess about her. What confused Yoshiko the most were the scorch marks—some still fizzing away with white fire in the mud or on the walls.

Wait, white fire?

Yoshiko stepped closer to look at the small flames sizzling out, never seeing fire like that before. *Where did it come from?* She could see where weapons had been dropped and picked up again, and where people had tried attacking but missed, hitting other surfaces instead and leaving dents and scratches, but this was different.

The hunters would have had torches to follow Asumi at night, but they wouldn't have caused those scorch marks and that much damage. It looked like fire had been thrown at speed. But nothing explained why it was white.

Yoshiko foolishly wondered whether her mother could breathe fire but managed a bitter chuckle at the thought. Would that even be possible? Her mother had said the curse brought powers of a dragon—though at risk of falling deeper under the curse. But Asumi had said she couldn't transform. Could one breathe fire without transforming? Could the human body do that?

Cursed or not, Asumi's powers hadn't held off the full attack. While it had dented the attackers, they had still caused her greater damage in the end, leaving her dead and mutilated. And now, they'd managed to escape to report to the council— her mother had been certain it had been one of them who'd betrayed them. Yoshiko furrowed her brow; the people who had sworn to assist Asumi in the governing and the running of the region, to carry out the ruling of the emperor and the shōgun for the benefit of the people and the domain, had betrayed their vows. Yoshiko cried out in frustration that she didn't know the council well enough to know who it was who could have done it. Whoever it was, the people who had killed her mother would be running back to them now. They'd send more soldiers. The towns would be more dangerous than ever now the soldiers knew the daimyō had been hiding in the area, and the hunts would restart, thinking she, Yoshiko, would be hiding there, too. Even if she could safely make it back to the caverns without being spotted or tracked by the dogs, moving about and gathering information and supplies would be difficult. And what if they already knew of the caverns? Had the dogs managed to track Asumi's scent there, too?

A chill ran down Yoshiko's spine. Was someone watching her, even now? She couldn't stay here—they could come back with reinforcements to search for her. Besides, they'd left the daimyō lying in the open. It felt too much like a trap—as if they had left her to be found by Yoshiko.

The wind gushed through the trees loudly and drew her attention deep into the forest where the thick, green treetops ruffled like waves. Could she go there?

She looked at her mother, staring numbly at the lifeless and mutilated doll in front of her. Her mother had said they couldn't live in the forest because of bears. But who cared about bears, now she'd seen what humans could do? The soldiers would deliberately kill her without honour—just because someone in the council had betrayed her family. At least a bear would do it out of instinct and need for food.

'I'd rather be food,' Yoshiko decided.

She sighed and rubbed her eyes a little too roughly. What should she do with her mother?

If she moved her mother, they'd know she'd been there. If she didn't move her mother, she'd live with the pain of never giving her mother an honourable send-off from this world to the spirit world. Yoshiko looked about her once more—deep into the forest this time. It was huge. So huge that, even should the soldiers return and notice their dead daimyō had been moved, they'd never find Yoshiko anyway. So Yoshiko carefully slid her arms under her mother's body and heaved her up.

Yoshiko never realised how heavy a human was. Asumi's doll-like corpse sought the ground, making it more difficult to carry. And, with Asumi's broken bones falling at awkward angles, Yoshiko's heart tore when she saw the unnatural set of her mother's body. *So much for trying to carry her like a princess to her final resting place.* Yoshiko cringed. Feeling guilty, Yoshiko refused to look at her mother's broken body—she couldn't handle it. Instead, she clamped her jaw and clenched her teeth, scrunching up her brow as she walked steadily ahead and only looked where she was walking or where she checked for enemies.

Sorry, Mother.

Hefting her mother's body like this, Yoshiko set her path forwards, deep into the forest and up the mountain, where nobody from the castle would look. This was the wild, where forest spirits, demons, and wild animals dwelt and where no human came.

Yoshiko scoffed. *Good job I'm not purely human.*

* * *

Yoshiko spent hours preparing her mother for burial. Wishing to burn her mother for a proper Hié burial, Yoshiko couldn't risk the smoke drawing attention to her location. So instead, Yoshiko made a bed of leaves on the ground, then, as gently as she could, she laid her mother's icy body on top and tried to adjust her limbs to make her look comfortable—as if she were sleeping. Then, Yoshiko gathered flowers and dressed her mother in their beauty to reflect how beautiful she'd thought her mother had looked in her life. Bitterly, she wished there were blue flowers so that her mother might take them to her father when they met again in the spirit world.

'I hope you both recognise and find each other again.' Yoshiko's voice cracked. And who knew what spirits looked like in the other world? Would they find each other?

With tears falling freely once more, her soul shattered as she covered her mother in soil and leaves to protect her from the elements and carrion-eating prey. On top of the burial soil, Yoshiko lay more flowers and muttered a wish to the spirits before leaving and marching alone into the forest, further up the mountain, searching for a place to stay—a place near a stream.

Yoshiko spent the following days aimlessly walking through the forest, hunting for food, and scavenging and foraging for berries or roots. Now, the only goal she'd had since being driven from the palace—of regaining the palace with her mother and driving the traitors out—had gone. Yoshiko wanted to take revenge for her parents, take back the palace, and make sure the domain was safe from whoever forced that fearful curfew, but how could she? She was just one girl. She didn't know who was involved; she didn't know how to go into battle. And Yoshiko had seen what they did to her mother. Even if she fought back, how could she have hope? Her mother was the strongest she knew.

Each night, Yoshiko looked up at the canopy and wondered how she could do it. Could she go back to the town and enact her revenge? Would she sneak in or barge in? Would she kill them or just maim and arrest them? Yet, each night, Yoshiko met the same issue. Who was *them*? Who had been the ones responsible for the murder of her parents and the takeover of the region? Who ordered the curfew and the bullying of the citizens? Her mother had stopped sharing what she found out, so Yoshiko had no idea what or who Asumi had been watching. Had it been that frightening that Asumi had worried about telling her? Or had she just become too obsessed to realise that she had been pulling away from her daughter?

So Yoshiko was alone now, but really, she'd been alone for longer. How hadn't she noticed it before? All that time she'd been secretly worrying about her mother, she'd failed to see how much Asumi was changing and pulling away; how secretive she'd become; just how careless and absent Asumi had been. Yoshiko clawed at the ground in the memory of it, beating herself up for not spotting or addressing it sooner. Unable to sleep for the self-doubt and punishment that haunted her, she got up and wandered the mountainside.

While wandering in the darkness, Yoshiko spotted something catching the moon's icy glow. Padding closer and cautiously looking about her, Yoshiko stepped out in front of it.

A polished stone statue had been what had caught her eye—a pair of small, stone lanterns stood on either side of a path that led up a long flight of stone steps. Moss blanketed the steps like something out of the mystical stories. With the forest on the mountain, the stone lanterns, and the ghostly light of the moon, Yoshiko could almost have sworn she'd accidentally stepped into the spirit world. But a breath of wind on the back of her neck reminded her it was still the world of the living. Even so, looking up at the disappearing steps in front of her, Yoshiko felt something drawing her nearer. Stepping onto a moss-covered step, she started climbing.

At the top was a wooden shrine gate: a red-painted, squared archway with a black plank on top. It was simple but powerful. As she stepped beneath it, Yoshiko could feel a thrum of power pulsing through the mountain, like the spirits who lived there were welcoming her. Despite the magnificent gateway, what lay beyond was a modest, wooden shrine, protected by two old kitsuné fox statue guards that looked like they'd come to life any moment. Yoshiko walked closer, feeling like the kitsuné spirits were watching her. She tried to focus on the shrine, so small and simple—the size of a tiny hut, with a few wooden steps leading into it. There, you could barely stand up fully, and a faded-colour rope hung waiting for someone to pull the bell.

Yoshiko looked around. Though she knew she was alone with only the kitsuné statues to see her, she felt if she rang the bell, someone could hear it and know someone was in the forest. But she never went to a shrine or temple and didn't ring the bell. Her arm stretched out as if the thrumming power was drawing her to ring it, but Yoshiko clenched her hand tight at the last minute. She couldn't. Instead, she looked up at the roof, apologised to the spirit who watched the shrine, and gave the rope a tiny poke with the tip of her finger. The bell made the faintest chime, barely audible, and she smiled before clapping twice, closing her eyes, and wondering what she should wish for. It took a while for the thought to come, but when it did, she smiled again and bowed before stepping down from the temple, knowing the spirits would help her never feel alone again.

Refreshed, Yoshiko explored the little mountain shrine more. There would be no priest or priestess dedicated full time to this shrine, yet it was well cared for. Ash lay in a neat pile on the incense platform, and little wishes flicked in the breeze from where they were tied on the wishing rope. Someone came here regularly, then, she thought. But was it a priest or priestess who travelled here to keep watch of it, or someone else? Without intending to intrude, some writing on one of the wish papers caught her attention. She didn't recognise the script.

Yoshiko took a step closer and fought an inner battle about being nosy. On the one hand, wishes were utterly private—only the spirits and shrine guardians could see them. On the other— another wish flicked in the wind, and she saw the same, strange script. It looked nothing like Hizen writing, a series of brush-strokes and symbols written vertically down the bamboo fortune paper. Instead, this seemed to be written across the fortune paper, small runes split into what Yoshiko could only guess to be words of different lengths, split with a gap between them, unusual for the writing she knew. She wanted to look closer, to see if she could recognise any of these symbols. Perhaps it was the writing of a small child before they knew how to draw the full symbols—but then the runes seemed too small to be written by a child.

Before her curiosity could get the better of her, something below in the forest made her jump. Her skin crawled when she heard several snapping branches, and she took flight. Bowing quickly to the shrine before she left via the wrong exit, wishing she could have gone down those moss-covered stone steps again, Yoshiko ran up the mountain and away from whatever was crashing through the forest below.

The trip to the shrine had refreshed her. Whether it was that new power she'd felt or a sense of normalcy. It brought the world back into perspective—that there was more to this than just her. Her parents had been killed, but that didn't mean Yoshiko was the only one affected. What had the old farmers said about people, particularly girls of her age, going missing? In her newly cleared head, she worried about Haruki. Her house looked like it had been empty for some time. How long had people been going missing for? Is that what had happened to her? Yoshiko knew she had to do something. And, though she felt alone and powerless on her own, hiding in the forest wasn't going to get her anywhere.

Yoshiko suddenly stopped. Something had tweaked inside her head, as if the shrine had already answered her prayers.

The farmers.

She wasn't alone. They'd been kind to her and were always welcoming, treating her like a grandchild, telling her to come if she needed help. Even just listening to them had been a pleasure. Her eyes watered again at the memories, and she realised she was desperate for their company. Yoshiko fumbled about in the little pocket inside her kimono. A small amount of coin was still there from when she'd last gone to visit them for supplies. Surely this amount would repay them for a meal and a blanket by the fire? Her stomach warbled at the thought of proper, warm food. How long had it been since Yoshiko had last had a meal? With a sense of urgency in her heart, longing for the companionship of the kind old couple and dear Mochi the dog, Yoshiko leapt on with renewed energy, south, down the mountain, and towards civilisation.

* * *

Yoshiko ran down the track that led to the farms. If anyone could lighten her heart, it would be that kindly old couple who always had interesting things to say, beautiful smiles, and a beautiful dog.

When Yoshiko reached their farm, she slowed to a trot and looked forward to the lovely dog that always ran to meet her, barking happily. But no dog raced towards her, tail wagging with a tongue hanging goofily from his mouth and eyes that looked more loving than anything you'd ever seen. Yoshiko stopped jogging and looked about. In fact, nothing was suggesting Mochi was there at all. The whole place felt empty. Yoshiko's heart dropped. Had there been a problem, or had they left? Perhaps they'd made the trip to the main town to visit their children? They'd often talked about how much they missed them since their children had moved away from the farm.

Yoshiko strode towards the door. But the spirits weren't exactly on her side these days, and her hopes weren't being met at all. Yoshiko paused; when she'd been at the shrine, there'd been that great energy. Maybe this time, her prayers would work. Yet, as she slid open the door, she was hit with the heavy smell of death and decay, and a mass of matted fur lay formless by the door. She knew that matted form was Mochi. His beautiful golden colour was dull and murky, but it was him. Yoshiko cried out, wanting to reach out and gather up the little dog in her arms, but at the same time feeling afraid to touch him. And with the smell as it was, she knew it wasn't just Mochi who was dead. Yoshiko swallowed her fear and, for the honour and love of the old couple who'd been good to her, she pushed further into the house, knowing what she'd find.

When did it happen? She stood inside the farmhouse, staring at what she didn't want to see. Looking through blurred vision at the old couple lying on the hard floor, she couldn't tell. Boots had trodden muddy tracks onto the wooden floors—boot prints that looked like those she'd seen at the site of her mother's death, too. Mixing in with the mud was spilt blood—darkened from age and exposure to air. The old couple had been run through with blades—perhaps even had their throats cut. Yoshiko's face scrunched up, and she tried not to cry.

If only I'd arrived here sooner. Again. She felt her lip quiver and took a sharp breath to try to stop her emotions from bubbling up.

Once again, she'd been too late.

Bitterly disappointed in herself, Yoshiko avoided self-blame by trying to figure out what had happened.

The killers—likely soldiers or hunters under the control of the council, Yoshiko guessed, thinking back to what had happened to her mother and how the situation was so similar— had burst in and likely killed Mochi first to stop him from getting in the way. Then, they'd attacked the old couple and marched straight back out again, leaving them to die. Now the old couple lay on the floor with their arms reaching out for one another, hands clasped. And in the freeze of death, their hands had frozen together. Yoshiko collapsed onto her hands and knees and heaved what little contents she had left in her stomach before bawling into the wooden floor.

How disrespectful, she thought, that the hunters had marched in here with their boots on. This house—so usually well-kept and warm and tidy—and these people deserved to be treated so much better. Instead, there was a dirty floor, furniture strewn everywhere, doors pulled open so hard that they hung unevenly in their setting, and belongings were thrown across the floor. Food from the pantry lay across the counters and floors, beginning to rot and adding to the smell of decay. She heaved again. This time, there was nothing left.

Then, Yoshiko rubbed the tears from her face and swallowed to try to stop heaving. She didn't want to be disrespectful by being sick in the presence of their bodies, just because of the smell. Yoshiko looked once more at the old couple, holding hands in death and seeking comfort in one another one last time.

If I'd been here …

She clawed her fingernails into the wooden floor in despair and frustration, and screamed into the ground. She screamed for the pain these good people had experienced; for their loss and the cruelty and dishonour of their deaths. She screamed for the anger she felt and the revenge she now swore. And finally, she screamed for the miserable loneliness she felt and the weight of being left alone, though she knew it was none of their faults. Then, throat raw, the screams died out, leaving an eerie silence that terrified her.

Shaken, Yoshiko looked up from the floor at the old couple in front of her. *I can't leave them like that*, she thought, distracting herself from a warning ringing in her mind.

She searched for the softest fabric she could find and collected fresh water. Then, crouching beside them and promising herself she'd not cry, she gently wiped the blood, dirt, tears, and stains of death from their skin.

Only when she felt they'd been properly cleansed did she stop, stand properly, and wipe the sweat from her forehead with her arm. Then, she wondered what to do about burial. She wanted to keep them together like this—with their hands held forever. So she stood once more and rummaged around in their clothing drawers, finding a beautiful handkerchief. As she searched, Yoshiko saw the rags of her sleeves and realised how awful her clothes had become.

She turned back towards the old couple. Surely, they wouldn't mind if she replaced her worn clothes with something of theirs? A selfish part of her wanted to take something of theirs as a memory.

Yoshiko found some clothes of the old woman's, who was a similar size to herself, liking the practical nature they had and visualising the woman wearing them to work in the fields. They were robust and, while simple, they were made to be long-lasting. These people wouldn't buy clothes often, but when they did, they'd make sure they'd last well. Yoshiko turned the green and blue fabric over in her hands, feeling the material brush over the backs of her hands and the woven texture caressing her skin like a memory she thought she'd forgotten. Remembering what her mother had said when they left the palace, to take two pairs—one for wearing and one for washing—she chose a green kimono and a dark indigo one, quickly dressing in the blue and making a bundle out of the green to take with her wherever she decided to go next. Back to the caverns, most likely.

Then, she returned to the old couple with the handkerchief and carefully wrapped it around their joined hands, tying it neatly.

Now they'll stay bonded forever.

Yoshiko stood, closed her eyes, pressed her palms together, sending a wish their way, and then bowed. She looked at the flames dancing in the hearth from where she'd lit a fire earlier to bring warmth and light back into the room. Yoshiko could just about feel the heat, and the glow of orange dominated her vision. She had an idea. She reached into the flames. Her hand didn't feel the heat, and it didn't look burnt either when she pulled a log out. Barely noticing what she'd just done, Yoshiko took a few trips—lighting new sticks and logs each time—and distributed burning logs about the house: lighting fabric, wooden floor, food, and paper doorways. Then, grabbing the old man's outdoor jacket and the old woman's outdoor shoes, she took her green bundle of spare clothes and headed for the front door.

Something stopped her in her tracks when she reached the door to leave the burning house behind her. And it wasn't the body of poor Mochi. On the door, where she hadn't noticed in her rush to come in, a message was painted in a large, black-ink script. Despite the heat of the roaring fire behind her, Yoshiko's blood turned to ice, and her heart spiked with dread.

They'd found her.

Wherever you're hiding, you'll be next. All who help you will die.

Yoshiko took a sharp intake of breath and tried to regain clear thought.

What if they're watching now? she thought, freezing.

The old couple's burial fire was getting huge and bright. It would attract people to come and see what was happening. But she had to get out of there soon before it engulfed her, too.

'The shadows are always darker where light is brightest,' her father always said when talking about poetry, the natural world, or societal issues.

So with a fire the size of a house offering the brightest light, Yoshiko slipped out into the night, remembering her mother's lessons to extend her senses and focus on the shadows.

11
Alone

With her head swimming with fear of the threat on the door, somehow Yoshiko made it back to the centre of the main town. Aware now of the danger she was up against—what her mother had known the entire time—Yoshiko understood what she had to face. It wasn't as simple as she had thought; people were dying around her. It was as her mother had said and Chinen had feared when he'd spoken with her that day in the garden. War had come. And closer than she'd realised.

Yoshiko crouched in the shadows of an alleyway opposite a cavern entrance, wondering whether the soldiers had found it yet. She almost didn't care now. If they'd found a way into the caverns, they'd likely get half lost. And then they'd try to kill her like they'd killed her mother and the farmers. But she'd do her best to go down fighting, just like Asumi had. She'd take them to the spirit world with her.

A vision of her mother flashed back into her mind, and Yoshiko set traps behind her at the cavern entrance. Then, she disappeared into the dark and cold of the underground, clutching a lantern until her knuckles became white. The note had scared her, and the tumbling feeling in her stomach didn't lessen while she dashed about the cavern tunnels and checked for signs of an invasion. But what she found disturbed her more—the caverns were undisturbed. They were as lifeless and empty and cold as ever, and that scared her more. In such a vast and confusing emptiness of stone tunnels, the knowledge she was fully alone amplified. Yoshiko wondered whether it hadn't been a better idea to stay in the forest. There, at least, the birds sang, the leaves rustled, and the sounds of nature continuing life—despite the woes of the human race—were comforting. But here, where the stone walls loomed, there was nothing.

Yoshiko huffed, and the sound seemed ridiculously loud. Deciding she'd go mad if she continued like this, she set up camp as always—as if no-one had ever gone missing—and pulled out the food provisions to check how much of it was still edible. As she sorted through the food, Yoshiko reflected on the plans that Asumi could have made, and what Yoshiko could do in her stead.

With the food laid out in front of her, Yoshiko realised it had only been days since her mother was killed, though it had felt longer. And this food that the kind-hearted farmers had sold her that same day was still mostly edible from the cool of the tunnels. She unwrapped the fabric that covered the extra vegetables they'd given her, and her emotions rocked. Satsuma sweet potato, cabbage, and a huge white daikon. Vegetables were expensive for the common folk, and she'd learned since leaving the palace that not everyone had the option to eat them. Yet this couple never failed to slip in an extra vegetable or two for her. That kindness— the pure kind—was something she never knew from inside the palace, and she never expected to feel such warmth from being given a few vegetables. It had always been something she'd easily had. And now, living in a world where people didn't have them, she knew the community that people lived by, in giving and sharing. This was special.

'Mother,' she whispered, staring at the food and wishing she could have shared it with her. Did her mother realise how kind the citizens of Hié were? Had Asumi known the strong sense of community that could be found outside the castle?

This whole time, Yoshiko had been blindly following her mother's instructions. She didn't know the information Asumi had been gathering and had stopped sharing. Whatever her mother had discovered recently had got her killed. Now, with weeks of information not having been shared, Yoshiko felt at a loss. Who was leading the mutiny at the castle? Which of the council were guilty, and who was innocent? How could she get back and guide Hié back to the right path and free the people from the fearful curfew without the latest clues?

Hadn't they meant to share information this whole time? Had Asumi become so buried in her grief and revenge that she'd forgotten what had been important?

Yoshiko looked once more at the vegetables. They felt so small and simple to her—things she'd always had easy access to and always enjoyed each day. Now they were so much more and a symbol of everything she loved about her region. She remembered Haruki, and how Yoshiko's favourite moments had been when Haruki shared stories from people's daily lives and the tiny treats from the town and how everyone worked together. Then, from the farmers and the shops she'd watched and hidden in to spy on the guards, she'd loved hearing people talk to each other normally and learning what lives people led. She wanted to build a domain that thrived on this—where people like her weren't raised so separately but could work with the people who truly built it.

And now, those people were scared. Yoshiko thought back to the whispers of the shopkeepers and their patrons about something feeling wrong in the region. Her people were suffering.

Kneeling, Yoshiko stared at the blackness beyond the light of her lantern. She still felt an icy loneliness, and now she noticed a hatred for the caverns that she'd never had before. Not even the memory of joy she'd felt at discovering the star streams could brighten this new feeling. But she'd stay here—where she could run easily to the surface and act in a way to help her people. She'd start from scratch. This time, she wouldn't focus so much on what was going on in the compound. She'd start from the foundation of a region—with its people. She'd help the people and work her way up—stopping them from being scared and from going missing. Then, she'd work her way up to retaking the castle and creating a region that could thrive on culture and community and true kindness. For how could she take the castle and feel pleased with her work when she knew she'd got there by ignoring the cries and the fear of those her family had sworn to protect?

A pang in her heart brought her lofty goals and determination to a pause. If she was so keen on community, she couldn't do it alone. Her mother had failed by trying to do it alone, and she'd had no-one to fall back on when she needed help, not realising Yoshiko had been there all along. Now, Yoshiko had to find her community, but she didn't know who she could go to for help. Her community was all dead or in the keep, or possibly her enemy.

Haruki had gone missing, her home empty and unlived in. Chinen and his group had marched to the western border town and wouldn't be back yet. Yoshiko often wondered whether they'd been safe and whether it would be possible to go there and ask for help, but she feared the journey would take her too long, and she didn't know the way through the countryside. Could she hire someone to be her guide? But it would keep her away from the town for too long, and she'd miss what was happening.

Being raised in the keep, Yoshiko realised, she'd had no true friends. People had either been hired to help and raise and educate her or were possible connections to the council that betrayed her family. She thought back to the families that visited her and her parents, and the people they went hunting with. Many of them lived out of town and visited for the occasion. Where did they even live? There was a family with three daughters that she loved to see when they came hunting—one girl, Moori Hisa, younger than Yoshiko, was particularly chatty with her and loved to show off her bow skills. She'd be fun to have around, but Yoshiko didn't want to get them caught up in this mess, and she didn't know where they lived. That pang returned. She'd never noticed how lonely her life had been before, outside Haruki, Chinen, and her parents.

Yoshiko put away the food again as she wondered who she could go to for help. It would have to be someone strong enough or willing to defy the guards, someone who wouldn't worry about that note.

For some reason, her mind wandered back to that shrine in the woods and the strange writing she'd seen there. What language could that have been, and why was it in Hié? Then, Yoshiko remembered a woman in a shop speaking of a hunter who always brought the best catch from the forest—a foreign man who could do anything if you asked him to help, be it fixing, hunting, building. He often kept to himself, seemed scary from the outside, but he was calm and kind, and she'd recommend him to anyone who needed help. The person she'd been talking to had seemed worried about him being a foreigner, but the shopkeeper had convinced her.

'He catches all the game that I sell here. It truly is the best. I'd trust him with any problem I have.'

'Oh, well, you *do* sell the best game,' the customer had said. 'He brings that? Does he help with anything? Since my husband died, I struggle preparing the house for new seasons. With summer coming, I'd like to get all the winter and spring stuff away.'

'Of course. He lives alone in a cottage on the edge of town by the woods, with hair as red as an autumn leaf. Ask any messenger for the autumn-haired foreigner, and they'll deliver your message.'

The shopkeeper's friendly voice echoed in Yoshiko's head. She remembered at the time she'd tried to imagine what someone with autumn-coloured hair would look like. It was like nothing she'd ever seen from the people of Hié or their neighbouring countries. But the woman had said the man could do anything. Could she go to him for help? It would make sense that he left the wishes in that strange writing if he lived by the forest and regularly went there to go hunting. And he was the first foreigner she'd heard of living here.

But the biggest hurdle that she kept coming up against, no matter how often she thought of it as she strolled the dark caverns, lay on the floor, and stared in frustration at the star cut-outs in the roof, was why he should help her at all.

12

Finding a Hunter

She had nothing to offer him, but she'd still try. After all, the shopkeeper had told that lady that he was kind, despite how rough he looked, and helped for a fair price. Yoshiko wasn't sure how much he'd want for helping her, but she knew even just a bit of help would go a long way. She could work towards finding more people another time. For now, the foreign man with autumn hair seemed like the only option. Besides, the shopkeeper had said he was a great hunter, hadn't she? The best in the country, in her mind. And someone who helped people and fixed things. Well, Yoshiko wanted a hunter—someone who could help her hunt traitors—and someone who could help her people and fix a domain.

Too much to ask? Probably.

Yoshiko set off towards the town when the sun started to set that same night. There was no point in waiting on her own in the caves. They were cold and dark and felt too haunted now. Dressed in the indigo kimono she'd taken from the old farmers' house and armed with several small blades and throwing blades, she emerged from the underground caverns to the north of the town and crept towards the edge where the foreigner was said to frequent.

His home was in a village near the forest to the north of the town, she'd heard. So whenever he came into town, it would be in this area. There were food shops, restaurant stalls, and saké houses—all casual and for the general citizens, but all perfect for someone to spend the evening at. Yoshiko hoped she'd come across him here sooner or later.

Yet Yoshiko was surprised by how difficult it was to find a foreigner with hair as red as the autumn leaves. She slipped through the shadows of the northern streets of town for three nights without sight or news of this man and became quite impatient. Yoshiko's only comfort was that she spent her time watching the people she was trying to save. She loved watching and learning about people. So Yoshiko's failure in finding the man became a delight as she watched a fish chef slice cleanly through raw fish, caught that day by fisherfolk. Her stomach growled at the thought of such beautifully soft fish, and she looked away by watching the happy, pink-faced patrons leaving the drink bar. She grinned for the first time in days and marvelled at how simple lives could bring such joy.

Each night, though, Yoshiko noticed a difference in people's behaviour as the night drew on. Shops became eager to shut, and people were hasty to head home. From her hiding places, Yoshiko overheard worried, whispered conversations and the sounds of heavy items being pushed against doors. Her smile disappeared.

On the fourth night, Yoshiko's patience paid off. The autumn hair certainly stood out; she chuckled when she saw a tall, broad man with lightly tanned skin and hair like deep red, dying embers stride towards the saké house, tucking his hands casually into the opposite sleeves of his light blue kimono, the pale blue only making his hair look all the redder. He held a deep grey *haori* in the crook of his arms, and Yoshiko was amused to see his ankles showing below his kimono, seeing as he was a little taller than the average Hién man. All about him, a mass of dark-haired Hién people wove around low wooden tables, some greeting him casually by calling out or bowing their heads briefly. The foreigner smiled and bowed his head, good humour and genuine warmth reaching his pale eyes. From this distance, Yoshiko couldn't see the colour, but she marvelled at them—she'd never seen light eyes before.

She followed him into the saké house, barely looking where she was going and stumbling into one of the low stools. She growled lightly to herself in frustration at her clumsiness turning heads and drawing attention, feeling her skin burn with embarrassment. Usually, people would sit on cushions in such an establishment. Yoshiko wondered why these stools were here and found herself admiring their style. Much later, she'd find out the autumn-haired man made them at the owner's request so that people could sit back more comfortably after a hard day's work. But, at this time, Yoshiko couldn't know, so tried to figure out where they had come from as she bought herself a small earthenware cup of saké to warm her bones and lift her spirits, waiting for the red-haired foreigner to leave.

* * *

'Well, I'm off.' The foreigner's voice sounded low and melodic.

Yoshiko focused on her empty cup and tuned her ears in to listen as the saké house keeper happily thanked the man for visiting again, both agreeing it had been a while since his last visit. Yoshiko was amazed at how well he spoke their language. She scolded herself, wondering what else she was expecting.

The man's name, she discovered, was Gora. Whether this was his first or family name, Yoshiko didn't know. But this Gora person seemed friendly with the keeper and his staff and told them to take care. With this, the tone in the keeper's voice changed, and he sounded dark and worried. The red-haired foreigner told the man to shut shop soon.

'Somethin' strange 'bout tonight,' Gora said, voice low and sounding as if he didn't want to disturb the people happily finishing their drinks. 'I can feel it.'

Yoshiko gestured to a worker that she'd finished her drink, and she was happy to turn her back to the talking pair and tried to make light conversation to thank them for the drink. She hoped it made her look more natural.

'You think? It's pretty early. Seems we're just going to have more and more problems if things have to shut up sooner. Business is hard enough with the curfew. You think it'll get worse?'

Yoshiko missed Gora's reply, but a nervous laugh from the shopkeeper drew her attention back to them. She watched them from the corner of her eyes as she rose from her seat to make ready to leave.

'Soon they'll be making us hide in our homes the minute darkness falls! Who will have any business then?' The shopkeeper was rubbing his rolled-up sleeve nervously but shrugged and smiled slightly.

The red-haired man clapped the keeper on his shoulder—Yoshiko wondered what kind of gesture it was—before both parties bowed and the foreigner left, calling over his shoulder as the other workers thanked him for coming. Taking it as the perfect opportunity to leave and follow, Yoshiko left too, thanking the workers and bowing and ducking under the curtain into the darkness away from the friendly environment within. It had been so warm and lively in there. Her heart wanted to stay.

Outside, her mission hit her. The saké had warmed her spirit and lightly numbed her body. She smacked her cheeks lightly and looked about, becoming wary that someone could have tracked her in there and waited for her to leave. None had. But the autumn-haired man had a quick stride, and Yoshiko had to rush to keep up. Careful to keep to the shadows, she followed.

Gora swayed slightly as he stumbled in the darkness down the track, zigzagging across the path and swinging his *haori* around casually. He sang to himself as he walked—a low, mesmerising sound in a language Yoshiko didn't recognise. *The language of his home*, she thought. Whether the song was right, she didn't know, but even drunk, it didn't seem wrong. The song seemed sad, though the notes had a strangely jolly and lifting feeling to them, and melodies she'd never heard before filled her ears. It flowed on the wind in a way she felt the Hién music didn't and made her want to cry and dance and laugh and spin all at once and watch the waves and the trees and stare at a fire. She was sure, in there, she'd see spirits dancing, too. She'd have loved for him to sing at the keep. This man's singing, she realised, could be beautiful—if not for the fact he was drunk and kept stopping or stumbling. His voice had become rough from the alcohol, but it was still uplifting enough to listen to. Yoshiko found herself wondering what it was about and whether a song could be both sad and happy at the same time. The song ended with a long, held-on note—held on as long as he could push the note from his lungs—and then it stopped.

Her heart pounded as the man stopped in his tracks with a scuff of his feet on the ground, and Yoshiko kept hidden and silent. He couldn't see her; he wouldn't know she was there. Yet, when he raised his chin towards the sky and sniffed the air, she doubted herself just a moment.

What can he smell? she wondered. Her nose was sensitive, and nothing unusual had caught hers. Could he smell *her*?

Yoshiko waited, holding her breath, not allowing herself to twitch even her nose. Eventually, he disappeared into a small, wooden stable by the side of the track. Yoshiko waited again and allowed herself to blink. Her mind raced at all the reasons he could be in that stable.

But this isn't his home. She thought back to what the shopkeeper had said to the old lady about where the autumn-haired foreigner lived. This wasn't it. There was much further to walk yet.

Yet no matter how long she waited, he never came out. A buzz of hot impatience bubbled through her, leaving her feeling inconvenienced and not even knowing why. What would her father say? The man who always taught her to be calm. Feeling more like her wild mother this time, Yoshiko emerged from her hiding place and silently clambered on top of the stable, looking through a crack in the roof to see why the man was hiding, thinking he'd noticed her and hidden in there to attack as she passed. *Not today*, she thought as she reached the rooftop, *and not me.*

She peered inside.

'You're sleeping in *here?*' Yoshiko couldn't help but call down through the cracks in the wooden roof, baffled.

Sure enough, the man with autumn hair had sprawled in the hay and had been snoring loudly beside a brown mare with a look of indifference on her face. Gora leapt up, crying out in shock and pulling himself into a defensive stance, adjusting his loosened kimono. Yoshiko almost giggled at how stupid it was. She'd been so tense that he'd discovered her and hidden to jump out and attack her, and here he was, drooling in the hay.

'Where are ya?' His voice had an echoing lilt to it that she couldn't place, like the foreign song he'd been singing, even in the Hizen language. 'I'll strike if I need to.'

The man wheeled where he stood, looking for the voice's body. Yoshiko was certain he wouldn't find her, but was wary, nonetheless.

'Why were you sleeping here?'

The man's thick eyebrows—darker in colour than his hair—arched up his forehead, and he continued to scan his surroundings, frowning when he still couldn't locate her.

'Why're ya hiding now?' he answered with his own question.

Yoshiko refused to speak.

Fed up with waiting, the man reluctantly responded. 'Rough times. Dangerous to be walking so far in the dark.' He waited for her response, body primed to leap out and hit anything that moved. 'It's your turn now!'

'I don't want to be seen yet,' Yoshiko answered carefully, wondering how to phrase it. There was a tense pause while he waited for her explanation. 'As you said, "rough times".'

'Fair enough,' he growled. Then, narrowing his eyes in thought, he plopped back down in the straw, kicking off his zori, and let out a sigh. 'Besides, damn comfy, this.'

Yoshiko wasn't sure he was talking to her at this point, though he'd spoken in Hizen. Still, she didn't know what to say back.

'So,' he continued for her instead, 'why're you followin' me? What's so important that you come out in the dark in rough times as these? No-one should be walking alone. Least of all a young lass.'

'Why were you pretending to be drunk?' Yoshiko shifted where she was perched on the roof and dared to get a little more comfortable.

'Huh?' He looked upwards, eyes watching the roof warily. She scolded herself for being careless. 'You noticed? People underestimate you then. If there's a problem, I can look after myself—or someone else.'

With that last bit, Yoshiko thought of the shopkeeper and what she'd said about him being kind. From the outside, he seemed careless and rough, and half-drunk, he even acted it. But she wondered if he wouldn't be a bad person to work with, after all, if the drinking wasn't too much of a habit. You couldn't predict someone who drank a lot.

'You should try remembering that.' He grinned easily and covered his pale eyes with his light blue sleeve, making as if he wanted to sleep.

'Remember what?'

'Actin' drunk makes people underestimate ya. Ya get away with a lot. Might come in handy.'

Yoshiko thought about that. It wasn't like anything Chinen or her mother had taught her, but from watching him earlier, she believed him.

'So, ya wanna speak? Be quick. I wanna sleep.'

Suddenly feeling off guard, Yoshiko wondered how she'd even go about asking it. In her mind, she imagined sneaking up to him, catching him off guard, and impressing him with her shadow skills. Then, just like her mother, she'd have given some impressive speech to convince him to work with her to save their region. Now she was here, Yoshiko felt awkward and not like that at all.

'Um,' she started, looking at his half-covered face. He already looked asleep. She wondered whether he'd even hear her now.

Gora grunted something from below, indicating for her to continue.

'I need your help,' she admitted. It wasn't smooth or persuasive, and her mother would probably be staring at her with a look of disbelief from the spirit world. 'I heard you were a skilled hunter and tracker and were good at all kinds of jobs, with a good eye and ear for things,' she gushed. 'There's something I need to do, and I can't do it alone.'

Yoshiko waited, the world about her silent—not even wind shook the trees. She shivered. The night felt so open, and she felt so suddenly vulnerable up here. It was time to leave.

'Where'd ya hear I was good?' the autumn-haired man said eventually, voice soft and hard to hear.

'A shopkeeper.' Yoshiko didn't want to admit she'd been eavesdropping.

He grunted and turned his head to the side, but he kept his eyes covered with his arm. 'Why should I? Got my own things to do.'

There it was. The point Yoshiko had been struggling to figure out a reason for. She still didn't have much of a convincing answer.

'I heard you were kind and took good care of people. People are getting hurt, and they're frightened. This curfew and the brutality of the guards are causing a problem.' Yoshiko thought back to everything she'd seen and heard, and somehow, words spilled from her mouth. She didn't know if it was the right answer, though. 'I'm sure it's a pain even for you, making things difficult—you're unable to return to your home safely. This isn't the Hié I was raised in. This isn't the life I was taught about.'

Yoshiko thought back to what Haruki told her of life in the town and how this didn't match up to what her maid had said. She had to fix it, and she had to find Haruki and make Hié a better place to live again. Then, she could return to the palace and find a way to punish the traitors on the council who started this all.

'It's a problem and a fuckin' pain, for sure. But I'm not sure how I can help with that. This sorta thing starts from the top. There ain't much us at the bottom can do.' The arm that covered his eyes struck out at the straw in frustration, and the poor mare next to him startled. He leapt up to calm her, hushing and humming at her.

'As you say,' Yoshiko said, thinking. 'It starts at the top.' She took a risk. 'Hear me out. Meet me tomorrow to speak properly. We can talk at a more decent time. I'll give you time to think it through.'

Gora grunted and plonked himself back in the straw once the mare had calmed. 'Fine,' he growled. 'I'll hear ya out. Where d'you want me to go?'

Yoshiko told him about a stone wall behind a plum tree in the eastern public garden. He was to go there, alone, and head between the gap when no-one was looking. From there, he'd see a place to move the wall aside.

'It's surprisingly light,' she told him. 'Go inside the opening and close it behind you. I'll leave a lantern for you. Just follow the passageway.'

Gora said something in a low voice—something in the language she didn't understand, the same one from the song—but she ignored it. Eventually, he agreed. Then, before he could change his mind, she leapt from the roof and sprinted into the trees on the other side of the track. She waited, hiding, certain he'd try to see. Sure enough, she heard scrambling and saw the red-haired man throw open the stable door and scan the track. Seeing nothing, he frowned, rubbed a hand through his fiery hair, and disappeared back inside. The last thing Yoshiko heard before she slipped away to make her way back to the caverns was the crashing of a large, heavy body into the straw as the man gave up for the night and fell asleep.

13

Gora

The man with autumn hair woke before the sun rose the next day, with the familiar and awful musty taste of dehydration after drinking spirits on his breath. Gora's mouth begged for a long draught of cool water, but here—not in his hut—he didn't know where to get one. He looked next to him at the sleeping mare huffing gently through her large nostrils into the straw.

Probably gotta trough o' water somewhere, hasn't she.

Gora wrinkled up his face. *Not that desperate to share with a horse, am I?*

Instead, he heaved himself up, shrugged on his *haori*, brushed down his light kimono, and kicked the straw about a bit to hide the obvious man-shaped dent. Then, Gora picked his way in the grey, pre-sunrise light down the track that led to his home. Home—to wash, drink, and change into something that didn't smell of a grim concoction of sweat, drink, and horse.

The morning air was cool and fresh, and the further Gora walked, the more his head cleared. He'd spoken with someone last night, he remembered, in the little barn. It had been a young woman—in her early twenties, probably—and she'd spoken well with the upper-class's dialect, using words only used in the upper ranks of society. Gora recognised them from watching the masked plays at Omatsuri festivals. But what would an upper-class daughter want from him and his services? Surely, she had better people to go to, like the guards or some authority figure? Gora doubted she wanted him to hunt for her or make her something. She'd not have snuck and followed him in the night and hidden if it were that simple, and she probably had enough good food from her birthright.

By now, he'd reached Yamamoto, the small village he lived in on the edge of the forest that climbed up the mountains of north Hié, and light had washed over the land. He stopped a moment to take a deep breath, as he always did near the forest, and rubbed a calloused hand through his autumn hair. He loved Yamamoto village and its home at the foot of the mountain with the houses and their steep, triangular straw roofs and simple tracks and rice paddies and vegetable fields dotted about. As Gora padded down the track, he heard the cheerful cries of children running outside and their parents calling them to focus on their morning chores first. He shrugged and smiled— life as always. Here on the edge, at least, things seemed a little less tense than in Hié town. That's why Gora preferred it here. That and its vicinity to the forest where he completed most of his work. He shrugged happily and shuffled through the worn pathways, past kids who called to him as he passed. He patted one on his head and gently tossed a cloth ball back to a young girl who'd cheerfully cried out his name and chucked it at him to try to catch him out and make him drop it. He'd caught it—just. When he walked down the paths to the houses, a few voices called out to greet him and teased him about staying out late and looking a mess. He jovially teased back and bowed good-naturedly, ducking into his small, wooden home.

He smiled to himself, slipping his zori off in the *genkan* and stepping up into the main home. Here, it didn't matter if he was a foreigner or looked different to anyone else. They'd accepted him anyway. Especially the kids. It was for that reason that he stayed here particularly—no longer the foreigner, just 'Gora'.

Inside, a variety of wood-carved furniture and tiny items scattered about from his attempts at learning a skill from the days of his childhood. Gora's life started far across the ocean, in a land called Eire he could barely remember from the length of time he'd been away. He scarcely remembered the faces of his family, and their voices even less so. Yet he had a strong memory of wood and of his father making all kinds of things. So, to keep that memory, he'd tried it. He wasn't particularly good, and many of his items were wonky or uneven, but the people here seemed to like them. They had a strange love for imperfect things, as they reflected the flawed nature of life. *Wabi-sabi*. People had been happy with Gora's items and requested more. Slowly, he'd got better, but he was still nowhere near as skilled as the famous Hié crafters. That didn't stop him from trying, though, and the random wooden items throughout his home showed he was growing.

It wouldn't be this that the woman wanted help with, either. She'd not have snuck out in the darkness to ask about wonky woodwork.

As he padded about his home barefoot, collecting water in a wooden pail to wash with and finally gasping at a long and refreshing drink, Gora thought about the woman and whatever her need could be. She'd been silent—creeping up on him was a rare thing, and something only the ninjas of this country seemed able to do. Discovering that secret organisation of night warriors had terrified him at first. He'd thought he was aware of what was going on around him, having been thrust into situations in his life where he'd had to develop a good defence and awareness—but the ninja were a different level. If the woman had snuck up on him, perhaps she was a ninja, too. But what would such an organisation need with him? He was a bumbling foreigner compared to them.

And though he could creep through the woods and hunt better than anyone, this woman had passed even his keen senses.

Gora tossed his kimono into a bucket, intending to wash it later. Then, dressed for a new day in his favourite dark green kimono and mid-grey *hakama*, trying to look a little more formal, he let his curiosity get the better of him—why was a rich girl hiding in a supposed secret tunnel by a tree? And what would she want with a man like him when she had a whole host of authorities she could turn to? A horrible thought flashed into his mind. She didn't want him to kill anyone for her, did she? Not wanting to go to the authorities, someone might want that sort of thing. He was a foreigner here, after all. People might think it was okay if the foreigner got caught doing unthinkable things, compared with asking a Hién to do it. If that were the case, he'd tell her where to go. Gora grabbed his boots from the *genkan*—and his twin cutlasses from days long gone, just to be sure, not knowing what he was walking into—and stomped outside, tying the sheaths of his blades to his *hakama* tie. Despite bringing them, he hoped he'd not need to use them. He was a forager and a forester, a huntsman and a man for hire—a man of many roles, including the creator of various wonky woodworks. But a killer? No.

He pulled his shoulders up to his ears and squinted into the distance towards the main town. Well, he wasn't a killer anymore.

* * *

The trek to Hié town took him well into the morning, and people were milling about their day. Shops were open—sliding doors wide, awnings propped-up, and goods laid out. The stomach-warming smell of mixed grain rice and toasted rice cakes wafted down the streets, and Gora's stomach gave a bear-like roar. He stopped to eye a small food cart on the edge of the road selling stone-oven-baked *satsuma-imo*. The naturally sweet smell lifted his spirits and the *satsuma-imo* seemed like the perfect way to satisfy his still-fragile stomach. Damn. He'd tried not to drink too much last night, but these days, he felt worse each time he drank. Maybe he was getting old.

Gora passed a coin to the tiny old woman at the cart and held out his hand towel. When she pressed a steaming hot *satsuma-imo* into it, his stomach gave another roar—this one loud enough for both to hear. The old woman's eyes crinkled as she laughed and patted his arm gently. He grinned and shuffled off to the side of the road where he crouched against the stone wall to eat. The *satsuma-imo* was deliciously sweet and so hot the steam looked like a dragon's breath. He puffed on it before each mouthful and devoured it far too quickly for his greedy tastebuds, which burned a little on the sweet treat.

Finally, ready to continue his journey into the unknown and find out what that upper-class woman wanted, Gora waved to the old lady at the potato cart and continued to follow the stone wall—reaching the garden the woman had told him about. He walked the perimeter of the park, occasionally stopping to swig water from his flask and lean against the wall to relax.

'There're lots o' damn plum trees in the eastern public garden,' he growled under his breath, looking along the wall and at all the plum trees. What would he do if he didn't find the right one? This place was huge.

But there was only one place where the stone wall seemingly met itself in a strange overlap. And, though it didn't look like anyone could go through it—it just looked like the wall had been built on a curve to accommodate the tree, rather than cutting the tree down to continue the wall in a straight line—upon closer inspection, and by pulling himself in the tiny gap behind the tree, Gora found there was indeed a space to slip through.

'Well, I'll be damned,' he breathed.

He looked about, ruffling his hand through his auburn hair awkwardly and trying to look natural and blend into his surroundings. Certain no-one was looking, Gora ducked through the gap and stood in a little crevice in the wall. How did no-one find this place? Running his hand along the stone wall in this little crevice, Gora gave a satisfied chuckle when his hand met another material—well-carved wood that had been cleverly made to look like stone. His heart leapt. This was just getting more exciting, and he felt the old, familiar feeling of adventure flush through his veins.

Gora slid open the door and met a darkness that disappeared into nothingness. Yes, as promised, a small lantern sat just out of the way of the door, giving a warm glow to the otherwise cold-looking tunnel. Gora felt that familiar sensation of his heart beating faster and a chill flashing through his spine. Then, he reached out for the lantern and shut the heavy wooden door behind him, taking his first step into the tunnel towards what he knew would promise adventure.

14

How Did it Come to This?

Yoshiko heard the autumn-haired man long before she saw him. She knelt on her cushion by the fire in the main cavern hall while she listened to the sounds of his footsteps and words that came in two languages—Hién and the one she'd heard him sing in yesterday. She wondered what the other language was called. But she didn't need to know it to understand he'd burst out with exclamations, questions, and the odd laugh. Yoshiko found it interesting. One day, she wanted to know more about the country this man—Gora—had come from and what it was like. She wondered how much like Hié it was, and what stories he had to tell. Her musings were interrupted when the man finally came around the corner, stopping dead in his tracks when he saw her and the cavern with a little stone village tucked away under the city.

'Well, I'll be—' His mouth dropped open, and he tried to look in all directions at once.

Yoshiko sipped her tea, holding the warm mug with both hands, and watched him warily. She was nervous about showing herself. Ever since fleeing the castle, no-one had known who she was. And the last pair of people she had regularly spoken to had been murdered in their own home. This man, Gora, was another innocent party, and her heart felt like it would run out of power with nerves. She closed her eyes for a moment and took a deep breath. How would her mother handle this? If she acted like Asumi, would that help her get through it? Yoshiko watched the man with autumn-coloured hair until he had gathered himself enough to speak.

'There's a village underneath the town?' he gaped and asked her, pointing vaguely at anything, dark green sleeve dropping down his arm a little. Gora still didn't walk any further into the room but spun on the spot to look about. He craned his neck to look at the ceiling.

Yoshiko hummed in affirmation and wondered what her mother would have said now, certain Asumi would have just waited to see what the man would do next and judge his reactions. But Yoshiko's mind was buzzing with questions. *Does everyone where you come from have hair that colour? What language do you speak? What was that song about last night? How far away is your home country, and why did you come to Hié?*

She managed to remain quiet.

The man stepped forwards, still looking up at the ceiling with his mouth hung open. 'There's light, somehow?'

Nodding, Yoshiko thought if she opened her mouth to talk, she'd burst and say too much. He looked at her now, face serious, and didn't speak again, clearly making his own judgement about who she was and what she might want. Instead, they remained in silence. She saw countless questions cross his face, and Yoshiko gestured to the other cushion by the fire and was happy when he took it—though his face told her he wondered why he had. Perhaps she had a chance to convince him to help her. Yoshiko poured him a tea and smirked at the look of confusion on his face, unable to wipe it from her face no matter how hard she tried.

Mama wouldn't smirk, she thought, but she couldn't help it.

His tea remained untouched while he continued to look around the cavern and back at her. Eventually, the man stared at her again, pale eyes piercing hers, and sipped his tea. 'How could you sneak up on me?'

There was a sting in his voice, as if he doubted it could be possible.

'There are many things we can't guess about someone from their appearance.' She thought of her mother, how she never thought Asumi would be cursed with scales on her body. 'People have many hidden strengths and secrets.' Inside, her heart leapt at how she thought these were words her parents would say.

'You speak like a rich girl but dress like a lower-class citizen,' he said.

'True.' Yoshiko sipped more tea to stop herself from bursting out with questions. Instead, she continued to watch him, wondering whether he'd accept what she had to say and help her.

The autumn-haired man waited, but she didn't say anything more. So he asked more questions. 'How did you find this place now? Where are we? What're ye doing here?'

'My mother showed me. It's complicated. I'm hiding.'

'Your mother? How did she find it?'

'Her family built it, generations ago.' Yoshiko felt him scrutinising her more closely, and her heartbeat rose, feeling uncomfortable at how much it felt like he could judge from just looking.

'Seems there's more to that story, but your face tells me not to pry. I know people have secrets. The damned know I have some myself. My name's Gora. What did you want me to come here for now?' He looked down at his empty teacup and raised a thick, red brow. 'Something's telling me it's not to drink tea with yerself.'

She felt a smile twitch in the corners of her mouth. 'I told you last night,' she said, trying to become serious again, holding herself like she'd watched Asumi do. 'I need your help. I want to make changes and help the people of this town, but I can't do it alone. As you can see'—she gestured about the cavern—'I'm a little low on allies.'

Gora looked about the room and let out a laugh. 'Just a bit, eh!' His face darkened over. 'So why'd I get the feeling you're that lost noble daughter they've been hunting?'

Yoshiko felt her body freeze. Gora looked at her warily now, and she noticed how rugged his face looked, though his eyes looked young. She tried to figure out how old he was—he looked weathered, like he'd seen many things, but his bright, pale eyes and energy meant he didn't seem too much older than her. Perhaps ten years older? A little more? It was hard to tell. She suddenly realised how large his nose looked, peppered with light speckles. He prompted again when she didn't answer.

'I'm right, aren't I?'

Yoshiko shifted uncomfortably on her cushion but straightened her back, trying to think of what her mother would say to make the situation one that gave her the best results. Nothing came to mind.

He grinned when she didn't answer. 'Yeah, I'm right. So, how've you stayed hidden this whole time now? They're hunting for you everywhere. Made a damn scare in our village. You been hiding under them the entire time?'

'Most of it,' she said, feeling suddenly ashamed of herself. Her energy left her, and her voice fell flat. 'Though I've been up into the main town for missions.'

'Missions?'

'To find out who betrayed us and killed my parents; to take back the castle. Gather supplies. To stop the people being frightened and killed just because they're hunting for me. That's why I need your help.' It all came out now, but it wasn't anything as inspiring as she'd have liked. Nothing like Asumi would say.

'And the daimyō? Is it true they found her dead?' Gora's light eyes of that unknown colour pierced hers, and she felt locked to the spot and unable to look away.

She froze, her breath catching in her throat and making it difficult to speak. 'What do you know?'

Gora shrugged and shuffled to sit cross-legged on the cushion, leaning back on one of his hands. 'Not much. Only snippets of news from people talkin'. They said the daimyō was found on Shogo's border. They say she must've been killed by a bear or somethin' running through the mountain pass, and was weak from hunger tryin' to escape. They say they still didn't find the daughter. Well, now I know why.'

Yoshiko growled—a noise that surprised them both. Gora jumped and looked at her with wide, startled eyes.

'Hey, now,' he said as if calming an animal. 'I'm guessing that's not true, then?'

Yoshiko shook her head and sighed.

'Well, ya never can just believe what others say. I figured somethin' fishy was goin' on.' He chuckled and relaxed again.

'Fishy?' Yoshiko said. 'What does this have to do with fish?'

Gora laughed again and explained that, in his hometown, it was a common phrase. He'd tried translating it into Hié because it was a 'handy phrase', but no-one understood him when he said it.

'It means something sinister is goin' on. Somethin' you don't trust—like fish. When fish goes bad, it smells. So, if a situation is bad, it gives people a bad sense—like bad fish.' He tried to explain it, and this time, Yoshiko understood.

He looked again at his teacup, and Yoshiko took that as a sign for more tea. She poured them both more, happily cupped the hot pottery in her hands, and sniffed up the reassuring smell. Gora made a noise like a wounded crow and hastily put the cup down, moaning of the heat. He looked at her strangely, but she didn't focus any further on it.

'So you want me to help save your domain, little noble?'

Yoshiko nodded and looked into the flames. 'Or, at least for now, those in it.'

'You know that could get us killed?' Gora's voice had gone dark.

'All too well,' she muttered and thought about those who had already died. 'But I know more will if I don't do something to stop it. I don't have the luxury of death; it won't solve my problem.'

Gora frowned and took a breath. There was a long pause as they both stared into the fire. When Yoshiko looked up at him, she saw sadness in his eyes.

'I just wanted a simple life. I didn't want to get involved in anything dark or strange or dangerous again. Wanted to get far away from the life I knew and start over—live quietly.' He looked up at Yoshiko. 'That's why I came here—to escape madness. The damned know I've known enough of it.'

Yoshiko wondered what he could mean by that, but he continued before she could ask.

'I like it here. I like my home, my village, my neighbours, and I have a decent job that I'm happy with and that helps people. It's so different to what I knew before. And I earn enough to live by, and enough to buy drink sometimes to avoid the ghosts. But now it seems there are different ghosts.' He leant back, propping himself up on both hands and looking up at the star steams in the ceiling. He spoke slowly. 'I've heard the stories, and I don't like what's going on. The daimyō's husband dead, and she and her daughter mysteriously disappear, only for the daimyō to be found dead, too. The daughter lives alone in the darkness, sneakin' around her own region where she should walk free and live the life of a young woman in the sunshine. There are stories of young girls disappearing—girls your age. People are afraid, goin' missing ...'

He sighed and closed his eyes. 'It's madness. Recently, a farmhouse near our village went up in flames. They were good people. I don't think that was an accident either. Fires like that don't just start by accident now.'

Yoshiko's heart quickened. 'That was me.' She spoke into the flames and tried not to picture the burning farmhouse in it. The familiar salty sting of tears burnt her eyes and her voice cracked, though she tried to hide it. 'That was me. They killed them, too. I burned the house to send them to the spirit world. I didn't know what else to do.'

Gora swore. He stared for a while into the flames, and Yoshiko waited out his silence, hoping he was thinking about an answer she'd feel pleased with. It was a little while later that he spoke again. 'If people like them are dyin', I want in. I don't wanna live in the sort of place kind farmers and innocent girls are killed. I saw too much of that before. I'll do my best to help, at least for the people. I can't promise much else.'

Yoshiko thought she'd be happy at this moment, but instead, her heart felt low. They met each other's eyes and nodded.

'How did it come to this?' He swore again and lay back onto the stone floor with his arm over his eyes.

Yoshiko looked up at the star streams, silent, wondering the same.

15

Getting Caught in a Scrape

That day, Gora returned to his home in Yamamoto in a daze and barely registered the journey. The voices of people passing him in the streets faded as if he were underwater, and Hié seemed to have lost its cheerful feel. Now, everywhere seemed tainted by this new-found knowledge, and he started to see the failings of the town—like the peeling paintwork on a shop sign and the abandoned house on the other side of the street.

He shrugged and shook his head wildly, trying to reinvigorate himself before he returned to Yamamoto. The people there would cheer him up.

The next day, he returned to the caverns. This time, much quicker in finding the entrance, he strolled casually through the public park on the edge of town, finding the section of wall that overlapped, and ducked through the hidden door. This time, instead of a flame torch to guide him down the dark tunnel, the girl herself was waiting, wearing a purple two-layered kimono and holding a closed purple cloth parasol.

'What the—how'd ya know I was here? Were you just standing there the whole time?' Gora gasped, stilling his heart. She'd looked like one of those ghost spirits in the stories here, and he leaned against the wall of the tunnel for support while he got his life back.

Her young face looked amused, and he wondered if she knew she'd scared him half to death. 'Heard you,' was all she said before stepping towards the door. 'Shall we head straight out?'

It wasn't much of a question, as she brushed past him, opened the door, and put out the flame, leaving the torch lying on the edge of the tunnel. With nothing else to do, Gora turned to follow.

'So what're we doin'?' Gora asked, tucking his hands into his dark green kimono sleeves casually. He leaned around and peered at her face as they walked, squinting. It looked different from the day before, but he couldn't tell if it was just that he was now seeing it out in daylight, rather than by firelight, half in shadows. He frowned in thought.

Beside him, the young woman raised her arm and fidgeted with her fringe, making sure it fell straight over her forehead. Then, she looked across at him and frowned back. 'What's wrong with my face?'

'Huh?'

'You're staring at my face. Is something wrong?'

Gora felt his eyebrows raise, and he realised she looked uncomfortable. He ruffled a hand through his own hair and looked ahead instead. 'Ahh! My bad. Just, you look diff'rent today.'

When he looked back at her, feeling awkward, he noticed a smile had replaced her uneasy expression. 'Good,' she chuckled. 'Means the disguise is working.'

When he asked her to explain, the young woman told him that her mother had taught her how to use powders and make-up to alter her face, changing the shape enough that people didn't realise it was the same person. She could make her face look narrower or more full, and Gora nodded, finally understanding.

That would explain why she looked different. Instead of a small, soft face with a slightly pointed nose and large, dark eyes, her cheeks looked rounder and her eyes looked narrower.

Lips were fuller with this make-up on but didn't quite show her expressions as easily as normal, and he found it strange that he could no longer read her face like he could yesterday. He shook his head as they turned onto a main street, wondering at the difference.

'Convenient! Can you do it to my face, too?'

Yoshiko stopped, and Gora looked behind to see confusion on her new, disguised face.

'Why? It's not like it would work. All of you is different.'

Now it was his turn to look at her with wide eyes. 'Alright,' he spluttered. 'I can't help if I'm different to all of ye.'

He saw the thought pattern flick through her eyes as she tried to defend how she hadn't intended it that way. This little noble lass was easy to read. Gora held back a smirk. Once she'd finished trying to dig her verbal hole, he held up his hands in surrender and grinned easily. 'Alright, alright. No make-up for the man. I get it. Just though' it'd be fun. Now, ye've still not told me what we're doin' today.'

Yoshiko looked at him and sighed, her whole facial expression, even disguised, showing she was already wondering whether bringing him on board would be worth it. He shrugged and held her gaze, waiting. He wasn't going to let a high-born push him around. But, instead of getting frustrated, she seemed to lighten up, and she gestured with her head to keep going, pushing up the parasol as a further disguise.

'I've been spending time in town, listening to people talk about what's happening in Hié. That's how I found out about you. Much is gossip, but some helps. Apparently, the hunt for me still isn't over, and since my mother was killed, it's only become worse. They know I'm here, and you already know of the curfew at night, and the guards are causing trouble. That's not what I want the samurai or Hié to be like.'

Gora hummed the odd polite response to show he was listening and looked around the streets. They were heading closer to the heart of the town, zigzagging towards the castle. He wondered whether she was taking him there. Before he could find out, she'd stopped and was glaring at a corner of the street, lowering her parasol closer to her face and turning to face a cloth shop as if admiring the wares. Not a moment later, three samurai guards stomped around the corner and into the shop street, and Gora watched as they surveyed the area. Their eyes fell on him, meeting his gaze as he stared at them, and he realised he ought to look away.

He sighed and rubbed the back of his head, turning to Yoshiko and resting an arm on her shoulder casually, joining her in looking at the shop. He felt her body tense, but she didn't move or look away from the shop.

She's terrible at acting, he thought, wondering how she'd got this far.

The guards stomped closer down the street, and Gora pointed with his other arm and muttered something about the cloth to Yoshiko. The guards were just behind them when she finally played along, reaching for cloth he'd pointed to. As Gora expected, the guards stomped on, stirring nothing but worry but leaving the people be. He turned back to Yoshiko, who had lowered her parasol to her side and was watching the guards leave, face pale beneath the make-up. Gora smiled slightly and moved the arm that was resting on her shoulder to rest his hand gently on her head instead. She flinched and looked up at him, brows furrowed, brushing the hand off.

'What are you doing?' she hissed, looking offended.

Gora was surprised. 'Just comfortin' you. Ye' looked like ye'd seen a ghoul.'

'Comforting?'

Gora furrowed his brow. 'Should I not?'

She paused, then looked away. The shopkeeper had rushed over and greeted them, and Yoshiko immediately switched on a bright smile and responded politely and eagerly. Here, she seemed totally different, and Gora noticed how much she lit up when talking to people.

This young girl should be walking in the sun and enjoying simple conversations like this without fear of being caught and killed, not hiding in caverns alone.

Gora let the two women's simple but happy conversation wash over him unheard and looked down the street at the guards marching further away.

He could help her, couldn't he? He knew what it was like to be trapped in a life you didn't want.

Later, Gora returned to the caverns and joined her in eating a simple meal. She'd prepared the food herself in a hot cooking bowl over the fire, and even watching her cook had been painful.

'You're trying to cook like *that*?' he cried out, unable to watch any longer and lurching forward to stop her from putting any more miso paste into the cooking pot. 'Have you ever cooked before in your life?'

She glared at him, pulling the ladle from the bowl. 'No.'

He was stumped, expecting some sort of long-winded explanation. It never came. Instead, he offered it himself. 'I guess up at the keep, the daughter of a daimyō doesn't need to do such things?'

'Not until they're forced to leave the castle.'

'So what've you done with food since?'

The girl flushed, face turning pink in the orange firelight. 'Mother did it mostly. Somehow, she knew. Though I didn't know enough to complain or know if it was wrong. And she never complained when I cooked, either.'

Gora raised an eyebrow, looking in the bowl at the strange-coloured liquid gloop that he guessed was meant to be a cross between miso soup and stew. 'Right,' was all he offered in return, resolving to eat back in his own home of an evening if he could help it, and cook for them himself if he couldn't. Until then, he'd have to brave what he was given and hope his stomach didn't reject it. He'd survived worse, hadn't he? He took his chopsticks out from his sleeve, cringing to see his hands shake as he reached for the offered bowl.

No sooner had he finished forcing the food into his mouth than Yoshiko padded over to a dark hut on the edge of the firelight. She returned dressed in the same clothes he'd seen her in when they met, a simple indigo kimono and black *hakama* with black *tabi*. He looked up as she strode back to the fire, knowing she was going to say they were heading out again, but not sure if his stomach was ready to move around without losing what he'd eaten. As expected, it hadn't been good, and he wondered if she even still had tastebuds at this point, and what her stomach was made of.

'No time to settle the ol' stomach, then?'

* * *

No time to settle the stomach at all. Immediately upon exiting the cavern entrance in the side of the building in the mid-town alleyway, the young woman ran off into the darkness, her dark clothing blending into the night. Gora bumbled about in the streets, spinning on the spot to look for her. She appeared a few paces ahead of him, looking at him blankly.

'How'd ya do that?' he asked, striding forward. 'You're like a damned ninja!'

The young girl, face now without make-up, looked confused, thin lips pulled into a frown. 'What do you mean? This is nothing like my mother wanted me to be.'

Gora's eyebrows raised. 'Right, well, either way, don't leave the peasant behind. How'm I supposed to help if you run off?'

The girl turned and continued, slower this time, up the hill towards the castle. Gora gazed at the tall, white structure, lightly lit up by the moonlight. It was completely different from the castles back home. Not that he'd seen many.

She coughed to get his attention, and he saw they'd turned to run along the side of the moat, down a street that circled the castle grounds, dedicated to large blocks of land to house the upper-ranking samurai and members of society. Here, the night was quiet, but more regular patrols took place as guards monitored the area and returned to their homes. They ducked behind a wall to wait one out.

'Where're we heading?'

'Guard tower,' she muttered, pointing to a building on the edge of the moat.

He nodded, then leaned around the corner to see if the patrol had gone. It had. And when he turned back to let the young girl know, so had she. Once again, he wheeled on the spot to search for her, exasperated. He saw her running the gap between him and the guard tower, let out a quick huff, and ran to join her.

'Don't just run off like that,' he growled lowly at her when he caught up, both ducking low against the white wall of the guard tower. He looked up at the slats of windows, wondering if a guard was on the other side, and kept his voice low.

'I thought you'd keep up. You're here, aren't you?'

'Aye, I guess, but an alert would be good.'

She turned to face him, expressionless. Then, she flashed a smile, one that reached her dark eyes briefly, too. 'Okay.'

Gora watched her for a moment as she looked up at the watchtower, and he wondered what kind of life she'd had before to not know she needed to tell people things. Now Gora was definitely curious as to what went on in that castle. He was tempted to ask. But his thoughts flushed from his mind when he saw her reach up and swiftly pull herself onto the sloped, dark-tiled roof of the guardhouse, and he stood up, hands on his hips, looking up in astonishment. She peered down, small face raising a questioning brow.

Gora flailed his arms in answer with an overexaggerated shrug and searched around them, now feeling quite exposed standing on his own. Then he looked back up at her and shook his head. She hopped back down to join him, and he leaned close to answer, noticing her edge back slightly as he did.

'I can't get up there!'

'Oh, really?'

Gora ignored the surprise in her voice and continued. 'What are we even doing here? Is it something I can do without clambering all over the place? I'm a big bloke. I'd break something!'

He didn't say whether it would be the building or himself, but either option was valid.

The young woman looked thoughtfully about; then her eyes flashed and she pulled him down and to the back corner of the guardhouse, crouching low on the edge of the moat. A moment later, footsteps of another patrol padded down the curved main street of this first upper ring of residences and headed for the guard tower.

Gora's heart thundered.

'Can you swallow any louder?' the girl hissed, sounding irritated.

What? 'As if you could hear that!' he hissed back, turning to glare at her. 'I thought you were a princess. Aren't princesses meant to be kind?'

He expected her to look annoyed. Instead, she looked as surprised as him. She clamped her lips together as if she couldn't believe she'd said anything, and her face had flushed as red as an autumn maple leaf.

'I'm not a princess,' was all she croaked back, looking as if she wanted to swallow her words.

The ridiculousness of it overcame Gora, and he swallowed back a bubble of laughter, turning to face away from her and clasping a hand over his mouth. A scuff on the road brought him back to reality.

Been a good few years since I was sneakin' around like this, he thought, narrowing his eyes and watching the road beyond the corner of the guardhouse. *Not sure I'm up to it anymore.* He knew if the patrol came past that corner, they'd be spotted. If the patrol went inside, they'd be fine.

Gora heard a shift of fabric behind him and felt a light tap on his shoulder, and he turned to see the young girl pulling herself back onto the guard tower roof. She gestured for him to urgently join her, watching the road carefully as if she knew something he didn't. She looked back at him with furrowed brows, gesturing again.

Still not thinking he could get up there, Gora ignored her. *She can speak to me if she wants me to do anything,* he thought, not understanding her urgency.

Well, not until the patrol came past the corner, and his heart flew into his mouth. He struggled to swallow it back down again and pressed himself against the watchtower, hoping he'd not slip and fall into the moat.

A group of armed guards in kimono and *hakama* walked past, chatting merrily. One good-naturedly ruffled the hair of another, and a female voice barked out for them to quit messing around. Gora wished the same—that they'd just quickly go by and not notice him—but things never went to plan. One turned her face to chastise the pair behind her, and he locked eyes with her, watching her face flush with surprise and then severity. She stood still, hand instinctively reaching for her katana. The others paused, and the playful man immediately stopped ruffling his comrade's hair and walked towards Gora.

Gora heard a frustrated tongue click above him, and a shuffle as the girl moved on the watchtower roof. He stood, preparing himself.

'What are you doing here?' the male guard storming towards him asked, face no longer jovial.

Gora tried to diffuse the situation with a lie. He bowed politely to greet the guard and then flailed his arms in a light shrug as he replied. 'Drank a bit much. Felt like a walk to wear it off and to admire the castle. Felt a bit sick, so had a bit of a rest. You know the time?'

The guard narrowed his eyes, and the others watched. The woman still had her hands resting on her hilt. Gora swallowed, knowing the guard wouldn't answer his question, wondering how this was going to turn out.

'You alone?'

'I am,' he replied, not even daring to look up to see where the girl was. If the guard had asked that question, it meant he couldn't see her. He'd not mess that up.

The guard looked like he was thinking, so Gora tried to press further.

'S'alright. I'll mosey on home now I'm feelin' better.' He tried to edge past the guards, but the first man stepped in his way. Gora winced.

A gasp went up, and Gora turned to see Yoshiko quickly run along the roof tiles, leap the distance to the ground at the main group's feet, breaking her fall with a roll, then launch back up and driving an elbow into the stomach of one of the guards. He stumbled back and doubled over in pain, face snarling and eyes watering. But Yoshiko didn't wait. She launched forwards, grabbed the man's shoulders, twisted him to the floor, and knocked him out.

Gora watched in surprise, and when she caught his gaze, he snorted out a laugh.

'Well? What're you waiting for?' Yoshiko asked him. 'We need to get out of here.'

He grinned. 'Aye, we do.' And he faced the man in front of him, launching himself forward, and before the man could even draw his blades, Gora had thrown a jab to the man's nose, a deep punch to his gut, and then tackled him to the ground. The man's head hit the floor, and he lay dazed.

Shall I knock him out, too? Gora wondered, quickly looking up as the remaining five guards dispersed to handle their two intruders. *Nah, hit 'n' run. Focus on getting away.* He rushed another guard—the woman who'd been waiting with her hands on her katana hilt.

She reached towards him to grab, maim, and arrest him, but Gora wouldn't let that happen. He leapt out of the way, crashed a fist sideways into her elbow to deflect her arm as it reached past, and then twisted to grab both her wrist and her upper arm. He swung her around and drove her to the ground, just like he'd seen other guards do to arrest people here.

Knowing this move, the woman resisted, and just as she was about to hit the ground, she caught herself, brought her leg around, and pulled him down instead. Gora rolled to his side, catching sight of Yoshiko fighting off two others as he did, and brought himself up onto one knee and then stood, grinning at the guard.

Her eyes flicked to look past him, and he heard a shuffle from behind, so he turned to meet it, quickly dodging a fist reaching for his face, feeling it narrowly scuff the side of his cheek. Gora grimaced and reached for the guard's shoulders, grabbing them and launching his knee into their stomach. He caught sight of Yoshiko again.

'You're not half bad!' he roared over the chaos, grinning. 'But—'

'But—?'

'You still fight like a noble—too fair. Damn the rules. Smash 'em.' Gora hopped aside, burying his elbow into the guard's side, then kicking the man's foot from under him while pushing his whole hand into the man's face and using it as a lever to bring the guard crashing down to the ground before punching him out.

He looked back over to the young girl, whose proper form would be slowing her down, and noticed it was only because she was unusually fast that she was able to stay on top.

How is she even moving that fast? he wondered, turning to the female guard again and spluttering as she buried a fist into his side. Frustrated and roaring out at the pain, he spun around and grabbed her arm, spinning her and locking her arm behind her, pushing her down onto her knees and twisting her arm against her back until she conceded. She didn't. She cried out to the guards in their guard tower, and Gora looked up at Yoshiko in shock. She didn't meet his gaze, already surrounded by three unconscious or maimed guards and dealing with the last.

Gora knocked out the female guard and rushed to help Yoshiko with the last, running and diving, pulling them to the ground. Gora sat on top and punched them out, looking up at the young daimyō's daughter.

She didn't look happy. He stared up at her, brows furrowed, wondering why.

Shouts brought Gora to his senses as people tentatively stepped from their homes and the guard tower to find out what had caused the chaos. Needing no further prompting, the two looked at one another and darted off back into the main town.

'What was that for?' Yoshiko spun to face him when they returned to the caverns.

Gora blinked. 'What was *what* for?'

'When you took down that last guard. I don't need saving like that. Did you not think I could handle it?'

Startled, Gora looked as her usually peaceful face lit up with anger. Her small nose flared slightly, and her eyes … he took a moment to figure out what was different about her eyes. Her usually dark brown, almost black eyes now had a spark of some sort in them. He could swear they looked like flames. Her brow furrowed more and he looked away, closing his eyes, letting a deep breath out, and scratching the back of his head.

'Ahh, it's not like I didn't think ye couldn't. You seemed to know what you were doin'.' He looked back up at her; the spark was still in her eyes. 'Just, that's what teams are for, right? Helpin' each other, even if they're good. Ain't me sayin' I think you can't. Just easier with two.'

She watched him, and he could almost see her trying to figure it out. Whatever she'd done before he'd joined her, it was like she'd been trying to prove herself to someone or compete with them.

Well, whatever. I ain't gunna be like that.

She sighed. 'Really?'

When he looked back, her eyes were back to their normal dark colour, and her face seemed more relaxed. He tilted his head, wondering whether he was seeing things. He looked at the flame torch in her hands and wondered whether the firelight had just reflected.

'Really.'

'Oh, well …' She trailed off, and he wasn't sure what she'd say next.

There was a long pause, and Gora found himself yawning, eyes watering. 'Well, whatever. I'm headin' back. I'm knackered.' He turned and strolled from the caverns. 'I'll see you tomorrow.'

Just before he entered the tunnels to leave, he heard a couple of footsteps towards him.

'Wait.'

He turned, wondering what was wrong now. Her face in the firelight looked almost embarrassed, and she looked to her side as she spoke.

'Thanks for today, and for joining me and saying you'll be back tomorrow. And for not thinking I couldn't handle it. I'm grateful.' As she finished speaking, she met his eyes for a moment and then bowed slightly.

Gora, stunned at having a noble bow to him, took a moment. Then, he grinned at her, and he noticed a small smile flicker across her face, too. 'Aye, yer welcome, lass.' Then, he turned, raising his hand in a wave.

16
Learning to Make Friends

He said he'd be back, but Yoshiko wasn't certain. That mission had been a failure, and she'd even insulted him twice—once by snapping at him about how noisy his swallowing was (as if was his fault she had accursedly good hearing), and the other by suggesting he'd deliberately dishonoured her by jumping in to save her.

Yoshiko curled up on her futon in the stone hut she and her mother had stored their belongings in. It felt safer to sleep in here, less out in the open than sleeping in the main cavern, especially now she was alone.

She kept thinking about what the red-haired foreigner had said: '… it's not like I didn't think ye couldn't … that's what teams are for, right? Helpin' each other …'

So he'd not thought I couldn't do it? Yoshiko stared at the roof of the cavern hut, unable to sleep.

The next morning, early, while Yoshiko was preparing to leave, she heard footsteps in the stone tunnels. Her heartbeat spiked, but she soon recognised them to be Gora's.

He came back, she thought, looking towards the carved doorway from the tunnels in that direction. A few minutes later, the orange glow of flame torchlight lit up the doorway and he stepped through, wearing his usual dark green kimono and grey *hakama*.

'Not ready, lass?' he called across the cavern. 'Thought you'd be waiting by the door again.'

'Nearly,' she responded, slipping her arrows into their quiver and picking up her hunting bow. She looked over at him. Just like yesterday, he seemed only armed with those strange swords of his.

She noticed he was looking at her bow.

'So what's the plan for today?' he asked, rubbing his cheek. He had a sleepy look across his face, and Yoshiko felt a spike of guilt. He'd not have had much sleep last night by the time he got home and then came back again.

'I'm surprised you're already here. I thought you'd be later.' She lit her torch with the fire before dousing the main flames.

'Didn't know when you'd be up and out. Forgot to ask. Thought it'd be safer to just come.'

I see, she thought, gesturing for him to follow her back into the tunnels. 'Well, I'm just going hunting. You can join me, and we can catch up on any questions you might have if you want.'

The man was quiet for a moment behind her.

'Yeah, I'll come and hunt.'

'I heard you help people with hunting?' she prompted to begin a conversation as they walked quickly up the mud track towards the woods, taking a short cut Yoshiko often used that wound through the town streets up to the foot of the hill where the forest started. You couldn't hunt well here, but it quickly got you to a good part of the forest where you could. It was steep walking, but that's what made it quieter.

'Aye, I'm pretty good at hunting.'

She heard the slight tug of his breath as they climbed up the steep slopes through the outer northern ring of Hié and towards the forest. He seemed fitter than most, she thought, but this walk would get anyone, particularly with the weather getting warmer and muggier.

'Where did you learn how?'

Gora didn't answer for a moment, and when Yoshiko looked over, she saw he looked slightly uncomfortable, and his face paled.

'Sorry,' she hurried to continue. 'You don't have to answer if it's uncomfortable. I just wanted to learn more.'

'You're alright, lass. Perhaps start with an easier question!' He fired a quick flash of a grin her way and then his face fell serious again, his blue eyes fixed on the floor where he put his feet.

She nodded, watching his face as she asked the next question, hoping it would help her read his reactions and figure out which questions were fine.

'What is the name of your home language? And where are you from? And how did you end up here?'

No sooner had all the questions tumbled out of her mouth, she tried to catch them, but it was too late. She'd only intended to ask the one. Yoshiko nervously watched his face to see a response, and he turned to face her once again but grinned properly this time.

'You sure have been holdin' back, haven't you?' His eyes met hers for a moment, and Yoshiko was stunned at just how bright they were, like the blue flowers she and her father had loved. 'I'm from Eire, and we call our language "Gaean". You heard me speakin' in it the other day?'

She nodded. 'The singing.'

He stopped walking for a moment and looked up at the sky, hands tucked into his opposite kimono sleeves. 'As for how I got here, I just ended up here. Decided I liked it and stayed.'

Yoshiko stopped and looked back at him, noticing a slight sadness on his face. She felt it wasn't the whole story, but knew not to pry. She hummed thoughtfully and turned to continue walking.

'What does your writing look like? Do you know the shrine further in the woods, slightly to the north-west of here? With the old kitsuné statues with moss at their feet?'

'Aye, I know that place. I go there. It's quiet. I like quiet places.' He continued walking, too.

'Did you write on the prayer paper there? In—what was it—Gaean?'

'I did. You saw it? You peekin' at my wishes?'

Yoshiko turned to face him, shocked. 'Of course not! I just saw strange writing and found it interesting. I couldn't read it.'

'I know, lass. I'm joking, can't you tell? What does it matter anyway? The spirits still get the wishes, even if others see them.'

'How is that a joke?' She pouted and continued walking, a bit faster this time. Behind her, she could hear Gora chuckling.

By the afternoon, they returned with a few wild rabbits and a bird. Once more in the caves, Yoshiko tended the fire and found her mind wandering. Gora was quietly singing to himself in lilting Gaean while gutting their catches of the day, and Yoshiko wondered whether she'd have been able to enjoy a free friendship like this with Haruki, too, if Haruki hadn't been her maid. She sighed, prodding the fire too hard, causing a couple of sparks to fly at her, feeling them less than Gora's outcry at her having had them fly at her. She looked up at him to see his light eyes wide with panic.

'Seriously, there's something strange about you, but I can't quite place it,' he growled as he went back to gutting the fish after she'd reassured him she was fine. 'You can hear too well, heat don't hurt ya, and there's something terrifying about your eyes when the light gets them or you're grumpy. You're not a demon or a spirit, are ya? Pretendin' to be a noble lass?'

Yoshiko felt her blood freeze, and she looked up at him.

'Aye, I'm right, aren't I? Well, if ye don't wanna be caught, don't react like that! What are ya?'

'Human, like you.'

'Pull the other one.'

'Other what?'

He let out a deep breath and tilted his head in frustration, and Yoshiko knew he'd usually run a hand through his hair in agitation if it wasn't covered in animal guts.

'Yer jokin', right? Humans aren't like that. That's more somethin' from the folk tales, surely?'

'Magic's dead—not sure what you're on about,' she bluffed, staring at the fire, feeling bothered knowing she'd just lied.

She looked back up at him when he didn't say anything, and his light eyes burned into hers.

'Aye, and I'm the son of the sun god,' he drawled, staring at the meat again. 'Call me Cú Chulainn.'

'Who? Is there a sun god?'

'He's a legendary demigod from Eire. His eyes were said to burn like a midsummer sun, but it ain't like yours when you look in the fire. What are you really? What are you hidin'? If I'm workin' with you, I need to know what I'm working with. I knew when you snuck up on me that first day somethin' was off.'

Yoshiko sighed. 'Still bitter about that?' she asked, only half feeling the joke she meant it as. She looked up at him, and the light-hearted man wasn't taking anything light-heartedly right now. He was completely serious, and his face was unreadable.

Knowing he had a lot to lose by helping her, she tried to tell him her family secret, but it was difficult to speak about it without it sounding like she was joking even more. She started from the top, how she experienced it, knowing she had heightened abilities but not knowing why, but then seeing what her mother was capable of when they escaped and how wild she looked at times, and then how her mother explained it as a family curse from the age of magic.

Gora was silent and never once interrupted with doubts about what she was saying. Instead, his light eyes pierced hers the entire time, and he processed it in silence. When she finished speaking and told him of the white fire at the place of her mother's death, more thinking aloud about what she'd wondered than telling him, a heavy silence followed. He stared into the fire again as he went through the motions of preparing the food, batting her off with his hands as she leant forward to help.

'I see,' he said finally, when Yoshiko was practically gnawing at her lips to stop herself from chipping in and breaking the silence. People didn't just process that someone had been given a family curse to be a mockery of the dragon spirits without needing time to think about it. 'That explains a lot.'

'You believe me?'

He looked at her now, eyes almost tired. 'I've been all the way around the world and seen many things.' There was another heavy pause, and his eyes went distant. She knew he was choosing what to say. It was times like this, when he spoke of his past, that his moods dropped. 'And the things I've noticed from you and heard about your family, even just the old stories of this country, seem to line up. I'll understand more with time, I imagine.'

Yoshiko was baffled. 'You mean you know other strange things from other places? Have you seen any other spirits or cursed people or magic?'

She'd thought the age of magic was over and that the spirits from the old stories hid from them these days. But what was it like in other countries? Did magic still exist? Did the spirits still show themselves to people? Yoshiko was excited to know more.

She watched him as he prepared the food, trying to swallow back questions. He looked up at her, eyes tired.

'So many questions. Do you just vibrate with energy all the time? Is a person not allowed to have a moment of quiet to catch up? Can I answer those later?'

Yoshiko, feeling a little chastised, thought for a moment before replying slowly, not knowing whether he actually wanted her to answer. 'I feel best when people are around. That's why the castle was lonely. Not many people spoke to me as a person, but as a duty. Other than my parents and my friend, Haruki. You're the only other person. Sorry. I can wait.'

She watched him look up at her again, eyes almost sorry for snapping at her, too. 'Aye, 's alright. If you need to talk, talk. 'S fine. I'll keep up. Let's just eat first. I still need a moment to process everythin' you said a moment ago.' He looked back at the food and gave her some, and Yoshiko hated to admit it, but he'd been right the whole time. She was a rotten cook, and eating his food made her shocked at just how much so. Trying not to feel embarrassed at what she'd fed him the other day, she dived into the meat, trying to store all the questions she wanted to ask him about the magic and creatures of other countries for another time.

17

Gora's Job Unveils a Horror

Several days later, Gora shoved his hands in his pockets and strolled up the city's main street, heading towards the castle compound. The shopping streets were busy, and Gora stopped to eye up some craftsmanship in the displays of a shop. Here, on the main street near the palace, things were beautiful but expensive. Even the food cost more, but the scents wafting through the lane were mouth-watering.

Today, Yoshiko wanted him to hang around by the main castle entrance and see what was going on: what things looked and felt like, who was moving in and out of the compound, and whether anything unusual was going on.

'What the—how do I know if it's unusual?' he'd protested. 'I'm not used to castle life.'

She'd just said to report anything that looked suspicious. It hadn't been helpful.

So, for days now, when he wasn't running errands for his clients, Gora had meandered through the town, spying on higher-ups, trying not to draw attention. Mooching about, he saw much: young women smiling at shop workers who glanced shyly back; older Hién people gathering to joke and play board games. But Gora could sense the tension. He wondered why there had been a sudden change. Such a peaceful country, founded on tradition, never changed too quickly without external influence. The people here would try to ignore it and continue as usual, put up with the hard times and hope they'd come to pass. But they'd never experienced other countries having the same problems like he had. They'd not seen what happens when an external force tried to break another. He had. He'd been there and, in some way, he'd been a part of it.

Gora shook his head and brought himself back to the present. He looked at the white-and-green keep rising on the folk-made platforms. Gora had seen the keep many times, but he'd never even stopped to wonder what it would be like inside. Now, he thought of Yoshiko and realised she'd have lived there.

'Damn, wonder what it'd be like in there.' Gora wondered whether it would be appropriate to ask her.

Drawing his eyes away from the keep, Gora looked about the upper market. One of the food carts in the middle of the street caught his attention, and his stomach gave an approving roar. Well, if he had to hang about here all day anyway, he may as well enjoy it. It wasn't often he got to eat food like this. A pair of guards standing watch by the palace bridge gave him a wary glare, but he shrugged and grinned back, and headed for the food cart eagerly.

'Yes, sir,' he called happily to the man at the counter who greeted him. 'Tofu bowl, please!' Gora pulled himself onto a stool while he waited and continued to watch the castle bridge. The guards had stopped watching him by now, giving up on the strange red-haired man they'd thought had been hanging about. He grinned as the cook handed him a steaming bowl of noodle soup, and he rubbed his hands together eagerly.

Gora was slurping the last of his soup and watching the people on the street go by when something finally caught his attention. It had been days of self-important-looking people entering and leaving the *oté-mon* entrance; nothing unusual, he'd thought. But, on this day, despite the warm weather and the sun, a cloaked figure slunk across the bridge and lumbered down the main street, barging past people and keeping their head low. Gora kept his eyes on this figure and lowered his bowl. Now and then, the figure raised their head to check they weren't being watched or followed. Whenever they did, a pale beard flashed into view. Gora scrunched his eyes in suspicion. People didn't grow beards often here, and they mostly had dark or black hair. This thick, scraggly, pale bush of a beard didn't belong to any Hién he'd ever seen.

Keeping his head low at the food stall until the cloaked figure got further away, Gora thanked the food-seller and ducked after them. Something wasn't right. Foreigners in Hié—other than him—and sneaking about like that (from the castle no less) in such times. He'd guessed external forces at play. Seeing a foreigner just made him more confident.

The pale-bearded man disappeared down a lane, and Gora ran after him. Hién folk parted as Gora rushed past, and they whispered to one another about why the 'hunter' was running in the town. The disruption caused the cloaked foreigner to stop and look around, and Gora skidded behind a shop to keep out of sight. His breath caught in his throat as he waited to be spotted. The shopkeeper looked at him strangely, and Gora apologised before rushing after the pale-bearded foreigner who continued at a quicker pace.

'Hunter, who is that?' someone called after him as he squeezed past. Gora muttered something about not knowing and continued, leaving the person confused.

Someone else called after him—a regular client of his, he realised as he glanced back at where the voice had come from and just waved in response.

Gora grimaced, knowing he was standing out too much. No doubt the cloaked man would know he was being tailed now. Gora dashed into a parallel alleyway and hoped to catch up with the cloaked foreigner this way, less likely to be seen. He hoped to spot the man as he wove through the streets but missed him once or twice and had to backtrack and run twice as fast to keep up. Gora's heart pounded from the effort, and he coughed into his arm as he stopped for a quick rest.

'Damn, too much drink,' he growled to himself, catching his breath, glaring down the street the cloaked figure had disappeared down.

Gora wiped the sweat from his forehead. He'd noticed a pattern in the cloaked man's movements—all downhill and in the same zigzagging direction. Gora looked at the ocean beyond, and it clicked. The port. Gora grinned and zipped off in another direction. Now, the man wouldn't see he was being followed, but Gora would easily catch up. So when he arrived at the port before the man—just in time to see him stepping warily down the final hill—Gora congratulated himself and hid behind an inn's stable door to watch what the cloaked foreigner would do next.

The pale-bearded man stomped past Gora's hiding place, and a deep voice called out further down the port. Gora dared to peek around the wall and saw another cloaked figure. This new person had his hood down, and Gora easily saw a pale face and a long, pointy nose, but he couldn't figure out which country they came from just by looking. Too far away to hear them, he saw both gesturing wildly and flailing their arms, clearly frustrated. In an attempt to figure out which language they might be using, Gora edged around the stable to get closer, but he tripped on something sticking out of the stable door and crashed to the ground.

Gora cursed under his breath and picked himself up, whipping his head around to scold a stable boy for leaving his shovel hanging out of the door. But he saw no stable boy, nor a shovel. Instead, he saw a small foot. His breath hung in his throat, worried someone had collapsed and needed help. Instead, he met worse. There were no horses in this stable, and there was indeed a young boy on the floor. But the boy was joined by a stable-full of cramped and terrified citizens chained and tied, unable to move for being shoved so tightly together. They tried to push away from the door weakly, terror in their eyes at the tall man who loomed in the brightness of the doorway. A child cried out, and a man wailed at him to leave them alone.

'Don't hurt us. Get away, demon!'

'It can't understand us,' someone else said, despairing. 'It's no use.'

Gora stepped further into the stable as best as he could, over the feet that poked out. More cries came in shock.

'Demon?' he spoke. 'I've been called that before, but not by the people of this country.' He frowned and looked about at them.

'It's the hunter!' a woman's voice cried out. 'Are you here to help us?'

But someone else didn't sound so convinced. 'Did you bring them here? They look like you.'

So many voices called out at once, and Gora worried it would bring the people who chained them up. He growled at them to be silent, rushing to explain it would bring the 'demons' back.

'I ain't never seen 'em in my life,' he growled, crouching and reaching for one of the chains, wondering how to break them. 'Can't you see their hair is different to mine?'

It was a weak argument, but the people here were used to having the same hair colour as one another and thought it was the same in other countries. But now wasn't the time to educate them otherwise—it would buy him time to figure out what to do if they thought he was on a different side to their captors.

'It's true!' one cried out. 'They have yellow hair.'

The others murmured before an older woman told them to listen and be quiet. Gora tried to pull at the chains and use his dagger to unlock them, but nothing worked. He cursed. He knew the minute he saw that creepy, pale-bearded foreigner sneaking about the streets that he'd be here for slimy reasons. And people chained up in a port only meant one thing …

Gora looked up at the young boy whose legs he'd tripped on. Fear wasn't a strong enough word to describe what he saw in the boy's eyes. Gora managed a small smile and ruffled the boy's hair. 'Sorry for trippin' on ya, lad. Must've hurt.'

The boy nodded mutely. Gora sighed.

'How long ye all been here? How'd ye get here without bein' seen? Why are none of the port workers spottin' ye?'

But no-one spoke up. They just looked about at one another— at anyone else but him.

Finally, a man piped up. 'I was locking up my shop! Two nights past.'

'I was walking home from my job in the castle,' a girl said quietly. 'But it was daylight. They caught me in the courtyard. They were rough and covered my mouth so I couldn't shout. Somehow, no-one noticed. In the castle! What happened to the guards?'

Gora rubbed the back of his neck and tried to think.

'Gora, will you help us?'

Gora knew that voice. He looked up, hunting in the group for a woman's face—one he'd regularly gone fishing for since her husband had died, as she had enough on her hands to run the shop.

He groaned. How could he make a promise like that? All the eyes rested on him, and the weight of their expectations and hope crushed him. Gora ground his teeth together and stood. He needed to see when the ship that would take these people away from Hié would leave the port.

'I'll do what I can. I need to go now. I need to try something.'

Gora didn't promise—he didn't say what he'd do. He couldn't. He closed his eyes tight before forcing himself to turn away from the frightened eyes of everyone chained behind him. He needed to tell Yoshiko about this. He recalled a part of their conversation where she'd mentioned something about the noble family having certain enhanced abilities, which is how she'd managed to stay alive this whole time. She and her mother had fought off the guards. Did that mean she could do something here? Refusing to look at the desperate hands reaching out for him as he left, he decided to get her help.

Besides, even if she couldn't do anything, she needed to know what was happening to her people. They'd figure out what to do from there.

He stopped and hid behind a warehouse wall on the edge of the port to watch the foreigners and find a clue of where they'd come from or what they'd do next. He was straining to hear what they were saying—even a clue of their language would help— when he realised he could understand it. They were speaking in traders'—the language all traders and merchants around the world spoke. If you wanted to trade internationally, you had to know it.

'… ready for when the ship comes in. Pack 'em up quick 'n' go, before we're spotted. We leave at the first hint of sunset … get the people loaded before then or lose a cut of your profit.'

The other man nodded before marching towards the far side of the port. But the bearded man came towards the stable, and Gora ran before being spotted, heading for the closest entrance to the caverns.

* * *

Gora was out of breath when he reached the caverns under the town and found Yoshiko just as she was starting a fire. She paused to look up at him. Gora stopped, almost bent double, clutching his side and taking great, gasping breaths.

'You—I need you to come with me,' he gasped, then rushed forward, pulled her up by her arm, and stomped out the small flames. The cavern plunged into darkness before the flame of his torch re-focused his eyes. Gora shuddered.

Yoshiko pushed him off her arm. 'What's wrong?' Yoshiko demanded, marching adamantly behind him.

'There's something you need to see. About the job you gave me.' He gritted his teeth as he thought about it. 'I saw a strange man—a foreigner—leave the castle. He's in the port now. Your people are in danger, but it's something I can only show you. I can't explain it.'

Yoshiko jogged to keep up with him as they headed for the surface, still asking too many questions. His brow was furrowed to the point he thought he'd have wrinkles tomorrow, and he felt like the damned were trying to pull him back to his old life, his memories swarming back.

Yoshiko grabbed Gora's arm and yanked him to a halt before he pulled open the tunnel entrance. He spun around and nearly swore at her. Her eyes once again looked like they were lit with flames of their own.

'I can't follow you down the street,' she said. 'I'll be seen. I'm not in disguise.'

Gora almost swore again—this time at himself at how he'd forgotten. He should've known. Yoshiko, voice softer as if she'd sensed his distress, continued, 'You go on as normal. I'll follow.'

Gora nodded. Light burst in when he slid the trap door open, and he turned to let Yoshiko through. But when he turned to look for her, she'd already disappeared. Scratching his fingers through his hair, he sighed and pulled the trapdoor shut.

* * *

At the port, he hid behind the stable and waited for Yoshiko to catch up. By now, the ship had pulled in, and he knew it wouldn't be long before the people were moved from the stable and stowed aboard. No, he needed to show her what was happening to her people while they were still chained up inside the stables. It wasn't something he could explain.

'Where is she?' he growled to himself, still staring at the ship.

'Here.'

Gora's body leapt from his skin mid-plan as her voice appeared by his neck. He jumped around, seeing Yoshiko standing patiently behind him.

'How did you—I could have attacked you!' he hissed. 'You made me jump!'

Yoshiko ignored his question as she looked about them and asked, 'What did you want to show me?'

Gora pointed to a ship and a hooded figure standing on its ramp. It was too far away for him to see the details, but he knew it was them.

'It's huge!' Yoshiko cried, leaning around him to get a better look. 'His beard is yellow?'

Gora squinted as hard as he could. He couldn't see any of the cloaked people from here.

'You kiddin'?' he asked her. 'How can you see that far? Curse stuff?'

Yoshiko shrugged before gasping and diving behind the wall again, pulling Gora with her. A cloaked man came from the stable around the corner of the wall and aggressively yanked on a chain. He yelled in a language Gora thought he recognised. It wasn't traders', but something from the west. Where was it he'd heard it before?

He and Yoshiko waited, hearing groans, wails, and cries mixed with a clunking of heavy chains and the dragging of feet. The pair dared to peek around the corner again. Gora winced as Yoshiko clutched at his arm, her grip like talons even through his thick jacket.

A bald man with a long nose dragged a line of Hién people from the stable—the man he'd had seen earlier, Gora thought. He had his whole face revealed now and was joined by a few other pale men, marching alongside them to the ship and uncoiling two long whips and snapping them at the feet of the prisoners who shuffled with the weight of the chain. The three shouted in that harsh, foreign language. Everyone on that port—him, Yoshiko, and the poor Hién people they had terrified and at their mercy—knew what sort of foul things they were yelling. You didn't need to know a language for that. Pain followed aggressive yells, and hard tugs kept them moving towards the ship.

Gora watched the back of the woman he knew and cursed. Where were the guards that were meant to be protecting these people? Where were the port workers to sound the alarm?

One of the Hién people stumbled and knocked into a man in front, and both tumbled to the ground. Whips lashed, and they wailed in pain. Gora rested his forehead against the wall, defeated. He'd heard this sound before, in his past. He'd failed them—he'd been too late. Knowing many of these people wouldn't survive what came next, he turned around and pounded his fist against the ground, biting back curses. He clenched his teeth and glanced beside him to Yoshiko, whose eyes were wide as she watched the horror unfold and whispered disbelieving questions under her breath.

Gora startled as she ambled forwards from their hiding place towards the ship. He lunged and grabbed at her shoulder and pulled her back behind the wall where she wouldn't be seen, hissing at her not to be stupid. But Gora's hiss of warning turned into a cry of pain—Yoshiko felt hot to the touch, burning hot—and he swore, wanting to tear his fingers away for fear they'd burn but not wanting to let go of her for fear she'd rush out into the open and be seen. Gora held on, biting back tears he could feel building in his eyes, not sure whether it was pain from his fingers and Yoshiko's heat or from watching helplessly as prisoners got loaded onto a ship he knew many would die on.

And the survivors? The cruelty and humiliation they'd feel afterwards would be worse than death. No matter where that ship ended up, those people's freedom ended here.

18

Gora's Past

Yoshiko couldn't tear her eyes away. Her head spinning, unsure of what to do or say, she turned in a daze to question Gora. Yet, when she turned, the autumn-haired man wasn't there. She couldn't even see or hear him slinking off, and she couldn't smell him. It was as if he'd never been there at all.

She clung to the edge of the stable, watching as her people were pushed onto the ship. Why couldn't she rush out there and help them, she wondered. Yoshiko scanned the area of guards. Those pale-faced men looked like brutes. Alone, she wasn't sure she could fight them off and save her people.

If only Mama were here, she thought, knowing her mother would know what to do.

Yoshiko wondered if she could run and get help from a local guard. But, with the way they had been of late, and how lax they'd been with the disappearance of the people, she doubted they'd believe her or help. To get permission to dock at this main Hié port, you had to have a special seal from the upper council. If this ship had docked, they'd have met with various official levels and been cleared by the council. *So*, she thought, glaring at the cloaked men go about their business on the ship, *either they lied to the council about their purpose here, or the council knows*. It wasn't good. And what was worse, Gora had gone. She'd just found someone who could possibly help, and they'd found this, and he'd realised they were in over their head, and disappeared.

She didn't want to give in to despair, but it was becoming increasingly difficult.

Gora had said the boat would leave as the light started to wane, and Yoshiko felt an urge to run and sneak on board—to go with them and find out a way to help them from there. But she had nothing to protect herself and fight off the foreigners with, and she wouldn't survive the trip from lack of food. Perhaps, had she prepared …

Instead, she blankly watched the ship navigate the shoals, heading out towards the Taiheiyō Ocean, and punished herself for her inaction. By dark, she'd made it back to the caverns, though she wasn't entirely sure how she got there. Memories of people chained and bound by ropes and forced to shuffle onto the ship distracted her. Men had cried, women looked struck with shock, and children wailed, screaming more when that earned them a strike to the head. She still remembered how a man pulled at his chains, crying and cursing as he yanked to reach his child, who had been knocked to the ground from the force of a strike. His attempts to reach his child only pulled at the others chained with him, causing people to flail and fall. His punishment had been lashings. The child screamed fearfully on the floor for the men to stop hurting his father. Nothing would ever make her forget this. She felt like she'd betrayed them.

Whoever had betrayed them on the council must have known about this to let them dock, and Yoshiko couldn't believe their cruelty. Who would let their people be kidnapped and taken away, chained, to some unknown place? If they knew, the fight she would face had become harder than ever, and her decision to put her people first, before reclaiming the region, became even more apparent. She had to bring those people back, somehow. But the person she'd asked for help had left, and probably rightly so, she felt. Originally, she'd only asked him to look for information and see if anything unusual was going on. He'd found it. Gora had never been asked to help her face strangers from another country, chaining, kidnapping, and exporting Hién people. This was too much.

With these thoughts haunting her, Yoshiko barely noticed she'd made it into the tunnels, stumbling on one of the steps in the darkness from her failure to bring a lantern. Heart in her throat, she felt her way down to the main cavern with her hands on the cold walls, ignoring her mother's lessons, feeling more hatred for this place with each corner she turned.

She smelt him before she even saw the light of his lantern.

Yoshiko followed Gora's scent, moving more certainly now. And when she got closer to the main cavern, the dim light of his lantern escaped the main hall and bounced weakly off the walls of the tunnel. The autumn-haired man was sitting on the cold stone floor, not even on a cushion, and leaning sprawled against the wall of a stone hut. He didn't often come in here, and she wondered if he didn't like the vast expanse of dark, preferring to be above in the light where his hut was near the forest. She didn't blame him. Yet here he was.

Yoshiko hadn't even spoken a word of greeting before he suddenly started talking.

'When I was a boy,' Gora started, slurring slightly, 'I was kidnapped. By pirates.'

He was drunk, she noticed. From where she stood, Yoshiko could smell the pungent alcohol. He swirled the bottle about and took another swig. Yoshiko waited, knowing there was more. Gora took a noisy intake of breath to continue his speech.

'Pirates took me from my family hut at night. Made me a slave on their ship. The things I saw …'

Yoshiko didn't know what to say, and, still numb from the

sight earlier, sitting didn't even register to her. Instead, she saw the flames of the weak fire Gora had made and walked instinctively to it, crouching and poking the flames to life. She stared into them as he talked.

'Four of us were taken from where I lived—a child from each village. They did it like that; I dunno why. T'was the same with any other kids they took. Anyway, it was me, two other lads, and a lass. They hid us in sacks, so we didn't know where we were 'til we were thrown in some tiny storeroom below deck. Rough way to be, like those sorry folks will be, stuck for days, weeks, months … who knows.' He sighed, staring into the bottle. 'They did terrible things t' the girl. I'll never forget her screams. We ne'er saw, but we heard, and even at that age, we knew what it meant. They threw her overboard when they finished with her. But I heard she'd died before that, and they still used her 'til she got too cold.'

They both shivered, and Yoshiko turned from the fire to look at him.

'A boy died shortly after. The same way.'

Gora looked as sick as Yoshiko felt, and they both fell silent, pale. He grimaced and took another gulp of the spirit.

Well, that explains why he drinks, Yoshiko thought, looking now at the stone floor.

'Your people.' Gora looked up at her now, and she returned his light-eyed stare. 'I don't know where they're takin' them, or why. But many won't survive. They're packed up with barely room to move and no sunlight. It's a ship for long-distance—part the way 'round the world. I can tell you it ain't nothin' to do with pirates, but the truth ain't much better.'

Yoshiko raised her eyebrows. 'So that's where you went? To check the ship?'

Gora watched her warily, his light eyes flickering with amber in the firelight, like an ocean on fire. 'Thought I'd run off, did ya?'

When she didn't respond, he continued. 'Well, I won't lie. I did consider it. Too many memories, ya know? But I said I'd do what I could to help ya and the people here. I knew one of the ladies—I couldn't do nothin', after all. So, yeah, I checked the ship.'

'You didn't worry you'd be taken too when it left? Or spotted?' Her body spiked with dread at the thought of being spotted by those huge, cloaked pale-faces. Like ghosts.

Gora scoffed into his drink at that. 'I'm used to ships, lass. Spent most of my life on 'em. I know how to sneak on one, snoop about, and get out. You learn that as a pirates' boy.' He flashed his teeth in what Yoshiko thought was meant to be a grin, but it looked more like a snarl.

'What's going to happen to them?' Yoshiko finally asked, settling onto her cushion and letting herself sit more comfortably than she'd have ever let someone see her sit before. She leant back onto her hands.

Gora glanced over at her, and she could see the pain in his face easily.

'They'll be taken far away and sold as slaves. I'm sorry.' He looked back into his bottle as he talked, not looking Yoshiko in the eyes.

Yoshiko mulled that word over a few times. 'Slaves … But who would do that kind of thing to another person?'

Gora shuffled and wriggled into a lower slouch, resting his head against the cold, stone wall. 'Plenty of people, my sheltered little princess. Plenty.'

Yoshiko rose from her place by the fire and slid down the wall next to him, and they sat in a heavy silence. Her mind couldn't comprehend a place where people were owned by someone else and forced to work for nothing, where people were chained up and loaded onto a boat, beaten and abused.

'So you were a slave, too? Before?'

Gora watched her from the corner of his eyes and scowled. Then, he took two long gulps of spirit before he answered with a tortured sigh. 'Yeah, at first. Even when they eventually paid me, though I was anything but free. They still owned and controlled me. That's why I ran away.'

'And you hid here?'

He nodded.

'Will they be treated that way all the time? Chained and beaten?'

Gora looked at the bottom of his bottle again as he nodded once more, more hesitantly this time, and apologised again.

'How can we save them?' Yoshiko could barely manage a whisper.

'I'm not sure you can.' Gora's voice broke, and both sat in silence, staring into the darkness of the cavern beyond the lantern.

Yoshiko bit back tears. She'd failed her parents. She'd not managed to take back the castle and keep her people safe. And now, her people were being transported overseas as slaves to an unknown place. Tense energy weighed upon her limbs, and she scrunched her fingers and toes up to make it go away. Instead of leaving, the feeling grew, and her body felt like it would be consumed by fire. Yoshiko gritted her teeth as her vision filled with darkness. If she let it take over anymore, it'd—

Yoshiko rushed to stand up, startling Gora into spilling some of his drink on him. He cried out, shaking the spirit from his hands, and stared up at her with large, blue eyes. He cursed. 'What's got into you?'

19
Chasing the Ship

Gora leapt up and stared, gawping at how dark Yoshiko's eyes had become and the tension emanating from her. She sighed and looked in the direction of the entrance, fidgeting.

'Don't even think about it,' he growled and grabbed her wrist before the young girl made any stupid ideas to run off. 'Can't go out there now.'

'Are you not going back to your hut?' she asked, voice tense, changing the topic in what he could tell was a distraction.

Gora shrugged and pulled Yoshiko with him as he plonked onto the stone floor by the fire. 'Figured I'd stay. Stop ya from doin' somethin' stupid. Tough times. Dangerous to walk alone at night. Might end up like *them*.' Glancing at her from the corners of his eyes, trying to remain casual, Gora shoved the bottle into her face. 'Here, get some drink in ya. It'll help.'

Yoshiko looked at him warily, but she took the bottle. Then, she shuffled closer to the fire and hugged her knees to her chest. As close as she was to the flames, he wondered why she didn't feel like she was burning. Gora watched as she sniffed the bottle hesitantly.

'Plum spirit?' she asked, surprised, and Gora saw her black eyes shine a little.

So she liked plum spirit?

Gora shrugged. 'Think I'd want bad-tasting stuff? We've had a shock—gotta have somethin' nice! Now, drink.'

He leant back on his elbows, looking at nothing in particular on the cavern walls, mind glazing over. Yoshiko took a swig of the spirit.

'It burns!' she spluttered, looking over at him with watery eyes. 'Don't you mix it with anything?'

'How else would it light a fire inside you now?' He felt a clumsy grin stretch over his face.

'Fire comes from the spirit!' Yoshiko countered.

'Aye, and this is just a different kind, lass.'

* * *

'We've got to go after them!' Yoshiko cried, jumping up from her cushion by the fire and almost wobbling in from the effects of the alcohol.

'Careful,' Gora slurred uselessly, watching his companion pull herself away from the fire and not rushing to help or do anything about it.

She turned to face him and put her hands on her hips. He looked up at her, warily, expecting some sort of lecture. None came. *What even is the point in her acting like that, then?*

'How'd ya expect to do that now?' he prompted more, teasing. 'Fly?'

She pouted, staring down at him. 'I'll fly one day, just you watch! Mama said other women in our family line could transform. Who cares about scales? I'll do it, too.'

Gora took a moment, boggled. He'd only been joking. She stood tall, as if it was meant to be impressive, but the drinking made her face pink, and he got the giggles. Gora roared out with laughter. 'Alrigh', little dragon princess. But when ya do, make sure ya give me a ride!' Her face went yet redder, ears flushing pink, and he stopped laughing. 'But whatcha gunna do *now*?'

Yoshiko sighed and looked up at the cutaways in the ceiling. 'A boat?'

'Are you guessing or deciding?' Gora took another swig of the plum spirit.

Yoshiko's eyes squeezed shut as she thought. 'Both?' She still sounded unsure.

Gora sighed and scratched his head, also looking up at the black abyss above them. 'That ship was a beast. Slow but steady. It's made for long-distance, will be worked by countless soldiers and sailors, and was a three-mast merchant vessel. Strong thing. Even if we did catch up with it, how do you propose turnin' it back? Fightin' all those big, hairy soldiers on board?'

Yoshiko said nothing but looked down at Gora and met his eyes. 'Your eyes look murky. You should stop drinking.'

He raised an eyebrow. 'How tactless of you, princess. Verbally attacking someone just 'cause they told you somethin' was difficult?'

'No. I agree it will be hard. I just noticed your eyes look different.' Her skin flushed red, and she clamped her mouth shut, pressing her lips tight.

His other eyebrow raised to join the other one. Then he laughed. 'Welcome to the inconvenience of drink. Or convenience. Whichever suits you best.' He raised the bottle as if to salute her but plonked it on the stone ground beside him instead of taking a swig. 'So, what d'ya want to do about that ship now?'

Yoshiko slumped back down to the floor to sit beside him. 'I need to go after them. Even if it's impossible. My mother would do whatever she could to make sure her people stayed safe. She always worked hard to keep war at bay so they could live in peace.'

She looked at her knees, expressions dimming again. Gora sighed.

'You don't have to be like her, ya know,' he said quietly, staring almost unseeing at the fire.

'What do you mean?'

'Well.' He paused for a moment to gather his thoughts and put them correctly. The alcohol made it blur all together. 'You always try to plan things based on what the previous daimyō would've done. But you're not her. You're a mixture of her and her husband, but you're also different. You have yer own way to do things. Everyone's different. You'll never do things right by you if you're chasing the impossible dream of bein' like her.'

'That's almost wise of you,' Yoshiko sniffed. 'But I've never led a region or gone on a rescue mission before. She always led the way and told me what to do.'

'But you fought, too, and found your way through it—like when we got caught at the guardhouse,' Gora pushed. 'So think of that. How would you, Yoshiko, not Asumi, handle this? What do *you* want to do?' His voice was getting louder in an attempt at motivation, but it just became a clumsy yell. And, from this close, Yoshiko wiped a bit of spray from her cheek where he'd leant close and yelled a bit too enthusiastically.

He leant away immediately.

Yoshiko lay back on the stone floor. 'How about a boat? Even if it means pushing to catch up. If we go now, we could, couldn't we?'

'Where d'ya think we're going to find a boat in the middle of the night?' Gora was astounded.

Yoshiko shrugged. 'Borrow it?'

'You're guessin' again, right? Cause it's harder than that.' Yoshiko looked at him blankly. He sighed and held his hand up against his eyes to think. 'Let's say, even if we did get a boat, how would we fight? We can't leave the boat just bobbing about on its own as we attack the ship. Boats are expensive. We'd lose someone's whole livelihood.'

'Have someone to sail it back?' Yoshiko guessed again.

Gora moaned and swung an arm about him to gesture at the empty cavern. 'Where will an exiled noble lass and a loner find people to help them chase after a foreign slave ship that kidnapped hundreds of people? It's not exactly the most tempting recruitment offer.'

'Well, I don't know!' Yoshiko hid her face in her hands. Gora was amazed. It was the complete opposite of her usual elite-member-of-society ways.

Well, I guess there's that ...

He scratched the back of his head, willing a thought to pop up into it other than the one he had. He didn't want to go with *that* option unless there was no other alternative. But Gora had lived here nearly a decade and was finally living a decent, normal-ish life. He wasn't about to let it all fall apart now that someone had decided to be an inhumane prick.

Damn, that would be their only option.

'Argh,' he growled, feeling reluctant about their option. 'Fine. I might know something.'

From beside him, Yoshiko perked up, her eyes immediately watching him closely, bright. His face flushed hot with the pressure.

'We might be able to go after that ship. Arm yourself well and bring a jacket. It's gunna be cold.' He let a deep breath out and watched as the young woman dashed off quicker than a child running after a treat, into the darkness without a second thought. *Her head must've cleared up enough for her to see in the dark again,* he thought, clicking his tongue at how fickle she was.

She returned from the darkness, slipping daggers and tying little belts of throwing blades into all sorts of places. Then, she tied her *tanto* and her katana to her sash. Gora's mouth fell open as she reached for more.

'I think that's enough. There'll not be a lot of space for *that*.' He nodded to her bow and arrows. She drew her hand back from reaching them, eyes questioning. He ignored her and stood, stretching, and then grabbed his own swords and jacket. 'Come on.'

* * *

Gora stopped at a small fishing dock, further along from the main trading port, and stomped along the wooden planks towards a single-masted Hién fishing boat. He pulled at some of the lines and jumped in, checking it was in order.

Yoshiko stopped at the edge of the dock. 'Are you stealing a boat?' she hissed.

'Huh?' He stopped what he was doing and stared up at her, incredulous. 'What sort o' man d'you think I am?'

Her eyes widened, but she didn't respond. Gora clicked his tongue and turned away from her, rolling his eyes.

'Get in,' he growled. 'It's *my* boat.'

He heard movement on the dock, and the boat rocked slightly, then a scuffling and a squeak as the young woman slipped in and landed on her backside with a crash. He spun around. A look of shock froze on Yoshiko's face, and her arms had splayed out to the side as she'd tried to break her fall. Gora threw his head back and laughed. She leapt up, brushed herself off, and scowled at him.

'Never been on a boat before, lass?' He continued to chuckle but held out his hand to her.

She narrowed her eyes at him but took his hand, clutching her katana tightly and looking about uncertainly. 'Never.'

Gora swore. 'Well, how the spirits do you expect us to go after that ship?'

'Can't you sail this alone?' She looked at him expectantly.

'Easier with two,' he growled, trying to block out her ignorance. How was she expecting to go after that giant fuckin' ship if she wasn't at least helping him sail? One person wasn't enough. 'Whatever. You're gunna help me, princess. Or I'll be feeding you to the sea monsters long before we catch up with that ship.' He pointed at her, not caring if it was rude. 'On my boat, I'm in charge. You do exactly what I say, when I say it, and not a moment later. Got it?'

She looked surprised. Well, good. He was going to lose his boat for this noble pain in the ass, after all.

'Understood,' she said coolly. But under her calm face, Gora could see a flash of fear in her eyes, and he caught her looking over the edge into the inky water.

'Don't look. Just go over there and pull in that line. We're off.'

She wasn't much help at all. She zipped around to follow each of his orders, almost a different person to the calm and collected woman she tried to be, or the innocent and excited young girl she could be when she showed sparks of her true self. Gora shouted himself hoarse over the sound of the ocean and the flapping sail and swore a great deal more than he had in a long time, in both his home language and Hién, but she got it done eventually. And, as the light came up and the glint of orange and yellow lit up the ocean horizon, Yoshiko's face lit up with awe.

'Sunrise at sea really is something, ain't it?' Gora smiled to himself as the sunlight filled his eyes.

From that moment on, no matter how clumsy Yoshiko was, he focused on the bigger picture. She was doing her best, a serious look on her face as she grunted to pull the lines and hold out against the waves that rocked the boat. Somehow, she'd managed to keep herself upright, and she focused solely on catching up with the ship, a dot on the horizon ahead of them.

Salt spray crashed across Gora's face, and the thrill of being in the ocean caught up with him again. He felt a familiar energy wash through his body, and it wasn't just the plum spirit. This, chasing a quarry, hadn't been the life he'd chosen, but the remains of that life perked up at the chance. The fresh sea air and the sound of the sea crashing around him lit his soul, and he urged the little fishing boat on. He saw Yoshiko glance strangely at him and realised he was grinning wildly.

'What?' he cried out. 'Ne'er seen an old pirate at sea before?'

'Never seen you like this, certainly,' Yoshiko called back, pushing her long, wet hair out of her face.

He laughed and steered the boat around a troublesome wave, roaring more when she wobbled over and caught herself on the mast. Her hair was plastered to her face, and she looked completely out of place. Instinctively, he ran his hand through his own hair and pushed it back with his fingers.

'How'd you get this boat?' she cried out to him at one point. 'Aren't they expensive? I heard most fishing families worked hard to keep them in their family.'

'Made it,' Gora said, attention fixed on the ship ahead.

They were pushing his boat to its limits, and he felt uncomfortable. Gora's eyes kept flicking about the boat, making sure it was holding together and an important part wasn't about to crack in half with the strain. It wasn't, so he dared to tug a little tighter.

'You made it? People can do that?'

'Where d'you think they came from?'

'I meant, isn't something only certain master craftsfolk can do?'

Gora shrugged. 'Depends. It's just a simple one. Took a while,' he admitted.

Gora looked about his boat, and his heart lurched at the thought of what he was about to do. He swore. Twice. When Yoshiko looked at him with a raised eyebrow, he looked away and said nothing.

'Let's focus on gaining on that ship,' was all he said, heart dropping a little. Then, 'Get down!'

Yoshiko's eyes flashed, and she dropped to the floor just in time for him to swing the sail right where she'd been standing. She glared up at him from the floor.

'You can get up again now. This'll be quicker with the wind.'

He doubted she'd understand. But that didn't matter. As they got closer to the giant, plodding slave ship, he saw the young woman cock her head, listening.

'They've seen us,' she said. 'Prepare for attack.'

Barely a moment later, cracks of gunpowder echoed from the slave ship, but Gora pushed the boat on. He grimaced at the thought of gunfire, knowing any moment something could go drastically wrong. But, somehow, with the smaller boat's lurching on the waves, those on the bigger one failed to hit their mark. At this distance, even Gora could hear their angry yells. The pair looked up at the looming ship, and Gora called for Yoshiko to duck once more as he swung the sail and tried to pull the boat alongside.

'What now?' Yoshiko yelled over the ocean crashing against the massive hull beside them.

'Grab that hook. Throw it over that ship.' Gora clenched his teeth and squinted his eyes to focus.

Yoshiko hefted the grapple and unwound the line that connected to it. Then, holding onto the edge of the line, swung the hook around to gather momentum, like she'd seen her mother doing once before. Gora watched her from the corner of his eyes, hoping she'd get it the first time. But then, it rarely worked out that way.

The hook launched high above them and flew over the top of the railing and dropped. When Yoshiko tugged it back to give it a grip, Gora felt his stomach knot in anticipation of a giant metal spike falling back on top of them. Yoshiko pulled. Nothing fell on top of them, somehow.

'You did it?' He almost couldn't believe it.

'You should doubt me less.' The girl was gripping the other end of the line tightly and had turned to face him. Her dark eyes were serious, and she reached for her katana with her spare hand, tying the casing to her sash. The incompetence with sailing had been replaced with the mindset of a fighter; the next dragon daimyō was ready to take her people home, no matter what was involved.

'I'll remember that for next time,' he said, teasing, but her change in attitude had caught him off guard, and he found himself blundering over the words.

There was a lurch in the smaller boat, and a cry came from Yoshiko as the bigger ship tried to pull away, and Yoshiko grabbed onto the line with both hands, gritting her teeth, planting her feet into the smaller ship and trying to hang on to both.

Gora swore. 'Forget that—you'll be torn in two. Get up there. Go!' he yelled and ran to pull the boat back around.

She leapt up, and the line swung her hard against the hull. But Yoshiko had planted her feet ahead of her and was already clambering up, looking back at him with uncertain eyes that asked if he was following. The gap between the two boats had already widened.

'Yeah, I'm coming!' he roared and took a deep breath.

He swore again. He'd spent a lot of time on this boat—the spirits knew it was true. Then, squeezing his eyes shut and urging himself on, Gora darted across his fishing boat, grabbed his sword, tied it to his sash, and pulled the line that would take his boat back towards the escaping slave ship.

His boat lurched forward on the waves, and the gap between the two boats closed in again. And, in one moment, he reached for the line they'd thrown over the ship. Yoshiko's eyes widened as she looked down at Gora's splayed fingers reaching. Then, he leapt and clutched the line with all his might, just in time for his boat to crash with a sickening crunch into the beast of a ship he hung from like a half-drowned spider.

The wake pushed his boat below the waves, and a splintering creaking drowned out his hearing as the weight of the slave ship and the ocean swallowed his boat to ruin.

'Well, shit.' He pounded a fist against the hull of the slave ship, and an alcohol-infused roar escaped his lips. When he pulled himself up the line and looked up at the young woman above him, her face was pale.

'That was your boat!' Yoshiko cried down at him, pausing on the line, eyes wide.

'No need to tell me!' Gora roared back. 'Get moving! What else did you think would happen when we abandoned it to get to this one?'

'I thought you'd tie it off or something.'

'To what? We're in the middle of the fuckin' ocean!' he cried, amazed at her lack of foresight. 'Just go! I'll make you buy me a pretty, new one when we're done.'

20

Trying to Keep a Promise

Yoshiko leapt over the railing, fire burning inside. Her skin was hot, her heart felt like it was scorching, and something burned in her head. She scanned the deck for yellow-haired sailors and soldiers, noting the number. There must be at least fifty on deck, a mix of guards and those to sail the ship. They all watched her, guards stomping her way, weapons drawn. In the corner of her eyes, across the deck, she saw a group of huddled Hién people, chained and looking at her warily.

Yoshiko glared as a foreign, pale-skinned man ran yelling towards her, his sword raised above his head to attack. She lunged forwards, drawing her katana from its sheath. In one movement, she sliced upwards diagonally across his stomach and chest to his shoulder. His blade clanged onto the deck as his body collapsed beneath him. Yoshiko didn't wait to see him fall. She pivoted and dashed to her right, running alongside the wooden banister towards the huddle of Hién women. A dodge to the side, an upper block and immediate strike back downwards, a pivot, and a long cut along another man's stomach sent two more foreign guards crashing to the floor.

Yoshiko scowled, trying to ignore the discomfort she had with ending a life. It was just like her mother had said: 'There's a time and place for honour and pity, and a time and place for letting people live. But, when it comes to war, you have to know when to kill. When it comes to protecting the people you swore to protect, when there's a blade held over the throat of a citizen of your empire, you do whatever it takes. Reflect on your actions in a time where you won't get killed.'

But she still never got used to it.

'Oy!' Finally, Gora had joined the party, and Yoshiko briefly turned her head to face him. Yoshiko saw him wipe his mouth with the back of his sleeve, and then he grinned. There had been a spark in his bright eyes since they'd been sailing, and now she saw a confidence come over him.

Her ears twitched as thumping footsteps from behind her made her turn again, and she swept her leg around in an arc and brought her blade sweeping diagonally down a soldier's body. The look of shock on the man's face burned into her memory before he spluttered blood from his mouth, and it oozed from the gash down his body.

She heard a low whisper from the people huddled together in bonds. Then, the crack of a whip and an angry cry in a language she didn't understand. But Yoshiko understood the cries of her people, and she darted around a man's side and pierced through his ribs with a double-handed side stab. She kicked him down and glared at the man beating her people.

'You ...' she growled, all politeness leaving her, copying Gora's rough speech, which seemed much more appropriate in this time. She wiped the man's blood from her face and ignored Gora's guffaws from behind her, mocking her improper language.

'Go! I can fight this ugly bunch of sea scum,' Gora said, barging into one man who lunged at her, cutting the man's sword arm, causing him to drop his sword. The soldier tried to fix it by barging at Gora himself, but the red-haired man had already dropped into a low stance away from the man and sliced across the man's thighs. 'Too bad,' Yoshiko heard him mutter to the dying man as he crashed to the floor beside her.

Yoshiko sheathed her father's katana, nodded at Gora, and darted off, grimacing.

She'd heard another scream from her people, and she raced towards them, fury filling her senses. She saw the pale man with the whip falter as he looked at her and froze.

Yoshiko kept running at him, dropped low, swept her arms up, and barged him to the floor with momentum. Then, she dropped to her knee and put the force of her weight into a palm strike to his forehead. His skull crashed against the deck with a sickening crunch.

She cringed. She hadn't meant to hit him that hard.

Yoshiko looked up at the Hién people, wondering if anyone would recognise her. Probably none. Few had seen her before, and no-one expected to see the daimyō's daughter running about on a ship and killing people. She swallowed, staring into their large, dark, fearful eyes.

'It's safe,' Yoshiko tried to reassure them. 'We'll get back.'

Gora was yelling something she guessed were profanities and war cries in his home language, barging into equally loud, yellow-bearded soldiers. When Yoshiko looked around, she saw sailors trying to keep out of the way, looking anxiously at the fight, to the captives, to Yoshiko, and back to the fighting. Yoshiko wondered how many of the people here were really in on this, or whether some were equally forced to do things as her people had been forced to get on the ship. One sailor had a massive welt across his face, giving her the answer. Well, if they didn't try to attack her or hurt her people, she'd leave them alone, too.

A yell from behind her and the cries of her people in front of her made her spin around and launch a throwing blade from her belt. Yoshiko heard it hit, and a thump on deck reassured her. Then, she knelt and quickly cut some of the rope bonds keeping these people together. Around their feet were metal cuffs she wouldn't be able to cut.

'Where's the key?' she asked the group. They looked at each other then looked about the deck to try to show her.

'Quickly!' Gora roared over to her, launching himself at another soldier: a man taller even than Gora and built like a tree. He pushed Gora, who crashed onto the floor to receive a branch-sized boot kicking his side. Gora yelled out, and Yoshiko flinched. She didn't need to look at him to know he'd been hit.

Then, from beside her, a cry broke out, and a figure in rags darted forward, ignoring the metal chains around his ankles, ploughing into the stomach of the tree-like pale-faced man, knocking the soldier over. The ragged figure immediately turned, his arms grabbed the sword arm of a surprised soldier to the side, and he shuffled his bare feet diagonally, strong, scarred hands twisting the sword arm and crashing the soldier down with a loud crack. The man's arm split at his elbow, and his face crashed into the deck. The ragged figure looked up, and Yoshiko saw the young face of someone from her country underneath unruly black hair. He looked into her eyes, then back at the remaining soldiers. Then, the Hién man crouched dangerously, like a cat ready to spring, his arms held up in front of him.

More of the Hién people Yoshiko had just untied rushed to finish what Gora and Yoshiko had started, shuffling awkwardly with the cuffs at their ankles. Gora was pulling himself up and clutching his side when a Hién man rushed over and helped him up.

'You okay, hunter?'

'Ah, thanks,' Gora said, looking across the space of the deck between him and Yoshiko.

She nodded to him, raided a soldier for the keys, and disappeared down the steps to the decks below, calling out for someone to come help her free the people below. Above deck, she heard the commotion continue. In front of her, a foreign yelling told her more soldiers were below, refusing to leave their posts and yelling abuse at the Hiéns trapped in the hold.

One peeked his head around the walkway, roared something, then ran towards her with a blade ready to pierce right through her stomach. She jumped to the side and parried it away, pushing it against the opposite wall, where the momentum carried it on past the people who'd followed her. It missed them, and she struck the man in the jaw with a punch. There wasn't enough room down here for her sword. Then, she grabbed the man's shoulders and drove her knee into his groin, grabbing the back of his head to push him onto the floor.

'Grab his keys,' she told someone, sheathing her sword. It wouldn't be much use down here anyway. Knives would have to do.

She and the others leapt over the man to continue to the storage deck below.

The smell hit her before anything else, a wall of unearthly stench—a mixture of death, disease, and decay. This smell couldn't have been made by her people alone, who had just been on this ship for a matter of hours. She didn't know how long some had been kidnapped and stowed away in an unknown place before being taken onto the ship. But even then, this smell didn't match up. This smell was like months or more of countless people being trapped here with no care. Her nose scrunched up, her eyes watered, and she tried to blink back the tears that followed. Someone behind her gagged and leant against the wall, heaving up nothing.

She heard someone's attempt to be silent as they waited for her to walk through the door, likely planning to hack her head off. She let a breath out and drew a dagger. Then, looking back at the three behind her, she signalled for them to wait. At that moment, Yoshiko ducked and rolled along the floor, swiping with the dagger to cut at legs. A roar told her she'd hit her mark, and she swept herself up onto one knee and plunged the same dagger into an inner thigh muscle. A particularly pale-faced man fell to his hands and knees in front of her, face twisted in a contorted look of pain and anger. Yoshiko ignored his yells and grabbed his sword, tossing it where he couldn't reach it.

'Eri!' a voice called out from behind her, and a woman ran forward toward someone in the room.

Yoshiko looked up and saw hundreds of Hién people bound together with no room to move. How could she have expected such a scene? How could she have prepared to see people like that, in different stages of disarray, beating, and despair? The tears that had threatened her at the stench now decided it was time to come again. That stench hadn't been her people. But they would have added to it by the time they got to wherever they were being taken. The stench was from hundreds and hundreds of others who'd been forced into this position. People who'd never been chased and saved. She wouldn't let it happen. She'd take them home and bring justice to whoever thought this had been a good idea.

21

The Return

Yoshiko watched the people gathering about the ship, frightened but freed from their bonds. Instead, their captors had been tied below, and the ship had been turned to return to Hié, sailed by threatened foreign sailors.

'So what do we do now?' she asked Gora, who slouched against the banister.

'Jump ship,' Gora said, staring into the water.

'And leave them?'

'They'll know how to sort it themselves. A bunch of kidnapped Hién people returning home won't be something that can be ignored. The guards can do the rest. Their families will be angry and want justice. We're taking them home, just like we promised. But if you're seen, you'll get killed. So, when we get close, we jump and hide and continue as before.'

'You'll stay?'

'I told you I'd help you find out the shit that's going on in that palace. We still ain't found it. Something here doesn't add up.' He gestured to the scene behind them. 'Plus, have a feeling I'm gunna be dragged into it whether I like it or not. Ain't enough redheads in your country for us to pretend it weren't me. Many here know me—or of me.'

Close to land, Yoshiko and Gora slipped away from the crowd and dived from the ship. With heavy swords, both struggled through the water and were exhausted by the time they arrived. They hid in the water and peeked around some rocks while the giant ship pulled up once more against the port. A racket erupted on land, and people raced to the ship, guards rushing up to see why it was there. The people of Hié poured off the ship, running to the guards and yelling.

'What are they saying? What's going on?' Gora asked her, trying to nudge closer. 'Use your weird ears.'

'Weird?' Yoshiko hissed back, but he flapped his hand to dismiss the question and gestured back to the port.

Yoshiko focused on what she could hear.

'They're trying to tell the guards what happened—and some of the port people,' she said, trying to combine what hundreds of people were saying into just one point. 'The guards barely believe them. The people are saying to check the ship for a few of the surviving crew.'

Gora just raised an eyebrow and kept watching the madness unfurl. It looked like some people were trying to flee up the hill from the port to their homes, and others were calling on help and trying to show them the ship.

Then, screams erupted from the hill to the left of the port and rippled through the crowd.

'What's happening now?' Gora hissed, straining his eyes and squinting.

Yoshiko stared open-mouthed, unable to believe what was happening. More cloaked people had come from all directions on the port; some guards just stood and ignored the pleading people, and others were pushing people back to the port. A flash of silver and more screams left one of the returned Hién people lying bloodied in a heap on the floor, and others ran to get as far away from the blade as possible.

'They're—' She didn't know how to say it. 'They're pushing them back. They're not helping at all.'

A line of cloaked people and Hién guards pushed the people back to the port. Anyone who tried to flee was dragged back—arms pushed behind them or pulled by their hair and clothes. Children were picked up or nudged back, and men who tried to punch their way out and pull others with them were beaten. The flood of people still trying to leave the ship stopped and stared.

'What the fuck?' Gora growled. 'What's going on now?'

'They're asking what's going on, why they're not allowed to go home,' Yoshiko whispered, unable to tear her eyes away from the scene. Why were there so many yellow-haired people here? She'd never seen them before. 'Are those foreigners normal in the town?' she asked Gora, thinking he'd know more about town life than she who had lived an excluded life in the castle compound.

He shook his head. 'Ain't seen 'em before. Only foreigner usually in Hié is me, and those who come on cultural diplomatic trips for you lot at the keep. None of them looked like this, though, I'll wager?'

It was Yoshiko's turn to shake her head.

By now, the group of ex-captives had backed into a circle, trying to escape lashes from all angles from the yellow-haired, cloaked men. Somewhere, a child was beaten and fell to the floor, kicked by the boot of a pale-faced guard. A man rushed forward to grab the child and pull it to safety but was kicked to the floor too. The captors yelled, hitting out at anyone in their way. Yoshiko looked about the port, wondering why no-one else had come to sound the alarm at what was going on. To her dismay, no-one else was around. Where were the workers? The fishingfolk? The merchants?

'What are you doing?' someone's voice rang out. 'Why are you with them? You're our guards—help us! They took us.'

Yoshiko tried to figure out what she should do next. What would her mother do? What would Chinen do? Should she charge in there and fight these people back, too? Or would it end up with an even worse situation?

Before she could decide, someone on the port decided for her.

'If you won't help us, we'll do it ourselves! We fought on the ship; I'll fight here too!' A man rushed forward with a sword taken from the soldiers they'd defeated on the ship and let out a roar. He dodged the pale-faced man's defensive lunge and darted to the side, slicing through the man's ribs as he slipped past to the side. Yoshiko's heart rose. Maybe they could fight. The yellow-haired man crashed to the floor, and the port silenced. He turned and called out to the waiting, fearful crowd. 'Let's go home!'

Soldiers rushed the man at once, surrounding him and plunging blades into him like a sweet potato being prepared to bake in a stone oven. He died, screaming and writhing in front of a trembling crowd. The crowd was overcome by the soldiers and forced back onto the ship, beaten and tied and shoved back into submission. But, they were told, they didn't have to worry. They'd be joined by more of their friends and family soon. And the ship would sail again.

'Well, fuck,' Gora said, making Yoshiko's insides feel like they'd leapt out from within her. She'd forgotten he was there. He pounded his fist on the rock they hid behind, bared his teeth, and rested his forehead on it, saying nothing.

22

A Damned Plan

'What have I done?' Yoshiko moaned when they returned to the caverns, leaning against the cold, stone walls and burying her face into the rock.

Gora felt much the same. He kicked over the water pail and roared, his scream echoing around the caverns. When he saw Yoshiko looking up, wondering whether other people had heard it, he didn't care.

'Oh, what would it matter anyway?' he heard her mutter into the wall. 'We'll all be caught and killed or transported anyway.'

Well, that wasn't like anything he'd known her to be like. Gora saw Yoshiko shiver, and he went to light the fire, glad when the heat flickered to life.

'What the fuck was all that?' Gora groaned and lay on the floor beside the flames, covering his eyes with his arm and ignoring the gross feeling of the wet cloth of his sleeve. He'd dry soon, here.

Damn, they'd been up all night, he'd lost his boat, and all for what? That? *That?* He cursed again.

'I brought their hopes up and failed them,' Yoshiko moaned, plonking herself wearily onto the floor by the fire too. Gora looked over at her a moment before covering his eyes again. She looked awful—pale face and long black hair plastered to her skin, almost like one of those ghost girls in the folk tales. He shuddered at the thought.

Then, who was he to complain? He probably looked worse. Heck, if he looked like he felt …

They sat in silence with death and fear weighing on their hearts, thinking of all those people.

'They're locked back up in that gods-forsaken ship. Soon they'll be cramped, covered in illnesses, dying. You've not seen it. You've never seen it.' Ghosts of the past flooded his memory, and his voice shook. Where was that damned drink when he needed it? He peered about the room for that half-drunk bottle they'd had earlier.

Suddenly, the young woman spoke. 'Tell me about it.'

'No.'

'I want to know!'

'No, you don't. Not this.'

'Yes. I want to know the pain and the conditions my people will be subjected to.'

'No, you don't! Trust me.' He was standing now, pointing at her and breathing hard. 'Let the world be damned. You don't *ever* want to know what sorts of things go on in those damned ships. You saw a smidgen of what it's like—people cramped up, boxed in. Remember the smell?' Gora felt a flash of satisfaction as her face paled. 'Yeah, now imagine that worse—with days and weeks of mess and illness gathered in one place without being cleaned. I saw it once and wish I hadn't. It'll haunt me forever, and you don't need to know. All you need to know is that *that*'—he gestured wildly in the direction he thought the port was above them—''is no place for even our worst enemies. Your people need to be taken from there and put somewhere safe.'

The ocean-bedraggled woman visibly paused and pulled her knees to her chest. But her black eyes remained locked on his as he saw her process it. Gora wished he could look away, but there was something unusual in her gaze—something unsettling and not quite human.

'They need to be off that ship.' Gora strode the remaining few steps between them and glared down at her, his lip curling in resentment for what he'd seen and what could follow. He waited for a solution.

'But how can we free them without them being rounded up, beaten, killed, and sent back again?' Yoshiko finally huffed and looked away.

Gora sighed and lowered himself to sit beside her, stretching out his legs and leaning back on his arms.

'I don't know,' Gora whispered, feeling the exhaustion from it all hit him. He just wanted to sleep. 'Is there anywhere we can take them on the borders? A village, perhaps?'

Gora thought of his own village near the mountain. It was still too close to the main town. But perhaps one a bit further afield could work? The young woman next to him shook her head, wet and matted hair sticking to her cheek. She pouted as she moved the strand of hair from her face.

'The rumours were that people had been disappearing from all over. I don't think it was just the main town.'

Gora lay back and let his head rest against the cold stone. It felt unusually comforting. 'It's a damned shame you can't turn into a dragon and storm the castle, all fires blazing.' He yawned.

'Even if I could, I'm not sure I would. I don't want to solve death with more death. That's not what my father taught me. Even my mother, warrior daimyō, would avoid dealing death unless there was no alternative. There has to be another way.'

Gora felt a spike of anger rise. 'But they're already dead! And more are dying! What other option do you have? You can't wait around and let more people die just because you're afraid to kill those who have shown they don't care about killing others.'

'I know, and I know! But—' She stopped, and Gora waited for her to continue. 'But that would only kill more innocents. And besides, I can't transform or spit fire.'

He looked at her. She seemed sad—like the spirit of some drowned and vengeful lost soul. Her face was pale, and she gazed anywhere but at him.

Gora huffed but knew she was right. They didn't have the firepower to storm the castle, or she and the daimyō would have done that to begin with. And, judging what happened earlier, the guards wouldn't be persuaded either. It was as if they'd been bought-out already. He saw a star wink in the ceiling up above as someone walked over the patterned street above.

Feeling sheepish, Gora looked over at Yoshiko. He knew she'd been determined to help her people, and now she was faced with this. For any country, let alone one in the middle of an internal upheaval with a council killing the rulers, this was a near-impossible mission. Invaders from other countries could tear apart their victim countries, their culture, and leave it broken. The girl's face looked blank and overwhelmed, and rightly so, he thought. She was staring at the fire with an expression he couldn't read.

'I'm going to get kidnapped,' Yoshiko said finally with a determined huff.

Gora nodded absentmindedly. 'Wait, what?' He sat bolt upright when he realised what she had said.

'I'm going to let them take me and put me on that ship,' she repeated, looking at him with confused, black eyes as if she genuinely thought he hadn't heard.

Gora stood up and waved his arms in panic, heart lurching. 'No. No, no, no, *no*! You can't and you won't. That's not how you'll save your people.'

Yoshiko just watched him with blank, black eyes. They looked almost empty, he realised. She'd not given up her hope that much, had she?

'What if they know it's you? What if you die on the ship? People die *all the time* on those ships. You just can't understand.'

'Then, I die trying to do something.' Yoshiko stood now too, grounding her feet and looking defensive. Gora flinched; he didn't know why. A weird strength emanated from her, and he thought back to the time she'd told him a bit about the curse and weird powers. 'If I get taken, I'll be transported straight to the country that's taking my people. I can find out who decreed it and why, and then try to stop it.

'Even if I try to stop it this end, the other country will keep doing it—here, other countries … it's all the same to them. So I have to stop it at the source—go to the palace or place where the people who run that country are. Find a way to get them to stop. Then, I can come back and sort the poison here, too. Only then will my people be safe, and then I can work on building the region from the bottom—strengthening the foundation and keeping the people happy.'

Gora felt lost for words. He stared up at her and opened and closed his mouth so many times he felt like a koi—his brain just as empty—and had no doubt that he looked like one, too. All he could think about what how stupid that idea was—as if she could do that, get there and ask them to stop. She couldn't just walk into another country's palace and expect to talk to the ruler. He tried to figure out the best way to tell her when she continued anyway, without his answer.

'You don't have to come with me. Thank you for your assistance over the last couple of weeks. You don't know how much you've helped.' She rested her hand on his shoulder and smiled slightly. Gora felt frozen. Then, she backed off and bowed slightly at him. 'I can't ask you to do anything more. It's too much.'

Then, with Gora's head still catching up with what she just said, Yoshiko said something about wanting to go for a walk to make plans and shuffled into the darkness away from the light, her footsteps echoing into the tunnels.

What?

The girl's footsteps were still padding away as Gora scrunched his eyes and scratched his head with both hands, trying to wake his slow brain up, but scratching so aggressively that he thought half his hair would fall out.

What?

She wanted to get kidnapped now?

What the fuck? It was madness! A girl couldn't just let herself get kidnapped away from her country to ride on some slave ship of death and risk dying just in the hope she could get to the country that is taking her people. And then she thought she could just walk off the ship and up to whoever was in charge and talk to them? Demand they give her people back? He pictured it and mocked her light voice:

'They call me Ii Yoshiko, dragon daimyō runaway of Hié and her mightiness of naïve stupidity. Thank you for your kindness in the future. I wish to ask that you kindly stop kidnapping my people. And, if you would, a discussion over green tea would suit me greatly. Do you have any desserts that would suit the occasion? I'm quite fond of them ...'

He stopped, looked at the cavern entrance she left through, and realised her footsteps had already melted away from hearing, and he kicked the fallen bucket over again and growled some more. He'd settled here because it was meant to be a quiet, peaceful, and sensible country.

And what makes her think she can just march off and speak to the ruler of that country, anyway? Gora knew if she was caught as a slave, she'd immediately be branded, sold, and packed off to work until the end of her days—unless she could buy back her freedom. There'd be no opportunity for some cheerful adventure to speak with the ruler.

'Damned princess. And she thought she could do it without me?' Gora scoffed and aimed a third kick at the damned, poor bucket. Then, he looked at it, felt guilty at his misaimed anger, and sighed. Gora stooped to pick up the bucket and brushed it off, checking for damage. Then, certain it was fine, he set it straight.

She was the first noble he'd ever met, if you didn't count that person who claimed to be the ruler of the pirates and the eleven seas. But then, Gora was never sure whether he could consider that person to truly be royalty. Most pirates in charge of a large-enough crew or fleet seemed to think they were ocean-spirit-claimed supreme rulers. But most of the time, they were just self-obsessed idiots who thought too highly of themselves and couldn't function without the help of everyone around them.

'Yeah, right. Mix naïvety, lack of worldly knowledge, a love of poetry, and utter foolhardy stubbornness, and you're perfect for a position on a throne,' Gora muttered to himself and stormed through the caverns, up the winding stone steps towards the entrance. He would look for the fool of this domain and try to set her straight before she did anything stupid.

She'd just said she was going to look for supplies, right? She wouldn't be getting herself caught now? A quick intake of breath showed Gora he didn't doubt it for a minute, and he soon raced up the steps and crashed through the cavern entrance, immediately shutting it and darting to hide behind a bush. For a moment, he wondered whether all these bushes and trees had been deliberately planted in front of the entrances, or whether the entrances had been placed where there had been lots of plants to hide them behind.

Yeah, right, like the old saying: 'What came first, the dragon or the egg?' He chuckled to himself darkly and smoothly darted into the crowd.

Noon was drawing in, and people were milling about, shutting shop for a break, and heading to eateries. The smell of boar hotpot wafted by his nose and made his stomach leap, guiding him to a restaurant before he'd noticed. When was the last time he'd eaten? He stared at the bubbled soup—the perfect mix of meat, vegetables, and miso broth. And was that roasted seaweed they were putting on the top? His stomach gurgled, and he realised people in the restaurant were watching him uncertainly and the chef had been speaking to him about whether he'd enter. Gora blinked, apologised, and quickly backed off before his stomach made him change his mind. He had to find her first, and then they could eat. Plus, he looked a mess—he was in no way dressed to enter a social food house.

What he *really* needed, he thought and daydreamed of the scenario, was an incredible wash, a long soak in a public bathhouse, and a fresh change of clothes. Instead, he stormed down the street looking like a nearly-dried drowned rat to look for the foolish girl who had walked off without a care.

Sure, she really thinks she can run a region like that?

A flash of pale flicked past Gora, and he stopped in his tracks, double-taking to look behind him. Someone was walking with their cloak hood up. And to make things worse, it looked just like the cloaks the slave catchers wore, and the large body filled it up just the same. Gora frowned and narrowed his eyes, scratching the back of his head as he watched the figure warily. He bared his teeth, hoping Yoshiko hadn't got caught up in all that again already. With the catchers on the prowl again, he didn't want to risk it.

For some reason, Gora ended up back by the port, running in the back alleys to keep out of sight of any guards or slave catchers who might fancy taking a grab at him. The port was still empty of workers, except for the traitor Hién guards and the cloaked foreigners lingering in small groups. The ship loomed in the lonely port. It was an unusual sight. Usually, this port was lively with ships and trade from up and down Hié's neighbouring regions' coastlines. As he ran past the port, Gora swore he could hear moans and cries from those shut away on the ship, but they were quickly shut down. He winced, knowing they'd be beating people to get them to shut up.

How could he ever let Yoshiko get herself caught and put on there? How could she even think it would stop her people from being taken?

Gora stopped to catch his breath, crouching over a little and coughing into his elbow. Then, he looked about. Where could the runaway be? He had a strange feeling she'd be near the ship, trying to scope it out, find out more, or stare at it and reflect on the world—that was the sort of thing people like her did, wasn't it? Meditate and reflect and join the bigger connections of the world through zen or something. Gora's eyes panned the view and saw a cliff that overlooked the port. Gora pulled himself back into a jog. It would make sense she would be up there and using her strange long-distance vision or whatever it was to watch over the ship and try to make plans. He wondered if she still thought she'd be able to escape it, or whether she was just mourning over the conditions her people were kept in. He'd know soon.

'Ahh, I was right!' Gora gasped, clawing for air as he ran the last stretch of the space between him and Yoshiko, who was kneeling on the top of the cliff. He cursed himself at his form. This couldn't be good for a hunter, he wondered, but also tried to think back to a time he'd run so much. Creeping about a forest was completely different, he thought, trying to make himself feel better.

Yoshiko turned towards him. As he'd guessed, she was looking out over the port. As he had arrived, she'd cocked her head but said nothing until he came closer.

'You're noisier these days,' she said. Gora felt disappointed that was all she'd said. 'Remember when you first joined me, and you kept trying to sneak up behind me? You tried to be quieter, then.'

'I'm not trying to sneak up on you anymore. I gave up. You're too weird. Whatever powers you have, I can't beat you. No point trying to compete with a dragon.'

'You were competing?' She raised her eyebrow and looked up at him as he walked closer.

Gora crashed down beside her with his feet hanging over the edge of the cliff. He looked down. Below, the waves crashed and lapped against the rocks. *Seemingly harmless*, he thought, *from all the way up here.* But he knew it would be a completely different story to be down there and in the water. Even the small waves could quickly grind you to nothing on the rocks, like rice polished beyond its shell.

'Woo, will you look down there? Pretty scary.' He looked down as he voiced his thoughts. Then a wild grin crossed his face, and he looked at her, but her face was still and looking far into the distance. He shrugged, and they sat in silence and watched the waves, the ship, and the sea.

Finally, 'You know I have to go.' Her voice came quietly, her thoughts far off.

Gora looked back at the ship. It was just a tiny model of a ship to him from up here, but she could see. What could she see? And how much? Could she see through the little galley windows and inside? Could she smell or hear them from up here? Probably. He thought back to what he'd do if he had the chance to save his people. If people had been taken from his village, and not him, what would he have done? He left when he was young, but would he have tried to run after them if so many people had been taken.

'I wonder if anyone tried to look for me.'

Yoshiko looked at him sympathetically. Gora felt like his heart had suddenly dropped. *Why all of a sudden?*

'I'm sure they did. Could you imagine they ever wouldn't?' Yoshiko said, her voice sounding far off.

Gora shook his head. 'They must have been so hurt. For years, I wanted to go back and find them—to try and regain that life and make it work.'

'Why didn't you?' She'd shuffled to sit in a more relaxed position. He noticed she was doing that more and more lately, unlike when they'd first met, and she'd tried to keep her rigid, formal kneeling.

Gora sighed and ran a hand through his hair. It needed a good rinse in a hot spring.

'I didn't know where to go. Which country is it on the maps? Which coast? Which village? Where you live seems so big and important when you're there; you know every nook and cranny, every person and every house. I thought I knew every area of that coastline from when I ran and jumped along the beach every morning as I went to help my pa catch fish or collect driftwood. But, when it came to it, I had no idea where I lived. I never expected to be taken so far away.' He paused and looked out to the ocean. 'I never expected that the further out you got, the more you draw back, and that large place you lived becomes a tiny speck on a map—like dust or sand. How many coastlines look the same when you look at them from out at sea or on a map? How could I have known that what we called the place would be different to what others called it? I know I come from Eire, I know that from other traders who sound and look like me and speak my language and sing my songs. But the village? Did it even have a name? It was too small a thing for other people to know, and it would take years to search all the coastlines.'

Yoshiko kept looking at him, and he felt his ears burning. Gora rubbed his head again to hide his awkwardness.

'I tried looking. But, in the end, I failed. I'll never go home.'

Gora felt like something was clawing at his heart, like a massive crow was sitting on his chest and digging at him. He shivered and rubbed his chest to be sure all his body was still in one piece. He heard Yoshiko sigh from beside him, and she pulled her knees up to her chest, as she always did when she was thinking or sad.

And, somehow, he knew what he had to do.

'I'll come with you.'

'Huh?' Yoshiko looked surprised—almost as surprised as he felt at hearing her speak so casually.

'When you go onto the ship, I'll come. I can't let you go alone. You'll barely manage. And remembering how it feels to be so far from home … that's what your people will feel, too—always wondering if they could come back, or whether they could even find it.

'Well, we know how to bring them back, and we know where to bring them back to. It's our duty if we know how to. I know I wished all those years that someone knew how to take me home. Well, maybe that's the world's sick joke—putting me here because I know what it's like.'

Yoshiko's face betrayed her by lighting up, though it seemed she tried to remain calm. Gora's mood lightened a little. 'Are you certain?' she said. 'You know what's at risk.'

'I do, which is why I can't let you do it alone. You'll die.'

Yoshiko scoffed. 'Thanks for the faith. And here I thought we were becoming friends.'

Gora let out a short chuckle and smiled, noticing her indignation and happiness all in one go. 'Yeah, I guess we are.' Then, he pulled himself up and brushed down his *hakama* roughly with his hands before offering one out for Yoshiko to take. 'Well, this is fun and all, enjoying the camaraderie of certain death, but we're not going to get ourselves kidnapped by sittin' up here, are we?'

23

Getting Onto the Death Ship

Yoshiko thought it would be simple, pretending to be scared as if she was scurrying home from work one night. She thought a lone girl at night would be an easy target for the foreign or bought-out guards. Instead, two nights she managed to get back to the caverns without being caught. The first coming across no-one dodgy at all, just seeing others like her fearfully scurrying to safety. The second, a pair of kindly guards on patrol hurrying up to her and warning her to get home soon and to stay safe, looking around hesitantly and carefully as they tried to make sure she was safe.

So there are still samurai keeping their code of honour and looking after the people, Yoshiko was relieved to discover.

But that didn't help her with her plan to ensure she got taken as a slave on that ship before it departed. She and Gora had reckoned it would only be in Hié a few days, so they'd planned and mentally prepared to get caught as quickly as possible. They'd even stowed their belongings away in the caverns where they could come back to collect them when they returned—if they returned. She'd guiltily put away her father's sword and other keepsakes from her mother, her friend, and the old farmer couple. She'd make sure to come back for them. Now, all Yoshiko and Gora had to do was make sure they were in the wrong place at the right time. It was harder than she'd anticipated. Gora, on the other hand, she hadn't seen since. She wondered whether he'd been caught already or was, like her, still trying.

The third night, she wrapped her hair carefully in a headscarf and pulled her jacket tight over her simple purple kimono to make sure she was as warm as possible. She clutched the clothes closer, kept looking over her shoulder, and took quick, shuffling steps in her zori. A wind suddenly blew up and pulled her headscarf from her head to reveal a youthful face and long, well-kept black hair.

Yoshiko allowed herself a small smile as a noise came from her right, slightly behind her. They meant to be silent—predators sneaking up on prey. She tried to pretend she'd not heard them sneaking up, ignoring her senses screaming at her that someone was going to grab her. Yoshiko continued to shuffle onwards without missing a beat, hearing shoes quickly pad up to her from behind on either side. *This is it*. Her ears twitched as she heard material scrap against itself as arms reached out, scraping the sides of their jackets. Strong, hawk-like grips grabbed at her arms and pulled her back, and before Yoshiko could fake a yell, firm hands clamped over her mouth and eyes. Shock flashed through her. She'd never expected it to hurt.

Yoshiko wriggled, pretended to try to break free, and kicked out. The two slave catchers hissed a laugh and dragged her off, moving just fast enough that when they pulled her, in her long kimono, it was all she could do to keep up without falling over. She stumbled, lost a sandal, stubbed her toe—genuinely crying out at this point at the pain—and tried to shake them off once more before pretending to concede.

A door opened somewhere, and her captors lurched Yoshiko forward and tightened their grips on her uncomfortably. She tripped on her remaining zori and stumbled forward a few steps before they picked her up by the arms and marched her at their pace. She let out a muffled moan—it was pulling on her arms too much that it hurt. Soon, a third voice hissed out.

'Where'd ya find this one?'

So the man on watch at the door was from Hié, she noticed. Not a foreigner? Yoshiko felt her blood boil. Why would they just sit here and let this happen—get involved, even?

'Scurrying home down by Koen Park,' the captor said without emotion. 'Tried to kick up a fuss.' So he'd been Hién, after all. With a bigger build—like the one on the left who regularly muttered in the language of the other pale-faced ones—she'd thought they'd both been foreigners. Well, he didn't seem happy with something, by the tones in his voice, Yoshiko thought. She wondered if he might feel guilty for taking her.

They shoved her with force—the hands coming away from her body and face. In a moment, she cried out as she fell forward, falling over something and landing roughly onto the floor. Pain stabbed up through her wrist as she threw out her arm and failed to break her fall correctly. The result was immense pain shooting up her arm. Yoshiko cried out, real tears springing to her face as she whirled around to glare at the person who had shoved her. But as she did, arms shot out and roughly grabbed at her ankles. Yoshiko tried to reach out and stop them with her unhurt arm, cradling the injured one by her stomach to stop the throbbing pain. But the person slapped her hand back and ignored her cries for them to stop. Rope bit into her ankles as they tied her feet and then grabbed both of her arms—causing another cry of pain as they pulled at her injured arm—and tied them together with the same rope they'd bound her feet with. Then, as roughly as they'd tied her, a pale-faced man shoved her out of the way until she toppled to her side, unable to balance, and left her struggling to sit herself back up.

'You'll shut up,' a voice growled from the side.

Yoshiko's heart lurched, and her body iced over. As her eyes adjusted to the darkness, she saw a pale-faced man with a scraggly beard sitting on a stool at the side of the room. He'd spoken her language. Too stunned to speak, she stared at him mutely. Then, she noticed many other people in various stages of sitting and lying down around her and in her peripheral vision. She'd not realised so many others had been taken since the ship had returned.

Suddenly feeling frightened, Yoshiko desperately searched for Gora—scanning the crowd of dark hair for that shock of autumn red she'd become used to seeing.

He wasn't there.

Wondering whether Gora had failed, loneliness crept into Yoshiko's heart like a fog in late winter. She wondered only too late whether this had been a bad idea after all.

<h1 style="text-align:center">24</h1>

Drinking Himself Onto the Death Ship

It was easy to get drunk. Gora had been doing that for years. Alcohol was the perfect way to hide from yourself and pretend like nothing mattered. And, after everything that had been happening lately, he needed a good drink.

Gora sat in a local Hién saké house and ignored the buzz of energy about him. People were still scared, and soon the realisation of life and the curfew would come back to them, but right now they were still enjoying the present—good drink. And good it was. All he'd known before, on the ships, was shitty-tasting gloop that was more suited to poisoning rats once they'd snuck into the galley or the storeroom. This, and most of the drinks from the country of Hizen, he realised, tasted good. It was so easy to drink.

And so Gora let another soft, crisp, clean saké slide down his throat and called out for more. And more. *Yep*, he thought as he eyed it up in the small, square, wooden container it was given to him in. This stuff was way nicer than even that bitter, dark red drink people raved about that came from the warm countries in the middle continent. Pirates, he tutted, knew nothing about good drink. Would drink anything if it got them drunk. Not that he had any reason to judge right now, considering his sole mission was to sit here, drink saké and spirits, and get drunk.

Gora thought of Yoshiko and wondered how she was getting on. Had she been taken yet? They'd planned for her to look like someone coming home from work, right? Would that mean she'd already been taken, if shops closed up already? He took another sip of the strong stuff—the plum spirit he'd got drunk with Yoshiko that last time he'd had a drink … or several bottles. How many should he drink this time for it to be late enough to go home drunk? Should he only drink a bit but pretend to be drunker? A tiny voice inside him said to opt for that—at least then he'd know what was going on and have some element of control, right? But, on the other hand, he didn't want to know what was going on. On this occasion, he was quite happy to let it happen to him without much thought. He'd end up in the same shit place all the same. Why worry?

He opted for somewhere halfway there—mostly because the owner got scared of staying open too late for fear of getting caught or guards punishing him for breaking curfew and kicked everyone out. And, before Gora left, the owner warned him about going home, that it wasn't safe to travel alone at night anymore.

Gora waved him off casually.

'No-one's bothered me for years.' He grinned, feigning confidence and thinking about how he'd hidden in Hié ten years already and not been found by the pirates. 'No-one's gunna bother me now.'

The saké house owner tried to persuade him otherwise, but Gora stomped out the door, stumbling slightly as he turned to bow to the owner. Then, he swerved down an alleyway.

Time to hunt for trouble!

Come on! he thought. Trouble, come find me!

Gora mumbled in his home language as he walked, as he often did when drunk, and cursed all the gods for letting him drink, for letting him be alone, and for letting him agree to this damned stupid mission he'd said he'd go on.

Well, okay, he'd not been alone much since he'd started helping that noble lass.

Fuuuuck.

He wondered once more where she was, whether she was safe or whether she'd been taken. For some reason, Gora hoped she'd failed and was sulking down in the caverns where at least she'd be safe.

Damn it, Yoshiko, he growled to himself as took a piss down an alley in the dark. *Let's just call it a night and figure out how to save the domain another way.*

Gora shuddered at the memory of that ship and waddled to the place they'd agreed he'd walk for maximum chances of getting caught. At the same time, he wondered why he was still going ahead with it.

Just quit now, save the girl, then save her damned region, he thought. Not that saving a region was going to be anything as simple as that.

But he didn't have time to 'quit now'. As he turned to head back to the caverns, he charged chest-first into the arms of a huge, pale-faced, slave-catching piece of shit.

Gora let out a roar and tried to back away, but he received a heavy fist to the stomach that made him double over in pain. Then, the scuffing of a second catcher behind him brought a foot stomping down into the back of his knee, and he crashed into the ground. Arms pulled him up and frog-marched him down a side street before he'd had a moment to realise what had happened. He spluttered, his stomach heaving from the punch and the swirling alcohol inside him. Maybe he'd drunk too much, after all.

25

On the Death Ship

The ship swayed, and Yoshiko sat with her knees drawn to her chest. She rested her forehead on her knees and habitually pulled at the chains that bound her arms. They wouldn't move much. Yoshiko closed her eyes and tried to breathe deeply and slowly, blocking out reality and focusing on a place she could feel calm. Instead, a wretched smell clouded her mind and overwhelmed her senses. She couldn't even concentrate on nothingness.

It must have been a few days since she had been taken and then pulled and marched onto this ship. It had been evening when they were moved—out of the prying eyes of port workers or citizens. Yoshiko was amazed by how this whole operation had happened without people noticing—or at least not talking about it. She wondered why no-one questioned the strange, giant ship kept in the port. Her wild thoughts told her that anyone who did was instantly silenced—a quick slip of a blade would do that. Her sane thoughts told her that it wouldn't surprise her had that been the case in current times.

Once marched onto the ship, they'd been lined up, stripped, and re-dressed in rags that could barely be called sacks for farm produce, let alone clothes. What had happened to the people's original clothes, Yoshiko would never know. Probably cleaned and sold for a profit without the buyers knowing where they'd come from, she guessed. Then, they'd been pushed below deck and hidden in every nook and cranny in the storage hold. With barely any room to move, they'd been bound to people either side and were unable to move. She could sit if she crouched or lie down if she fancied someone else's feet in her face—or worse. That was the extent of it.

When they'd first been taken down to the hold, a few people had cried across to each other—friends or family who were separated tried to communicate. But they'd been severely punished and beaten, and eventually, the communications stopped. The quiet was broken only by the moans or whimpers that everyone made at some point.

Yoshiko glanced up upon hearing a familiar, foreign whispering. Gora was cursing groggily in Gaean somewhere to her left, and Yoshiko peered over to look at him.

Gora had been in a bad state when he'd been captured and thrown into the room, roaring and wincing, covered in many wounds from where the catchers had beaten him up to make him easier to catch. It had been terrifying, and many of their fellow captives had cowered away. But soon he'd collapsed and become unconscious, and he'd not woken up until they've been brought to the ship. Two pale foreigners had dragged Gora on, and he'd finally come to only yesterday, now wincing and muttering to himself in lilting Gaean, still recovering from his wounds. She'd caught his eye from across to people between them shortly after he'd woken up and hunted about him in panic for her. Yoshiko had smiled slightly at him, though she didn't know why. It wasn't a smiling situation. But at least they'd completed the first part of their plan. Now, each time he caught her eye, she felt more and more uncertain and more guilty. Here they were, lying in their own messes and that of those around them, and he was still severely injured.

She'd never imagined it would be like this.

He'd warned her, hadn't he? What these ships were like. And she'd ignored it. Yet he'd still followed her. And now the only person she had to help her in the world was lying in pain in his own grime, probably wondering why he'd sworn to help her at all.

She stopped trying to catch his eyes, not caring if she couldn't communicate with him. She didn't want to see his usually light and humorous blue eyes turn dark and blaming.

Sighing at how dead and hopeless this place felt, Yoshiko squeezed her eyes shut and tried to think of the end goal: people safe, justice on the treacherous council, back at the castle. But now, what in the spirits' names had she got thrown into?

* * *

Yoshiko couldn't count the days she'd been here by now, and she—along with many others—spent most of her time drifting in and out of slumber with little energy to do anything else. Yoshiko had long given up on trying to find nothingness and meditate—in this accursed place, enlightenment felt far beyond realisation. The smell had multiplied way beyond the time she'd raided the ship previously and felt like she'd have been sick for even going near the hold. Now, locked in it for days and weeks, Yoshiko felt she'd never be freed of it and never forget it for as long as she'd live. She felt like she'd die among this smell—of human excrement and crushed, sweating, overheated bodies.

The man beside her coughed. He'd been coughing for days and was getting weaker each passing breath. Yoshiko was sure that lying in his own dirt and not being cleaned was a large part of his sickness, but their guards didn't seem to care about this at all. Then, before she knew it, a team of tall, pale men marched into the room, mouths and noses covered from the stench and eyes wrinkled from still being able to smell it.

The group of foreigners glared about the room and tossed their scraggly heads in different directions, splitting up and marching up and down causeways. They slashed their whips at anyone who moaned or reached out to beg for water and untied several Hiéns from their places in the hold. Then, the catchers pulled these people out, dead or moaning, and banged them up the steps to the deck. A moment of fresh air wafted into the hold, and Yoshiko closed her eyes to savour it. She could almost taste it; it was so clean. But her blissful moment was interrupted as the man beside her was unchained and pulled out by his feet and dragged away. Too weak to even moan, Yoshiko listened as his shallow breathing disappeared as he was pulled up the steps, head banging against the wood as the catcher dragged him behind.

Yoshiko held her breath, and she was sure most of the others in the hold did, too. From here, it was easy to hear the splashes as their comrades were thrown overboard, some screaming before they drowned. The hold was hushed. And, for keen-eared Yoshiko, she still heard them moaning as they sank to the depths—their gasps of stolen air would haunt her forever.

The sounds of their dying made something inside Yoshiko boil. She couldn't tell whether it was in her heart, her stomach, or deeper—in her soul, perhaps—and at first, she worried it was some tell-tale sign of a sickness taking her, too. Perhaps she'd finally caught it like the man beside her had. Her head felt a burning and her body went hot, but this felt hotter than any sickness she'd known or heard of. Yoshiko stared at the ceiling's wooden planks, knowing it led eventually to the outside—the outside where the air was fresh and the sky stretched on forever. Something inside her lurched. How Yoshiko longed to be up there. She dared to close her eyes and imagined flying. If she stretched out her arms and ran fast enough, could she run off this ship and soar? Even if it was for a moment, before plummeting into the harsh ocean below.

Even the ocean, she realised, *would be better than this.*

Yoshiko's body burned again. They'd pay. These people would pay for what they were doing to her people. She wanted to kill the lot of them and make them suffer. Each time a pale-faced crew member stomped down those steps or yelled in from above, she had the urge to snap their heads off. She was certain hunger and delirium consumed her. Where was the air? Why did her muscles and limbs scream and tingle? A fire rose and sank in her stomach, fuelling the desire to storm up, crush the ship, and eat the pale-faced crew whole, or burn them alive before tossing their remains over into the ocean. Thoughts of revenge for her people battled with fears of burning her people with those she wished to punish. And, not knowing where these thoughts arose from, Yoshiko moaned at the pain that this heat and this hate brought with it.

26
Slave Auctions

Fuck this. The world can be damned and take this damned ship with it. All kinds of curses in Hién and Gaean went round Gora's head as he lay in his bonds on the hard, wet floor.

What was I thinking? Why'd I let her come? A slave ship?

He'd seen these ships before; he knew what they were like. So why the fuck would he let her come here? Even to try to rescue her people?

The damned, old sea witch is going to eat well soon. He glared at a spot on the ceiling.

A bunch of the numbskull crew—lowers, no doubt—had barged in and dragged a load of the sick ones away. Trying to stop the spread of the sickness to preserve the profit they can make on those who remained alive, no doubt. They had been thrown overboard, and now everyone else knew what would happen if they died—or got too close to it. But he knew several people would rather jump over by their own choice than stay here. Better to die free than live in chains as a slave. There was a reason they bound you.

Now, Gora's main concern was Yoshiko. For some reason, he'd sworn to follow and protect her, even in such scummy places as this. Of course, he cared about the people of Hié—his neighbours and those he interacted with had no cause to be in places like this, as no-one did—and he'd do what he could to ensure they never had to be here. But right now, she was the one who had to stay alive the most. Unfortunately, she was also the one who lay in a disturbed rest, breathing heavily and sweating—severely overheating.

At first, he'd feared she'd caught an illness, and those around her still did. But she wasn't pale and limp like some of the others. Instead, she turned and fidgeted madly as if fighting an inner battle. What concerned him the most was whether the crew would think she was ill and just throw her overboard. While at least that would mean she wasn't in this place, it would mean certain drowning. No-one survived being overboard at sea for long.

He tried to raise his head from where he lay, bound, unable to move or sit up. He could just about see her like this, though it was a strain. In the first days on this ship, she'd been catching his eye, too, and they'd tried to communicate wordlessly—else incurring the wrath of the guards. But a few days later, she'd stopped for some reason, and Gora now wondered whether it was this illness, whatever it was, starting to take hold of her. Her temperature seemed to only be increasing, and those either side of her strained on their chains to lie further away from an overbearing heat. He frowned. The lass had said her family had powers of a dragon, hadn't she? She had strange abilities—like that sight, sound, and smell. And she'd said people in her family had been known to transform into dragons before. Well, now he wondered whether her body was hiding more than it looked. If she was fighting an inner battle with a beast—one that, in his mind, was a giant fire-breathing lizard that would burn and crush the entire ship—it really would be bad if the wrong one won.

For the rest of the journey, Gora fluctuated between listlessness, drowsiness, and a turmoil that resulted in him repeatedly swearing in his head, wondering how to achieve this impossible mission and whether the young princess was going to survive. Surely, it had been long enough to have got somewhere? The stupid amount of time he'd been conscious, at least, should have been long enough to arrive anywhere. Sea travel was slow, sure, but you could get to many places within a few weeks.

At least they got to go above deck sometimes. They were taken in shifts, pulled in their rows of bonds, for a moment in fresh air and sunlight, washed and scrubbed down to avoid more illness spreading and to keep their bodies healthy and decent for selling. Even the cold water was bliss after lying in your own mess in the dark and doing nothing but wait for the daily feed of tasteless gruel for days on end. Each time they were pulled up and taken to the deck, Gora looked out for Yoshiko, knowing she liked nothing more than going out into the sunlight when they were back in Hié. But she still avoided his gaze and looked more and more like she was closing in on herself as the journey progressed.

Finally, after another unknown number of waking periods, the cry went out above the deck. Gora sighed in relief and closed his eyes, listening to the muffled sounds of preparation coming from above. Soon, the yelling became angry, and Gora knew this meant those who had been stowed away on deck were being unloaded from the deck and marched off the ship. Shortly after, feet pounded down the steps to the hold, and Hié folk who'd been kept in silence for weeks were wincing at the suddenly loud yelling from those who controlled them.

Weary men and women were hoisted up, yelled at, barged into, pushed, beaten, and shoved in their chains into a movement they'd not done for weeks. People stumbled, cried out and moaned, and barely had the energy to move. Angry cries came from their captors as they hauled the Hién people up and flogged them to keep moving. When they pulled Gora to his feet, he looked about to see some people who would never stand again. Instead, they were cut and left—lying dead or half-dead—to be tossed overboard to the sharks when the line of people had gone.

Gora looked behind, anxiously trying to spot Yoshiko. He found her being pulled up by a young, peaky-faced crew member who cried out in pain as if burnt and then slapped her. The man swore, kicked her forward, and glared after her, rubbing his hands. Gora tried to look at her face and meet her eyes but felt the awful sting of the whip crash into his upper arm to bring him back to attention. He yelped and was pulled onto the deck into the blinding light. But he'd managed to get a glimpse of her face: eyes dark and almost unseeing. He swallowed down panic. What should he do next?

Gora and his fellows were pulled onto a stone port. Shouts came in an unknown language, and the bewildered and fearful Hién people looked blankly at this strange new world. Gora grimaced. So this was where they'd be sold.

This place was a well-built land, with cobbled streets and tall buildings made from stone and timber. The port lay in a little inlet, and he had no doubt this wasn't the main port of the country—there were no fishing or trade ships, and it was way too small for normal dealings—but a smaller one they'd made exclusive for bringing in slaves.

So they don't wanna cause a fuss in the main port, aye? Gora wondered, peering about him and then wincing as someone lashed out at him.

Gora stood on his toes and peered over the crowd, trying to look out for Yoshiko. He couldn't see her. As he looked around, Gora wondered whether he'd been here before. This place looked oddly familiar. Then again, wouldn't all slave markets look depressingly the same?

The weather, too, could be indicative of where he was. It was clouded-over, but not cold. Judging by the length of time it had taken to get here, they could only be near the middling continents. Based on this, they were still in the northern part of the world—above the centre-line.

Gora frowned. A few countries seemed to be getting more and more into slave dealing in this end of the world. But they usually enslaved their own or took from nearby countries. Why would they come from so far to take them? Tensions rising? Taking people from far-off lands would cause less of a stir as opposed to taking your neighbours.

As Gora thought this, he spotted the tall, slender figures of those from the south, with their warm and deep walnut and cedar skintones contrasting the pale ones from this country. He also noticed their simple dress, knowing that while the southerners wore no rags like the Hién people were being forced to wear now, they didn't seem to be much better off.

He grimaced as he watched a pair of southern men lifting heavy loads from the ship they'd been unloaded from. For some reason, at least they were now no longer slaves. But they hadn't been upgraded by much. Poor servants—still forced to work, but only given the bare minimum needed. Then, just as he stood onto his toes once more to try to look for Yoshiko, Gora was immediately pulled to the side and scrubbed down with a rough brush and an even more rough hand. The cold water and bristles of the brush pained him, and Gora roared out, receiving a sharp whack to the head before being pushed into the paddock with other men.

Great. How was he supposed to get out of here and grab Yoshiko now?

Across the other side of the paddocks, a crowd of pale men yelled and raised their hands to buy the fresh-off-the-ship Hién people at an auction. Gora's heart lurched. Panicked, he turned to watch, squinting to see what was happening. A line of Hién people stood at the side of the auction, waiting, with slave owners browsing to see those who would be called up next. Gora's heart stalled when he saw Yoshiko already standing in line. He cursed and noticed her eyes were just as dark as when he'd seen her earlier, and she was staring ahead, almost unseeing. Normal Yoshiko would be shocked by all this, looking around everywhere at what was happening to her people and trying to find a way out, trying to find him and meet her gaze so they could get out of here. But she wasn't. Something was wrong, like she was focusing on something internal—still that inner battle he thought she'd been facing on the ship.

A slave owner stood in front of her at the auctions on the other side of the paddocks, nodding his large head. She'd be taken soon, Gora knew. They took the quality ones first. He had to do something—fast.

Gora shuffled to the edge of the paddocks, keeping an eye on the black-haired noble beyond the crowd. He hoped someone would pull him out to be in the line next, but they kept grabbing others. Gora watched, stomach feeling like he'd swallowed the ocean, as Yoshiko was pulled onto the auction dais.

Several hands flew up to buy her before one—the pale-faced man who'd stood in front of her a moment ago—won the bid. She got quite a high price, by the sounds of it. A well-muscled woman of her class was a rare thing. Growing up in high ranking had meant she'd had the luxury of health, and these people could spot that a mile off. Then, with Gora trying to keep his eyes pinned to her, Yoshiko was pulled into a group of other Hién slaves, waiting to be taken by their owner.

Gora jumped as screams went up beyond the auctions. As slave owners left, taking their new possessions, people were branded with the sigil of the one who owned them.

He gulped. Not another one.

It was one of the worst feelings in the world, he was sure. Not just the pain—the unbelievable, searing pain—but the knowledge that your life and freedom were lost. And, right now, that little princess was about to find out just how bad it could be.

But, *fuck*, she was never supposed to get it.

Weren't they meant to have escaped once they got off the ship, before all this? Wasn't that the plan? Get caught, come here, escape off the ship, nose around to find out what's happening, then head to the palace to bully some royal shit into leaving Hié alone? But now that wasn't happening. If you got branded, that was everything over. Everyone would know, forever, what you were.

Gora was pulled into the line for the auction himself, but he didn't care. He peered through the auction crowd at the branding stations beyond. Yoshiko's slave owner was marching her and her group to the branding boxes, and he handed his mark to the woman crouched by the branding fires. A Hién man was dragged forth, shaking and crying, and pinned down by a large, brutish man. The woman held out the irons, pressed the scorching metal to his honey-coloured skin, and the Hién man screamed.

Heck, anyone who was branded screamed. There was nothing else to do. A hot, searing clenching of the skin sent bubbling flames through your body, making your brain flash over and your eyes cloud with a burning white. Your stomach lurched and clenched and tightened all at once. If these people had eaten much on the ship, there was a guarantee they'd lose the contents of their stomachs. But with most of the little food they'd eaten gone by now, most people here just bent double, crying and retching until an owner or guard clapped them over the head with something and yelled at them to move on.

Until it was Yoshiko's turn.

Gora was pushed forward in the line, but he still stared at her.

Yoshiko was pulled lifelessly over by a guard who clawed into her fair skin with his fingers and pushed her down. The guard nodded at the woman with the burning metal, who raised it from the fire's embers by her side. Even from here, Gora could see that Yoshiko just stared into the eyes of this woman—who had light hair the colour of a chipmunk, and a pale face that reminded him of the same, too. She didn't look like the sort of person to be here, but she was. For whatever reason. Gora could see an unforgiving dare growling through Yoshiko's eyes. When he flicked his eyes back to the chipmunk woman, he saw her falter. Her hand paused before she raised the metal, and her face closed in. Then, she looked away from the girl's eyes and raised her arm, pushing the metal into Yoshiko's chest.

The smile vanished from the face of the guard holding Yoshiko down. He peered down at the fair-haired woman pinning the branding iron on the Hién noble longer than it should, and then he looked into the eyes of the Hién girl. The girl wasn't screaming. Gora held his breath, sickness flooding through him even just watching. Then, as the metal left Yoshiko's chest, the burning mark of her new owner blazed for a moment before settling down into an ugly knot of red and white. Snarling, the guard pushed Yoshiko away and slapped the chipmunk-like woman across the face. The woman stood and threw the branding iron to the floor with a clang, cursed back at the man, and stomped away, glancing back occasionally, fearfully, at the black-haired girl.

Gora dared to release his breath, realising the auction had silenced, too. Hundreds of pairs of eyes watched the scene.

The slave owner slapped Yoshiko and shouted out at his entourage to leave. Gora watched as his friend was taken away.

27

The Work Farm

Yoshiko's ankles twisted over the stony streets as she walked bound in line with several other Hién people bought in the slave auctions by this foreign man. It was difficult to walk on these stones and keep the same pace as those tied about you. Yoshiko's muscles screamed out with an aching that couldn't be stopped—she wanted to run, to leap, and to feel the wind gushing about her as she dreamed of flying. She was sure she could do it this time if she ran fast enough.

Her leg muscles twitched at the thought, as if they had a mind of their own to dash off and swim in the air. But Yoshiko sighed and forced herself to continue. Could she even break free from these bonds if she wanted to? She looked down at them, certain she could. But as Yoshiko looked about her at the forlorn faces of her people about her—already dull and losing hope—she knew it wouldn't be that easy. What pain would it bring upon them if she did that? Would it be like the first time she tried to save the ship?

Now, Yoshiko looked to the people who escorted them—men only, she noticed. Where were the women? There weren't any foreign women in sight. And where were they being taken? Would they be walking for long? What if they couldn't walk all the way on these strange, stony roads? Looking around at some of the Hién people in line with her, she saw that some were grimacing at the stones against their feet and stumbling. And some of the men were carrying strange long, cylindrical items that looked to be created from metal and wood. It looked heavy and almost like a strange weapon, but not a blade—there was no way that could house a blade. Yoshiko thought back to the stories Gora had told her about lands overseas and his life as a pirate. He'd talked about a strange weapon that looked like a stick with a handle and could fire lightning stones at people to kill them. She tried to think back to the name he'd given it.

Gan? Gun?

If it was a gun, Yoshiko knew there'd be a hole at the end of the stick for the lightning stones—*rounds, he called them*—to fire out of, and there'd be a lever of some kind at the other side for a finger to pull it and fire the bullet. She looked closer to see if she could see them. She'd never seen a gun before.

A guard noticed her looking at the wood and metal stick he carried—she'd been able to confirm it was a gun, at least—and lashed out, slapping and yelling. Yoshiko winced and felt heat rise within her. He looked into her eyes strangely, like that man at the port who'd become angry and then scared when they burned her, she recalled. Whatever all that had been about.

Yoshiko could break away and make a run for it, she thought. That had been the plan originally, hadn't it, when she and Gora had been speaking of it. It had been an almost impossible plan, but the only one they could think of. Now, both were separated and heading who-knows-where. And in such a strange land, she wasn't certain she'd be able to figure out where he was and track him by sound and smell. Here, everything sounded and smelt different.

Yoshiko frowned and stumbled once more on the strange stony road, wincing as her bare feet were grazed. No, she'd have to be smarter than that. There was much more going on here than people just being taken. She thought about it as she walked; there was nothing else to do. First, her father had been killed returning from visiting the neighbouring region. Next, she and her mother had run away, and then her mother had been killed. People of the Hién domain had started to go missing, and the council had restricted her people's movements, ramping up the guards' bullying. Gora had said these foreign slave catchers had been seen leaving the castle compound—presumably after speaking with the council—and then been found with hundreds of her people in a mysteriously empty port. Then, when she and Gora had tried to save them, Hién guards had turned a blind eye and even fought back the Hién people, pushing them back onto the ships.

This was happening with the council's agreement and could be why her parents had been killed. But how had the guards been convinced to get involved? They were meant to protect the people.

Yoshiko had to find out what was going on and take her people home. And it couldn't be as boisterous an attempt as last time. That had failed. It had to be more subtle and well-informed. She needed to know who she was dealing with. If not, Yoshiko had no doubt another ship would simply head to Hié and start again, if it hadn't already.

Resolved that this could be the best solution, Yoshiko began to run plans in her head for how she could escape and find a way to investigate. At times, she reluctantly let the guards slap her when she looked about too much from trying to take in the area they were walking, and she resorted to looking at the stoned floor and peeking from the corner of her eyes. There were other people, too, she noticed, as someone not from the group caught up with them.

Yoshiko had never seen people like this before—they had beautiful skin that shone like polished cherry wood under the light of the sun. She'd heard the term *sun-blessed* before. This must be what it referred to—when the sun blesses someone with deep and healthy skin to be out under its rays without trouble. And these people were tall, slight of build but had fine muscles that were easy to see (from active lifestyles and work, she thought). They looked the picture of fitness and power, so why were they acting like they, too, were kept here? They didn't wear the rags she and her people did—instead wearing simple clothing—but something about the looks on their faces told her they were equally trapped.

A tall sun-blessed man strode past to the right of the slave group, and Yoshiko felt her face flush. His long legs looked like they had such power she was certain he could run for days. Yoshiko wondered whether she could beat him at running, not sure even her dragon-born curse could give her the power and speed to run against him in a race. And though even Gora was fit from being a hunter, this man looked more so.

Yoshiko looked away from the deep-skinned man's lean power to her right and glanced to the woman who overtook the group to the left, striding at a similar pace to the long-legged man. She, too, was tall, and she held a heavy basket of something on top of her head. Yoshiko wondered what she did. Was she carrying provisions? It didn't seem she'd be escorting the group of Hiéns to be used as slaves. From what she'd seen, this country seemed to only let the men—and the pale ones at that—fill such a role. And these new people didn't have those guns that the pale people did. What would these other foreigners do?

The tall woman's eyes slid to meet Yoshiko's, and her black eyebrow raised just a little up her contoured face. It was just enough for Yoshiko to realise the woman had caught her staring, and she quickly looked away, feeling her ears burn. Both continued walking, pretending not to notice each other, until the taller woman and the long-legged man strode onwards, overtaking the struggling Hiéns fresh from the death ship.

Yoshiko watched after them, soul aching to join them in walking free, but knowing they were likely anything but.

By the time they stopped among a great wall of trees, the soles of Yoshiko's feet burned from walking over all the lumps and bumps on the stones in the road. Within the great wall of trees lay a dirt road, and Yoshiko's relief flooded her body like a dip in a lake, and her feet sighed just as much. And, as they continued to pad down the first track, through a great, tall wall that broke through the trees, a large house with surrounding lands came into view.

It looked like a farm, but a wealthy one that spanned hectares.

The house was beautiful, in a way, but different to those they built in Hié, Yoshiko thought. Tall, many floors with many windows dotting the stone walls. It rose like a box—all the same level, unlike the tiered buildings in Hié. It dominated the landscape, which had several other buildings of weird and unusual shapes scattered throughout the fields. Yoshiko wasn't given long to wonder what the purpose of each building was, for as she scanned her surroundings, she saw people stooped in or walking through the fields, carrying baskets and heavily bunched or tied grains— some wearing the simple clothes of the two people who'd passed them on the road, and some wearing rags just like she was. And, to Yoshiko's dismay, she noticed that those wearing the rags were of the shorter, slighter stature she knew from back home, with black hair and honey-brown skin, just like the people of her country.

Hadn't she and Gora been on the first slave ship journey? Why were they already people that looked like they were from Hié already under the ownership of this man?

Mind racing, Yoshiko wondered whether these people could be from a neighbouring region in Hizen, and the ships were going about their land and collecting people from all the domains.

'Move!'

A man was poking people with the handle of his gun, and his face was pink and twisted as if he were angry. It took Yoshiko a moment to realise he'd spoken in her language.

Whether or not the others noticed, they showed no signs. They returned to their shuffle and moved as a unit down the track towards an outhouse. Here, they were given simple cloth suitable for working, yet still more like rags than clothes. Then, with pale guards sneering at them, they were ushered into separate buildings—one turning out to be an outhouse for slave women. There, they were met by a woman that looked like she was from Hié. She was gaunt, and her black eyes stood out against shadowed eyes. Yoshiko didn't need to search too deeply into them to see that the woman had given up on life, that her eyes seemed soulless. She gave their instructions briefly, and Yoshiko was sure she'd forget half of it. Yoshiko noticed the woman spoke unusually quickly and in a higher level of politeness that wouldn't usually be spoken in such a situation. Yoshiko wondered whether the guards could understand a little of what she was saying, and whether the woman was trying to throw them off a little with higher-level language.

With no chance to rest after their introduction, the women were to change quickly, even in front of a male guard, before they were pushed outside to work immediately. Some were taken to the house. Yoshiko was taken to the backdoor, where someone explained they were heading to the fields to help with the grain— it was harvest time, and there was much grain to be taken to the mill across the fields to be turned to flour. And, though Yoshiko initially expected the work to not be as bad as she thought—she'd seen maids working around the castle and farmers working in the fields—she soon learned it was a quite different situation.

Here was a life of no pay, no rights, constant verbal abuse and beatings by the guards, working from sunup to sundown, little food, and nothing to call her own. She didn't even own her own life anymore, she reminded herself, nursing a lash to the arm for being slow with the grain. Yoshiko grimaced. She couldn't delay or slow, though she had no idea how to do this work. And when she tried to whisper to the person next to her with a guard too close, even to ask for instruction, she only received more lashings with sticks.

Within mere hours, people learned not to even talk. And, though Yoshiko had been reflecting on whether she should make her moves that evening and slip away to get to know this land and complete her mission, upon reaching the broth pot the slaves gathered about to eat, she found what she least expected.

28

A Friend

'Eh? My lady?'

A familiar voice reached Yoshiko's ears as she sat about the campfire that a miserable pot of broth bubbled at. But, exhausted, Yoshiko watched the flames and figured the person was speaking to someone else. No-one knew her here.

To Yoshiko's left, a tall, slim, sun-blessed woman—from Qecla, Yoshiko remembered the Hién woman who gave them the introduction to the farm telling them the other people here were Qeclans—sat and looked up as a woman rushed to sit near them. No-one rushed here. Following the Qeclan woman's gaze and realising she thought she recognised this light smell, Yoshiko's heart lurched.

The woman sat down and whispered in her ear. 'Lady Yoshiko?'

Yoshiko agonised. 'Haruki?' She stared in disbelief.

It was Haruki, no doubt. Her short, shoulder-length black hair had grown, and it slipped in front of her ear and past her shoulder. Yoshiko noticed the shine had disappeared, and Haruki pushed it back behind her ear without thinking, like she always did.

'What are you doing here?' Yoshiko hissed. Her heart shuddered in her body, head running quicker than a warhorse to try to figure out how Haruki could have ended up caught, too.

'I was going to ask you the same thing, my lady. How could *you* be taken?'

Both kept their voices low; Haruki seemed tuned into keeping Yoshiko's identity quiet. *As always*, Yoshiko thought, *she looks after me well.* Yoshiko wanted to pull Haruki into an embrace but wondered if it was appropriate.

'I'm not quite sure what happened,' Yoshiko admitted, turning back to face the fire and looking down at the tiny bowl of watery broth she held in both her hands. It didn't look at all appetising. The watery mess of grains and leaves wouldn't stave off her hunger much, but she knew it was all they'd have. She swallowed weakly and tried to sip at it. 'But why are you here? I thought you left the keep? They said—' Yoshiko's voice cracked. 'They said you'd gone, that you didn't want to work there anymore. Everyone suddenly changed.'

Yoshiko had felt lonely when Haruki suddenly disappeared, and her solitude was enhanced by having to run away from her home. Through everything, she only wished she could have had her friend there to speak with.

Haruki also looked down at the bowl in her hand, face glum. 'We didn't leave,' she whispered. 'We were taken.'

Yoshiko looked at her, and Haruki's eyes slid to meet her gaze, but quickly returned to the broth. She kept talking. 'One night, we were finishing work and leaving the castle. The lady who took over duty for me until the morning was different; I'd never seen her before. I thought she was new. She looked nice. And then, as I left with a couple of others, we were taken before we could even leave the gate. Out of nowhere, we were shoved into a stable.

'There were a few people already there. A stable boy, a few maids—including your mother's head maid—and a guard. It looked like they were taking people away from the keep and replacing them. I realised then the new maid I saw must have been replacing your usual night maid and that I, too, was being replaced.

'I thought I hadn't served you well. We were told we dishonoured our positions and were asked to leave. That the daimyō was punishing us and sending us away. After that, we ended up on an awful ship. It was huge. They took us in the night to the small natural harbour to the west. You know, the one your history tutor said was once the centre of fishing before the bad storm? Well, the ship was there. I've been here ever since.'

Yoshiko couldn't believe her ears. She stared, not caring how obviously, at her friend. Haruki kept watching her bowl.

'But, Haruki, that was two seasons ago!'

Yoshiko felt heartbroken that her maid and friend thought she'd been abandoned and sent away—especially to such a place— and that the slave catchers had been dealing in Hié as early as that. But that was before her parents had been killed. Had people been taken from under their noses that whole time? From their household, no less? Had her mother known about it?

Haruki nodded. 'Lord Hitoshi was away, and Lady Asumi was in a series of governing meetings. I thought they did it then, so you and your family didn't have to see us after we'd disappointed you. I—I thought I'd angered you.' She took a shaky breath and turned to Yoshiko. 'And now you're here. I don't understand.'

'You didn't disappoint me.' Yoshiko rushed to say it. 'I was sad when you left. I thought you didn't want to stay with me anymore. I'd known you so long, then suddenly you weren't there. It was lonely. But this? I can't believe this happened under our noses and we didn't know.'

Yoshiko stared at the broth, not knowing whether she could even stomach it now.

'I'm happy to hear. I have been telling myself off for it ever since. Thinking I'd done something wrong.' Haruki's face had a small smile, and she glanced shyly at Yoshiko.

'Have more faith. Did I ever show signs of being unhappy with you? If I did, tell me how I can make it up to you.' She rested her hand on Haruki's shoulder and looked into her friend's eyes, trying to convey she felt saddened at the thought. Yoshiko racked her brain to think of what she could have done. She loved Haruki; she'd never have been unhappy around her, would she?

Haruki smiled and sniffed. 'Well, no, but ...' Then she stopped, and the smile edged higher up her face. Yoshiko's heart lightened. Haruki had such a bright smile. 'I'm just so happy to hear that.' Haruki wiped away a tear with her arm. 'How are your parents? How could you have been taken without them knowing?'

Yoshiko took a sharp breath and tried to swallow her heart back down to where it should be. 'Um,' she started, not sure where to begin. 'The day after you left the keep, Father was killed returning from Shogo. He never made it home.' Yoshiko heard Haruki gasp, and continued. 'Mother and I escaped because she thought he'd been murdered by someone on the council and thought they'd come after us next. We hid while they hunted us, and we tried to find out who had killed Father. But Mother was killed, too. She'd been found while gathering information and led them away so I could stay hidden.'

Haruki stared at Yoshiko, horrified. Yoshiko observed how peaky her friend's features had become. Haruki had lost a lot of weight.

'I don't know what to say. I can't believe it. Dead? But they were so strong and loved. I can't imagine anyone wanting to kill them. Or you.' She shifted uneasily. 'Do you know who did it?'

Before Yoshiko could respond, the tall Qeclan woman to Yoshiko's left leaned over and cleared her throat.

'Haruki, you know this woman?'

Haruki's face brightened. 'Nubia, I'm sorry. This is Yoshiko. I worked for her in my last life.'

Yoshiko noticed that Haruki was still hiding Yoshiko's identity. She felt grateful.

Nubia held out a slender hand, waiting as Yoshiko stared at it.

'You hold her hand, too,' Haruki whispered.

Yoshiko, blinking and feeling confused, held out her hand in front of Nubia's. Nubia, grinning, reached forward and clasped Yoshiko's hand. Reflexively, Yoshiko withdrew a little, but Nubia just smiled and held it harder. At first, this made Yoshiko panic. But then Nubia spoke once more in Hizen.

'This is the greeting from this country. Nice to meet you.'

'And in your country?' Yoshiko asked.

Nubia laughed a little, and Yoshiko realised how warm it sounded—like a hot dessert waiting atop a *kotatsu*. Yoshiko realised she hadn't heard laughter since before Gora had shown her the place her people were being taken before the ship. (She didn't count the guffaws of the slave catchers.)

'When we are all free, Yoshiko, I will show you. For now, we are here.'

'Are your people not free? It seems a little different.' Yoshiko looked about the fire at the two nations of people sitting together.

Nubia frowned. 'We were the same, before the fight. Now we work, and they say we are free, but we know we are not. We still cannot leave.'

Haruki chipped in and explained a little further—that the Qeclan people had been slaves before, but there had been an uprising. The Qeclans, being stronger fighters physically, overpowered their captors, the Acreins. Finally, more Acreins were sent from the capital, and many lives had been lost on both sides. After the uprising and a strike, some sort of agreement was made. The Qeclans had food, clothes, and money, and they were officially free, but what little money they earned went back into the Acrein pockets anyway for housing, and the Qeclans were still refused the freedom to leave. In a way, they weren't much better off, and they were still not free.

'We'll leave, somehow. Even if we have to buy our freedom.' Nubia finished Haruki's explanation.

'Then, Nubia, let's look after each other, and we may see your countryfolk's greeting yet.'

Nubia nodded. Yoshiko was impressed and wondered how much of that Nubia could understand. All of it?

'How do you know the Hizen language?' she asked Nubia.

'We talk. Copied the language. Gave lessons. Haruki is a good teacher; she speaks to me often.'

Haruki blushed and tried to hold back the compliment, stating that Nubia was just a good learner. Yoshiko dared to grin. How like Haruki.

'So can you speak their language, too, Haruki?'

'Only a little.'

Nubia made a noise, and Yoshiko realised it was a scoffing noise. 'Haruki speaks Qeclan well. She is modest.'

At this, Yoshiko let out a little laugh. 'I understand. She always was.' She and Nubia nodded together, watching a blushing Haruki. 'Will you both teach me? I love learning about other cultures.'

Her favourite part of her family being close with the shōgun had been all the diplomatic visits. She had meant it when she told Gora she'd have wanted to be a cultural ambassador. To visit other countries to represent her mother in Hié would have been a great opportunity, and she'd have taken Haruki along with her. Here, looking at Haruki sitting beside her, she now wondered whether her dream could still be possible. She couldn't believe she'd found Haruki again, and that Haruki had never left her. She'd do anything she could to make sure she could take Haruki away from here and take her back home.

Yoshiko paused. *How can we go home if I don't know where we are?* 'Where are we? What is this place?'

The other two women looked across Yoshiko at one another and frowned. Nubia rubbed her flat nose with her long fingers, staring at Haruki as if to suggest she should answer. Haruki did.

'It's a country called Acrein. The port town is Dunstrand— we're just on the outskirts of it to help produce crops for the people here and in the main town on the other side of the forest, Rödsted. There are lots of slave farms like this that feed Rödsted; that's why they took us. To have people to work the farms. Though some people do other jobs.'

'Rödsted is like Hié and has a palace?'

Haruki paused, and Nubia watched them while eating her now-cold broth. Yoshiko wondered how much of the language Nubia could understand, as she seemed to be watching and listening closely as if trying to keep up.

'Not like Hié at all, I think,' Haruki started slowly, 'but I've never been, so don't know much. This is just what I've heard. But the king does live there, in some kind of castle.'

Yoshiko nodded, taking a sip of her own broth, staring into the campfire in the centre of their seated circle. She watched the flames burn, thinking the main town would be where she would have to go to complete her mission.

Will Gora head there, too?

She looked back at Haruki. With Haruki here, her plans of escaping and finding Gora so they could follow the rest of their plan had changed a little. She couldn't leave here without Haruki, but it was risky enough trying to run away as just one person. Especially if the guards had guns and could shoot them if they tried to escape. No wonder Gora thought she was naïve with an optimistic plan.

There's just so much I don't know, she grieved to herself, wishing she were stronger, smarter, more powerful—someone she felt could save these people and take them home to safety. Looking around at the slave farm, she doubted even her mother would have much more fortune with that.

29

A Fever

Yoshiko chatted to Haruki and Nubia as much as she could over the following days, whispering to them and trying to avoid being caught by the guards. Mostly, she worked alongside fellow Hiéns, completing back-breaking work and collapsing by the river at the end of the day to wash the sweat and mud from her ragged clothes. They didn't see Nubia often; the Qeclan people had been given slightly better roles—if not by much—since their uprising.

'Yes, but we are merely indentured servants—there is no difference,' Nubia said when Yoshiko spoke to her about her role. 'These people would enslave anyone, given a chance, and they even treat people in their own country with a hierarchy—if you're low in the hierarchy, you're pretty much a slave.'

When Yoshiko quizzed Nubia further on this, the tall woman frowned and pursed her lips, and Haruki helped her translate.

'Even long before they took my people and me, they enslaved their own. But somehow, the lower Acreins refused and managed to work their way out of it. That is why they came to take us from our home. They realised taking from another country would solve their own people demanding to be treated correctly and paid. So they just took other people and made it so they had no choice.' Nubia then clapped her hand over her eyes. 'And yet, when we tried to free ourselves and fight for rights of our own, they merely repeated history. They went to take yet more people from yet another country—one from far away so no-one could do anything about it.'

She looked guiltily at Yoshiko and Haruki.

Yoshiko sighed. So if she freed her people now, the Acrein captors would just go onto yet another country and take more people?

These words rang in her head each day, and her body moved by instinct in the house or the fields, but her mind ran things over. She watched her people lose hope—even so quickly in the days they'd been there, imagining this was it forever—and their eyes glazed over. People cried at night and whispered for their loved ones, or blankly stared at nothingness. But Yoshiko's brain shifted through flames and tried to figure out how to save her people, and perhaps truly free Nubia's, without subjecting more people to this fate.

And all the while, something burned inside her body. She'd never shaken that fever from the ship. Her skin felt close to burning, and her head heated and felt it would burst. Yoshiko longed for some fresh, cool water and a natural spring bath to soothe her. Yet the river would have to do. And, disgustingly, the people here used it for everything.

Almost immediately, Yoshiko had become friends with the tall Qeclan woman, and she relished that friendship as much as the one she had with Haruki. Both these women offered Yoshiko freedom from the loneliness she'd felt growing up in the keep, a loneliness she was determined to erase and that had been melting away since meeting Haruki and then Gora. Nubia was a welcome member of her new social life. Nubia would join Haruki and Yoshiko at dinner if she could, and the three would sit and talk. Nubia learned about Yoshiko's position in the castle, hearing anecdotes of Haruki's life before she was here. In whispered tones, Nubia listened about the castle life they'd both led, and Nubia began to share a little of her past life before the slavers, too, of a simple life in Qecla, growing up in the bush and loving spear-hunting with her friends, then moving to a port town to learn trade and meet people from other countries. She'd been in this port town when the slavers came, and warlords from other areas bought and sold their neighbours for riches in an attempt to raise their own power. Yoshiko wondered how similar this had been to her country. She thought back to how her parents were killed and people were taken when the slavers came. Were neighbouring daimyō in on that, or was it just the council as her mother and she had originally thought?

The people here often talked about their life before being taken as their 'past life'. It was gone, dead, and they were unable to go back to it. But the more Yoshiko talked to these people and slowly learned elements of their lives and language, the more determined she was to help them. Here, it wasn't just her people she had to free. It was Nubia's, too. And she had to stop it permanently, from the source. If only she could escape, find out what was going on, free them, and take them home. Nubia had said that, though free, they weren't allowed to leave. That didn't sit right with Yoshiko. That didn't sound like freedom. They were still slaves in all but name, and the money they were given didn't amount to enough to support themselves. It paid for a bed in a shared room in a 'servant's quarters' on the farm, but that was it.

And more than ever, Yoshiko wanted to take Haruki from this place. She, like these people, should never have been here. Yoshiko had to take Haruki home and make up for the time they lost and the pain Haruki went through—thinking she'd been cast aside. She owed her friend that. Now, she just needed to figure out how.

One evening, six sunsets since the time they'd arrived, the workers and slaves of the farmland gathered in their usual place about the broth that bubbled over the flames. There was a hush over the camp and dark looks on people's faces. Something gnawed in Yoshiko's stomach. The heat inside her stirred, and she dreamed about soothing rivers and bathing in springs.

The guards had been tetchy all day—beating people more than usual, dragging them off, and returning them half-broken. No-one knew why their attitude was worse than expected, but the Hién and Qeclan people dared not speak a word and kept their eyes downcast to avoid the guards' stares. Who knew what would happen if the guards got them. Since Yoshiko had been here, she'd seen women slink back into the slave cabin, crying and hugging their bodies close, limping the next day as they tried to work. The guards and catchers leered at them, taunting and pushing. If a slave tried to back the woman up—man or woman, or even a Qeclan worker—they were beaten and dragged away.

Everyone knew what was happening, even the master. But he refused to do anything. One woman lumbered uncomfortably through the house and fields, belly swollen with the child of an attack long before Yoshiko had arrived. Still treated miserably, she was yelled at for not being able to keep up with the expectations. When Yoshiko asked what would happen to the child:

'They will be forced to work, too—an extra worker or slave for the Acrein pigs. Born into it is free for the master.' Nubia clicked her tongue and made a gesture with her hands.

Yoshiko had learned this was rude, almost like Gora's swearing.

Frustrated at how everyone was treated here, the fire inside her burned more. Yoshiko's stomach churned, and a burning feeling rushed up from within. She dropped her bowl and rushed from the camp, worried she'd be unable to keep the contents of her stomach where they should be. No sickness came, but the burning fever she'd had on the ship returned full force, and she collapsed into the grass beyond the campfire. Yoshiko's world faded to the sound of Haruki's panicked voice as she ran towards her.

30

In the Forest

'Damn that little princess.' Gora growled, kicked at some fallen leaves, and cursed. He was making a habit of that again. And he'd been so good at losing that shitty tongue since he'd started his new life in Hié.

Gora glared, shifting the damned heavy log on his shoulder. He'd been taken to the edge of a forest on the foot of a hill above the port. The view was great, he'd had to admit—the port, the town, and several farms and plantations spread out before him. But Gora hadn't been brought here for the view. Instead, all he looked at was a great expanse of dead, chopped-down trees.

As someone who lived by the forest and happily spent most of his time within it, he cursed. This was wrong. You don't chop down this much wood to use it. There were more sustainable and efficient solutions that yet kept the forest healthy.

He followed the trail of other enslaved men that walked ahead, each carrying logs over their shoulders as they stomped through the worn-down paths in the undergrowth. Their bodies were slumped and bruised, and big bruisers of men were walking alongside them and lashing out at any opportunity. You drop a log? You get beaten. You slow down? You get beaten. *Look like you have too much life in ya? You get it beaten outta ya.*

Gora remembered when he'd arrived at this place. Hién folks had already been here. When he tried to find out why, or how, they just ignored him. No-one spoke to anyone.

Damn. He and Yoshiko had gone and got themselves brought to a place like this and separated. Their big plans amounted to nothing if neither could escape or if one of them got killed.

'If she goes getting in trouble and dying, I'll kill her myself,' he growled under his breath, glaring at the giant of a guard eying him up dangerously. Gora kept moving. As he heaved the damned, stupid log through the trail, he thought back to how Yoshiko had looked in the last part of the ship—eyes dark, body burning up, restless, half-conscious.

A terrifying thought flooded fear through him. *What if she didn't make it?*

'Unlikely,' he huffed, treading carefully over the roots of a tiny tree stump. That girl was stronger than she looked. Being cooped up on that damn death ship had tainted them all. That was all.

His thoughts chattered away at him like an old person chatting eagerly to any young thing that would listen. And, finally, when the last of the chopped logs had been shifted to piles, he and the other Hié slaves were finally allowed to trudge back to the tiny, dark, damp sheds they called huts.

How could they call this shelter? It barely kept the rain out, and it smelt of sweat. He hated being cooped up inside it and hated the atmosphere of the sullen slaves who'd given up on life. Where was their drive to escape? Why weren't they sitting and stewing and trying to mull over every route outta there? That time he'd been on the pirate ships ... well, he wasn't going to go back there—even in thought—but he'd planned his escape so damn long he could still remember every detail.

He looked around. There was none of that fire in these men's eyes—not like the fire he remembered spewing inside of him that whole time. The look in his eyes had only reinforced the name the pirates gave him—devil's child. Fuck, they'd hated him.

Unable to sit here in this hut any longer in the heavy, empty silence, Gora got up and kicked open the door, muttering to the guard standing duty outside the door about needing to piss. He walked to the barrier that the slaves weren't allowed beyond and took a breath of the fresh, forest air.

Gora liked working in the forest back in Hié. In different circumstances, he was sure he could have liked this place too. The trees were huge, knobby, and ancient, with thick trunks and twisting lianas and ivy as far as the eye could see. The floor was rich with millennia of fallen leaves—so thick that the ground almost bounced as you walked. It was beautiful.

Yet here he was, bitterly hating the sight of it just because of why he was here. He'd seen the guards happily leap at any opportunity to lash out—one had beaten a slave until he bled just for stopping a moment to wipe his brow. Then, the slave had been made to trudge on—carrying the heavy log with his shaking and bleeding body. Gora spat on the ground as he remembered this and tried to take another deep breath of the fresh forest air.

Crap, they even had guns.

Guns weren't in Hié, yet. But it was only a matter of time, he thought, before trade brought them there, too. He wondered how the warriors of Hié would react to them: battle without honour. You didn't need to face your enemies honestly with a gun. And now, Hién people who'd never seen a gun before were face-to-face with brutes who'd be more than happy to blast a round of metal in their faces.

In fact, Gora wouldn't be surprised if it had already happened. Maybe that was why everybody here looked like a ghoul from one of the old ghost tales.

Gora marched back to the cabin—receiving a poking and a prodding from the guard to check he'd not armed himself in any way—to see it stuffed full of men crouching in the darkness around a bowl of gruel. They didn't look up when he entered, but he'd not expected them to. They'd given up. Gora knew that if he didn't get out of here soon, he'd end up the same. The last couple of days had been long enough. The guards had been on high alert for escapees at first. But give it time, and he knew they'd relax just enough that he'd be able to make his move.

Until then, he and the others ate their disgusting gruel in silence, and as each man finished his meal, he wiped away the dirt, lay his bowl to the side, and curled up to sleep without a word or nod to the others. Gora sighed and ran his hands through his now knotted and greasy hair, fingers catching in the curls, scratching at the itch. Then, he slouched his back against the cold wood wall to snatch some sleep before the eerie silence spooked him too much and gave him nightmares of the days of old.

31

Haruki

Yoshiko knew she'd spent too much time faffing—she'd been surprised by meeting Haruki here, and she'd been distracted, wanting to enjoy her friend's company once again. If she wanted to save her people, she couldn't hang around.

Since reuniting with Haruki and meeting Nubia, Yoshiko had regained a light that she felt she'd lost since she got separated from Gora and saw what it was really like in this life. The heat inside her threatened to overtake her. Her spirit burned to plunge those who had harmed her people into the depths so they could never escape. Death or suffering, she vowed they would pay. She refused to let anyone else die at the hands of the pale-faced guards.

So, as she worked, she searched for opportunities they could use that night: for places she could leave through, for routes she might need to take. If she could take Haruki with her, she could be sure to not part from Haruki again. Yoshiko also wondered where she would find Gora. Someone like him would no doubt be taken to a place that involved great strength—he was used to physical work. But where would that be? In this place, there were too many sounds and smells she couldn't identify. Even though his would be the only smell she'd recognise, it would be washed out by everything else.

Yoshiko thought about Haruki meeting Gora. What would she think? Haruki seemed to get on with everyone. In fact, she wondered whether they'd even met before. To Yoshiko's sheltered mind, Haruki seemed to have known everything about Hié town.

Recently, Yoshiko had spoken with some of her people about their daily lives from back in Hié and the things they most looked forward to. Yoshiko talked to a man about how he'd run a popular inn before the inn mysteriously burned down several months ago and he and his wife had ended up on the ship. Another woman helped make clothes before she was taken in the night. She wondered if her manager missed or blamed her, and she wanted to go back and mend their relationship and continue making clothes—with new ideas after speaking with the Qeclans. Yoshiko loved hearing all the stories of her people and yearned more than anything to take them back. So, before anyone else died, she had to leave and complete her mission. She hated to think what would happen to the people here as punishment for her leaving and felt like it would be betrayal. But she would come back. She'd save them.

It would have to be soon.

'You know, the last person who tried to escape was beaten and killed,' Haruki whispered as they crossed paths in the fields, one with a woven basket laden with collected foods, the other returning with an empty basket to start anew.

Yoshiko gazed at Haruki. She knew what Yoshiko was doing? 'How could you tell?'

'You're spying on all the guards and places that look like they could be ways out.'

'It's that obvious?'

'Only because we've all done it. But be careful the guards don't spot you.'

Yoshiko frowned. Surely her mother had taught her to be more careful with people reading her face and knowing her moves?

Haruki flashed a quick smile with a huff of laughter—and a short moment of the warm eyes of the days they'd last been together. 'You have an expressive face. You can't do much about that. Don't worry too much on it, and be careful with the plan.'

And before Yoshiko could question Haruki how she knew about her thoughts, Haruki had strolled off to continue her work. Yoshiko stared after her in awe for a moment before a spike of fear flooded her at the thought of a guard spotting her not working, and her back twinged in remembrance.

Haruki was right. The guards seemed worse than usual. Only the other day, Yoshiko had almost dropped bedsheets on the floor when pulling them off the line to be dried. She'd caught them, so no dirt had got on them, but the guard had reacted instantly, yelling at her for not paying attention. They'd pushed her, and everything had fallen to the floor. A Qeclan worker woman rushed to help, silent and with her eyes on the floor to avoid anyone's gaze. But Yoshiko had still been beaten for it. Her back still ached from the lashes, and it felt as if the fire she felt from the fever was leaking from her burning-up body through the wounds.

She longed for rain or a cold bath to cool her. But nothing came. The quick washes in the river were never enough to relieve how her body burned, and each day, she felt progressively worse. But she couldn't fall ill. If she was ill, how could she take her people home?

'Lady Yoshiko,' Nubia murmured at dinner that evening. 'You do not look well. Your body is burning. I can feel it from here.'

Nubia had joined Haruki in calling Yoshiko *Lady Yoshiko*, though Yoshiko had chastised them both for it. Here, she had no position.

'I'm just a normal person,' she'd said many times, to no avail. 'Call me Yoshiko.'

Yet, this time, Yoshiko just looked wearily at Nubia. She felt as if she were struggling. 'I'll be fine. It happens sometimes. I just need a cool wash.'

Yet Nubia touched her forehead in concern and clicked her tongue. 'I think it is your back. They hurt you, and your body is burning from it. It needs cleaning. What do you think, Haruki?' Nubia addressed Haruki now as she sat to join them, pushing her hair back behind her ear.

'My lady has always had hot skin. We joked that there were legends of dragon's blood running in the noble family, and that's why their sigil was a dragon.' Haruki looked at her now with her dark, caring eyes. 'But she does look unwell. My lady, you should rest.'

'Call me Yoshiko,' Yoshiko murmured, but she was spoken-over by Nubia.

'Dragon's blood?' The Qeclan woman's eyes lit like burning coals. She sat up straighter and leaned forward.

Haruki nodded. 'The maids often talked about the legends. The daimyō and Lady Yoshiko were always a little strange—like there was a power of something burning inside them. They could both hear things and see too easily—more than normal people— and had abnormally high body temperatures. And a look in their eyes that isn't fully human—which seems rude to say out loud, but we didn't know how else to phrase it at the time. We knew it was just old tales, but it was fun to talk about and see if the patterns fitted.' She turned to Yoshiko now. 'We knew you're just people, but it was a bit of fun to imagine you were something greater.'

Nubia's eyes glinted, but Yoshiko froze.

'That sounds exciting,' Nubia said, rubbing her ear lobe. 'In my country, there are stories of people who can turn into giant snakes. They are our gods—*naga*. They bring great fortune to those they like.'

Yoshiko's worry subsided to interest as Nubia told them more, and the three chatted for the rest of dinner about old stories and magical creatures. Until, at least, some Qeclan men began humming and singing in low tones under their breath, beating a rhythm onto the fallen tree trunks they sat on. Nubia told the two Hién women it was songs of the old legends from their country.

'They must have heard us.' She grinned her bright, toothy smile that covered her face—a hint of the Nubia they could have met had they met her in her home country, and not in this place.

Here, song was the only way to communicate or pass the time. If you spoke, they feared you were conspiring. But they couldn't stop you from singing. Especially if they didn't know what you had sung about. And so it was one of the few ways they passed the time, quietly singing songs.

Yoshiko loved hearing the Qeclan songs. Though she couldn't understand what they said, their sounds were so different from those from Hié. And she rejoiced at hearing the songs of her people when they sang, too—songs she'd rarely heard from inside the keep as they were songs of the common folk. Today, Haruki sang too, and Yoshiko's heart soared. She'd always loved hearing Haruki sing, especially songs from the common lives. What was best, today Haruki continued the mythical theme and sang of dragons and spirits and the ancient powers that had roamed their lands, and the world that lay alongside their own world, and of an adventurer who could pass through into the land of the spirits. It had been many months since she'd heard Haruki sing—she often imagined it whenever she heard Gora sing, of how these two people both sang so beautifully. Today, it gave her a feeling of freedom that ached in her soul.

An ache for flight.

And an ache at the fact that her friend had been stolen from her, and her people had been stolen from their homes.

And now, song was the only freedom they all had, and it struck her that perhaps that was why Gora sang. Is that why he continued to sing the songs of his homeland? From a refusal to give up when he was on the ship, to now, where he no longer knows how to return there? Was song all he had left of home?

She couldn't give him his country back—she didn't know how to return him there. But she could give these people their country back and take them home. And then, she'd rebuild it and make it stronger—starting with removing those on the council who'd sought to ruin it. She'd set up defences against slavery and ensure her people were safe so no-one would go through this again. She thought of this so deeply that it felt as if it had to come true.

Tonight, she thought, *is the night.* She'd grab Haruki, find Gora, and then find a way to make the Acrein people end this stupid slavery thing, and let the Qeclan workers return home, too.

But when the songs ended, Haruki cried out at how pale Yoshiko looked, and Yoshiko felt slick with sweat and overheated from that fire somewhere inside her. The guards, too, watched her—though dead of the concern that Haruki had. And when it came to finally being allowed to wash and rest, Haruki ran to help Yoshiko, who was struggling to walk straight.

'It's fine,' Yoshiko murmured to an agreeable Haruki, guiding her in a straight line to the river. 'I just need cold water.'

'I know. We're going now.'

At the river, Haruki helped Yoshiko and kept her chatting to keep her alert. Yoshiko's brain kept fogging over, and the world kept fading away.

'What's that?' Yoshiko asked when all she could hear of Haruki was a low buzz.

'I asked why you came here. I don't believe you were just caught.'

'I wasn't.' Yoshiko yawned and splashed water in her face to help keep her conscious.

Haruki made a noise to prompt her further.

'I came with someone. We got caught so we could come here and take people home.'

'Someone from the castle?' Haruki's voice sounded hopeful. Yoshiko felt bad for letting her down.

'No, a citizen.' Yoshiko wondered if Haruki knew him. 'His name is Gora. He's an autumn-haired foreigner who lives in Hié. Do you know of him? Lots of people seem to.'

'Gora?' Haruki made a thinking noise and squeezed water from her hair. 'I guess I've heard of the name. He's helping you? He's here? What's he like?'

Yoshiko let out a hiss as the cold water met her burning skin. But it felt so much better. She wished she could stay here. While she was in the water, she felt the burning fever ease a little and her brain un-fog. But when it came to Haruki guiding her out and back to the camp, the heat immediately returned. If only she could be free of it somehow. She thought, in her delirium, of those white scorch marks in the place her mother had died. If only she could breathe fire and release this heat. She still wondered if her mother had done that.

Yoshiko staggered, trying to focus on the cold of her wet clothes until they could get to camp where she could lie down. She frowned. She wouldn't be able to escape like this. But it had to be tonight.

Yoshiko looked at Haruki walking calmly beside her, wondering whether she'd be able to help them both escape. But before that decision could be made, a pair of hands reached out from the shadow of a building door and grabbed Haruki, pulling her into the darkness within and away from Yoshiko's reaching hand.

32

Time to Leave

'Move, rat.'

From the day he'd arrived, Gora realised he could understand some of the words the guards yelled; the language was similar to one he'd heard from his days on the ships. Not traders' language, but from a country he thought he'd possibly traded with when the pirates pulled up for supplies in some dodgy harbour. The people weren't from the same country as the language he'd heard, but Gora wondered whether it was a neighbouring country where languages developed and merged and some parts stayed the same. The orders and the curse words were the easiest to pick up, but then, those would be the ones he heard most on pirate ships. It wouldn't surprise him if he knew all the curses in most languages at this point, from those days.

The crack of the lash made the slaves wince, their backs curling and their heads flinching as if they'd all been hit, though it had only been the one. That person cried out from the bite of the lash. And then they pushed themselves to rush more, if only to save their skin a few moments longer from the Acrein tormentors.

Acreins, huh? Gora had wondered when he'd heard the name of the people who lived here. So they were in Acrein. If he had a map, he'd be able to figure out their location and how to get back. But it was a shame there'd be no maps in the middle of a forest. If the master had one in his large hut, it would only be of the forest and the surrounding area. One of the world would be too expensive and of no use to someone who made his money from logging.

No, Gora would have to return to the port for that kind of map—the one that showed the layout of the world. He knew he had to go east to return to Hié—that much was the only option. But how to get around the other countries and find safe waterways would be another issue altogether.

Certainly, to return, he'd need access to a map. And then a ship.

Gora wondered whether the country next to Acrein knew of its slave dealings. He wouldn't bet for a moment that Acrein didn't try to sell its slaves to the nearest countries for a profit. If that were the case, he and Yoshiko couldn't count on escaping to neighbouring countries to try to catch a ship back home. Now they'd been sold and branded, it would be bloody difficult to make their next moves.

Gora frowned and glared at the forest floor as he stomped over leaves and roots.

Any Acrein to see him or Yoshiko trying to move anywhere would catch them and call them in, resulting in punishment, killing, or taking them back to their masters for punishment or killing. So how could they move around Acrein and anywhere else they needed to go unseen?

Obviously, step one would be to escape this camp. But the guards and their hounds would make that difficult. Gora felt he could easily head deep into the forest and live there—he'd done that before—but it wouldn't help Yoshiko, so he'd have to emerge at some point.

Gora's axe struck hard wood as he pondered his escape.

I could kill the guards, Gora thought, eying up the blade of his axe. *And the hounds.* He struck the tree again and grimaced. That wouldn't work. They had guns—some of the guards carried them about instead of lashes. If Gora went on an axe-killing rampage, there'd be metal rounds shooting everywhere.

Gora's back muscles strained against another swing of the axe. Guns weren't accurate. If he stayed far enough away … Alternatively, he could rush and kill one of the gun-carrying guards and take the gun off him. But then, how long had it been since he'd fired a gun, anyway? He'd probably miss. It wasn't certain enough.

Onto another plan. During the day, they had shackles around their ankles that made it too hard to move far or quickly. It would make running and climbing a pain. If he could hit the chains and break them, then Gora could make his escape. But could he even do that? How many strikes of the axe would it take to break them? And by then, the guards would come running or just shoot him where he stood. He'd seen it before. A man who'd stumbled and was just trying to fix the chains into a more comfortable position after they got trapped against his ankle had been kicked, beaten, and dragged into the hut to starve for the next couple of days. If that was the normal treatment, how far away would Gora have to run before guards couldn't catch him or shoot him? And the chains would jangle and give his position away.

'… useless dog.'

Gora jumped at the guard's voice so close that he worried they were yelling at him. Instead, he turned to see a Hién man being pushed randomly into the ground by a guard. The man stumbled on the shackles about his ankles and tumbled towards the floor. Immediately, and to the Hién man's credit, he tried to roll and get back to his feet and keep going, but the guard caught him halfway and pushed him back down again, kicking. The Hién man blocked his head and chest with his arms, crying out as his sinewy arms were kicked instead.

That man must have been trained in martial arts back home, Gora realised. How did he get taken?

Dread sank Gora's thoughts about the escape. If a martial artist had been taken from Hié and kept here as a slave for who-knows-how-long—this man had been here when Gora had arrived—how could Gora ever expect to escape?

Gora shook his head and kept sinking the axe into the wood and grunting at the pain and aches that followed. He wiped his brow with his arm and stared up at the tree. Where was it going to fall best? An inner voice told him to crush a guard—pretend it was an accident—but he knew he'd be severely punished. It wasn't worth it. It would get in the way of escape.

It was back to that issue he'd come across before: how much could he do before they caught or shot him? He was a fighter—he'd never had formal training in Hié, but he'd fought and killed on ships. If he could escape the deadly grip of pirates on the restriction of a ship, surely it would be easier in a forest where he could run forever and have places to hide?

The tree crashed to the floor with a groan, and Gora's heart tugged in sympathy.

Gora knew there was only one solution: to leave at night, when the guards took the shackles off their feet and shut them in their hut, only allowing them outside to relieve themselves outside or in a tiny, putrid outhouse near their assigned hut. But then, the guards never expected them to run from the huts. The guards were posted everywhere—with guns—and the hounds lurked nearby. And the dark forest beyond the boundaries was enough for someone to get lost or scared. They'd be found when they collapsed the next day. But Gora wasn't like that. He knew forests at night.

He grimaced again as his back screamed at swinging the axe against yet another tree. That's what he'd do. He'd just pretend he'd given up on life until then—succumbing to a forever of chopping wood until he inevitably died young, either beaten or shot to death, starved, died of an empty soul, or was crushed by a tree and turned into mince for the hounds.

* * *

When evening came, Gora wiped his bowl and slouched against the cold, wooden wall as usual and pretended to drift off to sleep. When the last scraping sound from his hut ended and the final man fell into an uneasy sleep, Gora opened his eyes and blinked into the darkness.

All men were curled up or leaned against the wall.

It was time.

Under his breath, he muttered something about needing to piss—just to be sure that any man still awake enough to hear him move didn't pay attention. He picked his way across the bodies on the floor to the doorway and slipped out, sliding down the wall of the hut.

A guard stood watch between the huts, walking here and there to check no men came out—or, at least, not for long. Gora stood by the wall and pretended he was trying to piss. The guard walked back towards Gora's hut, and Gora could feel the man's eyes burning into the back of his body, watching. Feeling the burning get hotter, Gora willed himself to piss and make it look genuine. Somehow, he managed a trickle. The burning on the back of his head lessened, and Gora rubbed his hands down the pathetic scraps they'd given them as trousers and made a grunting noise as if disappointed that was all he could manage. Then, he turned and pretended to sidle back down the hut and opened the door. The guard watched and turned away as Gora's body half-entered the darkness.

Gora felt the corner of his mouth twitch upwards in a slight feeling of victory and darted back around the corner of the hut. *Lazy prick.* By the time the door had swung shut and the guard turned lazily back around to check his vicinity, Gora was already hiding around the corner.

Simple play. Did they truly think the slaves wouldn't try to escape at night?

The guards here were lazy, he realised. Being in the middle of the forest, they'd become lax and relied on the forest to do their work. The slaves here, too, given up on life, had long since given up on trying to simply run. Their feet storming through the undergrowth was an easy sign to chase. So no-one escaped here, and the guards' lives were made easy. So they became lazy, sitting together and chatting, laughing, drinking, with the odd one prowling between cabins now and again to look busy, but eagerly awaiting the time they could switch to join the merriness again. Besides, they never expected anyone to try to escape at night when the forest was dark.

Gora listened to the guard's footsteps and tried to match them as he snuck between the huts. The slave huts were close together and easy to move between, but these were the most monitored. He needed to get to the guard huts, or, better, the owner's hut. These were defended to stop slaves from attacking, but no-one expected the slaves to run away from here. It was because of this that the guards here paid less attention—there in body but not in soul. Perfect for running away.

So, aiming for there, Gora dropped to his stomach and pulled himself along the damp grass and leaves, trying to time his movements with the guards' footsteps. If he could reach the owner's hut, he could sneak out the back. It would take time, but it would be worth it. The best option and the least-watched. Fortunately, the ground was wet from rain and night-time damp, so it wouldn't crunch under his weight. But that brought with it the cold, and it soaked immediately into his body. Gora tried to ignore the uncomfortable feeling of wet that started to chill him and continued to pull himself across the distance, past the guards' huts, and slowly, eventually, to the owner's.

Gora paused halfway as guards by the owner's hut door watched out. Feeling wary, he shuffled further away from the huts, coming in wide to make sure they couldn't see him slithering in the darkness. He tried to take slow, deep breaths to steady the beating of his heart. Gora was sure they would hear it. It was just like a hunt. Except this time, unlike usual, he was the prey.

He continued to pull himself past the owner's hut, body shivering with the cold and the wet seeping from the ground through the thin clothes they'd made him wear. But he couldn't stop yet. Soon, he'd break the tree line. Nearer the slaves' huts, the guards sat a night duty along a line at the edge of the forest to be sure slaves didn't try to go into the forest at night. But here, by the owner's hut, they barely came. No-one expected slaves to be able to make it this far.

But Gora wondered how many of the others had ever experienced creeping like this in a forest. As a hunter, this was normal for him. Only there had been less at stake, then.

The guards at the perimeter did rounds occasionally, walking whenever they got bored or to stay warm. Gora hadn't seen a patrol since he'd been slithering through that area, and he knew one was bound to come soon. Better to stop and wait for the next guard to do some quick perimeter duty than get caught out by the laws of the damned—anything that could go wrong, would. So he lay in the shadows of the owner's hut, trying not to shiver too much.

Time drew on, too long for him to bear. The only sign to tell him how long he'd been waiting was the fast beating of his heart, signalling a time too long spent hiding at the foot of the owner's back window.

The camp was silent except for the guards' low laughter as they sat by the campfire on the other side of the camp and those muttering to themselves as they sat sulkily on the forest perimeter or near the slaves' huts, away from the warm fire. Gora waited for the plodding of one of these sulky guards. But still nothing. He grew frustrated. Night would disappear if he didn't move soon.

33
Burning

Yoshiko ran forwards to pull Haruki back out of the barn. 'What is this?' Haruki yelled out instinctively, though the grabbing hands wouldn't understand her.

Yoshiko stumbled in after her, fearing the stories she'd heard about others disappearing at the hands of the guards. *Grab Haruki and run away, escape*—that was her only plan now.

A sinister voice jarred both women. 'Punishment.'

The voice was Acrein but speaking in Hizen, and it was coming from behind Yoshiko. Haruki's eyes opened wide as she saw the person appearing behind Yoshiko. Before Yoshiko could turn, the person behind her kicked her into the barn. The door crashed shut.

'Punishment? What did we do?' Haruki cried out, pulling away from the hands that grabbed her and rushing towards Yoshiko to help her up from the floor.

The looming guard kicked Haruki to the floor, too.

'Your friend's been looking pretty sick, lately. And you've been scuttling about after her and talking too much.' He crouched beside them and sneered, grey eyes looking like cold, winter rain against sallow, hairy cheeks. 'We can't allow that. It might be a plot to escape.'

Haruki looked stunned, but Yoshiko propped herself up on her hands and tried to gather the strength to stand. Her head burned, and her eyes hurt.

'That's ridiculous.' Yoshiko sighed and looked into those soulless pale eyes.

'Is it?' The other guard, who'd kicked her in and shut the barn door behind them, pulled out his lash. 'You'd be amazed at what we've seen. We know it all. No-one escapes. We'll show you what happens to those who try.'

Yoshiko felt a shiver run down her spine as she looked up at this man; his scraggly mid-brown hair and beard made him look like a ghost or demon she'd seen at the plays—where only a tiny bit of a face showed amongst the rest.

The guards looked at one another and said something in their language. Haruki's face screwed up, and Yoshiko recognised it as the face she made when she was trying to focus or figure something out. Same as ever. Haruki reached out to grab Yoshiko's hand but was slapped away by the cracking of the lash in the scraggly-haired man's hands. Haruki cried out, and the burning rushed through Yoshiko again. She grimaced to fight it back. Understanding where this was going and what would happen to them if they stayed, Yoshiko pushed herself to stand and rushed at the man, driving her knee into his groin and elbowing his face as he doubled over in pain. The icy-eyed man stumbled back, and she kicked him away, watching with satisfaction as he fell to the ground.

If she could do this right, she should immobilise him first before handling the other man. But with Haruki at risk, she had to injure them both as quickly as possible and then aim for running away. So she wheeled about and rushed at the scraggly-haired guard before he could do anything with that lash. Her head felt foggy, and her body felt as if it were setting alight, but she couldn't let anything happen now. She could collapse later when they were safe. Now, they had to escape.

The scraggly-haired man flicked out the lash, and it stung her face before she could dive out the way. She cried out in pain but yelled out in anger at the man and rushed in close—too close to be hit by the lash—and drove several punches and elbows into his stomach and face. A burning anger inside her would have driven her to continue her attack until this man fell, unable to chase them, but a scream from Haruki halted her.

The icy-eyed man had recovered quicker than Yoshiko anticipated and launched himself at Haruki, crashing on top of her and pinning her to the ground, launching a punch into the young woman's face.

'Look at what you made me do.' He grinned, pulling his arm back for another strike and locking eyes with Yoshiko. 'You can watch what happens next and see what's going to happen to you once she's finished.'

A hand grabbed at Yoshiko's head from behind and drove her face-first into the floor. The voice cursing her told her it was the brown-haired man recovering too.

Yoshiko cried out, frustrated that she'd frozen when she should have quickly pushed the man off Haruki and pulled her friend out of the building. Now, someone heavy sat on her back and held her face to watch what was to come, nails digging in everywhere the hands grabbed at her.

Haruki thrashed and screamed, trying to kick the guard away. But he took the hits, anger pushing him on. His hands grabbed at Haruki's thighs and pulled them open, shifting forward to hold them open with his body while he wrestled with his buttons. Haruki panicked, eyes wide and face white. She tried to kick out again, but it earned her another punch to the jaw that cracked her head against the stone.

Yoshiko didn't need the family curse to have heard that. Human ears would have heard it easily enough. Haruki's head faced her, and her eyes—dazed—tried to blink away the tears. The burning inside Yoshiko's body sent a bright, white flash of pain and heat. She wriggled and roared and tried to get the brown-haired man off her so she could rush to her friend. He just laughed and dug his nails into her scalp more.

'Don't worry. It'll be you next,' he leered.

The two men joked and laughed about something in their language, and the grey-eyed one pulled at Haruki's skirts and ripped them out of the way. Panicked, Yoshiko cried out again and bucked her body to the side, almost toppling the man over. Her heart soared as his legs and arms released her, and she scrambled to her hands and knees to push the other man off her dazed friend.

But not before the brown-haired man caught himself and grabbed at her ankle, pulling her and causing her to crash to the floor again. He rolled her over and sat on her stomach, and only then did she see the damage she'd done to his face—it was covered in blood, his nose was broken, and he had a huge crack and bulge in his lip. There was a huge bulge somewhere else, too, and it pressed into her stomach as he pinned her down. He glared at her like a demon and spat bloody gob in her face. What he growled at her after, she didn't know, but she knew it wasn't good.

He slapped her face and clutched her neck to the floor with his hands. Yoshiko felt her eyes darken, and she cried out Haruki's name. She had to stop the attack on her friend.

But Yoshiko's eyes blacked over again, and she swore at herself for this fever that weakened her at such a critical time. But it didn't feel like she would faint. Instead, the burning boiled up hotter and faster than before and exploded beyond her control. The black vision exploded into white light that pained her eyes, and in an angry roar, she lashed out at the man pinning her down. Red and orange sparks surrounded her as if the fire she'd felt in her body for weeks had refused to stay locked away and escaped in physical form. The inferno that had been stored inside her with the fever pushed outwards, and she relished in the screams it created as the weight of the man on top of her lessened.

Instantly, she jumped out and rushed to where the grey-eyed man had pinned Haruki to the floor. He was staring up in fear, gross manhood in his hand. She yelled out and kicked him off before he could do anything else, letting her anger take control just enough to knock him cold.

At least, that had been the plan.

She choked at what actually happened. When she reached where Haruki had been lying, the burning white stopped clouding her eyes, and her vision cleared. The red and orange sparks hadn't been her imagination. About her, the barn burned in an inferno, and three burning bodies lay on the ground—two for the men, one for—'Haruki?'

Yoshiko cried out, rushing towards the smaller body. It was definitely her friend; it was where she'd been pushed onto the floor.

Yoshiko looked about again, not believing what had happened and trying to tear her eyes away from the smaller blackened figure on the floor, watching the flames swallowing the barn. It was strange. She couldn't feel the heat, and the light was so bright that her eyes felt they'd never know darkness again. The fire ate at the straw, instantly lighting and spreading to everything. The barn's wooden frame lit too, crumbling and groaning like the typhoons that thrashed her country.

Had she not just imagined that fire? How was it here?

She thought it had been in her head, reflecting the anger she felt and wished she could have unloaded onto those two awful guards. But now?

Yoshiko stared down at her hands.

'How?' Her voice came out as a croak.

She looked back down at the burning figure of the woman and crashed to her knees beside it. Tears sprung from her eyes but fizzled and evaporated almost instantly, licking heat against her skin.

She still didn't feel it.

'Haru-ki?' she asked, voice breaking halfway through. 'Haruki? No, you can't. I didn't mean to. It was them—I just wanted to get them off you.' Her body shivered despite the raging inferno about her. 'Haruki, no. Stop this. You can't. I can't let this happen.'

Nothing changed.

'How did this happen?' She bent over the body of her friend and screamed, feeling the heat radiating from Haruki's burning figure. 'Haruki, I didn't mean this to happen. I only wanted to save you. Wake up. Haruki?'

A beam from the roof dropped onto the burning straw behind her and made her jolt. She looked around. The barn was breaking.

Well, what did it matter? Her heart had already broken, too. She should just stay here. Instead of saving her friend, Yoshiko had sent her to a burning abyss. Why, then, did she deserve to live?

But what would happen to her country? Yoshiko had to save it, or more people would suffer at the hands of the council and the Acreins.

Yoshiko looked back at Haruki, torn. She let out a sob and stared at her friend.

'I don't want to leave you. I finally found you—I can't leave you.'

Haruki's grin flashed before her face—the smile from when they'd first reunited and the smile that flooded her face like sunshine whenever Haruki talked fondly of what could happen if they returned home.

'I wanted to take you home.' Yoshiko's voice bubbled and barely came out coherent. A bawl erupted and choked her up.

An urge drew her forward—to try to grab at Haruki and take her from this place. Perhaps she could still take her home, or at least bury her somewhere better than this—away from this place where she hadn't been free and away from the men who had made this happen. But as Yoshiko reached forward, burning skin seared her hands and came free from Haruki's body. Yoshiko recoiled in shock, staring at Haruki's skin that fell apart in the heat. She felt as if she'd be sick.

'I have to leave you here?' Yoshiko whispered, dazed. *In such a place?*

She looked about the burning barn—not even wondering how she didn't burn too. Her people considered burning a good burial. But here, surrounded by so much evil?

If the fire were hot enough, would it purify the place enough to give Haruki a good burial?

As if answering her prayers, the bright white fire that had flushed from within radiated about her again, stinging her eyes and burning even the memory of darkness from her soul. The inferno grew hotter, and the barn collapsed in. But Yoshiko was gone by the time it crumbled.

* * *

From the blackness of the night outside, the white fire engulfing the barn had attracted a crowd. People screamed and yelled; people of all countries—no matter the position—rushed to stop the flames. But they dropped their pails of water, staring in defeat at the tower of white fire.

Staring on, hidden in the tree line, Yoshiko glared at it all. It should all burn. At least that would purify this whole damned place. She looked out at the Qeclans and Hién folk, wishing they'd run and leave it all to rot. This was the best time, surely?

She stood unseen as everyone gawked up at the blinding white light from the barn. Well, she wasn't going to hang around. Yoshiko knew she'd only have a few minutes before the shock of it all made the guards realise their place and start a rampage to beat back the others. She wouldn't be here for that. She'd go while they were distracted and go to the person who ran this awful country and make them pay.

Somewhere, though, a figure made her pause. The tall, slender figure of Nubia, who looked about anxiously as if searching for something.

'For us …' Yoshiko breathed, looking back at the barn to Haruki.

And, in a spur-of-the-moment decision, her heart pushed her forward. Yoshiko sprinted towards Nubia, grabbed the woman's wrist, and pulled her away.

34
Waiting

Fatigue drowned Gora, and he knew if he didn't move soon, he'd fall asleep where he lay, get caught, be punished, never make it out, and wind up half-dead from a chill to top it all off. And, with the little care that was afforded to slaves, a chill could be the end of you.

Gora held his eyes open with his fingers for a moment and tried short, sharp breaths to give himself a rush of air. He had to stay awake.

Finally, after trying various ways to keep himself alert—including looking at the grass beneath him and trying to count the blades in the darkness—Gora froze as a perimeter guard stomped around the end of the camp, cursing to himself.

The guard walked as quickly as he could with his hands stuffed in his pockets to keep himself warm. His eyes scanned the area, barely taking in any of his surroundings. Then, he continued to stomp on, moaning to himself about how unfair life was and wishing he was in bed with some warm-blooded woman.

Gora rolled his eyes. *Boars, the lot of them.* And that was referring to them nicely.

Gora waited anxiously for just a little longer, barely daring to breathe as he listened for the footsteps on the grass to subside.

The top of the camp slipped once more into silence, with only echoes of men and hounds by the fire and snores from the owner in his cabin near where Gora lay. Then, Gora shuffled forward once more. And when he eventually made it to the tree line, he picked himself up and walked with a crouch, delicately placing his feet toes-first. He wished the forest would swallow up the sound of his movements, but echoes in the night were stubborn. Gora's efforts wore him out quickly. Foggy-headed, he refused to slip into carelessness and carefully continued to pick away.

The ground was damp from night-time dew, and the floor was soggy beneath his feet. This helped drown out any sound that leaves might make but left the danger of him slipping and causing a louder crash.

So Gora continued patiently on, pretending this was one of his hunts. Meat would be at the other end, he told himself.

A crack to Gora's left brought his heart sinking like an anchor through to his stomach. He paused and crouched to hide in the shadows of the undergrowth. Was someone walking around this part of the forest? A guard?

Another crack and he tried to crouch further, holding onto a tree to steady himself and blend into its form. Gora tried to smooth his ragged breath and listened, fear washing through his blood, tainting it, making it heavy and sluggish. There was another crack of a twig.

The steps sounded too fast to be a human and too light. Had one of the hounds at the campfire caught his scent or sound? But, had that been the case, Gora knew the hound would have got the attention of the guards, and they'd be crashing through here like Ishillian elephants after they'd accidentally eaten some over-fermented fruit.

A nosing noise snuffled and nudged at the leaves on the ground, accompanied by a low whine and huff. Gora relaxed, the side of his head resting against the tree trunk to gather his strength.

'Thank fuck,' he dared to breathe.

A deer.

Unable to wait on the whims of a deer, and ignoring the empty pocking of his stomach, Gora picked himself up and crept through the trees. By now, he'd be far enough away from the camp to walk, so he stopped occasionally to look for moving shadows and listen for signs of life. Gora looked around, trying to figure out where to go.

Find a clearing, Gora thought. *You can see the stars then.*

Then, he'd go as deep into the forest as he dared until he came to a town that wouldn't know about a red-haired foreigner taken as a slave. A place where he could get away as being someone from one of the ships that pulled in from overseas who was trying to jump ship or get a new job. He knew traders' language; he could communicate to any merchant or trader worth their salt with that. They'd never suspect a thing.

And that would only lead to one place: west—towards the city he'd heard the guards talking about beyond the forest. Where an extra man would go unnoticed, and the place the palace stood.

Hopefully, if Yoshiko had any sense, she'd also head there, because if she wanted to persuade the ruler of this country to give her people back, she'd have to head to the city the authorities reigned.

Gora ran his hands through his knotted curls and took a deep breath before ploughing on through the forest, hoping he could find Yoshiko and end this madness before it all fell to shit.

35

Escape

Nubia's hand strained against Yoshiko's, and Yoshiko finally heard a voice calling her name.

'Lady Yoshiko! Wait, Yoshiko. What is it?'

Nubia sounded impatient, like she'd been calling out for a while, so Yoshiko slowed enough for the hand to stop straining, and Nubia ran to keep up with her of her own accord.

'We have to run,' Yoshiko said, glancing over her shoulder at the sun-blessed woman easily loping alongside her as they darted through the trees that surrounded the farm. Yoshiko almost envied the long legs. 'Don't stop.'

'I won't stop. Just tell me, what is the problem? Where is Haruki? I could not find her.'

The words stabbed at Yoshiko's heart, and her voice cracked. 'Haruki's dead.'

Nubia didn't respond. Instead, she picked up a sprint beside Yoshiko, understanding she had no choice but to keep going.

The trees stopped flicking past them as they ran into an open track much like the one they'd been brought to the farm on, cobbled and unsettling to run on. Yoshiko halted, looking around and darting back into the trees where they wouldn't be seen. Nubia crouched beside her and looked Yoshiko straight in the eyes. Yoshiko realised how deep and observant her friend's dark eyes were. It was like they could see straight through her, and she wasn't ready for someone to see her yet, in case they didn't like the monster they saw.

'Haruki's dead?' Nubia asked, slightly out of breath, searching Yoshiko's face for unspoken answers.

Yoshiko nodded hesitantly, unable to speak and barely able to meet Nubia's eyes. It didn't feel like the right time to process things—Yoshiko knew she'd break if she acknowledged what had happened.

'I'm sad and angry. But I don't know the words I want to say in your language. It's … hard.' Nubia sighed and put her head in her hands, groaning in frustration.

Yoshiko looked over at Nubia to see the older woman's face struggling with the pain of not being able to gather the language she needed to express herself.

'I understand, though.' Yoshiko rested her hand on Nubia's shoulder, and the two women looked at each other for a while, finding a small comfort in the silence.

'Where are we going?' Nubia said eventually, sniffing and looking ahead of her onto the path.

'I came here with a friend. I need to find him. We came here on purpose to stop slavery. We didn't mean to get separated.'

Nubia looked like she was having a hard time keeping up. Haruki usually translated the more difficult language for her. But here, without Haruki, Nubia nodded when she'd processed enough of the language to decipher the rest.

'You're on a mission?' Nubia asked.

Yoshiko nodded. Nubia hummed in response and leant her shoulder against a tree as she crouched.

'Do you know who he belongs to?' Nubia asked, referring to the slave masters.

This time, Yoshiko shook her head.

'So you don't know where he is?'

Yoshiko shook her head again, and Nubia sighed.

'Then, how do you expect to find him? There are so many Hién slaves here; it will be hard to spot one among the rest.' Nubia pouted, thinking.

'He's not Hién. He's from Eire.'

'Eire?' Nubia's face scrunched up as she thought.

'From the other side of the world. Or maybe it's close to here. I'm not sure where we are. Do you know it?'

It was Nubia's turn to shake her head. 'I have never heard of it. However, that might make it easier to find him. If I don't know it, it will be rare here. And, as my husband and I worked in trade, we know lots of different people.'

This was the first time Nubia had mentioned her husband, and Yoshiko wanted to know more. But if the woman hadn't mentioned him before, when Haruki was around, too, perhaps she wasn't ready to speak of it. So, instead, Yoshiko said, 'I was hoping so. He has dark red hair. He will stand out.'

Nubia hummed. 'Most natives here have pale or brown hair,' she agreed. 'So a red-haired man will be easy to see.'

They rested in silence, listening around them and wondering where to begin. Yoshiko started to worry about whether they'd rested too long.

'I bet his hair is beautiful,' Nubia said, staring at the silhouettes of the leaves that rustled faintly in the night air. 'Like the sun, maybe, when it sets over the plains. I have never seen hair that colour.'

'No-one in my country has it, either,' Yoshiko said, reflecting on the time she and Gora were outside and the sunlight hit his hair and it shone like sparks of fire and autumn maple leaves. 'It *is* beautiful, but—' Her surroundings returned her thoughts to the now, and she thought of the way to return to Gora, not about the way his hair glowed. 'We should head to the river. That way, we can find out way back to the port where we came in. Then, we can start with inns and bars. We were planning to escape, so maybe he already has. If he has, he'll probably be in a bar.'

Yoshiko was thinking back to the first time she'd met Gora and his fondness for a drink whenever he needed to bury his emotions. Being locked on that ship had probably resurfaced a lot of them, so she was sure she'd find him in a bar.

Nubia looked disappointed and pouted again. 'We will look in every bar to find him?' She sounded doubtful. 'Remember, you are a fugitive slave, and I'm not much better—they still hunt servants. Remember when I said we weren't allowed to leave, even though they said we were 'free'. They'll catch or kill us if they see us.'

Yoshiko thought again, running her hands through her long, knotted hair and trying to untangle it a bit with her fingers as she thought. She wondered how they could find him. If they got close enough, she'd be able to follow his scent. But, from this far away, she had no clue.

'Either way,' Yoshiko began slowly, thinking it as she spoke, 'we need to move from here, towardsthe riverside. I can hear it somewhere to the left. Soon, they'll notice we're gone and try to find us.'

Yoshiko stood up and stretched her legs, listening carefully and focusing her hearing in a large radius. It was night, and no-one was moving yet. She strained her ears to hear the farm, hearing people still yelling about the fire. But they were a little too far off now to hear anything else.

'They'll come soon. Let's go. Anywhere. Let's try the port town before people wake up. Then, we can leave and hide before they find us.'

The two women fumbled down to the riverbank with Yoshiko identifying where it was, trying to walk along the edge and keep out of the water to avoid splashing. It was much too dark to try to swim, but it wasn't much easier to pick their way along the bank in the dark. When they reached a watermill, they ducked through the small gap under the axle and crept sideways along the edge of the stone building that sat close to the river. Yoshiko called out whispered instructions from the front, seeing where it was safe to walk in the darkness with her cursed sight and notifying Nubia.

'How can you tell?' Nubia hissed after a fourth warning about an area of the bank that slipped away.

'I can see it.'

'See? How? It's too dark. I cannot see. You're just a shadow in front of me.'

'Haruki told you about the dragon legend of my family? That the maids joked my family had a strange story?' Yoshiko prompted, trying to remind Nubia.

'Yes. Are you telling me it's true?'

'It's true.'

They carefully picked over another slippery bank.

'You are a dragon?' Nubia whispered doubtfully.

'No, but sort of.' Yoshiko wasn't sure how to explain it. Particularly after what happened in the barn, it was all too overwhelming.

'Can you use fire?' Nubia asked, pausing as she walked, her voice trailing off.

By now, they were close to the port. Voices of sailors roared from buildings all around them, and they had to whisper more quietly from fear of someone being around to hear them. Yoshiko paused too, both standing with their backs to the edge of a building by the river. Yoshiko peered into the swirling river's night-black water.

'I didn't think so until …'

'Until? So the barn …' Nubia was looking at Yoshiko now, and it looked like she could see Yoshiko a little in the dim darkness.

'I think it was me. But I'm not sure how. It was an accident.'

'Accident?' Nubia repeated the word, sounding confused and not understanding the language.

Yoshiko looked up at the stars and tried to think of a word that Nubia might know. 'I did it, I think. But I didn't want to. I just tried to stop the guards. But fire came.'

Nubia hummed in understanding, now staring down at the water. The lamps from around the port town and inside the buildings cast a faint glow on parts of the street and the river's water. It made things feel bright, but it also warned Yoshiko that they couldn't linger here too long. A voice came from inside one of the inns behind them. Yoshiko wondered whether those slave market workers would be inside.

'Stay here—I'll look in the inns for Gora,' Yoshiko said, determined to look as quickly as possible and leave. She didn't like this place.

'But what if they see you?'

'They won't. I'll come back. Hide by the riverbank.'

Nubia nodded, carefully inching down the slope towards some shrubbery. Yoshiko climbed up the stone walls of the nearest inn, peering in any window she passed. But inside anywhere she looked, she only saw the pale-faced, mousy-haired workmen, sailors, and guards that were native to this land. No autumn-coloured hair.

Yoshiko slipped away, disheartened. She dropped back down to the cobbled ground, stumbling as she tried not to land badly on her ankle. Then, Yoshiko slid down the riverbank's slope towards Nubia, finding her still behind the bush.

'Let's go,' Yoshiko said under her breath. 'We should get somewhere far away before morning.'

Nubia nodded. 'But which way?'

Yoshiko wondered where Gora would go if he escaped. She knew he liked quiet spaces with lots of trees. He spent a lot of time in the forest back home in Hié; there, he could also use his hunting and tracking skills to stay unseen, safe, fed, and alive. Everything about him had revolved around the forest until she'd asked him to join her in her mission. He made things from dead and fallen wood, he lived in the village at the foot of the forest, he hunted and tracked and collected food in the woods. So Yoshiko knew that would be the best place to start. And she and Nubia would be warmer and safer there, too.

'There's a forest nearby, isn't there?' Yoshiko asked Nubia, who looked at her with deep signs of fatigue. Yoshiko was feeling the same. She hoped she could get them both far enough away to rest safely.

'Yes. There is a big one that covers the area to the north. If we travel north-west, we can get there. Some of my people and yours work the trees there to sell the wood in town. They walk that way with carts of logs, so it's accessible.'

'Then, we'll go there,' Yoshiko decided aloud. 'We can hide and look for Gora.'

'The red-haired man?'

Yoshiko nodded and picked her way up the slippery slope of the bank. 'Just one problem, though. Which way is north?'

Nubia caught up with Yoshiko quickly. She looked up and smiled, pointing. 'This way. Now you will follow me. Dragon lady, keep watch for us.'

Together, they slunk through the streets, darting between buildings and looking out for anyone who might see them. Guards patrolled the area lazily, staring wistfully at the inns and not believing that anyone could escape without causing a ruckus obvious enough to be caught. The two women had to stop and wait several times for the coast to be clear, and time passed slower than Yoshiko hoped.

At this pace, we won't make it far by dawn, she worried.

As they zigzagged through the cobbled town, stumbling in the darkness on the pointlessly uneven stones, Yoshiko heard a noise in the distance to the east where the farm lay. Her heart froze. Had they finally come looking?

Dogs barked, men yelled, and windows lit up in the distance behind them as people woke up from the disturbance. Yoshiko pushed them faster, driving them to run down alleyways and up to the edge of town. Finally, the cobbled streets made way for a mud track, and it led up a hill that wound through some trees. Not the forest, but a patch of trees offered hiding places, at least, and they separated larger and more elaborate buildings. The strange buildings were huge, with large gardens and trees blocking them from view from the road. In any other circumstances, Yoshiko would stop to stare at such grandeur—even the white stone lit up in the dark of night—but tonight, she focused on sprinting into the safety of the woods.

The town echoed with distant yells, and Yoshiko's ears twitched at the sounds about them. She and Nubia wouldn't have much of a head start if the people on this hill woke, too. And, with dogs hunting them, they'd have no hope. Memories of the night the dogs had tracked her mother to the middle of nowhere and caused Asumi's doom flooded back into Yoshiko's mind, and her stomach lurched. Yoshiko bit back the emotions that flooded over her with it, and she frowned. She couldn't think about that right now.

'Sorry, Nubia. We need to be quicker.' Yoshiko grabbed Nubia's hand again and sped up, pulling at the Qeclan woman to go faster. The Qeclan woman hung on and drove herself forward, trying to keep up on her own.

Yoshiko could see the deep darkness of trees in the distance and didn't need Nubia to guide her. For now, the forest was thinned where pampered civilisation had cut it back, making way for more farms and large spaces where people from Qecla and Hié had chopped the trees down to sell for wood to build and burn. But eventually, trees became thicker, large houses were swallowed into the darkness, and the expanses of fields grew smaller as the forest loomed over them.

The yelling voices followed, and the barking dogs made sure Yoshiko's heart wouldn't slow for a moment. She swallowed down panic and tried to think logically. Water—they needed water. To hide in, to dive in, to drive off the scent. Surely the river that ran through the port town would run through the forest as well, originating from higher land and running through both?

Nubia's breathing strained as they slowed to a jog. Only Yoshiko's eyes could guide them through the trees that opened the forest up and then swallowed them whole. The darkness was uncanny. Everywhere, they stumbled against roots and felt branches and twigs and leaves hit at them and scratch them, but they didn't stop.

'Further,' Yoshiko growled, mostly to keep driving herself forward than anything.

Nubia moaned, tiredness settling in.

The forest was still dark, but the light became hazier as the dawn started to rise somewhere to the east. The outlines of roots, branches, and tree trunks became visible, and Nubia could guide herself. So they jogged separately and in silence, too afraid and tired to speak. Yoshiko couldn't tell how far into the forest they were, or for how long they'd been running, but she kept heading in the direction she thought was west—deeper into the forest. The barking of dogs, too, had faded until nothing but leaves and birds could be heard. But that didn't mean they could stop. Yoshiko knew she couldn't count on losing the dogs yet.

'Can you climb?' Yoshiko asked Nubia, both women leaning against tree trunks to rest sometime later, panting and gulping in air.

Nubia looked at Yoshiko through half-lidded eyes. She looked as if she'd fall asleep standing. 'Well enough.'

'Good, we need to climb.'

Nubia's eyes flashed upwards to stare at the canopy, wariness and displeasure evident on her face. Yoshiko apologised, but both knew it had to be done. There, they had more chances to rest safely and confuse the dogs with the disappearance of their trail.

Nubia seemed too concerned about her fate to argue and hesitantly reached for a branch. She pulled herself up fluidly, and Yoshiko nodded in approval, following shortly after, feeling the cool breeze brushing against her skin as she rose further above the ground.

The wind whipped Yoshiko's hair about her, and panting at the strain, they stopped in a tall tree—big and strong enough and hidden by many leaves—to rest. Nubia curled up, exhausted, into a crook where the branch met the trunk, sighing and watching Yoshiko with eyes full of questions. Yoshiko crouched into a nook, too, slightly lower on the tree to Nubia.

'The man we are looking for, does he have red eyes, too?'

Yoshiko startled at the question, being half asleep, and looked up at Nubia, who was resting her head back against the trunk now and looking into the distance.

'What do you mean?' *Why would he have red eyes?* Yoshiko wondered.

'If he has red hair, does he have red eyes? Or is he like the pale-haired ones who have different hair and eye colours?'

The question took Yoshiko off guard, and she laughed quietly. 'They are different. He is not like us with the same hair and eye colour. His eyes are like an icy sea: a pale, bright blue.'

'Red and blue,' Nubia said thoughtfully. 'He is colourful. Some folks in this country or those I've seen trading on the ships have blue eyes. But his colouring—red and blue—sounds more beautiful.' Then, 'Can we rest here?' She looked down at Yoshiko, face openly begging that Yoshiko say yes.

'Yes.'

Nubia's face washed over with so much relief that it flooded through Yoshiko's body, too. Both women slouched back with no energy to move or to speak, and Yoshiko's body finally released enough for her brain to wonder again. More accurately, to wonder things she didn't want to think about, like the barn.

Emotions that had been held back in the escape now overflowed, and tears pricked her eyes again. Yoshiko hugged her knees to her body and curled up as tightly as she dared without falling from the tree. She buried her face into her knees and sobbed, the picture of Haruki flashing clearly in her mind. How she had ever pushed that vision aside, even to run away, she never knew. She was sure she'd never be free from that image or the guilt.

'I killed her,' Yoshiko moaned. 'I just wanted to save her. How can I take her home now?'

Yoshiko heard Nubia stir from above but couldn't bring herself to look up. It felt like a blade was pushing into her heart and twisting—carving out a hole and crunching her chest. Her face convulsed with the pain and tears poured over wrinkles as she scrunched her face up against her knees. Yoshiko's teeth were bared, and she knew her face was red, ugly, with eyes blinded by the salty water that sprang from them. This crying face she had to hide. This person who had killed her friend could not be shown to anyone else. Maybe she had deserved to die at the barn, too.

A gentle tap on her head made her reveal her face to the forest, though, and she saw Nubia's long arm stretching down enough to touch Yoshiko lightly on the head with a single finger. It was all Nubia could do to reach Yoshiko without moving, and the touch made Yoshiko's heart lurch. She rushed to wipe her face, realising Nubia could see.

'Accident,' Nubia said, repeating the word Yoshiko had used earlier. 'Right?'

Yoshiko nodded miserably, and her voice crumbled into a high-pitched sound of pity as she replied, 'Yes. But I still killed her.'

Nubia ignored the pitiful sound and spoke again. She sounded exhausted. 'And the guards. Tell me.'

Yoshiko continued to hug herself closely and sniffed loudly. Her words tumbled in a blur that she'd be surprised if Nubia could understand. 'We were coming back from the river. Haruki helped me because I wasn't well. The guards grabbed her as we walked to the hut. They attacked us. They were going to rape her and make me watch. One was sitting on me. I got angry and tried to push him off so I could help Haruki. Next thing I knew, everything was on fire.'

Yoshiko looked up to see if Nubia had understood it all, and she saw the older woman slowly processing it, lips moving as she ran over words to keep up. Then, Nubia snarled and spat, tongue clicking with immense disgust and cursing in Qeclan. 'Then, they deserved to die,' she said, face wrinkling in disgust. 'And I wish I could have had revenge for my friends, too.'

'But not Haruki. I'd have done anything to stop her from getting attacked, but she didn't deserve to die. And it was a bad way to die, too. I hope she is spared in the spirit world.' Yoshiko felt the pain etch at her heart again, and she caved into tears again. She'd never see Haruki's cheerful smile again.

Nubia made a deep humming noise. 'Those boars. They think they can do whatever they want. I've seen it happen to their own women—free women! We are just sacks of meat for them.'

Yoshiko didn't know whether she could respond. She stared deep into the forest and accepted the tears as they streamed down her face, blurring her vision, dripping from her chin.

'You should've seen it. It was terrifying. I'd never wish that on anyone. She never deserved that.' Yoshiko remembered the burnt blackness and how Haruki's skin stuck to Yoshiko's hand as she tried to touch her. Yoshiko shuddered. Nubia's voice cut sharp and brought Yoshiko back to the forest.

'If you had not, she'd have died by their hands.'

Yoshiko sighed. In her heart, she knew that. 'You're right, but I wouldn't want her to die by mine, either.'

'Of course not. But you had no other choice. By your flames, or by torture and suffering and indignity at the hands of heartless guards. I think, if she could have chosen, she'd have chosen your flames.' Nubia's stern voice petered out. 'And so would I.'

'But—' Yoshiko knew it was pointless to argue back, but she couldn't help it.

'Was it quick?'

'Yes, instant. Though it must have been painful.'

'Then, quick is better than long, slow torture. She had a good death. As a slave, that's all anyone can ask for. Would you rather she died by those men?'

'No.'

'Then think of that. You did it to save her. As a slave, you have no choice in your death. I've seen so many—those I love and those I don't know. That fire was so hot. I've never seen anything like it. If I could choose my death, I'd choose instant fire, too, I think.'

Both fell silent, and the forest took over once again. After a while, Nubia spoke again.

'I saw my brother die. When we were first taken. My husband was away for trade, and my brother and I stayed in our country. Our town was sold off by a neighbouring tribe's warlord, and both pale men and warriors from the neighbouring tribe came to take us. My brother tried to fight. He was strong. But they beat him, clubbed him, crushed him. So much screaming and blood. I wish his had been instant. They had guns; they could have made it quick. But they didn't. They don't like it if you fight back.'

Yoshiko couldn't think of anything to say. Her insides twitched with sickness and anger, and the heat from before emerged in her stomach. She tried to swallow it down. Too many people had died. Yoshiko sat, swallowing raw feelings that would have her killing every pale person she ever saw again, and focused on her next plan. Inaction had caused people to die. Haruki would never have died if Yoshiko had escaped immediately. Instead, she had stalled.

Well, from here, no more stalling.

'Get some rest,' Yoshiko said gently. 'I'll keep watch.'

36

News in the City

'Did you hear about the fire in Dunstrand?'

Since his escape, Gora had found a small inn in Rödsted on the other side of the forest to Dunstrand port. With no money or decent clothes to help him blend in, he'd raided some sleeping guards and taken their coin purses and clothes. Now, with simple, local clothes and coin, he'd dived into the first inn he'd seen in the capital city and ordered the first proper meal he'd had in weeks and a large ale to wash it down with. The food had been half decent compared to anything else he'd eaten recently, and his stomach was full. Now, Gora hunched over a mug of bitter ale, moaning to himself about the foul taste it left in his mouth. He'd been spoilt with Hién spirits and saké, and in his grumbling, he barely paid attention to the gossip of the other patrons. That thing about the fire, though … someone asked that voice to keep talking, and Gora tuned in to the conversation more.

'Yeah, a barn on a farm mysteriously burst into flames. Burned white like nothin' seen before, apparently. Weird. Killed two slaves and two guards. Huge, like a tower of fire, they say.'

'An exaggeration!' someone else chipped in, leaning back in his seat and wiping ale from his mid-brown beard. His eyes were small, and he looked at the previous speaker. 'I bet it wasn't that weird. Just a barn fire got outta control.'

The previous speaker shook his hairy head, and Gora turned to look at him, seeing a face pink from drink. 'I tell ya! I trust who told me.'

'You think a slave started it to escape?' The man at the bar leaned on his elbows and hands, listening carefully.

Gora shifted uneasily in his seat and raised his mug to drink and hide his face.

'Who knows?' the pink-faced man spoke again. 'Maybe. But no-one could start a fire *that* hot. Seriously. No matter how many slaves tried to put it out, they had to wait for it to burn itself out.'

A woman beside them all scoffed. She had a tough build and short-cropped hair. Gora raised his eyebrow at her as she spoke. 'Pfft, perhaps alcohol made it burn brighter. Guards probably had a stash in there. Remember the inn that caught fire, and all the spirits exploded?'

'I'm telling you, that's nothing compared to this! They say it was white and as hot as the sun. And it burned all night and into the morning.'

Gora listened as the gossip became an argument about how one knew how hot the sun was and what the fire meant. Gora sighed into his mug. He was thinking about calling it a night and slipping away when he heard something else.

'I heard there was a strange slave on that plantation,' another woman said, smooth voice cutting through the brawling. 'They say she had eyes as dark as the goddess of death and barely flinched when they branded her. Never screamed—not a sound—and her eyes made the branding woman cry and run with fear. The woman's never been the same. My friend told me so. Knew the poor woman.' She brought her mug to her face and watched with stone-grey eyes as all attention turned to her.

It was silent for just a moment, until, 'Ahh, never! No-one could make a branding woman cry. They've got grit. Ain't gonna be any little slave girl gonna make one of them cry!'

The grey-eyed woman looked stonily at him, setting her face firm. 'It's true. The same slave girl has since disappeared, they say. Some think she died in the fire. Others think she started it and ran. She's heartless. One of her own died in that fire, and she still ran. She might kill us next.'

The tavern erupted with jeers and laughter. 'Like some ghost of a slave will scare me. What can they do? They're in the next town and ain't gonna come here.'

And, with that, cries for more ale broke out and the topic was left in the dust.

Gora slouched over what was left of his ale and watched it swirl as he wobbled the tankard around a few times. *Gross stuff,* he pouted. He threw the last of the bitter ale down, scrunching up his face as it went down. He slammed the tankard on the table and pushed it away.

So, the girl who didn't scream as they branded her, he knew that would be Yoshiko. But had she started the fire? He didn't know where they'd taken her, but the strange slave girl sounded like her, and it was in the direction of Dunstrand town, where they'd been sold as slaves. But Gora didn't know whether Yoshiko could make fire like that. Her family had the dragon curse on them, but that didn't mean she could breathe fire. Hizen dragons were water and air spirits anyway. Gora stared at the dregs of his cup and tried to remember the stories he'd heard about the Hizen spirits and legends of people turning into dragons. There wasn't much detail or anything of use. They only told of spurned women getting angry and wanting revenge on the men who'd left them.

'Oy, sailor. Whatcha glaring at my ale for, eh? Not good enough for ya?'

Gora glanced up at the barkeep, who was moving between tables to gather empty tankards and persuade people to buy more. The 'keep was headed his way and looking straight at him, warily.

Gora's story had been that he was a sailor on one of the ships that had pulled into the city harbour earlier that day. They'd believed him. All kinds of merchant ships pulled in there—unlike the small port of Dunstrand, which seems to be limited for the trade of slaves. All sorts of people came in on the merchant ships; an extra would go unnoticed. And it helped that he could speak traders' language.

'Ale's fine,' Gora answered gruffly. 'Thinking of the strange slave and fire. Ne'er heard anything like it. Demon's work, maybe.'

The 'keep's face lightened. 'Thought's enough to make anyone's face darken! It's not worth it to have slaves. Brings all kinds of trouble and bad luck, I'll tell you—too many problems. But then, who am I to tell the king? An' some seem to like havin' em.' He shrugged.

The barkeep nodded at Gora's tankard and asked if he'd have another. Gora nodded absentmindedly. Maybe it wouldn't be so bad to stay here a little longer, after all. Might hear something else.

As the 'keep wandered away, Gora mused. So some people weren't happy about the slaves. It was all on the king. Well, a nation catching and trading in slaves and servants would have to have it agreed on by a higher member of society. But for the king to be the one to choose it didn't bode well for him and Yoshiko. While Yoshiko's plan was optimistic enough at best, it would be even more challenging than they thought to stop it if it was the king who decreed it.

Again, Yoshiko's naïvety amazed Gora. He wondered whether her time here still made her think she could simply walk into a palace as a slave and ask for it all to stop. Here, she wasn't the daughter of a daimyō, not a noble or political figure of Hizen. Here, she was a nameless face among many forced to work forever against their will, no chance for rights, voice, or freedom.

Still, if she started that fire, the likelihood was that she'd escaped. No-one had mentioned the strange slave had been caught, so she must be loose. And then she'd be on the way to the palace, like they'd planned back in Hié, surely, to speak to the person in charge. That would mean she'd be on her way here, he hoped. Rödsted was the only place near Dunstrand with a palace.

Gora nodded to the barkeep as another foul ale was pushed in front of his face, but he hardly noticed the taste as he took a great swig and wondered how he'd meet Yoshiko again. Should he wait here and keep an eye out? Inns were always a good place to hear about things going on. Everyone travelling or drinking wanted a chat and to be listened to.

But then, what if she hid and no-one heard about her at all?

Gora took another swig and frowned into the mug as he rested it back on the sticky wood of the bar. Then, he looked up and stared at the door, running his hands through his hair as he thought. A great wall surrounded this whole city, and there were only two ways in: one was the open sea, the other was a bridge over a great slit in the earth where the ocean water washed in. The entrance closest to Dunstrand port town was the great, stone bridge over the moat, and would be the only way Yoshiko could enter the city. If he regularly patrolled that area, he should be able to bump into her. In the meantime, he could spend the night in local inns and hear more about what was going on.

For one, he wanted to know what happened to the Qeclans—how they'd been captured and then set only half-free, still forced to work. Finding that out might give him a clue as to why the Hién people had been enslaved next, and how he and Yoshiko could free them all.

Besides, he didn't mind the idea of sleeping on a proper bed, no matter how rubbish it was. After the ship and the hut in the woods, even a thin, bumpy mattress would feel like bliss.

Gora gulped down the rest of his ale and tossed a remark of gratitude over his shoulder at the barkeep as he strolled out the bar door and into the street. Now was as good a time as any to get his bearings, and he could go and eye up the ships in the port to see whether it would offer decent escape once Yoshiko had tried her optimistic talk with the king.

37

Journey to the Main Town

'Those damned dogs.' Nubia gasped and settled into the crook of a tree, hardly daring to whisper.

Once more, dogs roamed in the foliage below them, scouting the forests where they'd lost the trail of the two women. Men soon followed, cursing. Neither woman dared to move—not even to lean over to watch—for fear they'd be spotted in their hiding place high in the canopy.

Yoshiko was glad they'd hidden in the trees rather than keep running. She crouched on a branch, holding onto the trunk for support. Staring into the leafy branches ahead, she listened to what was happening below.

The dogs snuffled in the undergrowth, and the men carelessly kicked at leaves and swiped at branches with their hands and sticks.

Idiots, Yoshiko thought, grinning. *The dogs can't do their best with you making that noise.*

Not that she cared. In the end, it was in her interest that the men kept stomping through the undergrowth like clueless boars and interrupted the dogs. For if the dogs even heard the slightest disturbance where Yoshiko and Nubia hid, it would cause trouble for them. Yoshiko hoped the men would keep making their pointless racket.

Eventually, the sound of the dogs and men crashing through the forest faded away, but Yoshiko didn't dare move until it was silent and her ears couldn't even strain to pick up noise. She didn't want to know who could hear best: her or the dogs.

Yoshiko's heart thudded warily. She heard Nubia let out a shaky breath. Yoshiko met the older woman's glance and could easily see the question in them: would they continue now?

'If you're ready to go?' Yoshiko asked.

'Yes, and nature is calling; I don't fancy relieving myself up here!'

Yoshiko looked back at Nubia to see the massive hint on the woman's face. A grin erupted on Yoshiko's face, and she teased her friend. 'But urine is great fertiliser. It will help the tree to grow strong. Think of it as helping.'

'Absolutely not! It feels rude to pee on a tree! They are living beings.' Nubia's face was so expressive, and her voice hitched up a little.

Yoshiko grinned and began the difficult work of climbing back down to the forest floor.

* * *

A few hours into their walk, when their stomachs felt pocked with hunger and their mouths and throats sore and parched from lack of water, and all hope for finding water seemed lost, Yoshiko cried out in pleasure and started running to their right.

'It's water!' Yoshiko called over her shoulder, darting around a tree and crashing through large ferns.

Yoshiko halted at a slope, eyes wide and bright at the sign of a stream running clear as it bubbled over stones. Nubia appeared behind her, face just as lit up, with the biggest and toothiest grin Yoshiko had ever seen on anyone. They both looked at each other, started laughing, and were soon skidding down the muddy slope and crashing their bare feet into the water. Nubia made a high-pitched cry as she sat in the small stream.

'It's cold!' Nubia cried. Yoshiko laughed at the look of shock on Nubia's face, which quickly returned to its grin. 'Get in! It's so nice.'

Yoshiko crouched and eased herself in, but Nubia—who had other ideas—leant forward and pulled Yoshiko down. Yoshiko splashed front-first into the icy water. She, too, squealed at the cold. In an instant, both women were splashing their faces with handfuls of water. Yoshiko's face felt as if it had never been so fresh. She looked over to see Nubia cupping water into her hands and gulping it down, gasping at the cool refreshment.

'Drink it! It's so clean. Not like the river at the farm. I've not tasted anything so fresh since I arrived in this country.' Nubia took another handful.

Yoshiko paused, watching Nubia's satisfied face as she drank more and more of the icy water. Her own mouth felt drier in comparison. Yoshiko's heart froze as she realised how much this woman and her people had suffered, and she couldn't help but sit dazed from the realisation. That is, until her thirst became too much, enhanced by being so close to the water. She cupped her hands and drank deep. Nubia was right: it was beautiful. Like the water she drank back in Hié that came from the mountains. It was so cool and clean. If anything, it could almost be better—made better by their lack of good water since.

They drank and bathed and cleaned themselves and their clothes as best as they could, not knowing when they'd next get this opportunity again.

'It's a shame we have nothing to take some with us in,' Nubia sighed, unable to tear her eyes away from the glistening water that rippled around their ankles as she wrung out her tunic.

They'd both removed their clothes to scrub the dirt off in the river, shivering as the cold air caught their wet, bare skin. Now, Yoshiko squeezed the water from her clothes as best as she could and patted her body dry with them before ringing the clothes again. She put on her still-wet clothes and wriggled under the feeling of cold. At least she would feel fresh and alert for a while.

'You think we could walk by it a little while? Many towns build by a water source. It could take us to Rödsted and to meet Gora.'

'Is it safe? People could come.'

'We could stop before the town. But we need food somehow. And we can continue to drink until then.'

Nubia thought for a moment, face pulled tight with thought and anxiety. Finally, she agreed. They padded alongside the river, hidden among the trees for safety. It ran small for a long way, and Yoshiko felt herself becoming impatient. She had thought it would grow bigger by now. Yet the stream continued to run small, and the forest continued heavy and dark. And, as the afternoon light began to fade, the two women's shoulders slumped with disappointment and fatigue.

'Look, it *is* faster.'

Nubia's voice cut through Yoshiko's mind as she was slipping into a tired fog of uncertainty and depression. She looked up. It was! Yoshiko eagerly ran on ahead, darting through the trees and leaping over roots and low-lying plants. The fatigue from being awake for two days had suddenly left her as she ran, and behind her, Nubia struggled to keep up.

Ahead, the trees thinned, and the golden light of the setting sun seeped in. The forest was ending. Yoshiko halted to wait for Nubia to catch up. They had found a way out, finally! Nubia crashed into her from behind, bending double as she strained to catch her breath.

'Let's stop, now,' Nubia moaned, crouching and looking up at Yoshiko with large, begging eyes.

'Sorry.' Yoshiko crouched down beside her. 'I got excited.'

'You did. So what now?'

Yoshiko looked about them. 'Let's rest until full dark. Maybe then we can see if there are fields nearby to take food.'

'Steal?'

'What else do you suggest? We don't have money.'

Nubia shook her head and looked at the ground. 'I don't like it. But, if we have to …'

'We have to. We will only take what we need. Nothing more.'

So, that night, refreshed from a short sleep, a drink of water, and another wash of their faces, they snuck into the fields on the edge of the forest. The two women slunk in the darkness, edging along the bushes. Yoshiko could hear a dog whining as it slept on the other side of the field and instructed Nubia to be careful. Other than that, it was silent.

They stayed on the edge as they rooted through the plants, pilfering only what they could eat without cooking. Peas in their pods, a leafy vegetable, carrots, and apples from a tree. It wasn't much, but it was the best feast they could have had and would help them go that little bit further to Rödsted.

The river grew larger, and they walked on the track beside the forest, a few times darting into the trees as travellers or farmers came out early before the dawn. And, when the road became larger and paved with stones, they knew they'd be close to the city.

'There is one problem.' Nubia looked at Yoshiko in the pre-dawn darkness. 'If we arrive tonight, we will not have time before daybreak to search for your friend. We will be seen. They will know who we are by looking at us.'

Yoshiko hummed in thought. 'We will have to stop for the day, won't we?'

They both groaned, and Yoshiko became agitated at the delay. Who knew how many of her people were suffering and dying as she took her time to walk to the palace? What if more people from her home country were being snatched and shipped off again? A heat bubbled inside her stomach again, and she tried to focus on the memory of the cool river to stop it.

'Let's look for a safe place to rest,' Yoshiko said, finally.

They dived into the forest at the best opportunity and padded through the undergrowth. By the first light of dawn, Yoshiko picked a strong, thick tree and climbed, leading Nubia to a dense area of leaf coverage. Nubia was fearless at climbing the trees, but she still muttered to herself in disapproval and clicked her tongue. She didn't like sleeping in them.

'You rest first,' Yoshiko said. 'Tomorrow night, we'll head into the city and look for Gora.'

'Do you think he will be there?'

'I'm sure he will,' Yoshiko said, thinking of Gora's stories of his pirate days. 'I know he will have escaped. He's got out of worse places. And we planned to go to the palace. He will have gone to the city if there's a palace there.'

'What if this city doesn't have the palace?'

'Then, I'll go on to the next one.' *But,* Yoshiko thought, *Haruki said it did. So unless we have come to a different city from the one Haruki talked about, we should be in the right place.*

'On your own?' Nubia asked, her voice sleepy as she sat back in a safe position in the branches.

'Would you come with me?'

'I will. I will not survive on my own—your dragon hearing is too good. And I want to see the red hair of your colourful friend.'

Nubia grinned down from her place in the tree at Yoshiko—a wide grin that filled her face. Yoshiko dared to laugh. She didn't tell Nubia, but she was certain she couldn't survive without Nubia, either. If only for the fact she'd have succumbed to loneliness and anger and grief before she made it to the palace and made reckless moves. Yoshiko thought for a moment that she might finally understand how her mother would have felt all those months earlier, and how Asumi could suddenly make drastic and bad decisions. Unlike Asumi, Yoshiko chose to seek company, and Nubia kept her grounded and feeling human. She gave Yoshiko something to focus on and good company. Yoshiko would tell Nubia one day how important she'd been, she promised.

38
Fuck

'Well, shit.'

Blunt pain hit, and Gora doubled over and wheezed a cough. His eyesight speckled, and when he looked up, he swore again before the depths closed in.

'Fuck.'

39

The Bridge

Between fidgeting and the restless feeling of being so close to their target, Yoshiko and Nubia barely managed to doze. When they were sure it was safe, they talked about their past lives and what they would do each day, teaching each other words in their languages and talking about the history of their peoples.

Nubia was a knowledgeable woman with a great interest in natural things, hunting, and trade. She spoke of the days she lived in the safari bush plains or a coastal port town in Qecla, and how she went hunting often for meat and gathered foods for her and her husband to eat. She spoke of how they'd become betrothed, and how he'd given her the incredible wedding gift of a specially-made spear. She and Yoshiko laughed about how few women would find it an acceptable wedding gift, but that it sounded marvellous for someone like Nubia, who spoke of her hunting trips with her female friends with a light in her deep brown eyes and a huge grin stretching across her face.

Nubia and her husband had moved from the open plains of Qecla to the coast to get involved in sea trade. Both had wanted to see countries beyond their own, and they'd built a simple home in a local coastal port. It was there, when she'd stayed behind to help with a big community event and so not gone on a trading journey with her husband, that the Acrein slave catchers had come to her land, guided by warriors of a neighbouring tribe looking for profit. It was normal, at that time, apparently, for the neighbouring tribes to be at war with one another.

Yoshiko thought it sounded much like Hizen, where the days of feudalism were yet behind them and neighbouring daimyōs sought to expand their domain and start a war with the next. It made her more determined than ever to become a political figure, not a fighter, and continue the work of her father, mother, and grandmother in helping the shōgun bring peace to the domains and stop the fighting, to build a stronger, more united Hizen.

It was when Nubia was in the middle of telling her a funny story of a time she and her husband had been fishing, shortly after moving to the coast, that Yoshiko heard a stirring in the undergrowth. They fell silent, faces ashen and hearts thumping until the noises of the forest continued and they were sure it was safe.

'I am fed up with this.' Nubia muttered, leaning slightly closer to Yoshiko from the branch she sat on to whisper, hanging on easily with her long arms. 'Being on the edge of something I cannot control, unable to escape.'

Yoshiko nodded, feeling the same. 'Let's go as soon as we can. When the night quietens, we hurry.'

'I would run all the way to the palace if it meant getting out of this forest,' Nubia moaned, hiding her head in her hands for a moment.

'Be careful what you wish for,' Yoshiko teased, a light smile spreading on her face and her eyes crinkling. 'I can run a long way.'

'I know, and I will struggle to keep up. Me! Who ran so much with my beautiful spear.' Nubia reached up with her arms towards the sky as if she was calling upon strength. 'Maybe we can run a little bit.' Nubia smiled, turning to show the large, beautiful curve of her white-toothed grin.

When darkness seeped into the forest, Yoshiko guided Nubia down from their perch in the trees to reach the ground safely. Then, they tracked their way alongside the edge of the forest, next to the road, to the fast flow of the river meeting the gulley that separated them from the city.

It was a strange journey, and everything felt unusually still and silent. Yoshiko's senses stirred as they walked alongside the deep ravine that created a natural moat that made Rödsted hard to get into—naturally defended from any army that might want to raid. There was only one way in. Trouble was, outside the forest and the city, this meant there were few places to hide. When she reached the great stone bridge that would lead them across the river that roared below, they crouched and hid behind the stone wall, waiting for signs it was safe to cross.

The night felt heavy, and Yoshiko's heart throbbed with an anxiety she couldn't place. Was it fear of being caught, or something else? She looked back at Nubia, who was hiding close behind her. Nubia's face was closed, her eyes wide with fear and her mouth shut tight. Yoshiko turned back to look across the bridge. It seemed no-one was there, and the city felt too silent. Something wasn't right.

There, Yoshiko and Nubia crouched a little longer. Yoshiko peeked over the edge, looking far down the bridge. There was no-one. Then, she looked behind. There was no-one behind them, either. She opened her ears up to the sounds—her ears picked up a rumble in the sky, and she realised why the air was so heavy and no-one was around. A storm. She wondered what a storm would look like in this country and how safe it would be if they got caught in it.

'We need to cross now,' she said to Nubia. 'Stay low and run.'

Nubia nodded and shifted position. Another rumble, loud this time, came from the sky above. Both women looked up. Not wanting to get caught in the storm, Yoshiko darted around the corner onto the bridge, crouching low and keeping close to the heavy stone blocks that rose on the side of the bridge to stop people from falling over the edge. Her left hand brushed the rough stone as she ran, using it to guide herself. She heard the gentle padding of Nubia's bare feet behind her.

On a different day, Yoshiko would have marvelled at the size and build of this bridge. It was large, stone, and bulky. Nothing like the ones back in Hié. But, today, the rumbling sky made her nervous, and she wished to be somewhere sheltered.

Halfway over the bridge, she paused to look at the looming city walls. It was a fearsome sight of massive stone, and she felt dwarfed in comparison. She felt sick at the thought of her mission until a great gust of wind pushed her into the stone wall of the bridge, and sickness was replaced with a pain that flashed through her body when her fingers crunched under her body. Yoshiko held back a cry and crouched into a ball, looking back for Nubia. The older woman edged closer along the wall, keeping low, then joined Yoshiko crouching against the wall.

The wind began howling, whipping up and wailing through the stone gaps between the bridge and the city. Yoshiko's black hair lashed about her face, stinging her cheeks and blocking her vision. Frustrated, she stuffed it down the back of her shirt, barely stopping the wind's attack on it. It soon whipped up around her once again.

'This wind is madness!' Yoshiko said, pinning her hair down and feeling foolish that such a thing was bothering her when she had greater things to worry about. Surely, the fear of being pushed over into the river was worse?

'We are close,' Nubia reassured her. 'If we crawl, we can make it without being pushed over the edge.'

Yoshiko nodded and led the way in the slow journey to the other side. The perilous wind gushed over their backs like a river of its own. Below, they heard the fast-flowing river of water sloshing and roaring as the wind rushed it onto its banks.

'The sky is angry at something!' Nubia called from behind.

'Are storms often like this here?' Yoshiko called back. She saw Nubia shake her head.

'I think it is made worse by this gulley. It is folk-dug and changes the natural way of the wind. They made the ocean winds direct around the city to keep the city safe, but it made this path more dangerous. Be careful.'

Yoshiko wondered how Nubia knew this gulley had been folk-made. She'd thought it was a river. But Nubia's explanation made sense, more than what she had been wondering—the spirits being angry at this country for what it had done. The weather, she wondered, probably didn't even know what the people of the world were doing.

When they finally made it to the end of the bridge, Nubia and Yoshiko pushed their backs against the stone of the city wall for a moment to rest. Panting, both looked back over the bridge and saw trees in the distance bending like leaves and the sky light up white above them. The ground shook with the next roar from the sky, and heavy droplets dived from the clouds, attacking the ground with their heavy, cold wet. The women scrambled for cover under the city's entryway. The heavy rain still found them, and they knew they couldn't hide there for long. Surely, even in a storm, city guards would have to make sure the entrance was guarded?

40

Old Friends

'Well, look what the tide washed in. If ain't our old friend, Gora.'

Pain screeched through Gora's head, and he regained consciousness to the feeling of blood pooling into his brain and his eyes straining from hanging upside down by his legs. He blinked until he could see again and swore. How many times was he going to wake up captured on a damned ship? This time, he was surrounded by lumbering and smelly buggers on the deck of a ship he'd hoped to never see again and would recognise in an instant—even if he were hanging upside down.

'Fuck, what in the damned sea witch's curses are you all doin' here?' Gora growled, his insides freezing over with the knowledge of where he was—the accursed pirate ship he'd finally snuck away from nearly ten years ago. What the heck was it doing here?

A blond, greasy-haired pirate about Gora's age crouched inches away from Gora's face and grinned. The smell of the man's breath and the creepy grin made Gora shudder. 'Like we'd answer a traitorous cur like you. Thort we was friends, eh, and then what'd ya do?'

'Fuck you, Kipp. Get outta here!'

'Oy oy, that ain't nice. Just saying hi to an ol' pal. Bin years, mate. This where you've been hiding? Live 'ere, eh?'

'I don't fucking live here!' Gora roared, curling himself up at his core and trying to reach the binding on his feet. 'This place is damned. Get me down. I wanna leave.'

'Ain't no changin' some!' The greasy-haired Kipp stood up and gave Gora a push, making him swing and lose his balance.

Gora yelled out a string of profanities and thrashed out at any legs that were close. All around him, guffaws and jeers of Kipp's peers rang out, and the gaggle of pirates joyfully aimed kicks as he swung.

'That's enough!' a low voice yelled over the mayhem, and all on deck froze. Gora's insides did, too. 'Time's ready for talkin'. Our young devil's child has some asplainin' a do.'

Gora's rope stopped swinging enough for him to look around and see the wrinkled, old face of a man who had no cause to be calling anyone else the devil.

'Frewin,' Gora growled, glaring from where he hung. 'Maybe you'll answer me. I said, what you all doin' here?'

Frewin glared back down. This old pirate was naturally filthy in the slimiest way—attitude and all. His short, matted beard of mud-brown was now streaked with grey and hacked off below the chin. Frewin, ever impatient, had always had the habit of using his short sword for personal grooming. And matched with his abnormally large eyes—always watering, mostly yellowing whites showing and tiny, grey irises—meant he looked like some strange, washed-up corpse. Now, his eyes were yellowed more than ever, and Gora was amazed the old pirate wasn't blind yet.

'Foul-mannered and detestable as ever—you never were part o' the crew, were ya, boy? Shoulda knowen ye'd've run away.'

'That sort of thing tends to happen when you buy a kid as a slave.'

Frewin's face tensed with thunder, and he let a kick fly at Gora's stomach. Gora spluttered, and the rope spun again. As he coughed, his shirt billowed down around his chest. 'Amazed ye could still kick that high,' he wheezed as he tried to push his shirt from his face so he could see the next attack. 'Pretty spry for an old seaslug.'

'Cap'n, the bugger's got anuvver slave mark. Look,' someone on deck called out, and a muttering erupted. Gora tried to pull his shirt back up.

'Well, that one ain't mine, is it, lad? Got yerself cort when ya ran away, eh? Free life not for you, eh? That why yer here?'

'You'll all be damned; ye' know nothin'!' Gora yelled. 'I said get me down. I can't hang about here.'

Gora heard a quick intake of breath and the sharp sound of a sword leaving its scabbard before his shoulders crashed onto the wooden deck and his body piled on top of itself. When Gora sat himself up, Frewin was standing over him, glaring down. The watery-eyed pirate pulled out his pistol and pointed it at Gora's head. Gora swallowed.

'We heard this country be trading in invaluable goods. Ships turn up here, and goods are bought for a high price. Children from a country far away. All perfect for takin'. It's our turf—or did ya forget we control these seas?'

'Piece of shit,' Gora hissed, earning a sharp smack in the face with the butt of the handgun.

Frewin walked away, pocketing his pistol. Then, he paused and turned his watery, yellow eyes once more to Gora. 'Well, seems this might be our fortune. We'll let you go if you help us. Deal fer a deal—you know what it's like, by now. After all, yer one of us.'

'I ain't one of you.'

'Oh, aren't ya? With the things ye've done fer us?' Frewin grinned. 'We know what you are. We know what ye've done. Ye can't say yer not one o' us.'

The lads about him sneered, and some cracked their knuckles. Gora looked about him warily, wondering how he'd get away. He had to be back in the city to meet Yoshiko. Who knew when she'd be arriving and looking for him. 'Fuck that.'

'Suit yerself.' Frewin shrugged and turned away once more. 'Ye know how it works here, boy. Ye can stay here with th' lads; they'll help persuade ya. Ye'll help me once they're done with ya.'

Gora quickly tried to untie the rope around his ankles to free himself. Then, he could fight and run away. Before he could loosen the bonds, slimy Kipp was once more up in his face, unsettling as ever.

'So, Gora, how'd ye think yer gunna get out of this one after ye betrayed us?' Kipp's eyes bore into his, hate seeping into them. 'Ye think a brother should let a brother down?'

'Oh, go jump to the depths,' Gora said. 'I ain't yer brother.' The bonds finally pulled free. But when Kipp noticed it, too, the man grinned.

'Run again if you can, Gorey.' Kipp launched a punch at Gora's face. He managed to dodge it, crying out as it scraped his jaw and collided with his ear.

Gora's eyes watered, but he grabbed at Kipp's wrist and twisted it outwards, pulling Kipp down to crash onto the deck. The shock on the pirate's face sent a thrill through Gora—he'd learned that in Hié. If he could down Kipp, he might be able to get away. 'Sure, I'll run again,' Gora said with a grin as he stomped his boot down onto Kipp's hand.

As Kipp roared out and let loose a stream of curses, the rest of the pirates dived into action. Some lunged for Gora, hate scorching their eyes and blades and guns appearing from their holds. A young one ran for Frewin, and, upon seeing the young lad, Gora felt a hatred of his own rise from somewhere beyond his memories. They were still dealing with kids?

'Fuck this,' he spat, and he crashed his elbow into a pirate's to dodge the blade. The pirate roared as his elbow overextended.

He tried to grab his sword with his other hand, but soon found himself swordless as Gora whipped it from his grip. Gora slipped behind the man, grabbed his shoulders, and stomped on the back of his knee. The man thudded into the deck. But before he could deal with him a little more permanently, Gora was rushed by more of his old 'brothers', including a grimacing Kipp, nursing his hand but ready to deal out hell's depths.

'Ye have nowhere to go now we know yer here,' Kipp sneered. 'Ye broke the code. We'll get ye.'

Ignoring him, Gora parried the blades of two others and sent them crashing into one another, cutting through the upper arm of one to disarm the attackers. A crack echoed on the wind, and wood to the side of him splintered as a metal ball plummeted into it. Gora swore and spun on the spot, seeking the idiot holding out the smoking gun. A grey-haired goon with sharp eyes. Gora frowned and kicked out at someone beside him, looking for the nearest escape. He wasn't going to even try playing with guns. Before the old pirate could prepare to shoot again, Gora ducked, slashed out with his blade at a pirate's thigh, and dived across the deck towards the starboard banister. Weaving through the rushing seamen, Gora swore as he realised how far out their ship was. Land was ahead, but the ocean could still be treacherous. Another bullet ripped through the air behind him: those things always were bad for aim, but the next one could hit him. And how else was he going to get back to Acrein and then, hopefully, back to Hié? This was the only way he'd be free.

Squeezing his eyes closed to despair at his moment of madness, Gora launched the blade spinning at the pirate with a pistol, not even waiting to see how close it came to hit, and leapt over the edge of the ship.

41
Catching Up

Yoshiko and Nubia weren't huddling underneath the city's giant stone wall for long. Fearful of being found, the two women dared to jump out into the crashing rain.

They slipped through the cobbled streets, trying to keep to the edges of the buildings where there might be more protection from the driving rain. As Nubia had explained, the wind-break around the city meant the city itself was far less windy, and they only had to contend with the rain and the slippery stones underfoot.

Trying to work their way inwards and towards the centre, where they hoped the palace would be and they could find a starting point to look for Gora, Yoshiko stumbled and scraped her hands.

'This … this is difficult,' Nubia said with short breaths as she tried to regain herself. 'It would be bad enough even without the rain.'

The two were leaning against a slab of wall and hiding from the rain. Yoshiko's long, black hair was plastered to her head and face and had become a nuisance. She envied Nubia's short hair and wondered whether she could get away with cutting hers, too. She pushed her wet hair behind her ear to keep it out of the way.

'This place feels so disorganised. Where would we find anything? All the buildings look the same.' Yoshiko squinted about them, feeling hopeless.

But before Nubia could answer, the wind pushed a scent she recognised their way.

'It's Gora!' she cried, turning in the direction she thought she smelt it. Immediately, the rain pushed it back down again, and she sniffed deeply to try to catch it again. She needed the wind to pick up again. 'He's out in the storm, too.'

'Are you certain?' Nubia looked doubtful. Even with Yoshiko's strange abilities, smelling a man in a strange city in the middle of a storm felt a bit far-fetched.

'I'm sure. It's a smell I recognise. I don't know anyone else!' Yoshiko gestured for Nubia to follow her back out into the rain and down a nearby alleyway. Her heart thudded with the thrill of finally being able to see her friend again. Then, they could do what they came here to do and take her people home and it would all be over.

Wouldn't it?

'Well, ladies, you look like a pair of drowned *tanuki*.'

A lilting voice came from a dark alley, and Nubia spun with a gasp. Yoshiko grinned and rushed towards it. She peered inside, and a roughly-dressed and roughed-up Gora lumbered out. Yoshiko's eyes widened. Blood stained a ripped, soaked shirt, and his face looked like it was beginning to bruise.

'You look worse! What happened to you?'

'Awh, nuffin' really.' He tried to avoid the topic, but Yoshiko could see he was unusually shaken. She kept his gaze until his blue eyes gave way and he looked away awkwardly. 'Pirates are about.'

Yoshiko frowned. 'The ones who—'

'Aye. We had a bit of a catch-up. Managed to make it back before the storm hit.' Gora tried a grin, but with the injuries to his face, it looked more like a grimace.

'How did they find you? Are you alright? Can I help?' Yoshiko asked, feeling panicked at the thought of running into the group from Gora's tales. He waved a hand at her, dismissing the questions.

'They didn't. T'was coincidence. Let's try not to run into them again.' Then, Gora distracted her. 'Who's your friend now?'

Gora's attention had turned to Nubia, who was standing by and trying not to look like she was listening in too much, though her curious face showed it all.

'I am Nubia.' She stepped forward and introduced herself, holding out her hand the way she'd shown Yoshiko how to. Yoshiko was amazed when he smoothly took it and responded the same way as Nubia. Had he done that before? Was it common to greet people that way out of Hié? 'And you are Gora,' she said.

He grinned. 'I am. The little princess here been telling you much about me?'

'I'm *not* a princess,' she grumbled to him for what must've been the *hundredth* time since she'd met him. But her complaints were ignored as Gora and Nubia continued their introductions without her.

Nubia nodded. 'Yoshiko told me about you. Your hair is as she said.'

'My hair?'

'She said it was red. It's like nothing I've ever seen.'

Gora raised an eyebrow. 'Oh, aye? And am I as beautiful as she said, too?' He grinned now, and a glint flickered through his light eyes. Yoshiko rolled hers.

'Right, you're *the* most sought-after man in Hié, after all,' she drawled, firing back with the same humour she'd become used to from him. She was starting to get the hang of it, this humour that was so different to the humour of the Hié people—more teasing and dry.

Gora leaned casually against the alleyway wall and batted his eyelashes at the two ladies, smirking.

Nubia continued without a care. 'You are as she said. Your face is hairy, though. I did not expect that.' She looked him up and down, now. 'You look like one of *them*.'

Gora touched his face instinctively, Yoshiko recognised, and the joy in his face dropped. 'Well, it's hard for a man to shave when he's a captive, I'll tell ya.'

'It's fine. Lots of men look like that in this country; it's a good disguise,' Yoshiko told him, the mission back in the centre of her thoughts.

'Though your hair is a different colour. But they will not expect you to be a slave, at least. It will help you walk around freely,' Nubia added.

Gora frowned. 'It's true I've been able to walk around without too much bother the last few days. In fact …' He looked about them. 'I even managed to rent a room in an inn. We should go there. And you two look like you could do with some food and rest.'

Yoshiko and Nubia both lit up and looked at one another. Yoshiko's stomach pocked at the thought of food, and she covered her hand over it to try to tame it.

Gora guided them through more alleyways until they got to a stone inn near the port, and Yoshiko was glad to have him guide them. A ruckus could be heard from inside, and the smell of sweat and drink oozed out. From where she hid around the corner, Yoshiko felt a queasiness come over her as the smell wafted into her sensitive nose. She scrunched her face up, and beside her, Gora chuckled.

'It's rough, but it ain't too bad. Better than nowhere, and the food's okay. I'm on the first floor. We're gunna have to sneak you in. I'll go first, make sure the way is clear.'

He strode in, pushing the wooden door open without a care. The noise got a little noisier, and Yoshiko waited to see what kind of signal he'd give them. Not much later, two hats and a stained jacket flew out of the door, and Gora's voice reached Yoshiko's ears.

'He said to put those on and run inside,' Yoshiko told Nubia, edging forward and looking up and down the street. It was still stormy and raining, and no-one seemed in sight. Perfect time for a storm, in a way, she thought, though she wished she could have been out of it and dry.

Soon.

'You could hear him from this far among that noise?' Nubia's voice rose with her doubt, and her eyebrows raised, too. But when Yoshiko nodded, Nubia sighed and dashed forward, grabbing a hat and jamming it onto her head while scrunching her face up and visibly trying to ignore the thought of where it came from.

Yoshiko chuckled at the woman's face and rushed to grab the other. 'You take the coat. I feel you'll be more noticeable with your body shape. If I stuff my hair in my hat, I could probably get away with looking like a young boy!'

Nubia made a clicking noise but didn't question Yoshiko's idea. 'He could have at least chosen one from a *slightly* cleaner man,' she mumbled as she followed Yoshiko to the inn door. When they pushed the door open and peered in, Nubia took back her statement, Yoshiko easily seeing in the shadow of her face a look of shock. 'There are no clean men.'

Gora's hand rushed out from the side, and he pulled them up the stairwell nearby. There, he pushed them up and ushered them into a door. They didn't even wait to see whether they'd been spotted. A pair of heavy boots stomped up behind them just as Gora ushered Nubia inside, and he suddenly started whistling and slurring and fell inside the room, cursing as he slammed the door behind him. He immediately locked the door and propped it shut. Yoshiko chuckled at his old 'pretend to be drunk' trick.

'To be sure,' he said, catching her eyes.

Yoshiko watched him stride to the little, dirty window on the other side of the small room and peek out it before pulling two, broken shutters over it. The room fell black. Shortly after, and with a great deal of shuffling, the fireplace flickered into action and a soft glow fell over the room.

'So it was you that burned that barn, eh?' Gora asked, looking at the fire. He turned from where he crouched near the flames, warming his hands, and watched Yoshiko. 'Didn't feed you enough sweets or green tea, so you rebelled?' He threw an easy grin her way.

She and Nubia glanced at one another. Yoshiko wanted to bite back and toss a remark his way, too, but pain shot through her at the thought of the barn going up in flames. She felt the smile fall from her face and she looked at Gora, wondering what to tell him.

'I won't ask yet if you don't want. We can catch up after. You both need to dry off before you catch yer deaths. I'mma go find some food. There's not much in here to dry yerselves in, but you can squeeze the rain from your clothes into that bucket and try pat yourselves dry. When yer done, put this pathetic thing of a blanket around yerselves and sit by the fire to warm.'

He tossed a thin blanket towards them, muttering something about it being a single room, so there was only one blanket. Then, calling over his shoulder at them to not let anyone in unless they heard a knock of four then two, he left the room.

The two women looked at each other again, Nubia's eyes gesturing uncertainly towards the door. Yoshiko nodded and placed the stool in front of it, just in case. Then, as they took their wet clothes off and wrung them in the bucket, both felt an unmeasurable fatigue. The rush of escape had worn off, and they were in Gora's safe hands. Movements slowing and eyes drooping, they patted themselves dry and lay their damp clothes by the fire, huddling close together in the single blanket by the fire.

The heat of the fire and the exhaustion of their journey soon washed through Yoshiko, and by Nubia's head lolling and dropping onto Yoshiko's, Yoshiko could only assume she was the same. It felt like Gora had disappeared out of the room a long time ago, and Yoshiko's eyes kept trying to drop her into the abyss of sleep. Both women leapt out of their skin when the knock came: four then two. Then a pause. Yoshiko looked drowsily at Nubia, who returned the look. Another knock: four then two. Yoshiko looked down and realised she and Nubia were still in the blanket and their clothes were by the fire.

'Um,' she started, before realising other people in the inn shouldn't hear her. The knock came again, a little louder this time. Then, the door tried to push open. Gora had given up waiting. 'Wait,' she tried to hiss without being too loud.

Yoshiko ushered Nubia up and they hugged the blanket around themselves and shuffled towards the door. While Nubia tried to keep the blanket up, Yoshiko moved the chair and hissed at Gora to come in quickly but not look. When he saw they were hiding together in the blanket, his ears went as red as his hair, and he diverted his blue eyes elsewhere.

He kicked the door shut and, using his foot, moved the stool back in front of it. Yoshiko noticed he was carrying two plates full of food. Her stomach pocked, and she was sure she felt herself drool a little.

'Where did you get that?' she asked. She and Nubia shuffled back towards the fire and navigated sitting down while keeping themselves covered. Nubia looked nervous and had fallen silent, but she, too, was staring at the plates with the look of a hunter.

'The tavern below. Decent enough kitchen here. Figured you both had barely eaten in days.'

'You're right,' Yoshiko said, eying up the strange food on the plates. Her stomach rumbled audibly, and she felt her face flush. 'We haven't.'

Gora grinned and held out one of the overloaded plates. Nubia's long arm reached out for it, her other clutching the blanket around them.

'A plate for now, a plate for later,' he said, 'and I got enough that I thought you could reasonably share and last you a couple of meals. Was hard to get that much. Told 'em I felt hungover like anything and wanted to eat like a pig to soak up the alcohol. Might've been hard to get more, but see how that lasts.'

The women's eyes widened at the realisation this was all for them, and they dived in to enjoy the food.

'What is this?' Yoshiko asked, her mouth full of one of the hot meats and not even caring if it was against how she'd been raised. 'Meat and … what's this white substance?' She pointed at the mashed, white mound on the plate.

'And how did you buy it?' Nubia asked, eyes bulging at the number of meat sausages on the plate and then looking suspiciously at Gora. 'If you are a captive too?'

'It's local Acrein food—the food of this country. This'—he pointed at a part of the plate—'is sausage, filled with crushed and minced boar meat with spices to add flavour. And this'—he gestured to the white mash—'is a crushed and mashed root vegetable. They mash it after boiling it for a long time. Sometimes they add oil and herbs, or sometimes they add animal milk to make it creamier. Simple, but warming. And it's damned great when you're hungover.'

Yoshiko and Nubia watched as he pointed to the foods. But it wasn't long before their interest was back on devouring it—tasting the strange tastes and wondering at the magic of food that was more than gruel. The plate quickly emptied.

'That was surprisingly tasty,' Yoshiko said, wiping her mouth with her arm. 'I could easily eat more, though. Shame there were no vegetables.' She glanced at the second plate, before making herself tear her eyes away from it. That was for later, Gora had said.

'Says the woman I've seen eat three rabbits herself,' he muttered, which earned a shocked sound from Nubia, who lightly slapped Yoshiko on her arm and teased Yoshiko for her lack of noble lady-like generosity. 'I know!' Gora said, pretending to be unjustly treated. 'I thought she'd hunted it for us both to eat. But she ate it all. I don't know where she puts it.'

They both looked at Yoshiko's slender frame, huddled in the blanket. She pretended to look innocent. Then, Gora realised himself and looked away. He gave a nervous cough.

'Um, now you've eaten, your clothes might be dry enough from the fire. What d'ya think?'

They agreed, and he told them he'd go sit by the door and admire the plain, old woodwork while they got dressed. 'And while yer doing that, fancy tellin' me what happened since we parted? I thought you were done for, actin' half-dead.'

He sat himself down on the stool by the door, true to his word and facing the wooden panels. Yoshiko sighed and told him of the farm she'd been taken to. Her voice remained soft to ensure no-one else heard, and Gora hummed lightly and aimlessly by the door as he listened, probably trying to drown any of her voice out for anyone who might be walking past the room.

Then, Yoshiko told him of how she'd met Nubia and an old friend there—the maid she'd told him about before who had mysteriously gone missing.

'The one you said could have betrayed us,' she said in a low voice, still feeling annoyed that he could suggest such a thing of Haruki.

'I didn't say she did, just that it was a possibility,' Gora argued back. 'You know why I said it.'

Yoshiko hummed, discontented but knowing he spoke reasonably, and she continued. Gora had lots of questions, and they kept finding themselves taking tangents and having to track their way back until Yoshiko told him of how she'd accidentally killed Haruki when she was trying to protect her from being attacked, dishonoured, and killed, and then escaped with Nubia.

'And you?' Yoshiko asked once she'd finished and they'd all fallen silent in reflection. Nubia lounged back on the floor near the fire, looking as if she'd fall asleep now she'd been fed, hydrated, re-dressed, and drying. Gora looked at Yoshiko and tilted his head to think. He ran his hand through his autumn hair, like he always did. Yoshiko noticed how long it had become.

'Well, my adventure was much less dramatic,' he started. Then, he shuffled where he sat to lean with his back against the wooden door and crossed his ankle over his opposite thigh. 'I was taken to cut trees in the forest. After a day or two, I snuck out.' He rubbed his stubbly cheek and looked up at the dingy roof. 'Then, I travelled like you—through the forests—until I made it to the city. Some guards were sleeping on the side of the road by the bridge, reeking of ale. Took some of their money and a dagger. I was surprised you didn't bump into guards on the bridge on your way in, but likely everyone was sheltering from the storm. It's all anyone's talked about all day. No-one in their right mind woulda been out in it.'

'Yes, I don't know if my mind is right anymore,' Nubia chipped in, yawning and hugging her legs close. She stared into the fire, and her eyelids drooped again.

Gora leant back, watching as the two women relaxed and started to let their fatigue take over. Yoshiko's eyes drooped, too, and the world about her started looking more and more blurry. Gora's voice called out to them that they should rest, but it sounded distant and droning and far away. Her head sank to the hard, wooden floor, and the warmth of the fire lulled her to sleep.

Now and then, as she slept, her mind tuned in to the sound of Gora humming. It reminded her of the days he'd sung before. The songs Gora sang were different from the ones Yoshiko was used to him singing. They were sharper in sound than the songs of his people, and it wasn't Hién either—and it slurred and rocked about. She wondered whether it was a tune from the ship days. But Yoshiko dared not to ask in case it inspired sadness or bad memories of those days in him. And she wasn't even sure whether she had the energy to open her mouth to ask. So she remained silent, and Yoshiko found comfort in hearing Gora sing again, until she fell asleep.

42

To the Palace

The back of Gora's head lolled against the wooden door panels as he sat with his knees drawn up and his arms resting on them. The desire to sleep was surprisingly contagious, being in a room with others who slept so soundly, and Gora often caught himself drifting off and having to try to regain his alertness. Yet no matter how much he shook his head, rubbed his eyes, hit his cheeks, and stretched, the deep sleep in the room drove him into his own. Soon, he was faintly snoring and in a world of his own.

Gora blinked groggily and rubbed his whiskery cheek, staring out the tiny, fogged-over window on the other side of the room. Already, it looked like the light was dimming. If it had been getting light by the time he and the other two had settled down here, they'd slept all day. He looked over at the two sleeping women—curled up by the dim fire in their tunics and with the blanket pulled up as they huddled together. A smile pulled on his face—he'd only ever seen Yoshiko alone before. This was a nice change.

Feeling guilty, he crouched to rouse the two women from their sleep. When they stirred, he told them that the afternoon was fading and they'd have to leave soon. Yoshiko nodded, brushing sleep from her eyes.

'Okay.' She turned to Nubia. 'Nubia, will you be ready to go soon?'

'I will happily get far away from here.' Nubia took a final swig of the ale Gora had brought them from the kitchen. She screwed up her face. 'I do not like this drink.'

Yoshiko laughed and joined Nubia to finish what was left from earlier, eating quickly.

'It's not fully dark yet,' Gora muttered, peeking out of the door to see a full and bustling corridor with roars of laughter reaching from all ends of the inn. 'And why is it so full when we need to leave?'

'We could go through the window?' Yoshiko suggested, mouth full of crushed potato.

'Not much of a noble lady now, are you?' Gora feigned disgust at her bad eating manners.

'I learnt from the best,' Yoshiko said, swallowing, and raising her eyebrows at Gora. 'Hanging around a dirty, rough, foreign pirate will do that to you.'

Gora scoffed, and Nubia chipped in. 'You are a pirate?' she asked between bites of her last crust of bread, face dropping when she realised she'd finished it.

'*Was*. Never had much of a choice.'

'Sounds like we all ended up in places we didn't like,' Nubia said reasonably and left it at that.

Gora opened the window to look out and see whether Yoshiko's idea would work. It was a steep drop, and they were a couple of floors up. When he told them, both women shrugged.

'So what?' Yoshiko asked. 'Are there any people down there?'

'No, it leads to an alley. But there are people in the street beyond.'

'Then we go that way,' Yoshiko said simply. 'If we leave by the door, it will be worse.' She swallowed the last of her ale, mirroring Nubia's face. 'Really, how do people drink this regularly?'

'The water isn't clean or safe to drink,' Gora said. 'You get used to it.' He ushered them to the window and grabbed the blanket to help lower themselves towards the ground, which looked a long way away.

'Oh, it's just like when I ran away from home,' Yoshiko commented airily as she leaned out of the window before climbing out, dropping, and landing easily.

Gora guessed her dragon's curse helped her with that—she seemed to handle things easier than most folk. When Nubia went next, it looked a lot further down, and the ground seemed much harder. He gulped. He never did like drops.

At his turn, Gora pulled himself over the edge, trying to convince himself it would be like when Yoshiko jumped. Of course, it wasn't. The ground came full force, and he fell backwards as he struggled to maintain his balance on his feet. The hard ground met his tailbone, and Gora groaned into his elbow to stop people in the street from hearing his pain. The two women hoisted him up and pushed him against the wall, trying to hide in the shadow of the inn wall.

'Now what?' Nubia whispered, looking anxiously over Yoshiko's head as the people flashed past on the main road, past the back street. 'There are too many people on the street.'

Yoshiko hummed in thought. 'Well, the light is already dimming. People won't be focusing much—they'll be trying to get home before dark. So we'll look like two normal captives. They won't recognise much about our faces or brands in this light. We could pretend to be doing something, and that Gora is our master or guard?'

'I'm not sure that would work—' Gora started, but was interrupted by Nubia.

'It's true; he could look like one of them. And in the darkness, his hair doesn't look so red. It looks more brown, and he will fit in. If we don't speak, but act like in the fields, and he like a guard, we should make it.'

'But I clearly don't look like a guard,' Gora huffed, taking offence.

'You're wearing their clothes, though,' Nubia said, gesturing at him.

'I told you, I stole the first clothes I could find. It's not a full guard's uniform; it won't work.'

'It'll be fine. Let's go.'

The two women nodded together and started shuffling towards the street, hissing to each other about what they should be doing. Gora spun on the spot and implored to the sky with frustration.

'We're gunna die.'

* * *

'It would be much easier if you could turn into a dragon and just fly us there,' Gora panted as they dived into an alleyway to rest.

'As if I could!' Yoshiko retorted. 'And besides, a great beast like that spotted flying over the city towards the palace would cause an uproar.'

'But it's so dark, they won't see.'

'They would!'

'Stop arguing,' Nubia interrupted. 'You two are like bickering siblings. Let's go. The guards have gone.' She leaned around the alleyway and peered into the dark and empty street. Nubia frowned as she stared into the distance. 'We are nearly there.'

Here, the close and cobbled high street widened and the houses and shopfronts became larger and more well-kept. Ahead, a little further up the hill, the street divided into crossroads. This large clearing had a stone fountain in the middle, and Gora longed to drink from it after the difficult journey up the cobbled hill towards the high-society part of the city. But, knowing this kind of country and the lack of safe and fresh water in the towns, he held himself back. Yoshiko, however, ran to cup her hands in the water.

Nubia rushed after her, grabbed Yoshiko's wrist, and hissed, 'You can't. It's not safe to drink.'

Yoshiko's dark eyes widened. But she listened and didn't say another word until they reached the gates of the palace.

Eventually, the buildings on either side curved away and circled a giant esplanade that lay at the mouth of the palace ground's walls. A huge area, Gora could easily imagine military processions beginning from this space. Soldiers dressed smartly and, in their rows, marching pointlessly to the beat of a drum in circles to raise the morale and show off to the country folk. He never saw the point in this. He imagined a crowd of people gathering around the esplanade, and the commotion of clapping and cheering and calling as the band played, and the soldiers marched, and the drums beat, and the gun and cannon salutes pulsed through the air.

He started sweating at the thought.

They crossed the great esplanade, watching as the huge metal gates at the entrance drew closer. At the gates: guards. The trio edged to the side, walking along the circumference of the esplanade to avoid drawing attention. They peered across the expanse and at the building beyond. Gora felt his eyes boggle at the sight of the thousands of windows glinting with the light of the moon, some lit by the orange glow of flaming lanterns and candles within.

'It's so big,' Yoshiko breathed. She tucked a strand of long, black hair behind her ear and stared at the building beyond.

'Your palace was not like this?' Nubia asked—her mouth had dropped open, and Gora could see the bewilderment in her dark eyes that told of her trying to figure out what people would even do with a building of such a size.

'Of course not,' Yoshiko said. 'Nothing pointlessly large, for all things must have a purpose.' Gora saw Yoshiko smile for a moment and her face glossed over. 'It has beautiful carvings and construction: wood and clay, and tiles with carved spirits for protection and fortune. It's incredible workmanship that balances out the simplicity of the size. This'— Yoshiko pointed—'is a huge, stone demon. Like a cliff with myriad eyes lit to watch any who come near: it is a warning and a dare. I feel like I am being stared at. It's terrifying. It does not fit in with the natural world at all. There is no balance.'

At that moment, the peaceful silver of the moon in the windows looked like hundreds of cold, emotionless eyes. Gora shivered, wishing for the warm glow of spirits to fill his body and dispel the icy grip of fear. He rubbed his fingers against his scalp, roughing up his hair and invigorating his head back into alertness.

'Enough of this,' he said. 'Let's go.'

The three ran until they came to the great wall. Here, they tried to find a way in—a place the guards wouldn't be watching. On the far side, a small gate where a couple of slaves hurried in looked like a good option, but guards checked the brands carefully as they entered, making entry by anyone else impossible.

'Over there is a large stretch of wall with plants on the other side,' Yoshiko pointed out when Gora and Nubia were puzzling over what to do. 'I can smell them. It smells like a garden. We could go in there.'

'Of course!' Gora said flippantly, flailing his arms and looking at the young woman in exasperation. 'A section of the wall with plants on the other side in *just* the right place to climb. Not at all an obvious place for people to enter.' He let as much sarcasm as was needed to poison his voice, but Yoshiko, focused solely on the mission now, ignored it.

'The trees are on the inside and too far from the fence to be any use to people entering,' she said. 'But it may give us cover once we're inside.'

The three looked at one another, eyes unsure, wide, and sceptical.

'Right, well, we're gunna die anyway,' Gora groaned finally. 'May as well.'

Yoshiko glared at him but clambered up his back and lead the way up the wall, the three helping each other across. They were stopped at the first hurdle: thorns at the bottom of the drop into the garden.

Gora bit back a cry and countless curses, only letting out a tiny '*fuuuck*'. So there was a trap after all, most likely to stop bare-footed slaves from running away. Gora turned to his side at the anguished sounds of two women trying not to cry out in pain, but they curled and scrunched up their bodies, hands, and faces. Their bare feet had landed in the bed of thorns, which tore into their feet, and they'd dived from the thorns and fallen to the ground, writhing and reaching to pull the thorns from their feet and legs. Even Gora's stolen boots hadn't saved him from some stabbing into his legs and feet, and he winced as he stepped over to the edge, onto the grass. He pulled the little buggers from where he could reach and pulled his boots off to get the rest on his legs. The women whimpered and winced each time they pulled a thorn from the wounds, blood streaking their skin.

'I want to keep these thorns and shove them in the king's eyes,' Nubia spat, voice shaking. 'He is not a nice man. Stealing people to be slaves, setting thorns to punish those who try to seek their deserved freedom. What more is to come?'

She looked at Gora as if he had the answers, but he shrugged.

The trio winced through the garden and into the courtyard, watching out for guards and ducking whenever Yoshiko saw or heard signs of others. Her eyes darted, and her head tilted to the side as she picked up noises Gora couldn't hear. He watched, amazed.

'This feels too easy,' Yoshiko hissed, ducking as she heard something approaching ahead. Her face was set in determination, but Gora didn't like how worried she looked. He agreed. Though it was night, it shouldn't be this easy to steal into a castle.

They dashed between stone walls and dived through a small doorway—possibly used by staff—and entered the belly of the stone beast.

'The stone is so cold and heartless,' Yoshiko breathed, touching the stone and looking around the passageway. 'Who would be happy to live here, compared to the living warmth of wood and bamboo?'

They hid again as footsteps echoed—loud enough for all to hear—at the edge of the corridor where the two hallways met. But the footsteps continued and didn't turn down their way. At this point, no-one dared breathe without trying to control it, for fear they'd be heard. Gora's belly ached from the strain and exhaustion of the night, but they drove on, weaving to a place they believed would be the king's chambers or throne room—whichever came first, they'd start there.

Large doors towered over them in an entranceway—thick, heavy wood with carvings and metal fittings. Many corridors and routes led to this one, central point. Gora paused, pulling Yoshiko and Nubia back.

'If we get caught, we'll never get out. Are you sure you want to go in there?' He looked Yoshiko deep in her dark eyes and gestured towards the doors with his head. 'You said yourself, this feels too easy.'

'I'll do whatever it takes to save my people,' Yoshiko said. 'If I die trying, I can die with honour. If I give up now, I will never forgive myself—I will live in dishonour and have to face my parents in the spirit world and tell them why I failed our people.' Then, her face softened. 'You don't have to come with me. You have come further than I ever expected. Thank you.'

Beside them, Nubia shuffled and straightened her back until she was almost as tall, if not taller, than Gora. 'I'll come,' she said. 'The people of my country have already died for their freedom, but we did not get it. I will demand again. We will go home.'

Gora sighed when both women looked at him. He didn't have a choice, did he? How could he not, at the end of it all?

'Of course I will come,' he said, rubbing the back of his head. 'I let you get kidnapped, didn't I?'

Yoshiko grinned. 'I will make sure the people of Hié know what you have done for us,' Yoshiko vowed, then turned to look around the corner. She must have found it all to be silent, as she began to pad forwards, her bare feet barely making a sound.

Gora's stomach iced over and felt heavy, but he followed Yoshiko nonetheless—he'd come this far on the death ship, right? He couldn't stop here. His senses screamed out in the darkness— jumping at any tiny sound, heart pulsing beyond control when Nubia's hand reached out to touch his elbow. Gora squeezed his eyes shut and tried to steady himself. It was night. They were alone, weren't they? Yet something didn't feel right. He felt like prey being rounded up.

At the large doors, Yoshiko paused. She looked over her shoulder at Gora and Nubia as if seeking their permission. Even in the darkness, Gora could see Yoshiko's doubt. Her face was drawn, her body rigid. Nubia nodded, and Yoshiko breathed out, pushed the door, and slipped through the small gap. She disappeared from Gora's sight for a moment, and he panicked. He didn't want her to go where he couldn't see to protect her. Gora dived through the door, closely followed by Nubia. And when he caught up with Yoshiko, her face was frozen in shock. The three of them stared at the large room on the inside—the ceiling so high above them that they could barely see the carvings and paintings covering the cold, grey stone.

But it wasn't the incredible size of the room that froze Yoshiko's face.

It was the crowd of people watching in silence, and a young, blond man sitting atop a large, stone throne on a platform behind everyone else, observing with the amusement and cunning of a cat.

Gora swore.

43
Kiyohimé

A young man with perfectly curled shoulder-length platinum hair lounged back on his throne and grinned at the three trespassers like a wild cat. All about him, noble guests chuckled behind their neatly gloved hands. Everyone was looking at them.

Sweat iced down Gora's spine. He looked around, seeking an escape. Behind them, guards pushed the heavy doors shut, and other guards closed in around them. He returned his gaze towards the king's teasing eyes, and the young man grinned more.

'I heard little mice were sneaking around my castle. You didn't think we would let you patter in, did you?'

Gora stared at this strange young man—he was gaudily dressed in too much white, cream, gold, and flounce. *What a show*, he thought. But Gora knew it was the young, vain people you had to look out for most, for the praise and control they demanded was for more dangerous than the kings with a simple, military might. Young and spoiled princes had got their place by birth, not by earning it. Gora looked around—all around the young prince were people dressed in colourful dresses and suits, all flouncing, giggling, teasing, flirting. They eyed the young man on the throne and whispered about the three guests.

'Well, come forward. Enjoy your last moments while you can.' The young man in white grinned, looking around at his guests to lap up their praise and amusement. He propped a leg up on the arm of his throne.

Yoshiko strode forward before Gora could reach her to hold her back. Her face had set to determination. The guests looked on in amusement, but the young man simply rested his beautiful platinum head on one arm, a dangerous smile creeping onto his face. Gora hurried after her, gesturing for Nubia to quickly follow.

'King of Acrein, it honours me to be in your presence. I am Yoshiko, daughter of Asumi, daimyō of Hié, noble of Hizen. I have come to discuss the release of my people and the Qeclans.'

Gora opened his mouth to translate, but a voice beside the young man already echoed Yoshiko, translating it into Acrein. Gora was shocked to see a scantily clad Hién girl with chains around her ankles. Gora was pleased to see she'd been kept in good condition, but he knew in his heart why, and why she was kept so close to the platinum-haired man. He looked around the room and started to notice more Hién and Qeclan people, similarly dressed to this woman by the throne. Each was stunning, and now they'd become objects of beauty and bodily sacrifice. He frowned and glared at it all. This was disgusting. Just like the whorehouses the sea scum and pirates liked to visit, and at least they had the balls to call it what it was, unlike these people, trying to dress it up nicely and call it something prettier.

The young man smirked when the slave girl beside him stopped speaking, and she withdrew timidly to hide once more at his feet.

'You, the daughter of the daimyō? A slave? Hah—unlikely. I heard that family was killed by their own council. They didn't even see it coming.' The beautifully dressed man sent a look that was far from beautiful across his room.

Gora translated roughly for her, and Yoshiko's body stiffened. Gora swore he heard a growl. He put a hand on her shoulder.

'You know who killed my family?' Yoshiko growled.

The slave at the young man's feet translated, but he fired back another question without waiting for the woman to finish, smirking. 'You don't know? How pitiful.'

Yoshiko's eyes flashed, and Gora thought he saw a spark in them. 'How can you live with yourself?' she burst out, taking a step forward. Guards leapt to action and got to the ready, but Gora did too, and held out an arm, warning her. 'Taking people as slaves? Taking their freedom and taking them for your own? Our people aren't your belongings.' She gestured about them—to herself and Nubia, to those from their countries in the room. Those people leaned forward, mouths agape.

Once more, the slave girl at the young man's feet leant up to whisper a translation. He roared with laughter, and it echoed chillingly around the stone halls. Then, he stood up, kicked the Hién woman over, and she fell to the floor, struggling with her chains.

Yoshiko clenched her jaw. 'How can you call yourself a king if you treat them as such?' She gestured to the woman, and Gora translated. The Hién woman tried to shrink and avoid being seen.

'I am kind,' the young man said simply. 'I take these people, who live such primitive, awful lives in huts made of mud and wood, and bring them to my kingdom where they can live a better life. They were not true people. I give them work, shelter, food, and things they can do instead of rolling in the dirt, as they did before.'

The young man in dazzling white clothes stepped down from the platform and sauntered towards them. Guards closed in about him as he swanned over. 'Look at you,' he continued. 'Such poor, ugly creatures. Malformed. No hope in the world.' He gestured at Yoshiko, and she wrinkled her face in frustration. 'Now look at your people; you say I stole their lives? Do they not look like they have a good life? I clothe and feed them, make them beautiful. See? Some even share my bed when I am bored. How fortunate! And how generous of me. I'm *giving* them freedom. They just return my kindness by doing things for me.'

He smiled again, twirling his platinum curls around a slender finger, a jewelled ring flashing in the torchlight. He turned away and walked back up the dais, stepping over the Hién slave girl chained to the floor beside his throne, and he signalled with his finger for her to come closer. The woman looked at Yoshiko for a moment before draping herself over his knee as requested. Gora swore he saw the woman pleading in her gaze.

Yoshiko must have seen it, too. 'Our people aren't your accessories.' She gestured to Nubia, who stepped forward and nodded. 'Life here is worse than in our homelands. We are taken to work to breaking point. We live in huts, are yelled at, beaten, lashed, raped, and killed. We've watched our people suffer and lose dignity and hope. This is not a better life. You are deceived to think so. You may dress them in fancy cloth, but that doesn't make them suffer any less. Perhaps your people lie to you if you think the slaves are treated well. It is easy to see their pain by looking at them.'

Gora looked at Nubia, who was frowning and looking about her. She looked wary, and her body had adjusted into a distinctively defensive position. She was watching the weapons of the guards, large brown eyes flicking about. Gora was sure Nubia was barely listening to Yoshiko at this point, more concerned about their surroundings.

The young king snarled, and Gora's attention was drawn back to the dais. He pushed the slave woman aside once she'd translated Yoshiko's speech, and he stood again, in anger this time, not show. All amusement and beauty had left his face, and it now washed over with an ugly smile. *Deranged*, Gora thought, *as all overly spoiled leaders are, truly.* He looked flustered and wild and grabbed the Hién woman by her hair, pulling her up, deaf to her cries. Her hands reached up to grasp her head in pain, and she struggled to her feet against the chains.

Yoshiko roared out and marched forward, meeting guards who held out long spears to keep the trio back.

'Let her go. And let us all leave and take our people with us. Do you think you can do whatever you want? I will not let you do it anymore. Release her!'

Yoshiko grabbed at a spear to stop the guards advancing further, and they panicked, rushing and closing in a circle around her. Nubia cried out and leapt forward, but Gora grabbed her to hold her back. He looked about the room and searched for options. How many guards were there? Could they fight them all off?

A shriek made him and Nubia stare at the platform, open-mouthed. The king looked at the slave girl, pulling her head back roughly with her hair and telling her to translate. The woman cried out as she spoke, shrieks of pain punctuating her words as she stood on her toes to relieve the pain in her head. When she finished, the king's pale eyes flashed like winter lightning, and he kicked the girl from the platform. She fell with a sickening crunch, and a howl echoed in the hall as her body hit the stone floor. She lay whimpering and ignored.

Gora felt a wave of familiar energy emanating from Yoshiko. He was sure he'd felt it before and tracked through his memory to figure out when and why. *There's that warning signal again*, Gora thought. He hunted his thoughts while he watched her standing inhumanly still, staring at the girl on the floor, as the king returned to his throne, sitting heavily into it and glaring at his unwanted guests. His others were forgotten, left to watch in awkward silence.

'I let you come in. I said you'd never get out. I'm bored. Kill them. Even the slaves. She's tainted them for me now. I'll buy some more at the next shipment.' The king's face wrinkled in disgust and stared with a dark expression, cheek in his palm. The guards nodded, fanning out. The Hié and Qeclan people struggled against those holding their chains, trying to shrink back. The king spoke directly to Yoshiko, 'There will be another ship bringing your people soon. You can die knowing your people will never be safe.' Then he grinned. 'You don't even know, do you? I have friends inside making it easy for me. They agreed with me: money and weapons for slaves and access through the lands. They betrayed you. Those closest to you, and you don't even know who they are. Now, goodbye, little mouse.'

Gora looked back at Yoshiko, who was staring at the girl in pain on the floor. A single tear slowly coursed its way down Yoshiko's cheek, and before it could reach her chin, it fizzled and evaporated. He blinked.

What?

The girl on the floor stared at Yoshiko too, eyes wide and mouth open in shock. Then, a wave of heat hit him, and Gora furrowed his brows as the air rippled and shimmered around Yoshiko as if a veil between worlds was changing, and waves of heat undulated on the air. He looked back at the others in the room—no-one had noticed. The girl on the floor stopped sobbing and held her wrists gingerly, staring at Yoshiko. And in this woman's eyes, Gora saw an understanding that death would soon follow, and an acceptance. An acceptance of the fact that she'd rather die at the hands of one of her own, than an enemy. His breath caught in his throat when the woman bowed her head to Yoshiko.

Gora felt the surge of heat radiating hotter. It singed his arm, and he realised why the slave woman looked like she'd accepted death. It was about to be handed to them on a silver platter.

'White fire,' he whispered to himself, before bellowing at everyone in the room, 'Everyone, run! Get outta here.' Gora grabbed Nubia's hand and turned on his heels to race from the hall.

Nubia cried out protests about people always grabbing her to run and screamed out for Yoshiko to follow. The Hién noble didn't even flinch.

The guards at the door closed in to block their exit. Snarling, Gora wondered how to escape. They had to leave. Few people in the room had listened to him, and most loafed about confused, gossiping and drinking spirits. Even the king slumped back on his throne, drinking and glaring at Yoshiko. A few Hiéns and Qeclans and a panicked-looking Acrein noble, at least, had seen fit to slip away out a side door.

Gora huffed. He should have chosen a side door, but now it was too late, and he'd barge through these guards at the main door if he had to.

He didn't need to worry about that, though. A moment later, the guards looked behind Gora in fear and took a tentative step back. Gora dared to look over his shoulder to see why. The air around Yoshiko was thick with waves of light and heat, and even as he watched, it grew more intense. Not wishing to hang around to find out what would happen—*like the barn, ain't it?*—Gora swung around the door and into the stone corridors of the castle.

'Let go; it hurts. I can run!' Nubia called after him.

'Will ya?' Gora bellowed back at her. "Cause we have to, fast.'

'Why—why did we leave her?' Nubia was straining, looking back to the room where Yoshiko still stood.

Gora looked over his shoulder, too, and could see heat waves undulating in the air from the door. Laughter and chaos ensued inside, but he didn't know what would happen. He doubted the guards could kill Yoshiko at this point. He doubted they could even get close without their skin singeing. It wouldn't be long.

'Remember the barn?'

'Of course,' Nubia panted, pulling her hand free from his and running at her own power. Gora was surprised—she was fast.

'Well, it's goin' to happen again. Bigger.'

'Bigger?' Nubia looked behind her once more, and something in her stern expression showed Gora she believed him. She ran quicker, pulling ahead, and Gora had to push to keep up.

They sprinted down the cold, stone walls, not even noticing how dark it was this time.

'Get out!' Gora yelled to anyone they passed on the way out, not stopping to slow down. Nubia joined him in yelling at them, and some listened, immediately turning tail and running. But others stopped and stared, shaking their heads in disbelief before continuing. Gora snarled. He couldn't do much about it now. He'd warned them. They didn't have time to stop and persuade these people any further. They'd be lucky if even they got out. Perhaps he imagined it, but he thought he could feel a heat radiating through the air even out here.

They reached the doorway leading outside just as a thunderous roar and the crashing of stone made them both cover their ears and dive to the floor, crying out.

'My ears!' Nubia howled, curling into a ball and holding her hands tight to her ears.

Gora dared to open an eye and look, watching stone collapse inwards and fly outwards. The grey stone oozed with white-yellow light, making the two squint against the brightness. Even with his hands against his ears, Gora could hear a loud pulsing sound and a tearing. A great pillar of white-hot fire emerged from the stone, melting the inner walls into an orange and black smoking mess. The pillar pulsed out a red ball that washed through the palace like a liquid-flame wave. Gora wished he'd never taken his hands from his ears. Even from here, he could hear the cries of people caught in the blaze or caught too close. Their tortured screams crowed until death took them to a place they'd no longer feel pain.

Nubia tried to run further away to escape the heat, but she collapsed on frail legs. The two of them, helpless, watched the flames bring the palace in on itself as the thick outer walls seemed to about hold the flames back. But even from here, the heat was like nothing he'd felt before. Gora looked over at Nubia—her chest heaved visibly, and her eyes were so wide they showed the whites. She'd probably see the same in him, and he swallowed back the bile that threatened to heave from him at any moment. The smell alone of burning stone and people …

Eventually, the pillar of light weakened, leaving a simple fiery blaze to eat at the remaining stone. A titanic body stirred from within the fire—stretching out and clawing its way over the rubble like a shadowy serpent of death. Gora's breath caught. Nubia moaned, calling out to the sky in her language and reaching above. *There are no gods here*, Gora thought as he listened to Nubia's calling and watched the gargantuan serpent stretch upwards and tower over the burning ruins. Behind the shadowy figure, the sky rippled and waved with the heat, and the tearing noise Gora had heard before echoed louder. Shadows in the rippling sky loomed closer, hues of silvery colours merging with the night sky as the sky ripped open.

'The veil,' he whispered, staring.

Nubia stopped calling out to the gods for help and looked too. 'What is it?'

'The world between worlds.' She didn't understand, so he gestured and continued. 'There, where spirits live. And gods, and demons, and strange things.'

Gora missed what Nubia said next. The shadow serpent clawed its way closer over the ruins, and the firelight hit its body enough for them to see the inky-blue scales of an eastern dragon. The flames licked up the scales and lit them up like starlight, with different hues of blue rippling like ocean flames. From here, Gora could see the size of the beast, and he'd wager it could wrap around a ship a couple of times and squeeze it like a plum. This was the beast that had been hiding in Yoshiko? The one she'd been battling against as she burned up on the ship? Gora's eyes widened as he realised what could have happened had Yoshiko exploded like this on the ship if she'd not been able to control her fever back then, and how easily she'd have burnt that barn in Dunstrand.

The dragon turned its great face, long whiskers flowing on an invisible breeze, to observe the crumbling, smouldering ruins and narrowed its eyes as a crowd drew beyond the garden walls. Gora waited, feeling himself calming as the shock wore off, and he understood more that this was still Yoshiko. He wondered what she'd do next, and whether she'd calm down and return to her human form.

He hoped she would.

But the crowd came closer, and his hopes were dashed. Against the roar of the flames and the purring rumble deep within the serpent-like dragon that sat atop the ruins, Gora could make out words from the crowd. 'Monster' and 'kill'. He stared up at Yoshiko in shock.

'No!' He couldn't let them kill her.

Gora stumbled up, and behind him, a deafening roar forced him to cover his ears once more as the dragon let out an ear-splitting baying.

The crowd pushed against the gates, and guards and soldiers rushed forth with spears, swords, and guns. Gora's blood curled, and he couldn't move or draw his eyes away. Nubia clawed into his arm, and as he looked back at her, he saw her looking for an escape. He was about to rush aside and call for Yoshiko to join them when everyone stopped in their tracks and looked at the dragon.

The wind whipped up, and people had to ground themselves to stay standing. The dragon rose into the wind, staring at those around it, its serpent-like body curling on the current. It snarled. Fiery whiskers writhed like licking flames on the breeze. The waves of heat, hot enough to be visible, pulsed outwards, and Gora and Nubia sank to the ground to escape it, missing the moment the dragon soared into the sky, arching towards the city. This time, the roar echoed on the wind, bouncing on the stone walls of the city and the crumbling ruins of the castle. Everything else silenced. The eerie pause was heavy enough to choke Gora as he watched his friend dive towards the stone buildings, hot wind pulsing and the body glowing blue-white as a buzzing noise grew louder in the silence, becoming the only thing he could recall.

Gora saw the veil of the sky stretch out, and he saw the body of the dragon light up bright before the white flames plumed in the large, open streets of the upper-class quarter of the city nearest the castle. Somewhere among the pulsing buzz that filled his ears, high shrieks of the people emerged. There was another loud pulse of wind as the dragon flicked its tail and swam on the wind over the city. A louder buzz and brighter white-blue glow seeped through her scales. Another plume of white-yellow flame. More screams.

Gora cursed, shaking his head to get the high-pitched ringing in his ears to stop. Fear held him back. The hot, pulsing air and heavy buzzing pinned his body down, and all he could do was watch his friend burn the city, helpless.

He swore again. How could he compete against a frenzied creature? He wasn't one for grand displays of heroism and action. Yet the third time that inky body glowed white-hot through the scales, Gora's legs moved for themselves. The buzzing got louder as he sprinted closer, the pulsing froze his heart, and heat wrapped around his skin. White light burned into his eyes. His senses were overcome by how much of a threat his friend had become. He should be running away, but he couldn't abandon her.

'Yoshiko!' he yelled, feeling the pain of it in his throat.

This was his leader—the new warlord of Hié—he realised. Somewhere along the way, she'd become like a sister to him, the one he sought to protect, to fight alongside, and to fight for. Where she went, so would he. And so he ran towards her, into the mob of people who stood frozen—anger lost, replaced by fear—and past them.

'Yoshiko, no!' he bellowed. His throat felt raw from the heat. 'Stop!'

The third plume of flame crashed through stone, walls collapsing and melting. Gora could make out the tiny figures of people escaping in any direction they could. The dragon bellowed louder, eyes squinting orange in rage—a terrifying contrast to the deep blue scales.

'Yoshiko, I said "no"!'

The dragon curled lazily over a spine of tiles on a large building. The tiles fizzled and cracked, sliding down the sloped roof onto the floor.

Gora halted. He couldn't get any closer; the heat was unbearable. He yelled at her again, and she looked. Then, the giant dragon's body floated slowly to land on the roof of a building nearby, clawing into the breaking stone and curling the serpent-like neck down to look down at him. The orange eyes widened, looking like suns of their own. The maw opened into a snarl. All those teeth …

'We didn't come here for this! Look around you.' Gora gestured all around them. The dragon looked, eyes like slits again. 'They killed and hurt so many of your people—our people. You saw them die. But that doesn't mean you should do the same.'

The solar gaze returned to Gora's, and he squinted at the brightness of everything around him. He would never have believed it was night-time with all this light. Past the dragon, he saw strange shapes moving about in the ripped veil of the sky, and Gora swore he saw eyes. He looked away, terrified at what he'd see, back to Yoshiko.

The dragon huffed. Gora's legs felt like they belonged to a newborn babe, not a grown man. It was like the first time he set foot on a ship and swayed and wobbled about for days. He held her stare, setting his jaw, terrified, imagining the giant maw opening and reaching forward with a snap.

'You said to me before, when you told me of your family's curse, that you never wanted to use your powers to hurt or kill. Those with strength should use it to help the weak. Fire nourishes and brings growth, warmth, and light. You said yourself that the curse didn't need to be bad, and if it cursed you more each time you used it, you'd make sure to use it to your best. Is this your best? Do you want your people seeing their daimyō like this?'

Gora realised he was angry. He scrunched up his fists and kept from swearing. Everything they'd been through, for this?

'I feel let down, and scared,' he growled at her. 'Your people will, too.'

The buzzing stopped suddenly, and the pulsing air faltered. The crowd murmured behind him, most in confusion. But the Hién people looked on in fear and awe. They'd understood, and they waited.

Yoshiko's eyes shifted to them, and her eyes faded to gold. *This is a good sign*, Gora thought as his body melted into a puddle of relief; he was sure his legs would buckle.

'Shut it.' A guard clouted a Hién man around the head, knocking him to the ground.

The dragon's eyes flashed orange again, and Gora cried out. The dragon leapt from the stone, and the crowd scattered, leaving the Hién man who'd been hit trying to pull himself up and away while clutching his sore head. The dragon landed with a ground-rumbling thud beside Gora, wrapping her serpent-like body in a large arch around the two men, and she stared at the man who had fallen to the floor, waiting. Time stood still for both men.

Gora wondered if she'd been trying to protect that other man, in her own way. Yoshiko's eyes flashed back to gold, still staring at the Hié man on the floor, and a blue-white light licked like flames around her. The creature's body shrank and wrapped up in flames, becoming more human each moment, until a small woman stood in its place, staring sadly at the man. The woman wrapped her tunic tightly around her as if cold, her face dropped with a look of fatigue and sadness, and her legs trembled. Gora rushed to hold her up, taking her arm over his shoulder. Yoshiko opened her mouth as if to say something, but she paused. A tear took its place. She held a hand out to the man on the floor.

The silent surprise of the crowd didn't last long. A cry sent stabbing pains up Gora's spine. He looked about for Nubia, who was already yelling his name from the far side of the crowd and leading the way, running around the crowd and beckoning him with her arm to follow. Gora looked at a fatigued Yoshiko and knew she couldn't run. He squinted his eyes tight for a moment.

Gora opened his eyes. 'I'm sorry, my lady,' he said, letting her go.

As she swayed on the spot without his support, he drew his arm back, struck her, and caught her as she dropped unconscious into his arms. Within a second, he'd swung her over his shoulder and darted into the burning city away from the mob, following a yelling Nubia into the burning streets.

44

Escaping Acrein

'She is a monster?' Nubia grabbed Gora's sleeve once he'd caught up, both stumbling through the smoky streets, away from the burning flames of the palace and the upper city. 'She killed them all, and she did it at the farm, too. With the barn. Haruki …' Her voice trailed off.

They'd slowed to a walk to navigate the chaotic streets, Gora gasping for air from running with Yoshiko slung over his shoulder. Acrein citizens rushed towards the fires to see what had happened and put them out, ignoring people going the other way, even slaves. But Gora knew it wouldn't be for long. He had to get Yoshiko out of this country—and everyone else. Preferably on a ship that would take them back to Hié.

Gora reached over and patted Nubia's hand, but she instantly drew it back. He sighed. Fear filled Nubia's eyes. But if she was still coming with them, it couldn't all be bad. 'She will be distraught to hear she killed them. I'm not sure she'll recover. I don't think any of us will.'

Nubia nodded. Silence overcame them, and they came to a halt. Gora shuffled Yoshiko on his shoulder and strained, looking about for somewhere safe to hide her for the time being. He saw a small alleyway to the side and wondered whether it would do, guiding Nubia there and laying Yoshiko on the ground at the back of the alley where the shadows were darkest, furthest from the streets. He crouched beside her, feeling her burning forehead and scowling as it scorched the back of his hand—like that time she'd touched him at the port in Hié when they first found out her people were being taken.

'We need to return,' Gora said, trying to remember which way it was to the port from his explorations here while waiting for Yoshiko to make it to Rödsted. 'Back there, the guards yelled for the leader of the navy to be alerted, and the slave catchers. They'll be on their way to Hié soon. I have to take Yoshiko back to her country to stop it.'

'How will you get back? You have no ship. No-one to sail it. And you cannot beat an armada. This country is powerful. They have fast ships.' Nubia punctuated each point with a clap of her hands.

Gora grinned, and Nubia looked at him wildly. 'Aye, but ye forget, lass. I'm a pirate. Who said I had to get that ship legally now?' Nubia frowned at him, standing with her arms akimbo. Gora raised his eyebrow and sighed defeatedly. 'I'll do what I can. That's all. They'll need a few days to prepare the army and the ships at least. If I can get us a head start, we might make it and get our side ready to defend.' He rose to get going but stopped and looked back at Nubia. 'Could I ask you to stay and watch over her as she sleeps? Keep her safe?'

He felt nervous she'd not want to anymore.

'She will not attack me?'

Nubia's face was still ashen. Gora felt sympathetic.

'She won't. I promise.' He continued when he saw Nubia's uncertain face. 'Did she attack you after the barn or ever give you any reason to fear her?'

'No.'

'Then please think of her as who you have known. Yoshiko hates killing. She tries to solve everything through diplomacy—

too much so. She's probably going to be more scared of herself than you are of her. Please take care of her until I return.'

'Where will you go?'

'To find a ship and a crew. As you said, I don't have one.'

'You'll steal it?' She still looked dubious.

Gora flashed her a bright grin and threw his arms out casually. 'Of course.'

At the Acrein port, Gora acted like a casual sailor, confused by everything going on and slightly hungover—his go-to disguise. Behind him, yelling and action intensified as Acrein people tried to stop the fires and guards stomped about in a search for a Hién slave girl. He spun around, fearful someone had recognised him. What he saw was worse.

A Hién slave woman of about Yoshiko's age left a shop carrying heavy buckets of fish in water. Gora winced, wishing he could yell out and warn her. People screamed, and soldiers killed her on the spot, their swords stabbing through her abdomen and out the other side before pulling them back in gushes of red. Her body dropped, and the buckets crashed to the floor, spilling fish, blood, and water across the street.

Gora turned away quickly, taking quick and deep breaths. No Hién girls were safe. He tore through the crowd, not caring who he pushed out of the way, fighting to get to the port. *Fuck all this. Fuck all these people.* They had to leave. He doubted any Hién people—even the men, though they'd not been the ones who'd been seen turning back into a girl after being a flame-breathing dragon—would be safe at this point. People feared what they didn't know, and now they probably thought all Hiéns could turn into beasts of destruction, as stupid to imagine as that was. They were all going to die.

In the port, ships lined up at different stages of unpacking and repacking. Mostly merchant and trade ships, they were wide-hulled and would fit a lot of cargo—perfect for long-distance sailing. He tried to spot one that was repacking. As he did, Gora spotted a line of Hién slaves crouched, tied to a bench, waiting to be taken as labour for a ship. Behind them, Qeclan workers slouched about and waited, too, for measly pay and no better option. Gora had an idea.

He sidled over to the gathered Hién and Qeclan people and pretended to be occupied with looking about the port. When he got there, the bile he'd fought back from the palace and his fear of Yoshiko returned. What had happened to the slave girl brought it all back, and he tried to momentarily hide as he bent over to release his stomach of its contents by a wall. A few sailors laughed and clapped him on the back, teasing him about a rough night at an inn, but they mostly ignored him. When he'd stopped heaving, he wiped his mouth with the back of his hand and glanced at the nearest Hién man and spoke to him. Gora pretended he'd be sick again soon, leaning against the wall gingerly. The Hién man jumped at the red-haired man speaking his language.

'You, Hién, can you sail?'

The man tried to ignore him, but Gora pushed. To hide his speaking, the Hién man hid his head in his arms and bent forward. Gora grinned, wondering what the man would say.

'You dirty foreigner—putting us in such a place and then thinking you can speak in our language?'

Gora blinked and rubbed his stomach as he thought. But before he could respond, the next Hién man along hissed at them.

'Hunter? You mean you don't know the red-haired hunter?' Then, to Gora, 'So they got you, too? None of us are safe.'

They looked more downcast than ever when he next glanced over.

'Aye, it's me,' Gora said, and then he pushed again. 'And I said, "Can you sail"?'

They nodded and stared at the ocean. 'I was a fisher in Hié. What do you want, Hunter?'

'I need a ship and a crew. I need to take the daimyō's daughter home. War is coming.' He pretended to groan and crouch.

'The daimyō and her daughter disappeared before we were taken. You can't fool me.' The man sighed and fell silent.

Another overheard and joined in, whispering, 'Did you say the daimyō? She is here?'

'No, they killed her,' Gora said, spitting and standing up straight, wiping his mouth again. 'And her husband before that. But their daughter is here.' He turned and saw the anger cloud the Hiéns' faces, and even the Qeclans were watching.

'War is coming. You'll be killed if you stay. I saw a Hién woman murdered—she was just carrying fish. Will you help and leave?' Gora asked, spotting a man who'd noticed him loitering too long. He tried to hurry and get to the point.

'We are in chains. What can we do?'

'If I free you, will you help me find a ship and sail it to Hié?'

The sailors glanced at each other and then back at Gora. One bowed his head slightly, the others copying. Then, a hand grabbed Gora's shoulder.

'What you doin', sailor?' the voice growled in traders' language. 'No-one talks to them.' Gora turned to see who it was. The man's pale beard was a huge mess and smelt of stale ale, and his head lacked a single strand of hair. Gora swore he could see his reflection in the man's head, and he grinned, finding it amusing, causing a deeper snarl on the man's face.

'Sorry, guv'. I thought they laughed at me pukin' last night's ale out. Wan'ed to give 'em a piece of my mind.' Gora grinned, patting the man on his shoulder.

The man stiffened but glared over at the Hiéns and Qeclans, who were pretending not to watch. 'Yeh, well, get away while it's safe. Ain't good to be speakin'. They'll think yer up to summat. Heard there's an issue with slaves up in the city—don't get in trouble.'

Then, the man looked warily at them once more before he stalked off, waving his arms as he shouted orders at another group of Qeclans loading cargo onto a ship. Gora heard him yell something about the cargo being hauled today. 'Goin' too slow. Ship needs to leave tonight! Hurry it, ya sea slugs.'

Gora grinned and glanced at the others by the wall. 'Spread the message to as many Hiéns and Qeclans as possible this afternoon. 'S time to leave. And we'll get *that* ship.' He gestured with his head at the one the bald man just stomped onto and yelled at more Qeclans.

Then he looked about to make sure no-one saw him speak. Gora stuffed his hands into his trouser pockets and slumped past the dock and stalked the city, trying to pass his message onto as many others as he could. Many tried to hide from him, not believing him. He swore—it would help to have Nubia here now. And Yoshiko, if she was awake.

There were few Hiéns in the streets, already having heard about the threat to their lives. Gora saw the carcasses of a few already left in places in alleys—mostly young women. Their black hair sprawled over their bodies, and Gora felt his stomach heaving again. He found a group of Hiéns huddled in some bushes on the edge of the city and spoke in loud Hizen at them before they could run away. He passed the message onto them, too, and asked them to spread it, but he didn't stop to see if they'd understood. Then, he returned to the place he'd left Nubia and Yoshiko, uncertain whether he'd done enough.

'Most Hiéns are hiding. I'm not sure we'll have enough to be able to save them, but we'll have to leave this afternoon either way. I spoke to Qeclans, too—we're not leaving you all behind here.'

'This afternoon?' Nubia asked, daring to peek out from the hiding place.

'All ships are ordered to leave port before nightfall. The navy will come in tomorrow at dawn to prepare for war. They're headed for Hié. We *must* be on the ship this afternoon to make sure we're on before it leaves.'

'And the crew?'

'I chatted to some Hién and Qeclan sailors. All sorted. I wanna get as many of both peoples out as we can. So many Hién people have died already—' He paused for a moment, thinking of those bodies of the Hién girls.

'If they're killing Hiéns, do you think my people will be next?'

Nubia's face was clouded with worry, and Gora felt sad with her.

'I don't know. So far, I haven't seen it. But we can't be sure. That's why I want your people to come with us. We'll figure out how to get you home when we get out of this place.'

'Thank you.' They both looked at the pale, sleeping Yoshiko. 'Will she wake in time? What happened to her?' Nubia sounded stern.

'I punched her,' Gora admitted, rubbing the back of his head.

'You punched her? Why?' Nubia clicked her tongue at him and crossed her arms, giving him the sort of look a mother would give a child when she scolds them. He remembered that look from many years ago—from another life.

'I had to!' He waved his arms. 'It was for her own good. We had to escape, and she was too out of it.'

'Whatever, punch your leader.' Nubia flicked her hand at him. 'When she finds out, you'll be the one to face the fire.'

'Literally,' Gora chuckled.

And, when Nubia continued to scold him, he laughed all the harder. In the end, she gave up, nostrils flaring, sulking and waiting out the day. When mid-afternoon came, she was the first to stand. 'Let's go.'

'So you'll come, too?' Gora asked uncertainly, and he brushed himself down as he stood.

'Of course. I will not stay in a land I am not free. I will escape with you and those others of my people who can. I would be a fool not to. Then I can find a way home and find my husband. And I will follow her. Even if she is a monster of destruction.'

'Now, *that's* the spirit.' Gora grinned, earning another click of Nubia's tongue.

They held Yoshiko up together and picked their way towards the port, hiding when anyone came close. At the edge of the port, Gora ducked behind a stack of empty crates. Here, he could see the whole port. And when he looked around, he saw more eyes peeking out from places all around the dock, including the roofs of surrounding buildings. His heart lurched. People from both Hié and Qecla were waiting—they'd managed to spread the message to a large group, at least.

The mission suddenly felt impossible. With so many lives relying on him making the right choice, Gora felt uneasy.

'There are many people who have come,' Nubia whispered, also peeking over the crates.

'I worry they'll be seen if we can see them.'

Nubia shook her head. 'It is because they are looking for us that we can see them. They are making themselves seen to us so we don't miss them and leave them behind. Besides'— she stopped and gestured to a group on the docks—'if you're just seen as a worker, and you look like you're doing a job, you get ignored by those who do not wish to see you.'

Gora thought about this for a moment and realised many of the people trying to escape were pretending to look busy, particularly the Qeclans who had fewer reasons to fear being seen. Gora nodded to himself several times, running his hand through his hair as he figured out the next move.

'Which ship?' Nubia asked, distracting him again.

Gora nearly snapped at her but held his tongue. She was as anxious as he. He pointed to the one the bald man had stomped towards earlier. 'That one. Where the Qeclan man stands on the walkway with the box.'

Nubia followed his finger, squinting to see. 'How do we get Yoshiko there? There are many guards and sailors. If what you say is true about them killing Hién girls, she will not be safe.'

Gora tried to think again, spotting several small handcarts to the side that sailors used to load heavy cargo. He pointed to it and asked Nubia to bring it. She strolled out with her head low, stooping her shoulders and dragging her feet as if she'd lost hope and had no drive to do anything other than survive. Gora admired how easily she could act, and he marvelled at how different she looked than how she usually held herself up high. Gora caught himself staring and blinked back to the moment, wondering how to hide Yoshiko in the cart.

Spare sails, he thought.

'The spirits will kill me,' he moaned as he stuffed Yoshiko between layers of spare sail and rope he stole from a nearby ship. 'Pushing nobility around like cargo.' He grinned sheepishly.

Nubia gave him a funny look. 'If that is what will make your spirits or gods angry, I worry for your people. Are you not saving her?'

He shrugged and stood back. 'If I push it and you walk, it will look weird. You push—it will look like you're working. I'll walk with a pack and look like a sailor heading for the same ship. I'll bump into you on the way and help somehow.'

Nubia agreed, so she slowly bumbled along, dragging her feet, wheeling Yoshiko closer to the ship. Those who waited for an escape sign leant forward from their hiding places. As she got closer, Gora strolled out, bouncing across the port with a pack thrown casually over his shoulder. He whistled merrily to himself and scanned the port to see Hiéns and Qeclans watching him. The ones he'd spoken to earlier were still chained and sat on the side, watching his every move. He winked cheerfully and reached the walkway where Nubia was grunting and struggling up the ramp.

'Get outta the way,' he moaned at her loudly, trying to get past the side. 'Do yer job prop'ly.' Nubia muttered an apology but glared at him. 'Yer gunna fray th' ropes, idiot.'

Gora grabbed at some dangling ropes and threw them back in the cart, pushing her and the cart up the ramp to speed it up. Nubia stumbled forward, but made it up, rushing to the place Gora whispered as the likely storage area. Gora swore and strode to the cabins, redirecting himself at the last moment when no-one was looking and following Nubia into the hold.

They quickly hid Yoshiko and rushed back onto the deck with the cart, looking to see how many sailors were already on board. The bald captain was barking orders somewhere on land, pointing at parts of the ship and bossing foreigners to finish soon. Some of the last sailors would come as it was about to set sail.

Well, they'll miss it. Gora grinned.

The captain caught sight of him striding off the deck and called him over, squinting at him.

'Yessir?'

'Eh, I remember you. Pukin' your guts out, aye? Well, ye'd best be over it—we gotta leave. Get them slaves you tried to pick a fight with and get 'em doin' their jobs. I want this ship ready.' He thrust a key at Gora and stormed off, swearing, shouting at anyone to get him a drink or make the ship right. Gora couldn't believe his luck. The captain had unwittingly lost his own ship.

Biting back a grin and trying to keep nonchalant, Gora swaggered over to the chained sailors. They watched him warily, worried the red-haired man was coming straight over to them and would give them away.

'Oy, you!' he growled loudly in Acrein as he got closer, trying to keep in disguise. 'Cap'n wants you.' He didn't know much else of the language. Gora unlocked them.

Slumping and stretching, the workers looked at him knowingly and shuffled a little too quickly towards the cargo their fellows were already loading. He groaned to himself and yelled at them a few more times for effect. Then Gora looked about to see others watching eagerly. He'd have to start stowing them, too.

Gora gestured subtly to a waiting Hién, who slipped from the shadows and grabbed a cargo box.

'Take it on and hide ye'self,' Gora hissed, looking away and quickly yelling at another. The Hién bowed his head and did so, as did the next, and the next.

But from the shadows, Gora saw more, anxiously watching and leaning forward, fearful of being forgotten. Nubia was returning with the cart and more sails.

What's she doing?

'Oy, you!' he called. Nubia jumped. And, for a moment, she looked stunned to see him boldly stomping around. 'Got Captain's orders,' he muttered. 'What're you doing? Get yourself on!'

'There are more women,' Nubia said, gesturing her head. Her eyes were set with a determination that he knew instantly not to argue with. 'They asked me to get them on. Women can't just walk on board as easily as men in this country. They think women will curse ships if they sail.'

'How many?' Gora panicked, knowing he'd have had to find a way to get women on, but still not having figured it out. He looked around, trying not to get caught for talking to her.

'Many. Near the crates.' She left, heaving the cart up onto the ship and down into the hold.

Gora cursed again. He rubbed his palms against the scratchy stubble of his cheeks and looked around, wondering what to do. He waved an arm at some Qeclan men hanging around, trying to look busy but obviously watching him for a sign of their part in his plan. They eagerly jumped into action. They were tall and lean—perfect for this role.

'Those crates.' Gora gestured. They looked at the edge of the docks where Gora and Nubia had hidden. 'There are women hiding there. That Qeclan woman is trying to smuggle them on. Too many women working around the ship, though, and it'll look weird. So can you help hide the women and bring them on? Or find any other way. As quickly and as subtly as you can.'

They shuffled off, and Gora growled another curse under his breath. He saw more Qeclan and Hién men joining them, whispering instructions to one another. Gora put his hands over his eyes and moaned.

'We're gunna get caught,' he said to himself as he paced about to find something to do.

Gora frowned and monitored what was happening on the ships—many heavy crates were being loaded, and many empty ones were being removed from the ship before being loaded heavy again. 'Well, *they're* clearly women,' he mumbled to himself, catching a pair of Hién people carrying something on board. They'd covered their heads with hats, but the bodies were still clearly women—not that the Acreins would notice. Everyone foreign probably looked the same to them.

When Nubia didn't return from the deck, he strutted on board and pretended to observe the work in the hold. The captain shuffled off to talk with the master of the dock. Gora saw them process paperwork. *Fuck.* Gora rushed to find Nubia. They didn't have much time before the master called to leave. He found her crouching with the other Hién and Qeclan stowaways, by Yoshiko.

He gawped everywhere about him—in all nooks and filling the room, were stowed people.

'Some men told me to hide,' she explained. 'They will bring the rest of the women.'

He nodded. 'Good on them. We will leave soon. The captain is getting papers with the dockmaster.' People looked on at him in confusion. 'It means the captain thinks the ship is nearly ready. It's now or never.'

Hundreds of pairs of eyes widened at the realisation. 'Is everyone on board?' someone asked. Concerns flooded their faces, mirroring Gora's feelings.

Gora shook his head. 'Not yet. I need to get them on now while the captain is on the dock.'

He rushed back onto the deck and tried to look for the eyes that watched him from the shadows. What signal would he give? He looked about helplessly and tried to think about what wouldn't be noticed. At that moment, a Qeclan man pushed up the ramp with a cart. Adrenaline flooded Gora's blood. This was it! He ran to the Qeclan and signalled particularly widely with his arms and yelled overly loudly for the man to get the cart on, loudly cursing and saying it was time to go, to get the last on.

The Qeclan's eyes widened, but he nodded and looked behind him, gesturing to a few behind him also pushing carts. They hurried. From the deck of the ship, Gora watched as figures— Hién and Qeclan, men, women, and children—darted out, slipping and ducking and weaving between crates and barrels and talking sailors. As they reached the ship, they panicked and dashed up the gangway to the deck. People ran straight on, but there was no other option, and Gora knew it.

'Is that everyone?' Gora hissed, grabbing the last Qeclan with the cart and gesturing to the area the women had been hiding behind the crates. Gora's stomach flipped when the man shook his head.

'A few more.'

Fuck. Sailors were shifting and watching the ship full of slaves, pointing and chatting. 'Go,' Gora said to the man, and yelled for another to grab the cart off his comrade. 'Go, get them now. Walk there, run back. Run with them, and don't stop running. It's the last.'

Urgency and panic filled his voice and lit the same in the Qeclan man's eyes. The tall man nodded and rushed off. Gora dared not look. He rushed about the deck, hissing orders at any Hién and Qeclan who said they could sail—they had to get the ship ready to pull away.

On the port, people called out, watching, gathering attention. Still, Gora didn't look. He rushed about and directed people to get the ship to sail. It wasn't until a cry of alarm went out on the dock that he rushed to the port-side banister to find the cause of the call. Several more Hién and Qeclan men and women dashed across the port. Panic filled their eyes—he could see it even from up here—and guards and sailors rushed to stop them. To his right, Gora saw the tall Qeclan man sprinting with four more women— three Hié and one Qeclan—weaving between sailors and guards that watched in confusion.

A cry went up in Acrein, guards drew their swords and tried to grab at escapees, and the captain dropped his papers and strode out to yell at someone about the noise. Then, he saw his ship. He looked in panic, seeing stowaways running onto his ship, and looked up at Gora in shock. The bald man's face turned to stone. He ran towards them, yelling at everyone to stop them. Sailors began to flood onto the port from the inns, packs flung over their shoulders, a swing in their steps, ready to depart that afternoon for the navy to come in after them. They, too, stopped and stared at the riot that filled the port. Guards, sailors, and escapees pushed and punched and ran. Gone was their smooth escape. This was mayhem.

A Hién woman fell to a punch, crashing onto the ground and trying to crawl around legs. Holding her cheek, she pulled herself back into a crouching run between the legs of the sailors that pushed at people behind her. A Qeclan woman reached out a long arm to grab her and pull her up, and they both ran towards the ship, slipping through the grabbing hands of sailors and crying out in panic. Behind them, a mob of Acrein guards was close behind, heading to barge up the gangplank.

Gora bellowed to the Hién and Qeclan sailors on his ship to leave. Then, he called over for someone to help him on the gangplank, kicking and barging at the guards and holding them back. Ahead, screams echoed as two Hién men got caught in a blockade of guards, pierced by multiple swords, falling before they could make it. Gora's breath caught. So close.

Gora grabbed onto the rails as the gangplank rocked. Someone above cried down for him and the other man to come aboard so they could pull the gangway in and depart, but Gora saw one last Qeclan man—who'd been hauling cargo onto a different ship—diving towards them at the last minute—pushing through the crowd and shouldering large Acrein brutes out of the way. He roared in determination. But the crowd had pushed forward, blocking him, and Acrein sailors and guards crashed towards the gangway. Gora charged up the gangway to get out of the way as his stowaway crew yanked it up after him, all looking back at the Qeclan man blocked in the crowd. Gora didn't see what happened next, but he heard the screams.

45
To Hié; to War

Yoshiko tore her eyes open and sat up frantically, searching about her, hyperventilating and watching in confusion as the flames disappeared. Everything was dark.

Yoshiko forced herself to breathe calmly, but the memories returned, and she cried out again. *What have I done?* Yoshiko curled her legs up to her chest and buried her head on her knees. She felt hot tears burning in her eyes as she remembered the young king kicking the slave girl off the platform and then the world turning to white flames returned to her.

A hand reached out of the darkness and gently touched her shoulder. Yoshiko jumped.

'Yoshiko, we are safe now.'

'Nubia?' Yoshiko blinked and cried out again. 'Nubia, the fire—what have I done?'

The hand stayed on her shoulder, but the woman sat beside her without saying a word. Yoshiko dared not look at Nubia for fear of seeing hatred or fear in her friend's face.

'I just wanted to bring my people home. Yet, somehow, I've killed so many of them, and—' Yoshiko's voice broke, giving way to loud, ugly, heartbroken sobs.

Yoshiko covered her face and screamed into her palms. The screams of others from the palace and the city echoed in her memories. How could she have done that to those people? Nubia reached and pulled the screaming girl close and held her until the sobs subsided. If not for Nubia's embrace keeping her grounded, Yoshiko was sure she'd have drowned in the memories of the night. It wasn't like the time she burned the barn, where she only saw the aftermath. This time, she remembered it all.

Boots thudded beyond Nubia, and a man's voice cried out before a thud of weight crashed beside them and arms wrapped around her. He smelt like the sea.

Yoshiko barely heard what he was trying to say. Instead, memories of fire engulfed her, and the room became crumbling rocks with sprawling burnt bodies and flames so harsh and bright they could have only belonged in demon stories. The rock melted around her, and Yoshiko remembered a crowd as she clawed over the smoking stone ruins, and Gora and Nubia's faces below her. The horror in Nubia's face … Yoshiko's heart sank into her stomach and turned to stone. The looks on all those faces. Yet her anger had stayed with her, and she had launched towards the city, tumbling in the air and burning innocents and the upper city to a smoking ruin.

She'd flown, but it was nothing like the freedom she'd sought; instead, she'd turned everything into a burning hell.

Yoshiko heard the man's voice again. Was it in the memories or the dark room? She couldn't tell. She trembled against Nubia's warm embrace and wailed into the woman's shoulder, seeing only flames. A rougher hand shook her, calling out.

'Yoshiko!'

He'd called to her then, too, in the flames. A man had run to her, pushing the opposite way to everyone else, risking the flames to stand once more below her. Gora. She recognised him and his autumn hair—it looked almost like the fire, now—but she didn't recognise the look on his face. He was disappointed, and he spoke to her then, but his words blurred and echoed now when she tried to remember them, like they travelled through water as her mind faded back to the dark room she sat in now, inhaling Nubia's smell.

'Yoshiko, you're safe now. It's okay.' The rough hands took over both shoulders, pulling her away from Nubia and gripping her tightly, shaking her and becoming more insistent. The flames dissipated, and Yoshiko found herself staring at the autumn-haired man in the dark room. He was as panicked as back then, with distress marring his usually light and lilting voice.

Yoshiko held her breath and stared at him. The man's face relaxed as she calmed. Nubia too, beside them both, relaxed and shifted into a more comfortable position. Yoshiko thought about what her father had said about breathing and becoming calm. Gora nodded with her as she focused on her breathing, neither dropping their gaze. He kept his hands on her shoulders the whole time, staring into her eyes and keeping her grounded in this dark room, in this time.

'Aye, that's it,' he reassured her. 'Just breathe. You're safe. We're *all* safe.'

Then, Yoshiko gasped and made both Nubia and Gora jolt as she panicked and reached out to touch her wrists and ankles. 'Where are we?' Yoshiko asked, looking between them both and her wrists. 'Did we get taken again?'

'Taken?' Nubia asked, looking at Gora with a frown.

'It's a ship? Are they taking us somewhere?' She looked about the room, seeing a dim light seep into the darkness somewhere. She felt a rocking. 'But there's nothing chaining me down.'

The other two let out a nervous laugh, relief washing their faces. Yoshiko raised her eyebrows and egged them for an explanation.

'It *is* a ship. But it's fine. We're sailing to Hié.' Gora let a grin flash for a moment across his face.

'Gora is captain,' Nubia chipped in. 'We stole a boat!' Yoshiko noted pride in Nubia's voice and chuckled. 'So you are safe. And so are the others.' Nubia gestured around them at others sitting in the room, watching them or resting.

Yoshiko wanted to disappear from embarrassment at what they'd just seen.

Gora rubbed the back of his head nervously and sighed. 'We'll tell ya the story later. But for now, we sail home, but we sail home to war.'

'War? What happened?' Yoshiko looked between them again.

And once again, Gora and Nubia looked at one another, expressions darkening. Nubia clicked her tongue and gestured with her arms to Gora, who sighed and rubbed his face. He looked worn and stressed, with wild facial hair, hollowed eyes, and a haggard look. Yoshiko wondered when he last slept. He opened and closed his mouth a few times, looking at her and then looking away again, before finally returning a sad gaze at her.

'You killed the king, and they want revenge. They're sending an armada to Hié.'

'We started a war?' Yoshiko asked, trying to process it.

They both nodded, watching anxiously as they waited for her to return to her mourning.

'Fuck!'

Gora jumped and looked at Yoshiko in shock before bursting out laughing. He held his stomach and roared, wiping his eyes and laughing some more at the confused look on Nubia's face. 'Now, *that*,' Gora said between gasps, 'is something I never expected to hear from you. Been hangin' out with me too much, eh?'

Yoshiko pouted. Surely, if there was ever a time to express oneself in such a way, it was now? 'You curse all the time,' she fired back. 'Can't I?'

Then, Yoshiko stood up, brushed herself off, and put her hands on her hips, looking at them both. She couldn't mope and let her mistakes bring war and death upon her people. Every action had a consequence—she had to face hers. They looked up at her, Gora still with amusement on his face. The ship rocked, and Yoshiko swayed with it, having to catch herself and regain her stoic pose for the effect she hoped. Then, Yoshiko stormed out of the cabin, up the steps, and into the light. Behind her, she heard Gora and Nubia racing to keep up.

On the deck, Yoshiko looked about at everyone there. Qeclan and Hié; men, women, and some children. Yoshiko frowned. How many hundreds of each country's folk had been brought, and how many escaped with them?

'I wish we could have helped more,' Yoshiko muttered. Beside her, Nubia hummed an agreement.

People watched as the three strode about the deck, first to the stern to look behind—nothing was following yet. It was a vast expanse of ocean and sky. Then, Yoshiko ran to the bow, bare feet padding on the wooden planks, wobbling slightly as she tried to catch her sea legs. Ahead yet lay more open sea and sky. But this time, she imagined home. She wondered what the threat of the council was now, and how scared her people were to walk at night and disappear. Then, Yoshiko thought of the greater threat she brought to them from over the seas. What she'd sought to save, once again she'd brought the blade upon double.

Yoshiko cursed once more under her breath and turned to face Gora and Nubia, who gazed over the edge. 'We must make sure their ships don't reach the shore,' Yoshiko said to them, looking down the ship towards the stern side. Soon, Acrein would follow from there.

No-one noticed the single black dot on the horizon behind them, following from a distance too difficult to see.

46
Making Plans

The days passed endlessly on the ocean. Throughout the journey, Yoshiko, Gora, and Nubia met with people of each country and tried to learn more about their skills. They organised people to help with the care of others and the preparation of meals and rations; people to help sail; people to collect fish in ingenious ways on their journey to feed them; people to offer help in the preparation of the defence of Hié.

To Yoshiko's amazement, they'd received support from the Qeclan people to sail first to Hié to try to stop the war. Of course, the Qeclans had been upset that they'd not be able to go home yet, but with Yoshiko's promise that she'd do her best to accommodate and take care of them in Hié and ensure they had a safe route back to their country when she'd been able to stop the Acrein forces, they agreed. Nubia had been a wonder, here, translating and discussing with her fellow people. And now, Yoshiko was stunned as Qeclan people did whatever they could to support the journey back to Hié and the preparation of what was to come.

'It will take a lot of work to build things up again,' Yoshiko said one day to Gora as she slumped against the bow railing of the ship. She looked out over the water towards the east—to where she knew home was.

Gora, on a rare break, leaned on the railing with his elbow, chin in his hand and light eyes reflecting the blue of the ocean. 'If you're building it back up, you may as well build it better.'

'What do you mean?' Yoshiko looked at him from the corner of her eyes. He was deep in thought, and dark shadows clouded his tired eyes.

He yawned. 'Well, many countries and the people of those countries would do anything for a chance to make it better for all peoples. It's going to take effort to build it back up. You may as well make it better. Rare opportunity, I think.'

They fell silent as they stared towards the horizon. True, Yoshiko had always been interested in learning more about the people and interacting with them. In the time she'd been in hiding, she'd loved how they helped one another and had a joyful experience of life. They tried their hardest, had a simple and logical view of things, and were more honest than those in power had been. No matter what kind of domain it had been when her grandmother and mother developed it, something had gone wrong. Perhaps including the people in the rebuild would give it that joint interaction she wanted it to have.

'I have an idea,' Yoshiko said, stepping back and looking about the ship. 'Can we meet in your quarters? With those people we thought would be good to help us plan the defence?'

She referred to three people they'd previously met and identified as potential leaders for their plan, and Gora gave a single nod before walking off. Yoshiko went to find Nubia telling stories with some of her fellows and asked her to join them for a meeting.

'What is it?' Nubia asked as the door to the captain's quarters was pulled shut behind them. It was a tight fit with six people, and she nudged her way to stay standing beside Yoshiko.

'Do you have pen and ink?' Yoshiko asked Gora, looking about the captain's desk that Gora had claimed as his own.

Gora rummaged about in a chest and found a bottle of ink. Then, he unrolled the map he kept on the desk, put it upside down, and weighted it down. Yoshiko took the pen and began to sketch from memory a rough map of the coast and region of Hié and the neighbouring domains.

'There's a secret cove, here, the foreigners and council wouldn't know about. It was used by my ancestors to guide fishingfolk to feed our people in a siege when the harbour got blocked off. We'll land here.'

Yoshiko pointed to an area on the map and circled it. The Hiéns in the room muttered in surprise, and Yoshiko continued. She drew lightly on her sketched map to show the way.

'There's a route up the cliff we can take into the town. From there, we'll send people to warn their friends and family and bring them to the underground caverns.'

'You're sure you want to take them there?' Gora asked. 'You said it had been kept secret for generations.'

'It was made to be used in situations like this, to protect our people. And there needs to be a place we can gather in secret—to keep people safe and arrange the next steps. We can't do that with guards or the council sniffing around, so the caverns are the best place.'

'My lady, what are the caverns?' an older Hién man with salt-and-pepper hair, Ishikawa Morio, asked. He was brought to this meeting for his fighting experience in the samurai guards.

'Below our main town lies a network of caverns—an underground city. It's where my mother and I hid. There are many exits. It'll be the ideal place to operate.'

'But what of the ships?' a Hién woman with the family name of Fujiwara, another samurai, said. 'And how do we defend? We don't have a navy. We've only ever fought enemies from the land—other warlords of Hizen.'

'When we land, I want this ship prepared to go back out to meet the armada before it lands. Gora, you know the seas, and you know how to fight on them. Can you help our people to prepare with any other ships we have and go out with them?'

Gora frowned. 'Perhaps. I'll see what we can do. But with mostly fishing and trading ships, we're low on options. We'll have to fight dirty.' He grinned. She saw the same wildness from when they sailed his fishing boat to catch up with the death ship.

'Please, do whatever you can,' Yoshiko said. 'If we can get close enough to attack the ships in secret, sneaking on board or causing a hassle that will get them breaking from the inside, then we can take down as many ships as possible before they get close to the coast.' Then she looked at the others. 'While the ships are being dealt with at sea, I want a group of people dealing with the council—splitting up and picking them off one by one where they can't draw on each other's help. I refuse to believe all the guards believe in the council's vision. I imagine many will have been blackmailed. If there's a way to regain the samurai, I would do that. We need their help to defend and rebuild.' Yoshiko looked down at the map again and took a deep breath, wondering if there would be a way she could find Chinen, if he was still safe. If she could, she knew he would be able to help her gather the samurai to fight back. As one of the military leaders, he would be the best to lead them.

The Hién folk in the room looked downcast, and Nubia and the other Qeclan fighter looked confused. 'They are the great warriors you told me of, who swore to protect the daimyō, are they not? Surely they will help.'

Yoshiko nodded and looked blankly at the table. 'I know some were killed for their loyalty to my parents. Others would have killed themselves to die with honour, rather than live in dishonour and failure.' At this, Nubia clicked and muttered about it being a waste of good warriors' life, but Yoshiko continued. 'Some may have been taken as slaves if they were seen as a threat—immediately removed from the city—as many worked and lived locally and would have been able to return quickly and fight the council. I only hope some managed to stay alive without betraying my parents. I don't know.'

The room was silent, each thinking. Then, someone piped up, 'We were attacked.'

Everyone around the table looked to Ishikawa, who bent his head to hide his face. He bashed his fist on the table and bared his teeth as he spoke. 'They came to our homes in great numbers at night. Lord Hitoshi was on the way to his political talks with Shogo, and those of us who stayed in Hié went about our lives and duties as normal. But men came in the night, some were foreigners, and they attacked our homes. I, Ishikawa Morio, couldn't protect my family.' His voice caught and a tear slid down his haggard face. 'My wife … my wife and son died. My daughter was taken alongside me but died on the ship—an illness.' His voice hitched with pain, and he grimaced, rubbing his eyes. Then, he continued. 'No matter how much I and those of my house fought that night, we were overrun and refused all honour. Other samurai were taken onto the ship with me—all of us broken, grieving. Our families and homes and villages destroyed before our eyes. We had no idea Lord Hitoshi never returned from his trip. Or what happened at the palace.

'I dishonoured myself—I could not protect my people or my region. I gave up hope, thinking I deserved to live as a slave as punishment for my failures. But when I heard a ship was being stolen to take us back to Hié, I knew I had to do anything to return—to take my revenge and regain my honour by fighting again for our people.' He sniffed and finally looked up, eyes filled with tears. 'I don't know what happened to my comrades, but I'll fight for you with everything I have. I swore my loyalty and blade to the noble family. I'll fight for its last member as I promised.'

Yoshiko was stunned. Her eyes stung with tears to hear the man's story and see the pain on his face. She opened and closed her mouth, but nothing could honour what he and his comrades went through. Then, the female Hién who had been listening quietly until now piped up.

'My name is Fujiwara Masa. My husband and I were also samurai for the daimyō. He went on that trip with your father, Hitoshi. He never returned.' Masa looked Yoshiko directly in the eyes—her expression and posture strong.

Yoshiko froze. She remembered the name being called that day. The woman continued.

'I taunted myself when I heard the news. I thought he might yet come home, struggling and wounded, even if he had to crawl. For he was strong and skilled and determined. But I've learned it was a fool's hope. I wished I had gone with him, but my duties were elsewhere. I wanted to die with him in battle if need be. Instead, I was left behind. Only a few days after the news, I was stolen in the night. They set our holdings on fire, and my children and I ran to escape the flames. My children were slaughtered as we ran from our home—blinded by the smoke and unable to see the blades that awaited them. I was taken and put on the ship before I could fight. So I'll fight with you now—I'll regain my honour and join my husband and children in the spirit world.'

'I feel your time has not yet come,' Yoshiko whispered, unable to speak for fear of her voice breaking. She looked at the two samurai and couldn't hold back the tears. 'I had no idea. I wish—'

What did she wish? That she'd known? What would she have done? Would it have strengthened her or disheartened her to know so many of her parents' supporters, their families, and their villagers were being slaughtered?

I wish I knew more about my people, she thought, miserable.

'It is decided, then,' the sixth member—the Qeclan man, Ayodele, who was a large part of the Qeclans agreeing to sail first to Hié—said in a booming voice. He towered over the table, arms crossed on his great chest, and his soft yet serious, large brown eyes looked evenly at Yoshiko—like equals. Nubia had translated their stories for him and translated what he said now into Hizen. 'I failed to defend my home when the slave catchers came. We failed …' Ayodele looked at Nubia, who nodded with a dark expression. 'I won't fail again. There's a home that can still be saved. Then, we can return to our home. I'll fight, too.'

'If you don't destroy all the ships that come at us, we can take one to return to our homeland,' Nubia teased, looking at Gora now. 'You two are reckless. Keep one for us!'

'It is decided, then,' Gora repeated Ayodele's words, and Yoshiko bowed her head. He smirked. 'Let's pummel those bastards.'

47

Speaking with the People

A disturbance erupted on deck as fishingfolk among them ran forward. 'The cliffs!'

Feet pounded on the wooden deck as Hiéns and Qeclans alike ran to look, crying out in awe and relief. For Qeclans, it was a new world for them, and one they eagerly soaked up as Hién people who knew the coast excitedly pointed to areas they knew—the parts of the cliffs that looked like a bird in flight, the nooks the children played in in the rock pools. Few Qeclans understood what the excited Hién folk were saying, but the joy seeped through.

Yoshiko watched from near the helm, feeling a mix of relief and pride. She ran her fingers over new bumps and ridges on her shoulder and the back of her neck. It was smooth and hard, like a shell—the beginning of scales—and she knew it was spreading each time she accessed the curse's abilities, like her mother had said. Yoshiko remembered how her mother had looked when she died, with scales lacing her skin.

A lull in the conversations on deck brought Yoshiko's attention back to the present, and she moved her hand away from her shoulder. As the ship pulled through the network of jutting rocks towards the Hién coast, people pulled each other into embraces, crying with relief, smiling and chatting and finally feeling free. Yoshiko knew then she'd fight for her life to make sure these people would remain safe and happy like this. A few more scales wouldn't hurt her, would they?

Rubbing her neck once more, Yoshiko turned to Gora and a Hién man at the wheel and began the discussion about the route that would take them into the secret harbour. As she turned, Yoshiko noticed Gora watching her hand closely, seeing her run her fingers over the scales. She dropped her arm immediately and tried to act innocent. He raised an eyebrow but said nothing.

'Where's the harbour, my lady?' the man at the wheel asked, squinting into the waves beyond.

She pointed. 'Head for where the ocean disappears at that point, underneath the stone formation on the cliff that looks like a bird.'

A woman had pointed the bird's face in the cliff out earlier but not understood why it was there. Many generations ago, a carver had cleverly carved a rough hawk from the rocks that jutted out from the cliff. It took many of his years of experience to make it look like a chance formation of nature, and many people still marvelled at the supposed happenstance. Few alive today knew it meant a route into a small crevice.

The navigator frowned but guided the ship through the rocks. His face was still and stern, and peppered black hair caught the coastal breeze. He pushed his hair from his face and squinted once more ahead.

'But doesn't the coast join here, my lady? I've sailed these waters for years and never noticed a place even a tiny boat can sail to. The two cliffs meet ahead. We'll crash.'

'We won't. It's an illusion.'

The man raised his eyebrows in disbelief but continued, grimacing slightly as he pulled the ship towards what he thought would be its end. Then, he called out for three sailors to watch either side and the bow of the ship, telling them to yell out if he was to get too close to rock he couldn't see. Gora helped the man steer on tight turns, guided by the crying out of the sailors on watch. All people on the deck hushed. No-one wanted to be too loud to be heard on land now, or, worse, to cause the man steering them to mishear his guides and run onto the rocks.

She saw the fisherman's eyebrows unknot. 'The cliffs—'

The place he was certain the two cliffs and coast met fell apart to create a gap, wide enough for a ship to pass through and disappear into its valley. It took careful steering, particularly with the large Acrein ship, but soon, people were rushing once more to the edges of the deck to gawp at the cliffs separate ahead of them.

Once down the throat of the entrance, they could see a small, natural harbour—enough for the ship to pull around and drop anchor to let them people onto the stretch of rock and sand that circled the lagoon. The sailors ran about the deck, preparing the ship to land. Everyone else gathered in groups, trying to stay out of the way, eager for what came next.

Gora returned to the wheel after guiding the landing procedure and watched Yoshiko with a strange look. She raised her eyebrows at him, imploring him to explain. When he didn't, she spoke. 'Good luck.' She rested her hand on his shoulder like he sometimes did to her. 'Work well with the others, and don't try to take on a whole armada on your own. Our people will happily help you, I think.'

She smiled, and he returned the grin—and it filled his whole face. 'I can say the same to you. You be careful with the council. You, more than anyone, need to stay alive. Need a new daimyō.' Yoshiko nodded at him. 'And remember, it's okay to rely on others. You need your people as much as they need you.' He looked about them. 'They want to help you.'

Gora rested his hand on her head, and Yoshiko felt it calm her. Without thinking, she rushed in to hug him, burying her face into his shirt. It smelt of sweat and the sea, but it was better than the scent of alcohol that always used to cling to him when they first met. They'd both changed a great deal since then, she thought, and grown closer than she expected to. He'd become her friend—a true one—and someone she could trust. He'd followed her into the abyss and dragged her back out again. Yoshiko couldn't help but wonder what would come of their friendship when they stopped the war and began to rebuild Hié. Would he go back to hiding in the small village by the forest? Would they rarely see each other again—her in the city and him by the mountain? She wanted him to stay and remain her friend, not disappear as Haruki had.

But this wasn't the time to think of a future they couldn't guarantee. Who knew what would come next? Death was still a possibility.

'Don't die,' she muttered, muffled into his shirt.

'Yeah, you too.' Then, he whispered, 'And no turning into a giant ball of flames. You can control it. Plus …' he held her at arm's length now and looked her over. 'It's starting to show—there's a shine on your cheek. Happy for people to see you like that?'

She sniffed and pulled away. 'It's who I am.' Then, she bowed slightly and turned, walking down the gangplank and onto the stony beach towards the crowd of people waiting for her.

* * *

The people had divided. Some would head straight for the city; others would finish landing the ship and then head for the city. There, they'd go to find their families, show they were safe, and take them to the caverns. Then, those who could sail would go with Gora to arrange the attack of the Acrein ships and set traps.

Gora, with the help of Hién and Qeclan sailors, pulled in the ship and cleaned her down. For a moment, Yoshiko allowed herself to stand and watch, marvelling at his command. Then, she took that wonder and turned it into an effort to lead just as well, guiding the people up the steep zig-zagging path up the cliff.

At the top, Hién people ran to their families. Yoshiko looked at the Qeclan folk and sighed. The looks in their dark eyes mirrored how she felt, too. There'd be no running to families for them yet. Perhaps some would be like her, never to run to families again. She swallowed back that painful thought and waved for them to follow her.

Nubia caught up with her as she guided the group to the closest entrance to the caverns from here. There would be a garden on the edge of town, and even in the darkness, they could see the masses of trees that stood tall and a pond in the centre—they could hear the gentle rippling and lapping as pondlife darted about beneath. Here, between the wall and a tree, lay an entrance to the caverns. Yoshiko disappeared behind a section of wall and pushed a heavy door.

Within, she lit a torch on the other side, and a gasp went out among the Qeclan folk. She passed a couple of torches out and told them to walk straight for a while. Then, when the people had finished filing in, she pulled the door closed behind them.

No-one else should be coming this way tonight, she thought, catching up with the front of the group to guide the way.

People muttered to one another, asking questions about what would follow and how such a place was possible. But all muttering stopped when they reached the first main cavern. The massive hall carved into the rock opened out ahead of them, larger than some of the villages some of them had come from, with small stone huts dotted about a central, unlit hearth. Above, the roof curved into a speckled dome, and the people whispered in awe.

'This is under a town?' someone gasped.

Yoshiko couldn't help but smile.

* * *

Throughout the evening, people of Hié filtered into the tunnels, and as they came into the central cavern, all had the same response. People shuffled through the last tunnel to see the large, stone cavern, lit with a roaring hearth in the middle and lanterns around the edges as Nubia and her comrades had rushed about the room to give it light and more life. The beautiful orange glow gave the caverns a warm feel, and the lanterns around the edge opened it up considerably.

Praise for the caverns grew louder, and children cried out at how large and wonderful it was, wanting to run into the open spaces.

'The first three halls we found had no-one,' one woman said to Yoshiko, guiding her family behind her. 'We were worried.'

Yoshiko looked at the family's faces, seeing the remains of immense joy and sadness still visible. Their mother had come home. Yoshiko smiled at them and told them to find a place to settle and feel comfortable.

As more people joined, Yoshiko hunted for the joy in their faces, too, hoping many of the escapees had found their families safe and alive, and had rejoiced in the reunion. But each time people came in with heartbreak frozen into their eyes, Yoshiko's heart froze over a little more, too.

But she couldn't save everyone. How many times since she'd known him had Gora told her not to become too reliant on that hope? *Is that what it is to rule?* She wished she could ask her mother. How did Asumi remain sane, not taking on the feelings of the people?

In the back of her mind, Yoshiko knew the answer. Her mother barely met with the people. She worked mostly through the council and governors. This, as close as Yoshiko was now, was probably the closest a noble family member had been to the people for generations. This saddened her. How could they rule if they didn't know their people?

That evening, Yoshiko learned many things about being the one people look to for aid. As crowds of people flooded into the large cavern, they flooded around Yoshiko, having heard of who she was. They bowed, asked questions, asked to meet her, thanked her, wished to speak with her, sought advice, and all manner of business that kept her surrounded and occupied until the room buzzed with noise and Yoshiko saw it was full. It energised her.

Though she imagined most people weren't returned, she knew she had to speak to the masses while she had the chance. A war needed planning, and people had things to do, and Yoshiko felt she shouldn't wait any longer. It was now or never. She tried to find a place to stand to address the crowd, but she found nothing she could stand on. Ayodele looked over and saw her looking about. He gestured his head and she followed to a hut with a cut-away window and a slight ledge. This would do. She smiled at him, pulled herself up onto the ledge, and held onto the hut with her spare hand. Ayodele quietly closed in to be there if she fell, and the crowd began to hush.

'My name is Yoshiko, daughter of Asumi, late daimyō of Hié. I come with bad tidings and a plea for your help.' *Too formal.* She cringed, feeling her cheeks and ears burn and body begin to sweat. Nonetheless, she continued, 'Today, some of you had loved ones return to you. Many will already have told you where they've been. For those who don't know, I can confirm the terror. The council has been working with Acrein foreigners to take our people and sell them as slaves overseas.'

There was an uproar. Yoshiko waited.

'The council turned out the palace. They killed the daimyō and her husband; they kidnapped and sold many of the castle workers. And they kidnapped and sold many of us from our own towns and villages—sending us overseas to suffer at the hands of others. I have been there. I've seen how they treat our people and the people who are now our friends and allies.' Yoshiko paused here and gestured to some of the Qeclans around the room. There was an uncertain muttering between Hién people who had never seen these strangers before. 'Now, war comes to our lands to make us suffer more. We escaped, but they chased us.

'I need your help. We have war coming from the sea and a council in our own country that forces our warriors to act against their own people. Our country isn't safe. Nor are our people. I need your help to protect our home. Will you help me bring back peace?'

There was more muttering and silence, and people looked to one another for comprehension. Then, an old man in the middle of the room yelled, firing his arm into the air. People looked between him, Yoshiko, and their families. Then more hands went up. Among them, Qeclans, too, reached up their arms and cried out in their own language. Yoshiko spotted Nubia reaching up with both of her hands and crying out in a mixture of the two languages, making people look at her and chuckle in surprise.

Yoshiko grinned. Before she was taken to Acrein, she thought she had to regain the castle before she could do anything else, and she thought she had to do it alone. But here, with a crowd of people to help her, she wondered at how foolish she had been.

Then, someone asked, 'But how do we do it?'

The mutter went up again, but Yoshiko felt ready now. 'First, we must take down the council before any more damage can be done from the inside. I refuse to believe our military stands alongside them and believes what the council is doing is right. I wonder: how many are being blackmailed to keep their lives? To keep their families' lives? How can our own guards do this without feeling regret, and without some sort of threat to make them do it?' Yoshiko looked about at them again, thinking of the stories she heard on the ship from Masa and Ishikawa. So she asked, 'Who here has friends and families among the guards?'

Many hands went up.

'How many of them have you seen in the last year or so?' Yoshiko said, prompting.

The consensus was simple: most had not seen them in a long time.

'I wrote my brother off as a bad egg,' a man at the front grumbled. 'He refused to come home. He ignored his children. He acted with dishonour. But if he is being blackmailed, if he is suffering at the thought of his children being killed, I will feel ashamed for giving up on him.'

He looked up at her, and he received echoing agreements from people about the room; people passing on his message, and parents wiping tears from their eyes at the losses of their children to the military. The peoples' eyes implored Yoshiko for help, and she felt like she'd freeze under the pressure.

But in the end, her heart won out. She thought of her friend, Haruki, disappearing, and the disappointment and worry she'd felt then. It must be the same—even worse—if your family in the military was here and not able to see you, if you thought they'd betrayed you.

A foolish idea tumbled from her lips. 'I want to trap the guards and bring them home.' The cavern was quiet. She looked at the man, now. 'If your brother is being blackmailed to do the bidding of the council, at the threat of his family's life, then I want to know. We can bring them back and have them fight with us and help us remove the council.'

'But how?'

In the end, the people agreed on holding a last-minute festival to disguise their rebellion. People yelled out ideas, planned food stalls and ways to lure the guards in and then trap them and take them back to their families, and keep the council unawares with signs, games, and the full festival energy to distract them. And when the people split off into groups to plan it, Yoshiko tried to arrange her next mission: breaking into the keep to unseat the council. When someone came forth, a maid in the keep, Yoshiko grinned at her fortune and at how things worked when the people came together.

'Tomorrow night, will you be able to find someone to sneak myself and another woman into the keep?' Yoshiko asked the young maid, looking over at Masa, who had vowed to come with her.

The maid nodded, nervous but determined. Her small face was set.

Calligraphers, artists, and children offered to make signs and banners, chefs offered to open up cart stalls of festival foods, and dance groups offered the entertainment. This made sense, Yoshiko thought. Why not have a group of people led by industry or skill experts who could speak up for themselves and their fellow people? She sat down and watched the crowd as they spoke in groups and planned what they would do, wondering if there was a way she could form the new council to work like this. Ahead of her, Nubia and a Qeclan man picked their way through the lively crowd towards her.

'And what shall we do?' Nubia asked. Her dark chestnut eyes shone, eager.

Yoshiko decided to test her recent thought—leaving it with the people who knew best themselves. 'What would you like to do? What do you think you'd be best at?'

Nubia and the man looked at one another, both shrugging.

'We can cook, dance, play music, and join in the festival to distract the guards,' she said, translating her words to the man who nodded and agreed. 'We could wear masks and costumes so we don't cause suspicion. And some of us can fight and join you in taking the guards back or come to the palace.'

'Sounds good to me,' Yoshiko said, slumping where she sat and feeling like her body was diving into sleep. 'I trust you to organise that. Nubia, can you arrange it and report to me? You know your skills well. Fair?'

'It's fair,' Nubia nodded. 'I will talk to them and see how we can help.' She then told the man something in their home language, and he walked off. Nubia crouched next to Yoshiko. 'You need to sleep now. Everyone is sorting things out themselves. You need to know when it's okay to pull away.'

Yoshiko yawned and rubbed her eyes. Then, she massaged her temples. The noises were flooding into her ears, and she couldn't focus to block them out. It hurt.

Nubia chuckled and clicked her tongue as if she were scolding a young child. 'Sleep. I will have someone wake you at dawn, plenty of time, if you tell me how I will know what time it is down here.'

Nubia guided Yoshiko through the crowd towards a hut at the edge of the room, away from the bustling crowd. The noise was a little quieter, and the hut was dark enough away from the campfires and lanterns. In there, a group of children slept, curled up or sprawled out. The room had a peace inside it that drew Yoshiko in, and the sleep of the children ushered her own closer. She swayed under Nubia's grip and would have collapsed on the spot if her friend hadn't been holding her up.

'Can she sleep here?' Nubia asked a mother who crouched between a group of children.

The woman looked up and smiled, nodding and watching as Nubia gave Yoshiko a place in the corner.

'Please take care of her,' Nubia said. 'She needs sleep.' Then Nubia thanked the woman and turned away.

Yoshiko watched Nubia duck out of the small door frame, the darkness of the hut soothing her instantly as her head rested on the cool stone.

48

Omatsuri

Yoshiko was woken by a woman shaking her shoulder and calling out gently. It was still early, with people sleeping, eating, or rushing back up towards the city to begin the coup and regain the domain. People bowed as they noticed her, and she smiled back, enjoying being a part of this for once, even though the situation that enabled it was so horrific.

Someone ushered her to the fire for hot green tea and a serving of rice and miso soup, ensuring she gathered her strength. The woman feeding her was filling her for a long battle and chattered about what was to come. Yoshiko smiled and listened as she gratefully ate what had been prepared. Twice, Yoshiko rose to leave, mentioning her thanks, but the woman, in her middling years and with a kind, soft face, firmly insisted she eat her fill.

'You look like you've barely eaten in months. Extra will do you good.'

While basic and made out of simple ingredients they'd been able to bring together and carry down here, this simple soup with fish and vegetables was enough to feed several, and Yoshiko felt like nothing was tastier. Was this what cooking from the heart tasted like? A parent's cooking? Yoshiko thought back to the old farming couple and the food they cooked. It was like that, and she used that strength to drive her.

Yoshiko was pleased to see people had spread out and made themselves comfortable and safe. She headed for the hut she'd left her belongings in before they'd gone on the death ship. Yoshiko excused herself to those who'd taken it as their refuge and ducked inside. There, behind one of the corners, were her things. Gora's, she noticed, had already gone. He must have already been and gone again to deal with the ships and coastal defence.

She pulled her things from the hidden alcove: her spare clothes and things she'd collected along the way, her mother's things, and her father's sword. Then, she followed someone to a local bathhouse, enjoying her first bath for months and finally feeling clean.

For the rest of the morning, Yoshiko observed the planning of the festival. The region looked like it was going about its usual business. People scurried and strolled through the streets, shops and markets called out cheerfully and ushered people inside, and fishingfolk prepared their catch to sell. It looked normal enough at first glance, and Yoshiko hoped the guards and council wouldn't notice the change.

She admired the view. This was home. She could recall the streets and houses and gardens from the times she'd darted through streets and leapt across the rooftops with her mother and then Gora. Now, seeing and beginning to know the people, she realised she felt the buzz of life: one she knew she'd always wanted to be a part of and had been missing in the keep.

Yoshiko thought back to the times she had roamed the streets, disguised, after leaving the castle. She'd soaked up the energy of the people and wished she could have been a part of them. These people had been so free, she had thought. They could walk without threat of being seen, not being doomed to be caught and returned to the castle to be killed. But their buzz of life had been disturbed by the mysterious disappearances. People had become afraid and hurried, looking about them as they scuttled about their businesses, closing early and hiding in their homes. Now, finally, she and they would have their time. They were fighting back to regain the joy and buzz of life without threat.

A nearby restaurant ushered two guards in to enjoy a morning meal. 'Discounted, dear customers, to celebrate the excellent catch this morning! The fish is wonderful. Never seen anything like it …'

The guards went in, and Yoshiko was sure they'd soon be pounced on by a team of townsfolk, ready to confront them about their families. A woman ran into the restaurant, and a cry went up. Yoshiko wished to peek inside to see what was happening, to make sure the people were fine and the guards didn't hurt them. But she remembered what Gora told her. She had to learn to rely on others.

'I'll leave them to it,' she said, verbalising what Gora and Nubia had told her. It was time to let the people do it. They wanted to save their home as much as she did.

Feeling a pang of loneliness, Yoshiko wondered where Gora and Nubia would be. Gora would still be out at sea, setting up traps for the Acrein ships with the Hién fishingfolk and trade ships. So she searched for Nubia. She wandered the streets, watching as people pulled up lamps and banners for the festival and taking deep breaths to smell the vegetables, fish, and meats lightly frying at the food carts and rice cakes being dipped in soy or coated in a thick, sweet bean paste. Her stomach growled, but she kept looking for Nubia. She wanted to eat with her friend, anyway, to show her the tastes of Hizen and the local Hién regional foods.

Yoshiko peered through the crowd for a face she recognised. Ahead, the woman who had fed her the hotpot soup was calling out happily into the crowd, selling little paper windmills for children.

A figure appeared behind her. 'Take this. It might not be safe to show your face yet.'

Yoshiko jumped. 'Nubia? I found you!' She turned to face the older woman and grinned to see her wear a full stage costume and *oni* mask to hide her beautiful dark skin. Her heart already felt lighter to see her. 'Well, you found me.'

Yoshiko took the mask Nubia offered: a kitsuné spirit.

'I and some other Qeclans are performers.' Nubia gestured excitedly to the outfit she was wearing, did a twirl, and moved her mask to the side to speak properly. Yoshiko noticed Nubia's smile was wider than ever, and her dark eyes shone like onyx. 'The layered clothes cover our skin, and the masks cover our faces. No-one sees we are from another country. And the dancing is fun. It's different, but if we dress as spirits or ogres, we can dance as we want and people laugh, thinking it's the act. They don't know it's a dance from another country. And the children are cute. They join in.'

They laughed and walked through the festival streets as the stalls went up, Nubia covering her face again with the *oni* mask. Yoshiko smiled to herself, wondering of all the things Nubia would be remembering so she could tell her husband when she found him again. Yoshiko hoped they found one another.

The smells wafted closer again, and Yoshiko's stomach growled again. 'Well, this is my first festival, too, so let's enjoy it while we can, even if it is a cover! I want to see how my country celebrates! I want to eat as many sweets as I can before the war; I may never eat them again.'

Yoshiko grinned and pulled Nubia by the hand to the nearest stall selling toasted rice cakes, asking excitedly for two of both flavours. She then handed half of the sweets on sticks to Nubia, whose eyes bulged at the sight.

They lifted the masks enough to use their mouths and Nubia stared as Yoshiko devoured the rice cakes, soon left with just the sticks.

'You're like a child!' Nubia said, amazed.

'So tasty!' Yoshiko cried between mouthfuls of sticky rice cake, licking the red bean paste from her lips. 'Eat it.'

No sooner had Nubia finished hers did Yoshiko pull her up and to another food cart, and another, and another. Yoshiko devoured anything in her path, especially sweets. 'You weren't lying about the sweets,' Nubia groaned, managing a wobbly dessert covered in light brown dust. 'I will be sick. How are you managing this?'

Nubia looked over at her friend, and Yoshiko looked back, her cheeks bulging like a chipmunk. Nubia gawped.

'I'm catching up on everything I missed while I was away. And I've never seen so many commoner foods. They're delicious. How many different things can you make from rice? It's wonderful.'

Nubia flailed her arms and clicked her tongue. 'As if that's an explanation.' She put her empty bowl aside and held her stomach. 'I will eat no more sweets. I cannot manage it. I am craving the taste of vegetables and meat.'

Yoshiko gathered Nubia's bowl and returned it to the cart. 'I can go for that. Let's find a grilled food cart. There's one near the windmill stall. It smelt great.' They wove through the crowd. 'I wish I could just turn into a dragon safely. I want to eat it all. My stomach is too small like this.'

'Too small?' Nubia hissed, leaning closer to Yoshiko. 'I have never seen a human eat as much as you! Not even in my village after a long, tiring hunt!'

But their conversation cut there. Nubia cried out as a guard grabbed her and pulled her around. Yoshiko's heart leapt and she jumped around the fight him, but he quickly looked about him and leant forward with wide eyes and began to speak.

'Fujiwara Masa sent me. She says it's time.'

Yoshiko and Nubia looked at him through their masks, and he muttered his leave before bowing lightly and turning, disappearing into the crowd up the hill. He turned again, peering back at them, and gestured for them to follow him.

Nubia sighed, and Yoshiko could see her peering at the grilled food cart that was still so close.

'You keep handling things down here. Meet me later. Take this and make sure you try some of the savoury food. It'll do you good.' Yoshiko handed Nubia a couple of coins and grinned. She'd never been able to buy a treat for a friend before. Then, with a wave, Yoshiko darted up the hill towards the guard, who led her towards the inner town for the next stage of the coup.

49

A Name

'Are you certain I'll get in like this?' Yoshiko pulled at the indigo fabric around her legs, looking up at Fujiwara Masa in the back room of one of the restaurants in the upper circle, near the castle. The restaurant had been closed for normal business but was open for the people of the town to act out their coup and make it look as if it were business as normal. Yoshiko looked back down at the kimono. It had been months since she'd worn one, and the lack of legroom and movement instantly frustrated her compared to the looser skirts and clothing she'd been given from the Acrein slave farm, as rag-like as it had been. She'd have to get used to this again, though she wished she could put a *hakama* over it. At least, then, she could move a little more freely without worry of exposing too much of herself if she got too overzealous in her movements. She frowned.

'You look like a maid, don't worry,' Fujiwara Masa said, trying to reassure her.

Masa was dressed identically and would be joining Yoshiko into the keep to find the main perpetrators. She explained they'd be joined by a few others, along with a familiar face, who Masa said had offered to help them get into the keep after hearing the rebellion talks in the caverns.

'Suki.' Yoshiko's cheeks burned as the young maid raised the curtain separating the restaurant from the backroom and shuffled in, remembering the last time she saw Suki had been the time she'd abandoned her new maid in the gardens after running to meet her father.

Yoshiko hadn't been able to apologise for it, having been escorted by her mother's guards from the main hall after the news of his murder. As she apologised now, Suki was graceful and gracious and blushed at receiving an apology from the daimyō's daughter, explaining that her main relief had been discovering Yoshiko was alive. She agreed with Masa that Yoshiko looked well disguised. 'You'll be surprised at how you can go unseen in the castle grounds if you go as they won't expect. They won't expect the long-disappeared daughter of the daimyō to be there as a maid.'

Yoshiko nodded, hoping they were right. 'And the others? Didn't you say we had a few more to join us?' She turned to Masa and raised an eyebrow.

'They were waiting outside while you changed.' Masa leant out of the room and called out for someone to join them, and Yoshiko heard two pairs of footsteps coming towards the backroom and then smelled a strangely familiar scent. She couldn't figure out where she knew that smell from, thinking it was one she can't have known too well, when the owner of it stepped gently through the doorway, parting the curtain and stepping aside to allow the other in—two samurai, only one she vaguely knew. A young man with a slightly side-swept fringe and a lightly wavy, dark brown, short ponytail and a youthful, smooth face. She stared at him, recalling the day she'd met him in the gardens the day she'd heard of her father's death, noticing how his beautiful face looked more severe, haggard, sad, and she wondered what he'd seen since that day, when he'd been bright-eyed and youthful and obviously eager to go further. His deep brown eyes met hers with a frown, and she found herself thinking he'd changed a lot from back then when he couldn't meet her eyes, but he quickly caught himself and looked away again, the faint blush crossing his cheeks. Yoshiko looked at his comrade, a slightly shorter but older man with a shaven head and stubbling facial hair, and eyes hollowed and wrinkled with worry and age as if he'd seen the worst horror a man could face. He couldn't be much older than her parents had been, if that, Yoshiko thought, and with the way of Hié at the moment, she didn't need to think too much about what could have happened to make him grave like this.

'This is Daiki, captain of one of the samurai corps, and Ikeda,' Masa said, voice low. 'They say they have news to help us take back the keep.' She returned to the side of the room and stood beside Yoshiko.

She's like my guard, Yoshiko noticed, watching the older woman. Then, her eyes returned to the two men who'd entered the room and she bowed lightly to respond to their own. Yoshiko gestured for them to speak freely, and she watched as Ikeda looked cautiously at Daiki first. *What is their relationship?* she wondered, knowing that Daiki would be Ikeda's captain but confused as to why Ikeda seemed to be the guardian.

The young man spoke first, and Yoshiko was reminded of how smooth his voice had been back then, and how, given different circumstances, she might have even followed Chinen's suggestions to try to get to know the young warrior more. Now, she doubted it would be possible. She watched as he started carefully, looking regularly at Daiki to gauge his reactions before becoming more certain with his words.

'We think Chinen's at the centre of it,' the young man said, not even giving Yoshiko time to react. 'Too much has happened for us to ignore it over the past months. Things just didn't add up, but we didn't know what to do with our information until you said you were taking the keep back.'

Yoshiko, stunned, stared at him unresponsively for a moment. He waited, dark eyes meeting hers with certainty, no longer looking away. His thick eyebrows furrowed slightly as he waited for her response.

'It can't be him,' Yoshiko spluttered. 'He's been with our family for decades. He's guarded and trained both my mother and me. He's like family.' Yoshiko looked for someone in the room she knew would back her up. The only four in the room with her were new to her or the castle, and all looked at her expectantly. 'How could you say that? What evidence do you have?'

Daiki and Ikeda both sighed and met each other's gaze for a moment before Ikeda tilted his head to wait as Daiki explained further. Daiki's voice was low and sad.

'I know it's hard to hear, my lady, but Ikeda speaks the truth. We, ourselves, found it hard to admit. We've followed him for years, and he's been our mentor and leader. It hasn't been easy.' Daiki paused and waited for Yoshiko to say something, but she waited. He continued. 'He's always been active at the castle, as you know. Recently, he's been in more meetings than ever and not often at training or military routine. He slips out to meet diplomats. Before, he'd invite myself or another of his group to accompany him, always going in twos. Lately, he hasn't. In the last year, he'd often attend small meetings on his own, and he stopped telling us who they were with. He was always free and friendly with letting us know, especially as he'd have guards go with him. But lately …' He trailed off, sad eyes meeting hers.

Yoshiko still couldn't believe it. Chinen had been one of the only people who had been friendly with her in the keep and not treated her so rigidly for her station. He'd trained her, given her the skills to defend herself, been there with her the day her father had died. She blinked and thought again a moment. He'd left the castle that day, hadn't he?

'You'd come to get him ...' she said thoughtfully, looking up at Ikeda. The young man met her gaze and waited for her thought to finish. 'That day my father was announced as killed, you came to get him in the gardens. It's where I met you. You left with him. It can't have been him who killed my father.'

'True ...' he started. 'This is where we started to notice something strange.' His eyes bore into hers, and she saw only conviction. 'We were to go to the western border to ensure the lands there fared well. But we never got there. He turned us back and returned to the castle, where we found out you and the lady Asumi had gone missing. We never knew why he'd turned around, particularly as we were given orders by Asumi daimyō to ensure the western lands were well. He ignored her orders and returned.'

'He could have just received a message to tell him what had happened.' Yoshiko was feeling impatient. She rolled up her kimono sleeves and crossed her arms. She felt uncomfortable with these theories about the man her family most trusted, but more so that it seemed they were telling the truth.

Ikeda shook his head. 'But he couldn't have. We never received a messenger. We were the rear guard.' He looked at Yoshiko as if he were pleading with her to believe him. 'We saw no-one for days. At all. It was strange.'

The young man looked to his mentor for backup. 'There was something else, too. A weapon in his belongings that we'd never seen before. No blade, but a wooden rod with metal furnishings. We didn't know what it was at the time, but we've seen them on the foreigners, too. We figured it had come from them.'

Yoshiko uncrossed her arms. 'A gun? You've seen the foreigners? With pale faces and light hair?'

Everyone in the room nodded. Even Suki.

'How?' Yoshiko looked to the young maid now.

'They come to the keep to meet the council,' Suki replied, clasping her fingers nervously. 'We're not meant to see them, but sometimes we do. And people sometimes go missing if they're seen. We try to say nothing of it so we're safe.'

Daiki chipped in now, his voice quivering. 'They took my family. When we returned from that trip where we were meant to have gone to the western border, my household had been raided and my family taken. I was given a note—' His voice cut off, and Ikeda lay a hand on his mentor's shoulder. 'When I followed the note, I was taken by a foreigner with light brown hair. A Hién man, in diplomat's clothes, told me I had to follow orders or my family would die. Then they gave me this to help me fulfil my orders. I do not wish to use it.'

He untucked something from his armour and stepped forward, revealing it to Yoshiko. A gun. It was one of the smaller variety, she noticed, slightly curved to allow people to hold it and use it in one hand, like some of the ones used by the Acrein slave guards.

'They gave you that?'

Daiki nodded, pulling his arm back when Yoshiko didn't take the weapon. 'Seems they're offering to trade them here for something.'

'You know how to use it?' Masa asked, eyes watching Daiki's hand warily as he returned the gun to a holder on his *hakama*. 'I saw them when we were taken overseas, but …'

'I do. And I'll say again, I do not wish to use it. It is dishonourable. It is not our way to kill with such a thing. And I would not like to be killed by it.'

Yoshiko heard a faint sigh from Ikeda beside Daiki and, knowing no-one else would have heard it, tried to keep her lips shut. The young man seemed to disagree with her mentor, and she wondered why.

She returned to her original discussion. 'I do not know yet why you think Chinen is a traitor. But I agree the things you mention are odd. Is there anything further you wish to add before we head into the castle grounds? And will you be coming with us?'

The two nodded, Ikeda looking warily once more at Daiki. 'It's not just that. We put a watch on Chinen when things worried us. We hoped watching him would prove us wrong and that we could ignore it all, but it only made us more certain.' He looked around at the three women, young face serious and eyes slightly narrowed with disgust. 'It's true he meets with castle diplomats and foreigners, and he regularly meets other councilmembers. He's been at the castle more than ever, not returning to his homestead, and when we asked him when we'd return to the western border to ensure its safety, he seems as if he never considers it.

'I worry about the western border. My family is there. If the leader of the Hién military isn't willing to watch his home state, who else is there? I know not of another group being dispatched to check all is well. In fact, the other groups seem strange altogether. When was it our duty to lock our citizens away at night? When was it our duty to bully them and attack them? We saw the hunt for you, my lady, and the lady Asumi upon our return. We saw what the guards were ordered to do. When we told Chinen and asked him to stop it, he told us to leave it. As if we would do that!'

Yoshiko didn't know what to think. The young man's face lit up with rage, a contrast to the closed-off expressions he'd made this whole evening, where previously his only concern seemed to be his mentor. She looked to Masa for aid. Masa nodded.

'As you know, what they say about the guards is true. If Chinen was here, as the leader of the guards, it is also true that he would have had a say in their actions. If he did not stop them, then I consider him agreeable to it.'

Yoshiko's chest hurt. She stepped back and leaned against the wooden wall of the room, not caring to stand on ceremony. She took a moment to stare at a spot on the tatami floors as she ran things over in her head.

It's true that Mother and I thought it had to be someone high up in the council to know Father's movements for the political trip to Shogo. And who else knew Father was returning early? He only sent a letter ahead to Mother. Would Mother have told anyone? Yoshiko recalled her mother saying she'd expected her father's early return, but for one of the council to act upon it, they'd have had to have been told early and sent out the killers shortly after she received her husband's letter. Yoshiko hadn't known about her father's return, so Asumi must have kept it close to her chest. If she'd not told Yoshiko, her daughter, who would she have told? Only someone she thought she could trust. *It could well have been Chinen. He is someone my mother trusted, as her teacher.*

A shuffle from one of the others in the room caused her to startle and look up, and she noticed Ikeda's expression of rage had been swapped for concern, and his dark eyes bore into hers. This time, it was her own face she felt flush hot. She looked instead at Daiki, who had been the one to move, and he took another step towards her.

'My lady, we do not mean to concern you. We just wish to help. There is more to what my young friend was saying about the watch we placed on Chinen. He went nowhere without one of our allies following him. It was a small group of us. We could only ask those we trusted. One day, the watch failed to return. We found him dead with a strange wound—he looked like he'd been attacked with a gun. We had to stop the watch to preserve the lives of the others.'

At this, Yoshiko slid down the wall into a crouch, bringing her hands up together and up to her face to think. *What other strange things happened?* Suki shuffled forward and crouched beside Yoshiko, eyes full of concern and resting a hand on Yoshiko's shoulder, the unspoken question asking if she was okay. Yoshiko nodded and then realised where things stopped making sense to her. *The day Suki came.* She thought back to the day her father died. *Haruki never showed up, and instead, Chinen sent Suki to my rooms. He never sent people to my rooms, but he sent her.* Yoshiko remembered how wary she'd been of Suki at the time, but perhaps her worry had been misplaced and Suki was just a piece played by someone else—innocent but used. *Then Haruki never came, and Father never returned, claimed to be killed on the return, even though it didn't add up. Chinen left that day for the western border. Now I look back, it seems weird he left. Surely, had he heard Father was returning, he'd have held off to greet him and then left?*

Yoshiko looked once more at Suki, meeting the young girl's eyes. She smiled. The girl seemed worried. Yoshiko stood.

'It pains me to admit things don't add up, but I'm still not ready to believe. I want to see for myself and hear it from him. He's high up in the council. He could be the one pulling the strings. The others would listen to someone like him. If it was someone else, I hope he'd have shut it down. Unless people are going behind his back and he doesn't know what they're doing. But with the information we have, I doubt it's the case, though it pains me to admit that.' She looked to the two guards. 'Will you let me hold my final judgement until I hear it from the man himself?'

Ikeda bowed his head lightly, and Daiki did, too, but he added, 'My lady, trust me when I say it pains me just as much. He's the man I've followed for years, and the one I swore to defend. I looked up to him. But my duty is to my daimyō and my country, first. And the daimyō was killed because of this. By my honour I must do what I can, even against a man I respected.'

The look in his eyes told Yoshiko he was telling the truth, and she bowed her head, silent, not knowing much else to say.

50

An Unpleasant Surprise

Night was young, and Gora frowned and squinted towards the west. Dark sails just about disturbed the flat horizon line of the Taiheiyō Ocean, and he knew that could only mean one thing—war had come. He sighed and ran a rough hand through his auburn hair, turning to face the others on their stolen ship. A crew, of sorts. Only a moment ago, one of them, a Qeclan man named Jelani, had hollered from the crow's nest with the news of the enemy ships. Now, they crowded around Gora to find out what they'd do next. They'd hoped they could hold out until morning.

'Get the ship behind those rocks,' he gestured to a nearby island south of the Hié coast. 'We'll hide the ship there until the armada sails closer. Spread the news to the others.'

As the ship cut through the waters and closer to the island cliffs, Gora strode about the deck and assessed what they had. The main Acrein merchant ship they'd stolen, sailed by a smaller crew than it should have, and several fishing and trading boats from Hié. It wasn't much, not against a powerhouse like Acrein, but it would have to do.

Later, when full darkness fell and a skeleton crew remained to monitor their little army, Gora left the captain's quarters and padded to the deck. He always struggled to sleep on the edge of a raid, and nothing cleared his head like a walk in the night, hearing the lapping of the ocean and feeling the fresh, sea air against his face. At the bow of the ship, he stopped and looked up at the stars, listening, wondering where the Acrein ships would be now. Would they be close enough for them to see or be seen? Would they be sailing or stopping for the night?

A scuff of boots on the wooden deck ripped Gora from his thoughts, and he jumped to see who the noise had come from. A pale face split into a wide, deranged smile in front of him, and Gora's heart crashed through his ribs. He leapt back and grabbed his dagger defensively.

'The fuck you doin' here, Kipp?' Gora growled, trying to steady his voice and sound threatening. In reality, fear flooded his body like a wave crashing on rocks; if Kipp was here, Frewin was, too.

"Ent pleased to see me, eh, Gorey?' Somehow, the smile split wider, and the pale pirate stepped closer, throwing his arms out wide in a casual greeting.

What did Kipp expect Gora to do, hug him? Gora huffed.

'I said, the fuck you doin' here? How did you get here and find this place?'

Kipp shrugged. 'Followed you, din't we? You din't see us?'

Kipp turned casually and, once again, dread flushed through Gora until the hairs on his neck tingled. Gora looked about too, warily, expecting to see a host of pirates slipping out of the darkness, grins borne, blood dripping from blades. Instead, all he saw was the blackness of night and a light red glow of a lamp ahead where his night-watch crew waited. *What're they doin'*, Gora wondered, *letting this seascum on board?*

'They 'ent seen us,' Kipp sniggered. 'Paffetic.'

At least his crew was alive, for now. 'What do you want, Kipp?' Gora growled, still waiting for an answer.

'Heard there was a good fight comin' up. Chance for a good haul, innit. Frewin's as excited as that ol' Red Beard bloke you 'n' me heard in stories as kids!'

Gora rolled his eyes, wishing he didn't know what Kipp was talking about.

'Besides, wan'ed to fight with my old pal again, din't I. See how well you lasted on land, you soft bugger. Bet you got a pretty wifey waitin' for ya, ent ya.' Kipp stepped forward and grinned wider yet, and Gora took a step back, glowering.

'None of yer business. None of it. Get outta here. You'd better hope you're alone.'

'Nope, I's here, too.' A creaky voice stirred from behind him, and the heat disappeared from Gora's body.

Kipp wheezed with laughter at Gora's face. 'That's Birchall. Comes everywhere with me now. Like a team. Like you and I was before you left.' Kipp stepped forward and dug an elbow into Gora's side the way he always did when he tried to be friendly. Gora let out a grunt.

'Shouldn't you get back to ol' Frewin?' Gora wheezed, trying to get them off his ship. 'He'd flay you alive if he knew you'd gone.'

'Nah, he's good. 'E knows. We're here for the fun. So long as we all get the goods, he'll be fine.'

'Where is the odd seaslug, anyways? Hiding behind some rock like a coward to blast us to smithereens and rob our corpses?'

There was a hissing laugh by his ear, and Gora felt a shiver through his whole body. 'The cap'n's doin' what he does best, Gorey!'

'Killin' and stealin'?'

'Aye! Ye know it.'

'I don't think a battle is the best time. But you were always best at buttin' in at the worst times.'

'Wot you on about? You forgo'en? Profitin' from chaos is wot we do. An' this is the best sort of chaos. There's battleships like we've never seen. Riches better than waitin' on some Ishillian border for a silk trader. And a new land to pillage …'

Kipp's voice trailed off, and Gora knew he'd be grinning like some crazy spirit in the old Hizen folk tales, waiting for a reaction. He didn't want to give him one. It would only make Kipp more eager.

'So, if you're that excited, shouldn't you be with your dear cap'n? Why you here on my ship?' Gora said, trying to keep his voice steady.

Gora wanted to do anything to get them away from his crew. He didn't have time for their rubbish. Birchall let out a low, gurgling chuckle and shuffled closer.

Kipp's voice came right by Gora's ear; he could feel the breath against his skin. 'Nah, I'm stayin' with you, old brother. Figh'in' like ol' times. See how paffetic ya got. You know th' deal. Wha'll happ'n if ya say nay.'

A dagger appeared at his side where the 'friendly' elbow had been, and Gora knew when to give up. He scanned his eyes across the dark deck, thinking about what would happen to the crew if he said no. Even if he said yes, there was still a likelihood of trouble. But he agreed to let them stay, knowing he'd have to figure out a way to get the pirates away. It seemed the only way was to help them get the Acrein riches, and if that meant they'd help take on the armada—with the pirates' notorious foul play and dirty tricks—then he'd have to settle with it for now.

A night watch ran up to Gora on the deck, shocked to see the two foreign pirates. Her eyes narrowed as Gora explained in Hizen what had happened, and she stayed quiet. Then, she relayed a message to him about the Acrein ships.

'Speak in a language we all understand,' Birchall hissed in traders' language. 'You don't want us getting the wrong idea and sticking ya, do ya?'

Kipp sniggered.

'Enough! They don't know it.' Gora glared at them and took the rest of the message. The woman looked warily at their two guests. 'The armada's coming.'

Gora hissed at the woman to spread a message to douse all lanterns, to hide the boats, and he and the two pirates ran to the banister to watch the Acrein forces sail closer. *To be sailing at night,* he thought, *they'd need a large crew to take the shifts.* He saw Hién folk returning to their boats from the island and dousing their lanterns. It fell dark. They waited, listening to the lapping of the ocean, watching for the first of the Acrein ships to appear ahead.

'It's them,' Birchall sniggered.

Sure enough, large shadows with floating lights sailed past, cutting past the island without seeing the small, hidden Hién fleet.

Time dragged as the Acrein force slipped by, and in the night, the massive ships felt like an ethereal force of giant demons. *A close enough assessment.* Gora yawned, heart beating with anxiety that someone on one of those ships could notice them.

Yet they went unnoticed, and Gora managed to slip the signal to those on his ship, getting his team ready. Before the last Acrein ships passed, smaller Hién boats would slip out, unlit and hopefully unseen, to sneak aboard an Acrein ship each and take control. From there, the rest of the Hién force would create a blockade.

'It's time,' Gora muttered, climbing down the rope ladder into a boat waiting below, and to his disappointment, Kipp and Birchall followed.

A boat of eight—Gora, three Hiéns, two Qeclans, and the two pirates—rowed stealthily through the undulating evening waves. Ahead, another giant shadowy mass loomed, and the lamps on the deck and in the portholes swung far above. Gora raised his arm to signal to the others to pull up beside it, trying to keep pace. At the speed the boat was going, they only had a short window for getting aboard.

Two grappling hooks were flung and caught along the banister of the ship, Gora wincing at the thud. He pulled himself up quickly, followed by the others, before the final member, a Hién woman named Yonemura, abandoned the boat to the waves, hauling herself up, too. They wouldn't be needing the boat to get back. Their mission was either win or die.

The eight slipped among the unsuspecting Acrein sailors—a skeleton crew to keep it plodding on through the night, unaware anyone could come aboard unnoticed—covering their mouths and cutting their throats and lowering their prey to the ground to avoid a racket. Dirty work Gora hoped he'd never have had to do again, and dishonest, cold-blooded killing. But this was war, and Gora kept count each time he killed; he'd atone for it somehow, he hoped, and place himself before the spirits at the forest shrine. But now wasn't the time to lament if he wanted to protect the country he called home.

'Not too bad for a land-loving softie,' Kipp sniggered from behind him, grinning as he jumped out at a man pacing on the deck.

The man's eyes opened in alarm, but no sound escaped the victim's mouth as Kipp expertly slashed out, metal slicing the neck. Blood spewed from the flaps of skin, and Gora's stomach lurched. There was a reason to cut necks from behind, but Kipp lapped up the sight—he absorbed it and turned it into killing fuel, eyes already darting for his next victim, grin widening. Too dangerous. Gora remembered all too easily why he'd been determined to leave pirate life as far behind him as he could. Though they'd known each other from a young age, Gora had no doubts he could quite easily become Kipp's next target, body sliced open with his contents spilling about him.

Gora sprinted down the deck to charge the team of sailors who'd spotted them, trying to put as much distance between him and Kipp as possible. It was no use; the man followed and dived into conflict with glee.

'Where's your skulking friend?' Gora growled, breath heaving from the effort of the fight as the last Acrein sailor fell to Kipp's blade. The deck was finally clear.

'Went down t' the sleepin' quarters,' he said. 'Prob'ly killing people as they sleep. Just like 'im.' Kipp giggled, wiping his sword on the slacks of the corpse at his feet.

Gora's skin crawled. Such was war: kill or be killed. But Gora knew even he would struggle to kill someone in their sleep, even to protect someone else. 'Speaking of the devil,' he growled, eyes watching a hunched form slinking up the steps onto the deck, covered in blood and lips curling into an unsightly smile. Birchall was followed by Jelani and a Hién man, both with greyed, closed faces.

'Galley, storage, and sleeping quarter cleaned, sir,' Jelani said in stilted Hién, voice thin as if nauseated. He looked uneasily at Birchall.

Gora nodded gravely. 'And the captain of this ship?'

'Fed to the sea witch.' Birchall grinned knowingly, and both he and Kipp watched Gora carefully.

Not for the last time that long night, the heat from Gora's body all but disappeared, and he nodded curtly, amazed he could keep himself upright, and plodded heavily over to the wheel, ignoring the guffaws of the two behind him.

51
Taking Back the Keep

Masa broke the silence, clearing her throat. 'Excuse me, but if we are to succeed tonight, I believe we will have to leave now.' She looked to Yoshiko for her agreement.

'Daiki, Ikeda, do we have your help tonight? Even against the council?'

The two nodded, faces serious once more, and so Yoshiko took it as a cue to leave, smoothing down the maid's kimono she'd been given and grabbing a basket covered in piling, tumbling cloth to hide her sword was balanced atop it. She nodded to the others and stepped from the room and out of the restaurant, into the main street.

Masa and Suki followed, then Ikeda and Daiki, all faces serious. Suki shuffled ahead, looking up at the sky. 'My shift to monitor the keep at night starts soon,' she said. 'We have to hurry. We are punished for being late. Councilman Inaba is not a forgiving person.'

'Inaba?' Yoshiko asked, remembering the list she and Gora had worked on collecting when they spied on all the councilmembers. 'He was on our list.'

'Yes,' Masa stated. 'We used the list you gave us to form a plan this morning. We found maids in the houses of these people and recruited their help to sneak members of the rebellion into their homes. They'll handle it from there.' Yoshiko made a noise of satisfaction. Masa continued, 'We also discovered a few others from speaking with the guards we won back. It was quite surprising.'

The word *concerning* more came to Yoshiko's mind.

'You can guarantee that information is genuine?' she asked as they shuffled up the streets.

'Oh, yes. Our interrogators were persuasive.' Masa's face crinkled into a deadly smile, eyes glinting.

'Interrogators? We have such people?' Yoshiko had never known there to be such people in Hié.

'Of course. Anyone will tell you anything if you get their mother or grandmother involved.'

Yoshiko shivered at Masa's grin.

Suki giggled behind her hand. 'Mothers can be terrifying!'

Nodding, Yoshiko recalled the scorch marks. After what had happened in Acrein with the white fire, she was now certain the white scorch marks had been from her mother, but she couldn't imagine how her mother had done that. As far as she knew, Asumi couldn't transform.

'So what were these extra names we learned?' Yoshiko asked when they shuffled over the bridge, pausing a moment while they were cleared to enter the castle. Daiki and Ikeda had slipped behind a few hundred metres to avoid drawing attention by entering at the same time as the maids. The guards on the bridge let the three women through. Never once were they suspected, and Yoshiko felt vaguely disturbed by how they could sneak into the grounds. She glanced guiltily over to Suki, remembering the time she met her new maid and had suspected her, too. If this was how lax the palace was with maids, Yoshiko would have to make changes.

'Minamoto and Ichimura, one of whom will be in the castle this evening, at a supposedly secret meeting with another councilmember, Masa muttered as they padded through the courtyard towards the steps. 'We don't know who it is yet, though. Apparently one of the councilmembers has been taking up residence in the keep, playing daimyō. If what Daiki and Ikeda say is true, I'd wager it's Chinen.'

'Ichimura? But he was so friendly!' Yoshiko recalled Ichimura; he had been close to her father. The two men got on well, regularly drinking saké together and discussing the arts and latest plays. Then, Yoshiko's face fell when she realised it had been Ichimura who had told her father about the famous philosopher and poet visiting Shogo during that tragic trip. *Was that him trying to set things up?*

They fell silent once more as they cleared the top of the steps, bowing their heads to shuffle past guards. Glancing from the corners of her eyes, Yoshiko realised the guards looked uneasy. Then, she saw a dark cloak with a barely visible pale face and straggling light brown beard—a foreigner, controlling the slave trades. Looking back at the guards, Yoshiko understood. They were unhappy with the situation and orders, too, it seemed. Once they were past them, Yoshiko heard Daiki and Ikeda's footsteps reach where the guards stood, and a slightly friendlier exchange took place. But still, the hint of stress lingered in the guards' tones, and the two samurai soon followed the three women, not far behind.

Finally, they reached the top platform, breath slightly strained from the number of steps. Yoshiko felt faint as she saw the *tenshu* keep again, doors and courtyards and gardens all as she remembered. She let out a shaky breath. She was so close to the dream she and her mother had all those months ago.

'The others will be attacking the councilmembers in their villas when the moon is halfway through the sky, right above,' Masa whispered, leaning against Yoshiko's shoulder and peeking through an inner stone doorway. 'If we don't all act at the same time, they may spread word or cause trouble. Suki, where next?'

'This way.'

Suki directed them through the passageways and up the wooden steps inside the keep to the higher inner levels, past the tearoom Yoshiko sat in with her mother on that fateful day. Yoshiko frowned. If this didn't work, and they failed to stop the traitors, they'd be surrounded by guards and have trouble leaving alive. Even with Daiki and Ikeda to help, she wasn't positive of their odds in a full fight.

Yoshiko's ear twitched as movement came from behind Ikeda at the back of their group. She pivoted and raised her arms to attack or defend, but found people who looked like workers rushing about on all floors. A pair of girls with their kimonos tied for easier movement bound up the steps, a little pink-faced, and the flash of a man from the kitchens darted across the landing of the floor above. Yoshiko held her breath for a moment. This was the keep's attack. Those who had been working here would join them in taking it back in one swoop, inside and out. She never imagined taking it back like this, only ever thinking she had to work alone or with just Gora. But this, with an army of people who lived and worked here and had as much right to help in the revenge of it all, was something she could never imagine. She almost wanted to go and watch, to rush about and run through the building to see the maids turning out the council, run outside to see their belongings strewn on the ground, but that wasn't going to get the demon at the heart of it, whoever it was. She caught Ikeda's eyes as she turned back, both then looking away.

'It's time,' Suki whispered, gesturing for them to keep moving and glancing out of a window at the moon.

Yoshiko nodded and looked at Masa, who was still smiling.

'Time to enact our revenge. Those who kill and betray will face their justice.' Masa's sleek black eyes bored into Yoshiko's. 'Let's regain our family honour.'

Yoshiko's heart soared. This is what she had wanted all along, even before this all: to be surrounded by people of all creeds who felt no need to paint their words around her. To be treated normally. She pulled at her kimono for more legroom, and they padded softly to a room with the faint glow of a burner leaking through the thin paper frames. Inside, voices and laughter erupted. She extended her senses and noted three people inside, hearing their voices strain from too much drinking.

A guard stood by the door, and Yoshiko's battle mind readied herself to kill him before he could sound an alert. Her muscles tightened, and before she could rush forward, Masa grabbed her arm. The guard caught Yoshiko's eyes, bowed calmly, and stepped aside.

'One of ours,' Masa mouthed to her, eyes serious.

Yoshiko's eyes widened, impressed. And then she looked towards the sliding door, wondering who on the other side had been the one to betray her parents and her domain, selling their people to work without freedom or identity on the other side of the world. Quickly looking back at Daiki, she wondered whether she was even ready to find out if it was Chinen or not.

Yoshiko shuffled forward and reached out to slide open the door, calling out to all the spirits, praying that she wouldn't see Chinen on the other side, that he hadn't betrayed her family. And yet. After all this time, she knew she couldn't rely on prayers. She had good people around her to help her, more than her mother had those months ago. Yoshiko knew she could do anything with the right people to support her. Even open this door.

52

Fighting from the Boats

Other than the two pirates, who were a law unto themselves, Gora and the other five of his group donned the jackets of the sailors as extra cover for when the dawn eventually came. Not that Gora thought it would completely stop the neighbouring Acrein ships from noticing they weren't Acrein, but from a distance, people rushing about in the right clothes might just avoid suspicion for long enough. Besides, if he and his forces kept to the plan, and the other boats were also in their places, a great chunk of the Acrein armada would be gone before the night was over.

'Gora, we don't have enough crew to sail a ship this size,' a Hién fisherman, Yamato, asked.

Gora was watching the swinging lamp of the next Acrein ship over—their next target. 'We don't need to sail it well, just enough to keep up and cause havoc on the others,' Gora replied. 'Make ready the cannons and collect all weapons you can use. Spread the news to the others.'

Yamato ran off, alerting Jelani, and both spread the word. Later, Gora ducked below to the cannon deck to check on progress.

'Cannons set,' Jelani said. 'And others close by.'

'And weapons?'

'Prepared and ready over there.' Yamato gestured towards the door where Kipp and Birchall were fingering swords and guns.

Gora's blood ran cold to see those two protecting the pile of weapons like blood-hungry hellhounds.

'Kipp, Birchall.'

They looked over with steel in their eyes.

'Yes, *sir*?' Kipp spat.

'I want you two in charge of firing cannons. We need to rip through as many of those ships as we can. I trust you can do that? Don't lose too many to one ship, though.' Their grins came back. Gora addressed the others. 'The rest of you, grab a couple of weapons and head on deck. I need you all looking lively and steering this hulk.'

'Sail with just five people?' another Qeclan, Quinni, asked, towering over the others.

'It'll have to do. Go.' Gora said, and the others rushed into action and ran above. Gora watched the two pirates crouch by the cannons. 'You can break those ships, right?' He was unsure now.

'Who d'you fink we are? We've broken enuff ships in our time. Easy.'

'Two of you are enough?'

Kipp spat. 'We don't need your *fishingfolk*.'

'Right, I'll leave you to it.' And Gora was all too eager to run up the steps away from them. They could fire the cannons all they wanted. Their love of destroying things would work to his advantage. And while they were down there, he had fewer worries about them killing his crew. He wasn't even fully on deck before an ear-splitting boom from below rocked the ship and crunched into the one next to them, bringing yells from the next ship and a cacophony of alarm. A second one followed closely, and amongst the ringing in his ears, Gora could hear the two pirates giggling like little children, and they yelled up at him gleefully.

'Pull ahead, cap'n! Let's get the next one.'

The small crew pulled the monstrous ship ahead quicker, passing the chaos beside them as the crew cried out about losing water. Gora knew their position was revealed now but doubted the Acreins would realise it was one of their own ships firing. For now, while it was still dark, they had the advantage.

Another shot ripped straight through the hull of the next ship, which immediately began taking on water. Gora grimaced, admitting it was a great shot, and he immediately relayed orders for the ship to turn about and get out of the way of returning cannon fire, to sail ahead. Two more cannons blasted from below, tearing through that second boat until it could no longer float.

'Gora, there's more cannon fire in the distance,' the Hién woman at the helm, Yonemura, called out. 'Is it the others?'

Another covert Hién boat had sailed to the other side of the Acrein forces to mirror the same attack. Then, they'd have ships firing, two on either end, pinning the Acreins from both sides.

'It had better be.' Gora marched to the banister and watched the flashes of cannon fire across the dark gap.

Below, another couple of cannons spewed forth and crunched through distant wood, bringing Gora's attention back to his own ship. Flashbacks of times he'd been forced to sail with the pirates, sending cannons to tear through their victims, left Gora with a chill. These fellows had no mercy. They could destroy this armada, but if they ever turned on Hié, he wasn't sure Hié could ever defend themselves.

His blood froze further when another crashing roar came from way behind the Acrein forces, and another guffaw of laughter came from below, Birchall and Kipp giggling about their captain joining the fray. Gora's heart froze next. Frewin was here.

Yonemura lurched the ship between the Acrein hulks, lining them up for the two below to fire. Jelani and Quinni loped about easily on deck, acting as runners to pull the lines to keep them steady. Gora's heart pounded, anxious for them to get as far to the front of the group as possible, away from Frewin behind.

'The fuck are they doin' here?' he muttered to himself, watching the first sliver of blue light up the night and reveal the shadows they sailed with.

A cannon whizzed past too close for comfort and plopped into the ocean ahead of them, coming from behind. Gora cursed, realising the stray cannon had come from Frewin's ship.

'Sugano, get a boat ready for evacuation,' Gora called to the Hién nearby, who ran off immediately. 'Those fools could sink us.'

Even at the first hint of dawn, he could see Acrein ships dropping boats to escape the smoking wrecks, and Acrein soldiers jumped into them to row to land, where Yoshiko's defences would hopefully be ready if the trade and fishing vessels couldn't stop them first. Gora looked ahead, seeing they'd come close enough to see the cliffs of Hié in the distance, and looked back to see several Acrein ships pulling ahead from the safety of the centre, letting their comrades act as a protective shield. It was still too many for the other boats ahead to take on before they arrived at the Hién coast, and Gora knew that would mean thousands of Acrein soldiers storming the land if they arrived. He growled.

'Yonemura! Take her starboard.'

Yonemura turned the ship, but Gora could see the concern in her eyes as they sailed directly to a point where they'd collide with one of the inner Acrein ships sailing to the coast. Below, the pirates had stopped firing, and Gora dreaded finding out why.

'Goin' to sail right into them, cap?'

'Kipp!' Gora leapt at the voice in his ear again.

The man started cackling. 'I like it. Full speed, boys!'

All eight aboard Gora's ship stared at their course, a direct collision with one of the Acrein ships. As they got closer, Gora ordered the wheel to be tied on course and the crew run into the boat Sugano had prepared. They piled in and pulled away just as the target Acrein ship screamed at what they thought was their comrades. But it was too late. The escape rowboat had pulled away far enough when the crunch of heavy warship colliding with heavy warship made them cover their ears, and splinters of wood threw about the collision point. Gora bellowed at them to row ashore, away from the firing zone and back to somewhere safer: to the war. And as they rowed, ignoring the screaming of the muscles in their backs, all eight looked behind as their other small group in the ship on the other side fired yet more cannons into the chaos. Gora wished they'd stop and get out of there, not knowing whether they'd be safe or hit by the cannons the Acrein ships finally sent back their way.

'Are they going to be alright?' Sugano gestured with his head towards the next line of defence, the merchant ship they'd escaped Acrein on.

Gora shrugged, feeling the fatigue set in but knowing he couldn't stop rowing. All eight of them watched in silence. The merchant ship had moved ahead to block the way of the remaining six Acrein ships that escaped the cannon fire, stopping directly in the way of two Acrein warships. The merchant ship had no cannons but, with its sheer size, would damage anything that rammed into it.

'What are they doing?' Yonemura cried out, turning to face Gora with her face raw with panic. 'They'll be crushed.'

'I left Shingo in charge of that ship,' Gora said, remembering the capable Hién sailor he'd planned this with. 'He'll have it sorted.' The words spilled from Gora, but when two Acrein warships ploughed straight through the merchant vessel, pushing its remains ahead of them as they sailed on to the coast, his confidence left him, and he hoped Shingo had it covered. 'Come on, it's a long row back.'

53

The Traitor

Yoshiko slid open the wooden-framed door and rushed inside without a word. Before the three drinking traitors inside had the chance to respond, Yoshiko and Masa had kicked away the swords that lay on the floor by their knees and then kicked two on the sides of their heads. One, the lord Minamoto, not even struck by an attack, let out a gasp at the sudden intrusion and fell, crashing into his saké and spilling it over the tatami, cowering on the floor. The other, councilmember Inaba, was caught from behind by surprise and took a direct hit from Yoshiko, and the sound of the strike alone would have been enough to knock the man out. He slumped, unconscious. But the third, the one Masa had struck, raised himself from the floor, clutching the side of his head, glaring.

'Chinen? But—' Yoshiko felt sick, like the floor had disappeared beneath her. She stared, stunned. All along, Ikeda and Daiki had been right. She'd hoped they'd gotten it wrong. She glanced quickly at the two samurai in the doorway, both watching carefully, clearly trying to figure out when to engage.

Chinen roared, still pressing a hand to his head, and leapt up to face Masa.

'You wretch!' Chinen yelled, uncharacteristic of anything Yoshiko knew of him. Her blood turned to ice at his aging face marred with hatred, wiping all memories of the friendly smile she'd known from before.

Chinen lunged at Masa, reaching for her sheathed katana. Instinctively, Yoshiko kicked his stomach, and as he bent over with the pain, Masa pummelled the handle of her sword into his temple. He spat out, turning to glare at Yoshiko with eyes filled with death. Then, as if he finally recognised her, 'You!'

'Yes?' she asked, grounding herself and standing as tall as she could, drawing her sword slowly, watching for signs of what was to follow. She tried to shut her brain up. So it had been him all along. She looked over at the third member, Minamoto, an elder male merchant cowering in the corner with Masa's blade now pointing at him to stay where he was. He wouldn't be a problem yet. But Chinen …

'How are you still alive? We searched everywhere. You should be dead.' He snarled, steadying himself. Then he looked into the doorway at the two samurai from his group. 'You found her? I knew you two were up to something.'

Ikeda's face was blank, and he stared at his old commander with defiance. Yoshiko wondered what Chinen meant about them finding her. She turned back to her old teacher, wondering how to handle this. If it hadn't been him, she felt she could have handled it better. Now he was here, she worried she'd hesitate.

Masa bared her blade at Chinen, her face like stone. Chinen looked between the two women. Then, he smirked and eyed the blades. 'You should know better than to come into a tearoom with swords drawn. Even those two know better.' He quickly gestured with his eyes at the two in the doorway, swords still away but their hands at the ready. 'Put them down. You don't draw blades against unarmed folk.'

Yoshiko felt a low growl escape her lips and a heat rise from within. *Feigning innocence!*

'You don't betray your friends or sell people as slaves, either,' Yoshiko said curtly, trying to hold back the fire she felt at seeing his face at the centre of it all. 'Yet here you are. This is no time for manners. It's not a happy reunion, Chinen. I can't believe it was you who betrayed us all along.' She paused, watching him for even a sign of remorse. None. 'I didn't want to believe the others when they told me. I was foolish. I've learned these last months to trust in others. I should have remembered that now. We're taking the castle back. Come quietly or come by force.'

Chinen laughed, eyes darting to where his sword lay. 'As if you could stop me. You were always weaker than your mother. Maybe she could have stopped me if she could have managed to stay alive, but you couldn't.' He ducked, grabbed a cup of saké, and launched it at Masa before diving towards her. The woman cried out, turning her face away as pottery smashed against her face, her sword arm raising in defence.

The older man reached to grab the sword from the woman's hand, but Masa predicted his movement and pulled her arm out of reach just in time, pivoting and firing a quick kick to his hip joint. Chinen faltered just a moment, and Yoshiko stepped onto the low table in the centre of the room—ignoring her manners and trying not to step on the saké pots—and fired a low kick to the side of Chinen's knee before grabbing at his collar with one hand and pulling him away from Masa, stepping back with her foot to use her lower body weight to move him.

Not one to be manhandled, Chinen easily swiped down at her outreached arm and twisted her hand off him, twisting it further until it was behind her back. She slashed out with her blade and he caught her other hand, stopping the blade short of his body. Yoshiko cried out in frustration and kicked back against his legs, watching Ikeda dive in from the doorway, hands bare, looking past Yoshiko towards his commander. Chinen spotted Ikeda and moved Yoshiko between the two men, leaving few openings for Ikeda to attack past her.

'I knew you had a soft spot for her, back in the gardens, remember?' Chinen smirked. 'If you want to strike me, you have to strike her first.'

'You!' Ikeda glared at the man, putting up a guard and looking for a new opening.

I'll never let that happen! Yoshiko growled, moving her head to the side with a speed even Chinen couldn't prepare for, and his grip on her sword hand loosened. In the time Yoshiko managed to lean away, Ikeda closed the distance between them and fired a punch to the side of Yoshiko's head, straight into the old man's face. The young man wrapped his arm around Yoshiko and prised her away from the stunned man before his senses came to, which, with his skill, was within an instant. Yoshiko swiftly turned and raised her katana again, standing warily beside Ikeda.

'You alright, Masa?' Yoshiko called over, allowing herself to quickly look towards Masa, who had wiped shards of pottery from her face, blood trickling down from her forehead by her eyes. She still had her katana, Yoshiko noticed. *Good.*

'Perfect,' Masa called back, eying up the situation. She looked at Chinen and then back at the two other councilmembers, one cowering in the corner. 'Daiki, keep your eye on these. Don't let anyone leave this room.'

Daiki made an affirmative sound somewhere behind Yoshiko, and Chinen snarled.

'I take it you won't come quietly, then?' Yoshiko asked him, wanting to give him another chance to make the right choice.

The old man took a deep breath, eyes weighing her up, and then spat at her feet. Beside her, Ikeda's body flashed forward, stepping lightly around the low table and firing a jab to the old man's face. Chinen deflected it, but Yoshiko watched Ikeda's other hand come up and grab the arm Chinen defended with and quickly stepped aside to twist it and then push the councilmember down by his elbow. But Chinen quickly caught up, lunging forward as his body bent over and pivoting his opposing foot to spin forward and bring his arm out of the elbow lock, launching his opposing elbow at the young man's face. Ikeda blocked, but Chinen used that moment to take the hand that had grabbed him and push the man down himself, bringing Ikeda crashing to his knees onto the table in front of him. Yoshiko saw the young man wince as his knees met the hard wood, and she stepped in to look for an opening. This tiny room made it too hard to fight. They'd get in each other's way.

We've got to end this soon, she thought, eyes darting to where Masa too looked for an opportunity.

'Don't forget, boy, who taught the person who taught you.' Chinen snarled, smashing his elbow down on Ikeda's shoulder muscle. The young man cried out and tried to move out of the way and roll to the side, eyes meeting Yoshiko's, but Chinen pinned him in place, and the table got in his way. Yoshiko was preparing to fight over Ikeda when Masa stepped forward and dug a kick into the back of the old man's knee, bringing him momentarily off-balance and using that to grab his head and arm and pull him off and to the side. Chinen was pulled to the floor, and both Masa and Ikeda leapt back and out of the way while Yoshiko rushed in, leapt over the table, and brought an elbow cracking down on top of him.

We just need to arrest him, she thought, bringing her arm back around to strike him with the pommel of her katana. *But it looks like we'll have to knock him out first.*

He blocked, and Yoshiko leapt back out of the way before he could step in and do anything else. She couldn't get in the way by wrestling with him here; he'd win. She knew her advantage was speed.

The three watched their target warily, knowing Daiki had their back when it came to watching the other two councilmembers. Even then, Yoshiko checked the one cowering in the corner. His beady eyes were watching the fight, visibly trying to figure out how he could benefit if either side won and constantly darting to the door to see if Daiki had left an opening to run. Yoshiko rolled her eyes.

Chinen, too, looked towards the third councilmember, and a small smile crossed his face. Wondering what he was thinking, Yoshiko watched him carefully, as, it seemed, did the others, as they too held back and remained at the ready, waiting.

'So Inaba really won't wake up? You must have got him good, woman,' Chinen said, eyes meeting Masa's glare. 'So there were good women in the forces. I always wondered whether it was worth it, though the daimyōs insisted. That's the trouble with female leaders, I guess.'

Yoshiko stared in disbelief. *Seriously? The man who trained me thinks that?* He'd been so kind, the only other person to treat her normally, and he'd been hiding this terrible personality the whole time? She felt the fire burning stronger inside and almost felt like using it. Almost. If it weren't for the innocents in the same room and knowing she couldn't control it, Yoshiko thought she would have.

Chinen met her stare and smiled, and Yoshiko shivered. Even the look on his face now made her shudder. She wanted this done and the man out of her sight, and she'd apologise to Daiki and Ikeda for ever having doubted them.

Chinen kept his gaze on her as he reached forward towards the table, testing her, and took hold of the bottle of saké. He dared drink straight from the bottle as he kept his eyes locked on Yoshiko's, and she felt the two beside her fidget with unease. She felt the same. There had to be something she could do while he was distracted, but at the same time, she knew he was using this moment to plot and benefit himself. He wanted them to think he was distracted. His eyes quickly darted to the side, and she saw him looking at the three blades Masa had confiscated from them and moved to the side, out of the way.

So that's what he's going to do, Yoshiko thought, switching her stance.

The old teacher flicked his wrist, and the bottle flew from his grasp and launched itself into the air. Thinking it'd be another attempt like the time he'd thrown the pottery at Masa, all three watched to see where the bottle would go. It fired towards Minamoto cowering to the corner, whose gaze was still looking to Daiki for an opening to escape. Ikeda lunged forward to attack the old man, but Yoshiko knew Chinen would skirt around the young man.

The fire scorched somewhere in the pit of Yoshiko's stomach and she took a breath, thinking of her mother's lessons on how to predict moves. And as Chinen dived to roll on the tatami and reached for the black handle of one of the discarded katanas on the other end of the room, Yoshiko lunged and sliced her blade cleanly through the man's outstretched arm. He crashed into the floor, unable to grab the katana or roll on his arm. Chinen cried out and quickly got to his knees, holding his bleeding stump and staring wide-eyed and white-faced at this *feeble* noble lady.

Yoshiko smirked now. 'Not a chance, Chinen?'

Beside them, Masa rushed to pick up the three men's swords, passing them to Daiki, who tossed them out of the room. Blood still oozed from cuts on Masa's face, but she still held up her own blade with one hand and raised it to Chinen's neck, blocking him off from attacking or escaping the room. Ikeda stood behind Chinen and took his uncut arm, twisting it harshly behind the old man's back, pushing his face into the floor. Finally caught.

'Your position on the council has ended,' she said through gritted teeth, pushing down the flames she knew would otherwise leap forward and burn it all down. 'You will face punishment for your betrayal and the trading of our people. For now, until your punishment is chosen, you will be locked away where you can't hurt or control anyone.' Yoshiko called out to the young guard outside.

'We're not going to kill him?' Masa's face fell, watching the traitor with disgust.

Chinen almost sounded disappointed, too, as he spoke into the floor. 'Yes, do it. If you want revenge, that's how true warriors work. Your mother would have killed me.'

Yoshiko ignored his taunts and slid her eyes to watch Daiki grab the old merchant Minamoto, who cowered and mumbled a string of incoherent pleas to the samurai. The guard from outside stepped inside, looked briefly in surprise at the three councilmen—one unconscious, the other cowering in Daiki's grip, and the other livid and pinned to the floor with half an arm bleeding at his side—and he bowed his head. 'My ladies, sirs,' and then he stepped in beside Ikeda, struck Chinen until he fell limp to the floor, and dragged him away, unconscious, by his foot, leaving Ikeda wiping blood off his hands and watching after them in disgust.

'Well, it can't be helped,' Masa sighed, sheathing her blade and looking at the other two councilmembers left in the room. 'Let's take them to the prisons. Though I must admit, that was a little anticlimactic. I expected more.' Then she turned to Daiki and Ikeda. 'Can you two help us?'

'You know, that was the plan,' Yoshiko said, wiping her blade clean on Inaba's kimono sleeve. 'To arrest them, not kill them. He wants us to kill him, and I won't give him what he wants. We can get honourable revenge with justice. These men will face trial and questioning, though I admit I wish I could just kill Chinen for what he did. You'll still have use of your blade and get to enact revenge on those who took your family: remember, they come from the sea. Those who fooled even Chinen and got him to do their dirty work from the inside.'

The four of them looked at the two remaining councilmembers and wondered how to move them.

'How can you be so calm when he betrayed your family and country?' Masa asked, sounding still frustrated.

Yoshiko shrugged and thought of her father and the peace he'd have sought, the alternatives he'd have found. So she wanted to, too. 'I'm not calm. If I go by my emotions, I'll burn everything I care about. If I try to go about things step by step, thinking about how I can help my people and solve it, then maybe I can do good instead of burning things to the ground.'

What happened at the barn and the Acrein castle couldn't happen here, the place she had to protect. And each time she let the powers take over, the spirit of it took over her body more. She fingered the bumpy scales on the back of her neck and stared at the lord on the floor.

Masa sighed. 'Come, let's find a way to get these pathetic lugs to the prisons ...' Masa said, accepting Yoshiko's answer and smiling, looking at Daiki and gesturing for them to continue.

A shuffling in the corridor drew their attention to the doorway. Yoshiko listened, then a small, pale pace appeared in the doorway, peeking inside. Then two more. Three young maids stopped and bowed.

'Do you need help cleaning up, my lady?' the first asked when Yoshiko said nothing. The girl looked no more than fifteen years, yet her dark eyes were sharp and keen in her soft face. Her eyes rested on Inaba on the floor. He groaned a little but didn't come to.

'Would you?' Yoshiko asked, taken aback by the maid's offer.

'Of course, my lady.' The third smiled as she raised her head and padded over to the man.

Yoshiko watched in amazement as the three young girls bound the two men in colourful sashes, Minamoto whimpering to himself, the maids whispering to one another about ways to stop them from moving. Then, excusing themselves, they slid their prisoners along the floors, dragging them down the steps where a pair of guards came to take over, flirting with the girls, admiring their handiwork and strength. Yoshiko and Masa followed, with Daiki and Ikeda trailing behind discussing something with one another. The guards threw the two councilmembers into a cart, which would be driven to the prisons on the edge of town when the purge of the castle grounds was finished. Already, several people were bound in colourful silks and left in the cart.

Around them, castle workers rushed past with carts of the council's goons or heaving burly foreigners over their shoulders. Yoshiko called out for the castle and grounds to be searched for any stragglers and put a watch on every gateway and to patrol the grounds. Masa was sent to carry the message to the festival that the castle had been regained, finally.

After all these months, Yoshiko thought to herself as she turned to look at the castle, white paint looking ghostly in the moonlight. She'd missed this place.

A footstep scuffed on the stone pavement behind her, and Yoshiko turned to see Daiki and Ikeda waiting. Both bowed as she turned.

'Permission to speak?' Daiki asked, still bent at the waist while he awaited formal permission.

'Of course,' Yoshiko said, feeling caught off guard that they'd asked. Would she be going back to a life of such formality already? She didn't know if she wanted that.

'What Chinen said about us finding you and knowing we were up to something: it's true. We told you we put a watch on him. But we also sent one for you.' Ikeda paused and looked at

Daiki again before returning his gaze to Yoshiko's. His face flushed slightly again, and for a moment, he looked a little more like the young man she'd met in the garden before all this had happened. Then, his brow furrowed again.

Daiki continued for him. 'We had a feeling you were still alive. The reports only mentioned your parents being dead, but nothing mentioned you. We thought it would have also caused a stir if you'd been found dead too, but you weren't. Ikeda here told me he thought you'd be strong enough to stay alive, and perhaps your mother had ensured your safety, so we sent out riders, one at a time, to find you. We couldn't afford to have too many go at once as it would be suspicious that our ranks were smaller without orders, but we could at least do that.'

Ikeda jumped in. 'A group of us were all certain. We were suspicious of Chinen, who seemed to not have any drive to find you, and we were all certain you were still alive. So we took turns. But'—he looked away, frowning—'things started to keep getting in our way, and Chinen seemed suspicious. For some reason, he stopped us from looking for you.'

Daiki nodded, eyes closed and sighing. 'He ordered all my ranks back to base. We were monitored until you somehow returned and the festival was put on to distract people. It gave us the chance to slip away.'

Yoshiko didn't know what to say. *Someone came looking for me?* She felt her eyes start to burn and bid this feeling back, and the two men's faces looked most panicked the longer she took to respond. Daiki took a step forward, hands reaching out as if to embrace her, but then stopped himself. Yoshiko realised how much like a friendly uncle or father he looked and remembered he'd said his family had been taken. No doubt he was hurting greatly too, but he'd still taken the time to help her. The gratitude she felt was even stronger, and she forced herself to reply, even if her voice threatened to break. 'I can't believe someone looked for me. Thank you.'

Feeling nervous, she looked again at the palace, not knowing where else to look. A small chuckle distracted her, and for the first time, Daiki's face let a small smile break across it, and his eyes crinkled and shone, even in the night. This time, he put an arm on her shoulder and smiled reassuringly. 'And we'd have done nothing differently. Though you'll have to give most of the praise to young Ikeda. He's the one who pushed the most.' Daiki gave an overexaggerated sigh and made his face look pained. 'He meets you once and becomes devoted for life. Young men these days.'

Daiki turned his head to look at Ikeda, and Yoshiko's gaze followed. Ikeda flushed and turned his head away, trying to ignore them, and Daiki gave another overexaggerated sigh, shaking his head.

A laugh slipped from Yoshiko's lips. Maybe she wouldn't be going back to such a formal life after all.

Feeling better and embracing their first accomplishment, Yoshiko bid Daiki and Ikeda farewell as they left to gather the guards. With Chinen gone, Yoshiko put Daiki in charge of the Hién samurai for the time being to ensure they had someone to rally them and prepare them for battle. With instructions on how to get them ready for the incoming ships from Acrein, Yoshiko needed someone she knew would stand by her to ready the guards. Daiki seemed to have this respect. And though she could see he was still fighting demons of his own, she knew now why Ikeda stuck so closely to him. The young man would never let his mentor down. Right now, those two were her best hope to lead the Hién guards.

For now, finally, Yoshiko padded the corridors of the *tenshu* keep, with workers rushing about her to return it to a suitable state, bowing as they passed her. She slid open the door that led to the governance hall and sat on the dais on an ornate cushion and admired the beauty of the room ahead. Tonight, no lamps burned to light up the carvings she knew adorned the wooden panels with old lore and beautiful trees and dragonflies flying over a pond. The wall hangings with elaborate ink paintings of storks, beautiful artisans, and birds in the bamboo went unseen. Instead, Yoshiko knelt in silence with the moonlight seeping through the windows, feeling comfortable now she was alone with no-one to see her to allow her tears to burn at finally making it home.

54

Keep Them Portside

The next morning, Yoshiko and Masa strode through the streets towards the port, finally in a thicker kimono and a *hakama*, glancing at the guards, samurai, and citizens who walked among them. All were set for one thing: defend home. Daiki had prepared the guards well. Archers waited on walls and slopes in view of the port, ready to send a long-range attack at anyone who stepped from Acrein ships. Katanas and *naginata* lined the harbour and the streets.

Yoshiko looked around, anxiety gnawing her stomach, muttering to Masa only about her worries.

'We have something to protect,' Masa said. 'That's far more powerful than an army coming to attack. The enemy has less purpose, and purpose is what's important. It brings strength.' She turned her head to look at Yoshiko and smiled. 'We've had enough of our families and friends being taken. We have a chance to fight now. We didn't before. People want to stand.'

Masa's eyes were bright, and she burned with an energy like all those around them. Yoshiko nodded, understanding. 'You're right. I shouldn't underestimate the people. I'm still learning.'

Yoshiko looked back at the streets behind them; the streets and homes and little shops lined the path that led up the slope to the top of the hill where the palace stood tall and white in the dawn light. She, too, would protect her home like she couldn't before, and she felt comfortable knowing Ikeda and Daiki were up there with some of their group, preparing cavalry and protecting the castle from being invaded again should they be overrun by the main force at the port. And she still didn't trust the council. She never knew when someone else might still be lingering uncaught to take control of the castle again. Yoshiko knew she'd have to do a full review of those given power in the Hié region and discuss it with the shōgun, but for now, she had other things to worry about. She focused back on the mission at hand, looking over at Masa for reassurance, and feeling yet more comfortable when Ishikawa Morio from the ship met them at the harbour, bowing as they arrived.

'My ladies,' he said. 'We have three ships coming in. We should get the archers to shoot first to reduce those who enter. The one beyond with black sails, though we're not sure what it's doing.'

'Black sails?' Yoshiko mumbled, turning to look to the sea. None of the Acrein ships she'd seen had black sails. *Pirates?*

Sure enough, she could see a fourth ship off to the side, with black sails and a flag with bones and a red mark painted on it that she guessed could only represent blood. She pushed her eyesight to see further, certain it was pirates. 'If only Gora was here to ask,' she muttered, wondering where he was. She'd have expected him to have checked in with her by now, and she felt uncomfortable he hadn't.

Yoshiko gripped her bow nervously, then they stood and waited as the ships grew larger on their approach to the inland port. Before the three white-sailed ships got any closer, white clouds on the distance crept close enough to reveal more Acrein ships.

'If it's not getting any better ...' Masa muttered.

Yoshiko narrowed her eyes to squint into the distance. The black-sailed ship was doing something strange, and a smaller boat was hanging to the main group's side, out of sight.

An explosion close to them incited a yell to the crowd on the docks. One of the closer ships, the one to their left, had caught on something underwater and lurched towards the centre ship, splinters flying upwards and raining back down. The foreign troops yelled out, and as their ship scraped the centre one, the cry got louder.

'Gora?' Masa asked, watching wide-eyed.

Yoshiko grinned. 'Gora,' she confirmed, thinking about Gora saying he'd lay traps. Then, as the three ships lurched closer and the cries of the Acrein army grew louder, Yoshiko raised her bow and watched those around her do the same.

Ishikawa gave the signal, running to stand with a group of swordsmen to the side. From slopes and walls surrounding the docks, longbows were pulled back and arrows loosed towards the three ships pulling and creaking into port Acrein soldiers started dropping before the anchors could, and an alarm was called out on deck. More Hién arrows fired into the ships, and though not all hit, enemies fell. Yet, despite the chaos onboard and sailors falling to volleys of arrows, the three ships landed. Soldiers from the ship streamed out, feet stomping, shields raised, swords held high.

Yoshiko shivered at the barbaric roar coming from the pale foreigners. In the distance, out at sea, the mass of white-sailed ships grew closer, and Yoshiko heard more of the explosions and cannon fire that meant Gora and his group were still alive.

'Keep firing!' Ishikawa roared at the archers, his tanned face screwed up like a nut as he roared orders over the noise of battle. The archers pelted the oncoming enemy with arrows.

Acreins fell, but more leapt over them, charging the blockade the Hié people made. Behind them, Yoshiko saw gunmen coming from the ship.

'Steel yourselves!' Yoshiko yelled, handing her bow to the boy beside her and drawing her katana. He ran off, away from battle, she hoped.

Yoshiko stepped out to meet them, bringing her blade low to her right side and stepping with her left leg leading. Then, as an Acrein soldier held out his bulky shield and raised his sword to attack, she lightly shuffled to the side and sliced upwards through his descending arm, cutting it off. The soldier's eyes flashed as he saw his arm falling in front of his face, crashing behind Yoshiko. He barged his shield into her body as he yelled out in pain and frustration, pushing Yoshiko back a few steps before she could regain her stance. She swung her sword back around in a loop over her head and sliced through his neck. The man fell, headless, as his legs crumpled beneath him.

It had only been a few seconds, she realised. Yoshiko took a deep, rattled breath and held her sword ahead of her, watching the incoming army. Behind her, Hiéns ran forward to join her and crashed into the Acrein army with a clash of spirits. The noise was immense. Somewhere ahead, the sounds of what she thought was thunder clapped from behind the Acrein forces. She knew it was the guns, and instantly, too quickly, Hién people fell.

Yoshiko pivoted to her right and sliced through the back of the Acrein soldier beside her, then dipped her sword and shifted her weight to her left leg to cut the outer leg muscle of a man in front of her. She pushed through and forced his weight to drop onto his injured leg, slicing next up his torso to his opposite shoulder. His eyes caught hers as his sword fell, followed by his body shortly after. Yoshiko learned then to never look at face-level in battle, the man's grey eyes already haunting her.

'Push them back!' someone yelled. 'Into the water.'

The crowd cut and pushed, trying to drive the Acrein force back. But the Acrein force was bigger, stronger, and had greater numbers and guns. Their brute force hacked right through the Hién people and forced them aside, carving a way through. The

Acrein forced filtered through the streets beside the storehouses and away from the harbour.

From her place among the horde, arms already aching and sweat streaming into her eyes, Yoshiko dared to look behind her to see the force of pale soldiers running through the streets and into the town. She cursed. They'd head to the castle and kill anyone in their way, raiding homes and killing families. She had to try to stop them.

Yoshiko turned to run up the slope towards the town, pushing her way out of the mass. Someone pushed into her from the side and she stumbled, but she brought her blade crashing down onto a pale-faced man ahead of her with the force of her fall and swung her arms to stab sideways into the soldier who'd pushed her. The two fell, and Yoshiko pushed through to follow the Acrein wave into the town, elbowing, barging, and cutting as she ran.

'Masa! Ishikawa!' Yoshiko cried out, gasping for breath. 'To the town. We have to block them off.'

She didn't see them, but she heard their replies and knew they and their forces would follow.

Yoshiko's time as a fugitive in her own empire had paid off. Instead of following, she led a group of Hién people around the Acrein horde, taking the back streets and cutting down some of the soldiers who'd strayed. Families leant out of the upper windows, throwing pots and cups to break in shards on the heads and faces of the enemies. Everyone chipped in.

'Just a couple more streets,' she shouted, breath coming in short bursts. 'If we head down that alley, we'll meet them from ahead.'

'My lady, behind!' Masa cried, and the small group looked to see a group of Acrein soldiers following.

'They followed us, the bastards,' Ishikawa growled.

'Doesn't matter; keep running,' Yoshiko ordered. 'We must get ahead.' She'd heard the pattering above; older children were darting over the roofs above them. She could hear them catching up, then the grunts and clangs as soldiers fell behind them having things launched at them from above, or ninjas leaping down on them and cutting them with knives and projectile weapons. And as soon as the following soldiers were down, the defenders melted back into the shadows, disappearing into the alleys and rooftops.

Yes! Yoshiko cheered inwardly as they made it to the turning to overtake the main Acrein group running up the main street. Diving out of the alley and onto the main street, Yoshiko saw the soldiers approaching, kicking down doors into houses to kill those inside. In return, ninjas swung in through the windows, killing those who broke into homes and pushing them back out through the windows. Yoshiko noticed one Hié ninja crash through the window with an Acrein man, both falling onto the group that ran and fought below. She cringed. Both died.

Just in time for the Acrein force to reach them, Yoshiko heard a clatter coming down the main road from the castle. Daiki's cavalry was finally ready. The small group rushed out of the way, and a cry went up from the surrounding homes and Hién citizens cheered as the samurai atop horses clattered past. Before the horses hit, Yoshiko saw fear in the Acrein army's eyes, some trying to dive out of the way but meeting resistance by others in the same dilemma as them. The horses smashed into them, and the soldiers fell, crushed beneath the weight and momentum of the cavalry or cut by the swing of a katana or *naginata* as the cavalry took a chunk out of the mob, riding straight through towards the port. But her victorious feeling didn't last long once she heard the thunderous clap of Acrein guns ahead.

'We'll take the stragglers,' Yoshiko said, running back into the road and charging at an Acrein soldier with greying hair who'd avoided the cavalry by hiding in a doorway. Though he was quick to raise his weapon and charge at her, she sliced through his chest as she ran past. Another Acrein soldier yelled from the other side of the street, charging her with a war cry and rage. Ishikawa leapt in front of her, parrying the sword and bringing his own back up to slice diagonally against the man's neck. Masa and the rest of their group ran to join them, picking off those the horses had left.

Yoshiko groaned as she spotted a felled horse and its rider crushed beneath it. She blocked an attack from her side, struggling with the force and tumbling over a body onto the ground. Masa leapt behind the soldier before he could attack Yoshiko and stabbed him through his chest. Then, she held out a gloved hand to help Yoshiko up.

'What now?' Masa asked, wiping her mouth with the back of her gloved hand. 'The main street is clearing.'

'We head back to the port, closing off any stragglers. Then, we can see how the main force in the harbour is doing, and what might be happening with extra ships.' Yoshiko wondered how Gora and the fishingfolk were getting along in their marine battle.

'And what if they get through the side streets?' Ishikawa asked, eying the broken-down doors to family homes and shops.

'Likely they have,' Masa scoffed.

'The ninjas will get them. I saw them earlier. And the teenagers on the roofs. And if we go to the harbour, we can send some of the riders to patrol the streets.'

On their return to the harbour, they met an Acrein barricade across the road. Yoshiko and her team met it before they even realised, and Yoshiko cursed to herself about how she'd not been able to single out the sounds to know it was there.

'A trap!' Ishikawa yelled, diving to the floor and pushing a young man down with him.

Cracks of thunder ricocheted up the streets towards them, and Yoshiko skidded to a halt, crashing onto her arm and rolling to the side behind a shop awning. Masa followed a moment too late, collapsing under her own weight as something fired into the side of her knee. She crashed beside Yoshiko with a scream of pain, curling up to clutch her bleeding leg.

'Masa.' Yoshiko dived to help, but the woman pushed her back. Her ears still roared with the sound of thunder, and Yoshiko knew the blockade had guns.

'No, it won't help.' Masa scrunched her eyes shut and gritted her teeth to hold back a yell. 'This is it. I'll return to my family with my last push of strength.' Masa managed a grimace at Yoshiko and patted the young girl's arm before looking over at Ishikawa on the other side of the street. 'Ishikawa, it's your turn to guard her now!'

Then, with one final glance at Yoshiko, Masa hauled herself to her feet, dived out from behind the awning, and ran towards the barricade, limping on her injured knee. Yoshiko's heart shuddered as more gunfire came from the barricade, and she looked out to see guns pointing at Masa, who screamed but kept forging forward. Yoshiko saw Masa slash out at the first soldier she reached, parrying his long gun and cutting into his stomach with a stab to the side. Some of the Acreins pulled out hefty blades, pointing them at Masa, who dodged a sword to her side and dug her blade into the ribs of her attacker. She stopped, unable to tug it out again. Yoshiko cried out, trying to warn her, but Masa had already ducked out of the way and barged the man with her shoulder, pushing him to the ground.

But the man had pulled Masa with him. Bigger and larger, he grabbed with a roar and held her still as a comrade of his stuck a sword through Masa from behind. Yoshiko froze, knowing she'd never forget the gargling cry as the tip of the sword appeared through Masa's chest and disappeared again in a flow of blood as the soldier pressed his boot against her back to wrench the blade out again. Masa dropped to her knees, coughing and heaving, her face contorted with pain.

Two soldiers raised their swords above a small-looking Masa as the remaining soldiers of the barricade marched past them towards Yoshiko and her small team. Masa looked at the men marching past her in shock, face looking ghostly against the red smears of blood on her cheeks. She screwed her face up, reached down for a sword dropped by a dead Acrein, and swung it in a large arch at the legs that marched past. Two men fell, clutching at their legs and roaring out. In the same moment, the two swords held above her were thrust into her, stabbing into her spine and through the back of her neck.

Yoshiko's frozen body watched the way strands of Masa's thick, black hair dropped to the ground as the swords thrust into the nape of the woman's neck. The light shone in the black as the hair flitted into the mud before its owner crashed down on top of it. Blood oozed, covering the beautiful black hair in sticky red before being sullied by the trampling boots of soldiers.

Why did she do that? Yoshiko wondered, staring at Masa's lifeless body. Couldn't they have worked something out for her to remain alive?

'Lady Yoshiko!' A voice carried through the haze of thought as Yoshiko was torn from her terror to see Ishikawa signalling her from across the street. She didn't listen to him. Fire burned within her, and she looked at the four soldiers Masa had killed. Yoshiko would take the rest as payment for their brutality.

Before Ishikawa could say anymore, Yoshiko had pulled herself up onto the shop roof and run across the top towards the soldiers on the ground before launching atop of them, crushing one and not giving them time to aim their guns at her. She elbowed one and cut through the arm of another, watching a gun tumble to the ground with a thud. Then, Yoshiko kicked and pushed to disperse them.

With the main group distracted, Ishikawa and three more ran down to join her, finally able to approach without gunfire slicing through them. By the time she reached the dead woman, Ishikawa had reached his lady's side. Yoshiko crouched down to lay Masa gently on her back and closed the woman's eyes.

'My lady, you're not hurt, are you?' Ishikawa grabbed her shoulder and looked at her with grave concern.

Yoshiko shook her head, trying to bring herself to leave Masa where she lay and process just how hopeless things felt. And when they reached the harbour, the mayhem, head-splitting racket, piles of bodies, and rancid stench made her wonder how anyone could think of battle as glorious. Hizen had been in a feudal era for centuries. Regions fighting each other like this thought this was honourable? She stared, baffled. Riders and horses had already joined the mounds of the dead, even with their strength, and gunfire still shot ear-splitting thunder. Her ears strained as she heard a familiar voice; a wild string of curses roared as steel hit steel and a body was pierced and fell. A flash of red hair appeared behind the falling corpse.

'Gora?' She blinked, barely believing it.

'Well, young princess, I finally found ye. Took a while.' Gora swung his legs over the bodies between them and joined her. 'Couldn't see yer pretty head. Worried you may've been buried somewhere.' He looked pale and haggard, but Yoshiko felt the familiar warmth and a needed rush of calm as he placed a large hand on her head. She noticed his breathing was shallow.

'You're hurt?'

'Only a little. Though I'm more worn out than anything. Barely made it back to shore in that tiny boat.' He cursed again, jumping back as Yoshiko lunged to the side and pierced an Acrein soldier who thought they could sneak up on them. Gora laughed. 'Though you seem energetic enough.'

'Barely,' Yoshiko murmured. 'I feel hopeless. Mother never said how tiring fighting was.'

Gora's eyes widened and he opened his mouth to speak, only to be interrupted by a ball of flame and wood spewed from further along the harbour, flying above them and hitting a warehouse. The ball of flaming wood crushed many, from all sides of the battle, and a cackling laugh erupted from somewhere among the fray. Gora's eyes narrowed again in a way Yoshiko had never seen before, and she followed his terrifying gaze. Pirates.

'Just keep at it. People will follow you. I am. Others are. We're fighting for home. So keep leading.'

Yoshiko knew he was trying to be reassuring, but in the sight of the flames and with the ringing of metal in her ears, the flames within were threatening to rise again. She scratched the scales on the back of her neck and tried to swallow, to keep calm, but the orange glow of fire drew her energy too much. Her mind felt like it was struggling to hold back the heat.

Frustrated, she cried out, 'I've never seen a war. I don't know how this works. I'm just trying to protect my people from any more being taken or killed without accidentally blowing anything else up. But their guns are doing that well enough for me. It's all too much.'

'So why don't you use those powers? I can see you struggle. Rather than holding it back, guide it and use it to help us win this.'

She knew he was trying to be helpful, but she worried she'd burn too much again. Yoshiko shook her head.

'Too many people have already died by that power. I won't win this war or the trust of my people by turning into a monster and burning and killing everything. It would destroy our home, our town, our port—everything.' She sighed and looked into his tired, blue eyes. Against the grime covering his face, they were as blue as an ocean in the height of summer. 'I know you think I can control it. But I don't think I can. I don't think I'm meant to. In all the stories, those like me explode into something monstrous and set fire to everything. There's never a good story.'

Gora shrugged. 'Depends who wrote them.' Then he wiped his brow, smearing the grime across his face. 'They're already dying. They're fighting and dying. Trying to live. Look around us.' He pointed to the mounds of people at their feet and the people who collided ahead of them, then buried his own blade deep into the stomach of an Acrein soldier who charged them. Gora snarled. 'So much death.'

'But—' Yoshiko panicked, staring helplessly about her and swallowing back the flames within. 'I won't kill my own people. I want to help them. People are afraid of power they don't understand. If I use that power now and it goes wrong, they'll turn against me instead of against the enemy.'

Gora roared out in exasperation as he dodged another attack and kicked the attacker away from Yoshiko. 'Yoshiko, this is ridiculous. Of all the times!' He slashed out at the attacker. 'You have a power that can save your people. All along that's all you've said you wanted to be able to do. So just fucking do it. So what if people are afraid? They're already afraid. And at least you'll have stayed true to yourself and done what you wanted to do. What you said you wanted to do when you first met me. I'm here because you wanted to save them. So fucking save them.'

'But I'm scared! I don't like not being in control of myself. I don't know what happens then. You saw it! I'm afraid of myself. I can't do it.' Her blade lowered to her side and she watched the flames. Gora groaned.

'Then, it can't be helped. Raise your sword again, lass. Rally your people. Put up a final wall. They'll come to you: that's the strength of home.' Gora turned his head and nodded to Ishikawa, raising his sword high. Ishikawa raised his in response and called to the Hién and Qeclan people to pull back.

The fighting crowd melted apart. Gora nodded to Yoshiko, guiding her down the side once more to the front. Her people were tired, muddy, bloody, hurt. Eyes were dim and people panted, licking their lips for water they couldn't at this moment enjoy. Some had tear-stains streaking their dirty faces. Yoshiko's heart lurched, and the flames within boiled. She turned then to look at the Acrein force, and her eyes widened at the realisation they looked the same. They weren't all that different at all. Even they looked like they just wanted to leave and go home, like her people. Only, the Acrein people were much further from home. Why did they even come in the first place, then, if this was the case?

'Don't look at them too much; you might find it hard to fight them,' a voice said from behind, and a tall, dark, slim figure stood to Yoshiko's other side.

'Nubia?' Yoshiko called out, her energy suddenly returning as she looked up into the stern but familiar face of her Qeclan friend. She saw more joining them, standing heads above most of the Hién force. 'Where have you been?'

'Chasing runaway pigs in the streets.' Nubia clicked her tongue in disapproval and nodded to the force ahead of them. 'That's enough letting them prepare, don't you think?' Nubia smirked as Gora chuckled. The three smiled, and Yoshiko realised she'd never seen the Qeclan people's fighting style. She peered at the weapon in Nubia's hand—a *naginata*, aimed already at the enemy force ahead.

'You're right,' Yoshiko said and then snarled, raising her own blade to the enemy. 'Time to tidy up Chinen's mess. See you at a feast when this is over. We can eat as much meat and dessert as we want.'

Before Nubia could even protest about dessert, Yoshiko grinned at them both and darted forwards, readying her katana. And when cries came up as people followed, Yoshiko couldn't help but watch as Nubia loped ahead, aimed her spear, and launched it at an Acrein soldier running straight at them. It struck smooth, stopping the soldier in their tracks. Nubia caught up, yanked it from the Acrein's chest as they fell, and turned to stab it into someone else. Yoshiko was in awe. If Nubia could gather the strength to keep going, then so would she.

55

A Hold on Life

The sun was barely at the top of its daily arch, yet her muscles burned as if it had been days, and her whole body ached. Her sword felt heavier than ever, her throat was parched, and her stomach groaned for food, feeling weaker each time it moaned. And, as Yoshiko parried a blow from a pink-faced Acrein who looked as if he were struggling as much as she, she stumbled on something beneath her feet and tumbled down onto something softer than the stone she expected to fall on. A body. Yoshiko fooled herself into looking down: a hand. The emotions she'd tried to hide away for the sake of getting through this bubbled up and broke, and tears burned her eyes as emotion welled up in her throat at the thought of standing on someone.

It was pale and pink—an Acrein.

Yoshiko slid down off the body in a hurry, worrying about sitting on a corpse, and landed hard on the stone ground. She made the mistake of turning her head to see the face. She froze. The man's pale face was marred by the dirt, sweat, and blood of battle. Blood matted his light brown hair, and his mouth was open as if he'd been gasping for breath in his final moments. His eyes would haunt her forever, and she saw the tracks of tears down his dirty face and the remains of a tear stuck in his thick, blonde

451

eyelashes. Beyond the tear, blue eyes, paler than Gora's, had lost their life and shine to death.

Tears streamed down her own cheeks, and her attention was brought away from the dead young Acrein to one looming over her, stooping and struggling for breath. It was the man she'd parried away earlier, before she'd stumbled. He was back, struggling to raise his sword properly and utterly exhausted. Blood seeped at his side from where he'd been hit, seemingly a moment ago before she fell, but not by her blade. Yoshiko felt sorry for him, and when she looked up at him, it wasn't anger in his eyes, but desperation and anguish. She bet he didn't want to fight, either. Yet he raised his sword and stared at the young girl beneath his feet with a pained look in his eyes.

'Yoshiko!'

She should never have looked at their eyes. How often had she scolded herself for that? But she couldn't help it. And now the anguish in his eyes had frozen her, leaving her staring up at him to see what decision he would make. She could always block it, couldn't she? Yoshiko curled her fingers around her sword handle and listened to the voice calling her name.

Yoshiko knew she should be swiping at this Acrein's legs, rolling back onto her knees, and slashing through his stomach. Her mother would have. But she wasn't her mother. She knew this now. And her kindness and intuition looked up at this man and realised he didn't want to be there. They had invaded her land, but at whose order? That young king's? Had the people wanted to? Did the soldiers want to fight as little as the Hién guards who had been blackmailed by the council at the threat of harm coming to their families?

'Yoshiko!' that voice called again, and she heard someone pushing through a crowd and calling her name desperately, feet and blades pounding closer. But she couldn't turn. Both she and this Acrein were locked, neither one able to move. She knew it now. He couldn't kill her. Yoshiko could see his arms shaking to hold his blade, eyes as haunted as hers. The man opened his mouth as if to say something—an apology, perhaps? But, before anything could come out of his mouth, his eyes flew wide as a sharp blade pierced him from behind. His sword crashed to the floor, and the blade was removed from his body before he crumpled at Yoshiko's feet. A tall woman stood above him. Her face was stern, covered in grime and sweat, but Yoshiko still recognised it.

'Nubia?'

'Snap out of it!' Nubia said, crouching and pulling Yoshiko up. Her eyes were dark and angry, and Yoshiko saw the tell-tale signs of Nubia's fury as her nostrils flared and her jaw tensed. 'This is not the time to feel sorry for people.'

'But he didn't want to kill me.'

'Who does?' the woman said, trying to control her heavy breathing, picking up a blade again. She'd lost the spear, Yoshiko noticed, and blood oozed on her arm. 'Few here actually want to kill.'

Yoshiko blinked. 'Then why are they here?'

Nubia looked at Yoshiko as if she couldn't believe what she was hearing. 'To protect those they love from those who do want to hurt people. Them. Us. You. We all have something to look after. If we can force the enemy to surrender and go back, that's all we can do. And that's all anyone here is thinking.'

Yoshiko stalled, wondering how she never realised.

'How do I do that?' Yoshiko asked, earning a confused look from Nubia, who was scanning around them. 'Get them to surrender and go back?'

Nubia shrugged and wiped sweat from her brow with her forearm. 'Overwhelm them? Show them they can't win?'

'But more of them keep coming! And their guns are undefeatable.'

Out to sea, where Gora's fishingfolk fought and set traps, they'd held off the main ships. But now little boats pulled into Hié, the soldiers joining their comrades as a seemingly endless, replenishable force. It was too much for the people of Hié. And, even then, out to sea, the black-sailed pirate ship coursed about, firing flaming balls wherever they pleased, seemingly happy to cause chaos.

It was too much. Her people were suffering. How could she think they could have won this?

Hiéns and Qeclans alike were panting, not giving up, but falling. Gora had lost his strange swords and grabbed an Acrein broad sword. His teeth were bared and his eyes fierce as he spun and hacked, swearing in all the languages he knew. Then, he'd yell out something in the Acrein language, over and over but earning nothing from the Acreins around him except more anger and more resistance.

Then, a scream from a voice she recognised, and her heart faltered. She and Nubia caught each other's eyes, then both looked in the same direction. Ishikawa was holding his arm in pain, a deep gash spilling blood from his sword arm. His fist was white from clenching his katana, refusing to let go.

'Ishikawa!' Yoshiko yelled, running forward, jumping over the bodies of the dead to get to him.

How often had he defended her today? She was alive because of him. She had to defend him, too.

A large Acrein man—big even by Acrein standards—hulked over the samurai. The man pushed Ishikawa, sending the Hién flying and crashing into a pile of corpses behind him. The Acrein boar rushed him before Ishikawa could stand, and though Ishikawa tried to get back to his feet and keep grasp of his sword, he stumbled in the tangle of limbs. The Acrein giant's fist bashed into the side of Ishikawa's head, leaving Ishikawa to collapse to the side, katana finally tumbling from his bleeding grip. Yoshiko yelled and pushed to get to him, but her path was blocked by another large soldier. And though she hacked at him with all her might, the man wouldn't fall.

She called Ishikawa's name again, and Gora caught her eye. He spun to where she was staring and ran to help, colliding with another Acrein soldier fresh from a boat. Yoshiko slashed at the man ahead of her, and when he finally fell, she ducked to the and ran to Ishikawa. But the Acrein giant had grabbed the samurai by his neck and hauled him up, lifting Ishikawa off the floor and grabbing Ishikawa's katana with his other hand. Ishikawa, face set, though a little dazed, tried to kick out and smash his fists down onto the elbow of the man to let him go. But the Acrein didn't flinch, drawing his other arm back and running Ishikawa through the stomach with his own blade.

Yoshiko screamed, but Ishikawa didn't—his voice stuck, gasping for air. The giant pulled the sword up through Ishikawa's stomach through to his ribs, and the samurai's body spasmed. Still holding onto his large enemy's elbow, Ishikawa glanced over at Yoshiko as she ran towards him. He crinkled his eyes, somehow managing his kind, old smile at Yoshiko reaching out across the air for him. Her breath caught in her throat. How could he smile so kindly at a time like this? She hadn't managed to save him.

The katana was pulled from his ribs, and the Acrein giant tossed Ishikawa's corpse to the floor like a useless rag. The giant turned to face the person the dying, old samurai had smiled for. He stomped over the bodies of friends and foes alike to get to her.

'No!'

A roar came up from behind the man and Gora jumped onto his back, stabbing two swords into the man's huge shoulders. The giant cried out, throwing Gora off and wheeling around to face him, swords still sticking out of his shoulders. The Acrein pulled one out, blood oozing down his arms, and pointed it at Gora. Gora fumbled on one hand, holding one injured beside him. He hunted for a blade, reaching out for one still stuck in a dead Hién woman beside him. The Acrein giant rushed him, but Yoshiko was faster. She gathered her remaining energy and leapt to the man's side, slicing at his waist as he raised his sword at Gora. He yelled in pain but still pushed on, so she swung again and cut across his spine. Now, Gora was ready, and he hacked upwards into the man's thick arms. The blade caught in the man's arms, so Gora let go and dived out of the way. Yoshiko darted around to meet him and sliced up at the man's neck, yelling out as if it would push it through further. The giant stumbled, stopping enough for her to wrench her blade back out and cut again before Gora pushed the man to the ground. He wrenched the sword free from the giant man's shoulder and hacked into the back of his neck, near severing in the combined effort.

The giant crashed into the floor with a thud, drawing the attention of other Acrein soldiers. For a moment, the fighting stopped.

'Seems we killed their Fionn Mac Cumhaill,' Gora said, wheezing and clutching his chest.

'Fion Maku—?' Yoshiko panted, feeling her hair sticking to her face and not even caring to move it out of the way anymore.

'He was a giant.' Gora could barely speak, and Yoshiko saw him leaning to his right, protecting his side. Blood stained his shirt.

'You're hurt!' She rushed to his side, but he nudged her away.

'I'll be fine. Can't stop yet.' He stood and yelled something in Acrein again. It sounded the same as what he yelled before. This time, some of the Acrein soldiers listened. Yoshiko wondered what he was yelling.

The Acrein soldiers looked around, uncertain, clutching injuries, some fresh from the boats but wide-eyed at the scene ahead of them. And, for the first time since the start, Yoshiko properly looked, too, given time without fighting to process her surroundings. Her people were ragged, hurt, exhausted, scarred, but still stood strong in some sort of wall to protect their home. They raised weapons once more as the Acreins looked at them.

Gora yelled again. The Acreins shrugged, muttering to one another. One finally stepped forward, clutching a bleeding arm, and replied to Gora. His face looked desperate.

'What are they saying?' Yoshiko asked Nubia, who stumbled to her side.

'He's telling them to surrender and asking where their leader is,' Nubia replied, face scrunching up to focus and leaning her arm on Yoshiko's shoulder for support. 'They don't know.'

Other Acreins called out to each other, faces aghast. Nubia translated roughly. 'What? Why did we come then? He ordered the attack.'

Gora laughed, but it sounded more like a choke. Nubia translated again, seeming a little surer and more confident this time. 'He used you and abandoned you—to claim victory if it looked good. You want to die for him?'

Many of the Acreins shook their heads and looked at their fallen fellows. Someone fresh from the boats, looking tired from the battle out at sea, looked down, and his face flushed with horror. He screamed and ran forward. Yoshiko's heart sunk to hear it.

'Sieb!' The man dived to the ground and pushed the neck of a fallen horse from a man's chest. He cried something into the man's chest, hugging the man to his body and weeping. Everyone froze and watched. It was as if a flame went out and an emptiness remained. The man cried out to his comrades, gesturing at the Hién people and all around them. The other Acreins, pale-faced and tired, slumped and nodded. The sobs in the following silence were eerie, and somewhere out of

Yoshiko's sight, a Hién woman cried out too. The silence broke, and people fell to their knees.

Someone called out to Gora and marched at him. Gora twitched to defend, but the man held his hands up. The Acrein soldier looked like a broken man as he spoke with Gora. Yoshiko ran up to them, watching as the Acrein soldier dropped to his knees in front of Gora, followed by other Acreins about them.

'Gora, what are they saying?' she asked. She hoped they were surrendering but was unable to believe it until he confirmed it.

'They surrender, my lady,' Gora said, suddenly formal, face still.

A light ember flickered in her heart.

'Really?' she whispered, barely daring to believe it and feeling what could be relief. She looked at the man, seeing honesty and misery in his face. He nodded.

Acrein soldiers dropped their weapons, many flopping to the floor in exhaustion. Gora cursed, thanking the spirits. Behind them, Nubia did the same. Yoshiko looked at her, gave a small smile, then turned to face her waiting defence. Their dark eyes staring and expectant—many able to guess what was happening but, like her, unable to believe it until someone said it aloud.

'It's over?' someone nearly whispered.

Yoshiko nodded, a teary smile filling her face. 'They surrender,' she said, and then again, louder, brushing her hair out of her face and nodding. Then, among the chorus of people calling out to thank the spirits and clapping each other tiredly on the shoulders, she bowed to the Hiéns and Qeclans and turned and bowed to those they had fought. And though many of her people had dropped to the floor from exhaustion, many rose to bow with her.

Beyond, Acrein faces froze with uncertainty, and they watched their supposed enemies bow to them. Many Acrein men cried and others dropped to their hands and knees or looked numb. Yoshiko understood that. All these emotions and more coursed through her body—relief more than anything—and she felt if it weren't for Gora and Nubia beside her, or her people being so gracious behind her, that she'd be feeling as numb. Instead, she stood beside them, exhausted, thankful for their part in the peace they'd gained.

Until a high-pitched scream cut through the port. Everyone, Acrein, Hié, and Qeclan alike, collapsed, sitting, standing, turned to see what had happened: a child kicking and screaming over the shoulders of a strange-looking man—a pirate, Yoshiko thought, as he looked nothing like the others here—who was running towards a large, black-sailed ship that had used the mayhem of battle to pull into to the far side of the docks. In the distraction of the fight and surrender, the pirates had done what they did best: thievery and kidnapping.

'No!' Gora yelled, eyes flooding with recognition. Hand still clutching his bleeding side, he scrambled towards the pirate ship, stumbling. Nubia lunged and grabbed him, chastising him for his injury bleeding far too much to be safe. 'But they're taking them!' he cried out. 'They can't. Yoshiko!' He was desperate. No other word could describe the wild look on his face as he recalled dark parts of his history and looked at the young children being carried onto the ship. Three of them. A mother raced after, calling out her son's name, only to be blocked and kicked down by a young, blond pirate in a brown jacket. 'Kipp? Kipp!' Gora met the young pirate's eyes. The pirate returned it with a daring look, holding out his arms innocently, before grinning and running onto the ship.

Gora yelled something in a language Yoshiko didn't understand, but it sounded like he was pleading. He bellowed, desperate, pulling in Nubia's grip. As was the mother, who scrambled back to her feet, kicking off her sandals to chase the ship before it pulled out of the docks. Even the Acrein soldiers looked on in shock.

Nubia called out for help as Gora struggled in her grasp, and two others rushed to pin him down while she ripped some cloth from the kimono she'd been given to bandage his bleeding side. His pained roar cut through the defences Yoshiko had put up to stop the burning inside her. She'd tried to hold it back in the battle, and when she heard him and the mother scream; she tried to hold it back when the screams of the children cut through everything else. But now, with the shattered look in Gora's eyes as he looked at her from where Nubia and the others pinned him down, she could no longer hold it back.

'Yoshiko, please. Help them.' Gora's pleas sounded like they were travelling through water.

The docks faded to black and the people's voices merged into one before it all washed away in flames.

'I'll go,' she said, barely recognising her own voice.

56

Her Power

Yoshiko's skin burned with white fire and a light exploded in her soul, giving her one last rush of energy. This time, she'd control the anger, she told herself. This time, she'd watch what happened through her own eyes and not let it all take over.

Yoshiko watched as the world faded and people turned to look at her, eyes dark with fear. The same, familiar feeling of burning pains and muscles expanding overtook, and the nebula of fire within coursed through her. But this time, she focused on that heat and the exploding light and refused to let go of it. She watched the golden, burning light turn white, and she felt the scorching of her body as it grew. She imagined things she thought were good, and how it felt to fly, imagining the wind wrapping around her and floating on the breeze; the sound of Haruki and Gora singing; Haruki's smile and Yoshiko's own hopes to have saved her and brought her home. Yoshiko clung onto that, refusing to fail again, and when the burning stopped, her vision returned, better than ever before, and her people had sunk far beneath her.

The heat was still there, but it wasn't as scary as before.

Somewhere beneath her, people on the docks screamed and scrambled to get away, but she didn't look. She didn't want to see their fear. Instead, she raised her long, snake-like neck and lifted her head to the breeze. She sniffed. The air smelt rancid, but among it, a freshness of the new winds came in from over the sea. Yoshiko followed that breeze, and it cooled her burning body as she rose higher into the cool, wet clouds. This is what she'd been searching for that whole time. Something to cool the burning. Undulating her long, serpentine body in the clouds, that huge ship with the black sails looked incredibly small.

Yoshiko twisted her snaking body and dived towards the pirate ship, wind rushing past her face and whiskers. She dived into the ocean and beneath the ship, twisting underneath and grabbing onto the wood with her claws. As she pulled them out, timbers creaked and holes pierced the hull. Small bubbles plumed about her, the ship taking in water. She didn't care. Yoshiko clawed her way around to the other side of the ship. It rocked with her weight, and the crew cried out as they stumbled about on the deck. As she climbed the side, a man leant over with a fear-filled face to look out for the monster, meeting it face-to-face. He paled and screamed.

Taking that as her opportunity, Yoshiko leapt onto the deck and smiled, showing her sword-like fangs. The old captain with yellowing eyes yelled something to the crew, and they darted forwards, guns pointed at her, ready to burst thunder through the tips. She brushed them aside with a swipe of her tail, sending them flying. The captain's face went from a sneer to a disgusting gnashing of his yellowing teeth. In a moment of rage at what he'd done all these years and the remembrance of the fear on Gora's face, Yoshiko pounced on him, pinning him down beneath her front claws. She roared, sending burning air across his skin that burned and bubbled. The old man screamed in pain, trying to thrash out but failing beneath her weight.

Feeling satisfied, Yoshiko looked across the deck to where the children had been taken below. Knowing she'd have to be human again to follow, she tried to recall how she'd changed back before. She couldn't remember. What had made her calm that day in Acrein, before she burned the city, and Gora with it, to the ground? She took a deep, huffing snort out as she thought, recalling a vague memory of Gora's panicked face as he yelled out to her, arm gesturing widely at the mess around them.

Yoshiko's heart stung. She'd felt shame and shock, and a few of her people, dressed as slaves in the crowd, had looked terrified, wary, and hopeful that the autumn-haired man's pleas to his friend would work.

That's it!

Gora's words and the faces of her people had calmed the anger, and the fire in her stomach had wavered, dimming the heat and the light. Maybe that would work. Yoshiko looked down once more at the pirate trapped in her claws who had collapsed from the pain of the burns, leapt off him, and focused on letting go of that burning light. She felt the world grow around her as she shrank in a release of white light, the heat dissipating, and Yoshiko transformed back into a human. She ran down some stairs at the end of the deck, entering the belly of the ship. Pirates jumped out at her as she navigated the corridor, but she'd been expecting this. Rats always hid in the dark. Yoshiko held out her human hand and focused on the burning heat she still felt within, willing it to her fingers, trying to push the heat away like she had that time she'd accidentally burned down the barn. Her mother had been able to call fire in her human form. So much made sense now. Asumi had defeated the men and dogs that time like this, hadn't she? That's why there had been scorch marks about her death place.

Knowing she could do it, Yoshiko focused on the heat, and the tips of her fingers glowed red and white with a searing spark, and jets of spewing flame shot out in a beam like the star streams of light in the caverns. The beams of flame hit the pirates, burning straight through them. They fell at her feet, and she leapt over them to where she guessed would be the cargo hold and the place they'd hidden the children.

As Yoshiko skidded into a room, holding the doorframe to turn at a sharp angle, a blade struck out from the darkness. Heat spilled from her shoulder, and metal struck her bone. Pain and burning flushing her body, she turned to barge into a large figure. The blade fell to the floor. As her eyes adjusted to the darkness, Yoshiko found herself face-to-face with the man Gora had yelled at. Kipp, wasn't it? The young man, Kipp, grinned, grabbing her shoulders and pushing her down, rolling on top of her.

'Gora's—' he said. She didn't understand the rest. The man's grin had a sly, sickening look to it, just like the men in the barn, and she knew what would follow.

Yoshiko kicked at the man's knee and shoved him off, then leaping up and kicking at his head, not risking anything this time. She'd made that mistake last time. Yoshiko dived for his blade by the door and launched it at him. It stuck in his thigh. Kipp roared out, and with a flick of his hand, a dart of silver flashed in front of her eyes, and Yoshiko dodged just as a dagger whistled past and buried itself in the wooden doorframe behind her. A sound to her right made her turn to see three terrified children, mouths covered with filthy rags, limbs bound.

The slimy young man said Gora's name again, but Yoshiko vowed it would be the last thing he said. Kipp rushed at her, limping and lunging, grabbing, pale eyes leering, so she held out her hand and focused the heat through her hands again, this time to her palms. She dodged to the side of Kipp's reach and grabbed his head from behind, sending the burning heat through his skull with her hands. Kipp screamed and clawed at her hands, burning his fingers against hers. Yoshiko stopped when he became limp and fell through her grip, his skull sunken and black and melting.

On any other day, she'd feel sick. Not today. She had children to save. Yoshiko freed them from their bonds, whispering words of comfort to them. She'd probably frightened them more than the pirates had, she realised, hoping in the darkness of the storeroom they'd barely seen what she'd done. That wasn't something she could think of now. Guiding them back onto the deck, the children clung to her, their grips tight on her clothes. On the deck, the three children looked at the pirates and screamed, hiding behind her. A man yelled out, but she ignored him—she didn't understand anyway. Instead, she crouched and turned to face the children.

'Have you ever seen a dragon?' she asked them, trying to smile. Inside, the burning rose again, and she feared they'd hate her forever. The children shook their heads, tears streaming down their faces as they snivelled. 'Well, did you know they protect the oceans? If you're in trouble on a ship, you can ask a dragon spirit to help you. Shall we try?'

The small children hesitated. Behind them, the captain was up, yelling and clutching his red, bubbling face with a rag, and others loaded their guns. Yoshiko swallowed, hoping this would work before the guns were fired. The children tried to look, but Yoshiko blocked their view so they couldn't see. One of the three, a little girl of only several summers, looked at her with a determined face, taking a deep breath. Then, she let go of that breath and yelled out for a dragon to help them so loudly Yoshiko's ears rang. The other two joined in.

Smiling, Yoshiko focused on the heat and the bright light and called on the curse. The heat took over, and once she'd focused it, the children and the rest of the deck had shrunk far below her, her neck lengthening and towering into the shrouds, the ship creaking. Yoshiko bent her long neck to look down at the three children, nodded at them, and then scooped them up to hold them in her front legs before leaping from the deck and soaring into the sky. Behind her, guns fired into empty space, unable to reach.

The children squirmed in her tight grasp, but Yoshiko held them tighter. She didn't want them to fall. Instead, to distract them, Yoshiko flew closer to the ocean, and a young boy cried out in awe, trying to touch it. So Yoshiko flew lower, letting them brush the waves with their fingertips. The little girl laughed, and the flaming light in Yoshiko's soul felt softer.

Maybe this isn't so scary after all, if a child can find happiness in it.

Yet, as they reached the shore, Hién, Qeclan, and Acrein people healing and waiting and mourning together turned their attention to the returning four, and Yoshiko's moment of bliss evaporated. Her people looked frightened. They ran to grab the three children and backed away, some rushing forward to point blades at her, their faces dark and emotionless. Gora and Nubia ran to stop them but were held back.

'What are you doin'?' Gora cried out. 'She saved them.'

The bright light inside flickered out, and Yoshiko fell to the floor, human once more. Her body was tired, her shoulder ached and bled freely again, and she couldn't move. The blades pushed closer, but all she could do was watch. Yoshiko lay her cheek on the cold stone, wondering if this would be her last resting place. It wouldn't be so bad, she thought; the stone was cool against her bleeding shoulder. She shivered, realising the stone was taking her heat, and she wondered whether she was going to join her parents. She felt as cold as her mother's body had been the day she'd buried her in the forest.

So much has happened since then, Yoshiko thought, eyes heavy, *Mama.*

'She led you to battle. She saved your people.' Nubia's voice clucked in the distance somewhere, sounding tired and frustrated. 'You should be ashamed.'

Yoshiko chuckled to herself, sure Nubia would be standing tall and brave as always, chin in the air.

Another voice rang out. 'And yet she's a monster? A *Kiyohimé* cursed to seek vengeance?'

'Why would she burn and destroy something she worked so hard to save?' Gora's voice was weak and tired. He needed urgent care beyond just binding his wound, Yoshiko thought, trying to push herself up to help him and tell him to rest. But she couldn't even twitch her finger. Instead, her eyelids shut, and she couldn't find the energy to open them again.

The voices lulled again, and she missed what came next, until a thudding sound of someone landing beside her and a calling out in a high-pitched cry. A woman. The woman rested a hand gently on Yoshiko and rolled her over. She felt a wetness on her burning shoulder, clean and light against the sticky heat that spilled from it. The woman was dabbing her wound, and though it was soft and caring, pain flooded her body until her energy failed.

57
The Aftermath

Yoshiko woke in a futon in a room in the castle, feeling the same pain in her shoulder and an ache in her whole body. *So I'm still alive somehow.* She opened her eyes to see two faces peering down at her.

'Gora? Nubia?'

'Be lucky, lady Yoshiko,' Nubia said, grinning and reaching out to brush a strand of Yoshiko's long, black hair from her face. 'The effort it took to get Gora into a lady's room … He caused such a fuss to make sure he was here when you woke up. I think he worried you'd die.'

'Of course I was!' Gora pouted, sitting cross-legged on Yoshiko's other side.

'Your injury —' Yoshiko started, staring at Gora's stomach. He was in clean clothes and sitting straight, but unnaturally so.

'Pretty rough. Good job Nubia helped when she did. Can barely move. How troublesome.' He cursed, rubbing his cheek. 'But, you should worry about your own,' he added, face serious as he frowned down at her.

'Eh, I seem to be alive, at least. Better than I thought. And at least you could finally shave again. Don't look like a dirty pirate now.' Yoshiko managed a grin and watched his face. Gora cried out in protest, but his ocean blue eyes glinted. Beside them, Nubia chuckled and agreed. 'And you, Nubia?' Yoshiko pulled herself to sit up, wincing at the pain in her shoulder, but running her eyes over her friend to make sure she was well.

'I am recovering well, thanks to your people,' Nubia responded reassuringly, passing Yoshiko water and telling her to drink.

Yoshiko hummed in response, feeling the water refresh her. She stared thoughtfully at the pottery cup, wondering how many others were injured or killed and what they'd lost.

When a medic reviewed Yoshiko and allowed her to leave her futon, she padded through the halls of the palace with Gora and Nubia. 'We lost so many,' she mourned, finally voicing her concerns and listening to the empty castle walls, seeing few workers around.

People would still be tidying and mourning after battle. It would take a long time, she knew, but they'd pick up eventually. For now, she needed fresh air, so they walked to the gardens.

'Woah,' Nubia muttered.

The gardens took Yoshiko's breath away. She'd forgotten how beautiful they were, the colours as vivid as always and the great trees bringing peace as the wind gushed through them. The seasonal autumn flowers waved in the cool evening breeze against a backdrop of golden leaves, and for a moment, Yoshiko felt transported back in time, as if nothing had happened. As if she could step into that garden and join her parents on that bench by the pond to watch the ducks, terrapins, and koi.

She sighed. That would never be. Instead, she walked through the gardens with her two friends, eagerly pointing out some of her favourite places. Nubia's face lit with awe, and she often stooped to smell the flowers, claiming to find a new love and a new favourite in each flower they found. Yoshiko and Gora laughed, both teasing the tall woman and picking vivid pink and yellow flowers and lacing them into Nubia's short, curly hair. And when Yoshiko looked at her friends laughing together, she felt positive about forging a new lifestyle of her own back in the keep, where she would work with the people to build a region they could be proud of, and where she would never feel alone again.

Yoshiko now realised her mother had kept her within the confines of the compound to keep her safe from the effects of the curse, which had already taken a great toll on both Yoshiko and those around her, but it wasn't the life she thought was best. Yoshiko ran her fingers over the scaling on her jaw. The people knew about her and what she could do now, and yet they were still here, and she was still here. Eventually, she knew it would consume her, especially if she used it as much as she had done recently. After less than a year of using it, she'd already surpassed the effects of the curse that her mother had had. Yoshiko knew she'd have to watch her changes from here on, but reflecting on the *tenshu* keep, her friends enjoying themselves, and those she'd worked alongside, she knew the change was worth it. Scales and all.

* * *

'Why did you do it?'

Yoshiko had come to the prisons on the lower level of the castle grounds where people were temporarily stored until their punishment was decided. Death, exile, or labour, no-one was kept here for long, so they were basic buildings with simple cells and a regular guard to watch them. Here, Chinen and the other traitors were kept there until their verdict. All the foreigners who'd been taken with them in the raid on the keep had been returned to the Acreins to face their judgement in their own country, and here, she'd have to help decide what to do with those from Hié. Now, she stood by Chinen's cell, arms crossed and awaiting his answer.

Chinen stirred, sitting on the floor, staring at her through the bars but refusing to speak. Yoshiko had never seen such an ugly look on his face. He was like a changed person, and she growled and pushed again.

'I said, why did you do it? Answer me.'

Behind her, Gora leaned on the prison walls. Arms crossed and foot against the wall, he looked the picture of casual. But his ocean blue eyes were piercing, and his face held back a sneer. 'We should chop off a finger each time he refuses to talk,' Gora said, leaning his head back against the stone wall and closing his eyes. 'See if that helps loosen his tongue.'

'I'm tempted,' Yoshiko muttered, glaring once again at her old teacher.

'And your mother wouldn't hesitate to do it.' Chinen smiled slyly and watched her from the corners of his eyes. 'You always were too soft, like Hitoshi.'

'We're not here to talk about my parents. For now, the fingers stay. I won't resort to the gruesome violence you'd enjoy.'

'You're such a fool. No wonder we could collapse the domain without your family noticing. It will happen again. People are done with the ruling class. They want a change. Revolution comes without your control. It's already happening.'

Yoshiko nodded, much to Chinen's surprise. His mouth dropped into a frown, and he watched her carefully.

'Yes, there are many things that need to change. Things my family couldn't see or adapt to. And the council was no better. We could have done more. But that doesn't explain why the council, there to guide and offer *counsel* to the noble family, chose instead to go behind their backs and betray them. When the foreigners came, we should have formed a united front—turned them away and defended our lands. Instead, what did you do? You met with them. I know this. I've already spoken to them. And now, I'm asking you why.

'Why, when my mother turned the foreigners away and refused to make agreements with them, did you and some of your fellows meet with them in private and make arrangements with them? I know you did it. I heard from Inaba, and Daiki and his crew can confirm that they saw you meeting with foreigners and carrying a gun. What did you gain from meeting them?' Yoshiko waited, feeling her patience thinning. She took a breath and forced herself to outwait him.

'So you know that?' Chinen asked, smiling again. 'Clever girl.' Yoshiko wanted to snap at him not to patronise her, but he continued. Instead, she simmered. 'The foreigners were offering us good trade and a chance to reflect on our place in the world. They came in on large warships with rods of iron that shot metal thunder that could kill someone far more effectively than with a katana and were quicker and had a longer range than a bow, and they brought riches and offered to trade, giving us the opportunity to have it, too. As the military leader, my role to help protect our country and find the best ways we could defend ourselves, how could I not meet with them? And those rods of iron—those guns, as you know they're called—would help us against the other feuds from other regions, like the western domain. We knew we were hopelessly behind against these foreigners with their war machines. Your mother knew it and hated that we were behind, saying she'd discuss it with the shōgun and other warlord leaders. But she turned a blind eye and ignored my suggestions to listen to the foreigners. But I knew; I knew we couldn't ignore them. They'd turn it all against us. You've seen their guns. You've seen how they kill people.'

Masa's death replayed in Yoshiko's mind. Behind her, Gora snorted.

'Because that's the noble reason to sell your own people,' he said dryly, eyes opening to look unforgivingly at the old military leader in the cell.

Chinen frowned and responded with something unsavoury, and Yoshiko wondered where this true self of his had been hiding—how long had he been like this? From the start, or had he become like this over time with working at the castle? It disgusted her to think they once thought of him as family.

'He's right,' Yoshiko said, voice hardening. 'It's no reason to give up our people. Our people and their safety should *always* come first. As the military leader, that was your role. You don't agree to sell people for the sake of new weapons or control.'

Chinen shrugged. 'There are many of them, and that was the agreement to avoid having the foreigners storm the place anyway. What do the lesser people matter? It's the result that matters. In a world of instant war and death, making the right friendships is important. Your family couldn't see that, so some of us took it into our own hands. If the noble family couldn't bring us into the new age, we'd do it ourselves, and rid ourselves of the inconvenience of a noble family who couldn't see the truth. So Hié suffered a little at first. In the long term, we'd thrive.' He glared at her. 'We'd do better without your family. I can't believe I was reduced to the position of teaching little girls. I worked hard to do better! The time of the nobles and the warlords is over. A new age is needed. There are many who think it. This will happen over and over, people going behind your—'

'You shit!' Yoshiko smashed her hands against the bars to interrupt his self-gratifying monologue, the crash ringing through the echoing stonework. He jumped, shock on his face at the language she used. 'You were like family! And you do this? You bastards think you can actually do that? That you're better than them? *Lesser people?* Our people are greater than you'll ever be! They rose to protect their homes and loved ones. You have no idea of what they lost and how hard they still worked. You just let the enemy walk in, taking bribes. They're precious, and they inspire me to be a better person *and* a better ruler. You don't understand them at all.'

Yoshiko, feeling as if she'd get nowhere, turned on her heels and stomped from the prisons. Behind her, Chinen rushed to the bars and growled out sick profanities, earning a nose-crunching punch from Gora before he followed her.

'He is a shit, isn't he?' Gora agreed when he caught up, spitting on the ground with a disgusted look on his face. '*Lesser peoples*? Does he even know what those lesser peoples do? A country wouldn't last a day without them. Tending crops, growing and raising food, making, cooking, mending, selling, building—'

'He doesn't want to know it, that's all,' Yoshiko said, voice stiff from the anger that built inside her. 'There's no use even trying. I can't believe that's who he was all this time. I never saw it. I'm going to build a new council. One made of true representatives of the people, not those like him who don't even give a damn for those they look after. I want people who can guide and inspire me, not those who sneak about and try to upturn me. How can a country thrive off that? And how did my mother not see it?'

Beside her, Gora shrugged, looking simply ahead and offering no real thoughts on that until they'd walked—and in Yoshiko's case, stomped—some distance. 'Depends what they allowed her to see.'

He sounded stressed, and Yoshiko saw the same haggardness when he was exhausted, and a stiffness in his stomach. 'Is it causing you trouble?' She nodded down to his waist where he'd been injured in the battle. He nodded. She understood his fatigue. Her own shoulder still gave her pain and grief, and with his injury being in his side, it would be even more restricting. 'It's been a long day. You need to rest. You need to be well for Nubia's leaving day. Come.'

He sighed and rubbed his neck, following her back up the steps to the top level and the *tenshu* keep where he'd been given rooms and fresh clothing. Yoshiko watched from the corner of her eye as he plodded, energy depleting visibly on the last set of steps. At the cost of his own health, he'd accompanied her all day, making sure he was there for when she met Chinen. She smiled, thinking of how her life had changed.

* * *

The whole domain worked together. It was just as Yoshiko had seen in the time since she left the castle—people helping people. How the council had never seen that amazed her. And now, with their efforts, the region was being put back together. Even the Qeclans continued their massive efforts to help, though Yoshiko had tried to insist they rest—they'd done more than enough.

Soon, the Hién and Qeclan people had repaired the Acrein ships so the Acrein soldiers could return home. With agreements for their people's freedom in place, the Hiéns and Qeclans supplied the Acreins with provisions for their journey and sent them home.

And then, for Nubia and her fellow Qeclans, an Acrein ship was left for them. On their final day in Hié, a convoy escorted the Qeclans to the port, where their ship awaited them.

'Now you can finally go home!' Yoshiko rushed forward to hug her friend.

Nubia wrapped her long arms around her to hug her back. 'Yes, goodbye. And thank you. If not for you, I'd still be on that farm with no hope. Now, I'm determined to bring my people back to our homeland and rebuild. And I can finally try to find my husband.'

'I couldn't have done it without you, though. You kept me sane. If not for you, I'd probably still be burning a hole somewhere in Acrein into the underworld!'

Nubia laughed. 'Yes, you would be!'

Yoshiko pointed to several boxes her convoy was carrying. 'These are gifts from the castle. Thank you for staying with us and helping us. The people of this town worked hard to make these; you and your fellow countryfolk are quite popular here. You will always be welcome back to visit.'

Nubia peered inside one of the boxes, 'Sweets? I shouldn't have expected anything else from you!' She grinned. 'Thank you for looking after us. We will always remember it.'

Yoshiko looked behind Nubia at the Qeclans excitedly rushing about on the ship to prepare for it to leave. Their numbers had also reduced, but she was glad to see many would be able to return. Their eyes had lit once again and large, toothy grins stretched across their faces as they called to one another merrily. Some leaned over the edge, waving to the crowd of Hién people who had gathered to bid their new friends farewell, and Yoshiko grinned with them. As sad as it was to see them leave, their joy was infectious, and she was excited for them.

'I hope you find your husband as you wanted to and that you are able to build a new, great life back in Qecla. Safe journeys. I'll remember you always, and perhaps, if I can, even try to visit. I'd love to see the place you described to me, and maybe one day we can hunt together.'

'I'll even show you my special spear!'

With one final hug, Nubia turned towards the ship. Yoshiko felt a part of her dim as her friend stepped onto the deck, and the Qeclan sailors pushed the ship out to sea. Many Hién people had also come to wave them off, so among this cheerful and thankful crowd, Yoshiko watched until the ship slipped past the horizon. At some point, Gora strode up beside her to watch, too.

'I knew she'd have to leave at some point,' she said to him. 'But I think I was avoiding how much it would hurt.'

Gora tilted his head to the side, thinking. 'True friends don't need to be in the same place. It doesn't matter where you are in the world; you can still look up at the same sky and think of them, knowing they can see that sky, too. I bet she'll also think of you forever—and Haruki. Distance isn't something that can change that, particularly after all we've been through with them.'

His voice was light and lilting again, like it was before their adventure overseas. Gora was relaxed again, and Yoshiko smiled.

She grinned and nudged his arm with her elbow. 'So deep and poetic for such a barbarian as you!'

Gora laughed and his eyes crinkled. 'Hey, I'll have you know I'm a very deep barbarian. There's much beneath this beautiful face.'

They walked back up the town hill to the castle compound, laughing and joking, Yoshiko feeling her mood lighten again. 'I hope so. I'm making you the captain of our new Hién navy, after all. There needs to be some sort of brain in there. And now you have a position to fill in society, you can't just get drunk and hunt.'

Gora shrugged. 'Well, true. I'm sure your other form would be much better at hunting than me. I'd have been out of business if I didn't change jobs.'

'I don't think I'll be turning back into that form anymore. I hope not. Now my people are safe—and the rest will soon be returned home—I don't need it. I'll guide them myself, with my head and with them to help me.' She rubbed the scales on her jaw and paused. 'There's no point risking the future for the sake of being able to use different abilities. Humans have strength enough.'

'They do, indeed,' Gora hummed in agreement, looking about him at the keep, and Yoshiko could tell from the look on his face that he was still unable to believe he was here. She chuckled.

'Things are changing, captain. Get used to it.'

58

To the Future

Change? he wondered, looking about him at the castle scenery. Gora had never been around places so grand. The garden hummed with life and energy, greenness everywhere, and the white Hién *tenshu* keep stretched up elegantly ahead of him.

Since when did he get to such a place? To be allowed to walk around here so freely?

The closest he'd got before was standing on the road beyond the moat, looking over the bridge and peering at it as an outsider. It was a place he and many other citizens would never step foot in. But now his whole future was mapped out ahead of him and so much grander than he could have imagined. *Captain of the new Hién navy? Ocean's Guard?* He liked those titles.

'I understand why you have to go, and give you my full support,' Yoshiko said from beside him as she too paused to look up at the keep, hesitant. Gora wondered whether she still felt unable to believe she was home. A lot had happened since she had to run away, after all. 'Hunting down pirates, trying to end the capture and killing of children, and keeping the seas a little safer is a noble cause. I'm proud Hié can stand alongside you to do it. And I know how important it is to you after everything that happened to you. At the same time, of course I'll be sad you'll not be staying here.' Yoshiko turned and smiled at him. 'Make sure to come back home now and again. When we met, I never could have guessed how much of a friend you'd become. Now, I can't imagine you not being around.'

Gora grinned. 'Of course I'll come back. As Captain of the Ocean's Guard and Hién navy, I'll have to report progress to my daimyō, won't I?' She looked at him and a pink flush washed over her cheeks. Gora knew she still wasn't used to being called that. He teased a little. 'And, true, when we first met, I thought you'd be a snivelling little princess who'd need me to do everything for her. You didn't turn out to be *so* bad.' Yoshiko acted affronted, and he chuckled. 'I'll always come back, and I know you'll do just grand around here. You'll give me something to be impressed with when we first return home, won't ya?'

Yoshiko nodded, and then the pair waved when they were hailed by the group of guards waiting at the main entrance. Among them, Daiki stepped forward to bow and greet them, and Gora saw Ikeda close to his mentor as always. He'd got used to the two being together, and he looked over to see Yoshiko smile at the group. He'd been told the story. In the two short weeks since they'd helped Yoshiko take back the castle, these two had been helping to rebuild and strengthen the Hién guards once again. They'd also become trusted friends to Yoshiko, and he was glad she'd have good people to watch over her when he left.

While Yoshiko was speaking with some of the guards, Daiki stepped over to Gora and asked to speak with him, putting an arm around Gora's shoulder and leading him away a few steps. When Daiki felt comfortable he might be out of earshot, they stopped, and Daiki released his arm from Gora's shoulder and turned to face him. Gora saw his face serious, and Daiki's voice was low.

'I want to come with you. With my family dead, I have been struggling here.' He looked back for a moment at the group speaking behind him, and Gora followed his gaze. Then Daiki looked back. 'I know I can help you on your mission. I have nothing left for me here, and I want to do my best to stop others from suffering what I did. If you're going to stop the pirates and the slave ships, I want to come with you.'

Gora took a moment to process this, taking a deep breath and looking at Daiki's face. His eyes were still shadowed from his mourning. Gora looked over at Yoshiko and Ikeda, the two people he knew would be most impacted by this, before responding. 'And what about your lad? Ikeda goes everywhere with you. He would be sad to see you go.'

'I know he wants to stay by the young daimyō's side. He feels obliged to watch over me, and he has suffered a lot in the last year from what has happened. I am indebted to him for his care. But I can't cause him any more worry. His future is here; he wants to rise in the castle ranks and watch over the lady Yoshiko. Whether he admits it or not, I can see it. He never once gave up on her when we heard she'd gone missing. Even after the rest of us gave up. I can't ask him to give that up to look after an old, jaded man like me.'

Gora sighed and ran a hand through his hair, thinking. He'd hoped Daiki would stay and watch over Yoshiko, knowing Daiki's care and skills. But he understood Daiki's need to redeem himself and how being here could cause him pain. He let a quiet curse word slip from his lips as he looked once again at the group ahead of them in the castle entrance. Yoshiko's eyes were lit up as she spoke with the guards, and Suki had come out to meet them. He smiled. She thrived around people and was always most energetic around others. This was what she needed the whole time. He looked for Ikeda, but the young man was already walking towards them, his face serious and eyes locked on Daiki.

'Ikeda—' Daiki started but was interrupted by the young man.

'I know what you're asking him, and I'll ask the same.' The young samurai turned and bowed to Gora, locking eyes with him once he stood again. 'If Daiki is coming with you, I'll come, too. It's my duty to follow him.'

'Duty?' Gora said, as Daiki spluttered the young man's name once again.

Ikeda ignored them both and waited for a response. Gora rubbed his cheek as he looked at the pair of them, wanting to despair at them both for leaving the person he wanted them to protect behind. 'Ahh, you said he wanted to stay!' He looked impatiently at Daiki, whose brow furrowed, looking just as baffled as Gora felt.

'Ikeda, you have your own goals. You don't need to come with me. I'll be fine.' Daiki's face looked almost pleading, as if he was trying to persuade a child to do the best thing for them.

The look must have softened Ikeda's resolve a little, because he turned to look back at the young daimyō. When he turned back, his eyes looked pained, and Gora knew the young man was struggling with making the decision and what he truly wanted. 'Right now, this is what I need to do. I told you I'd be with you while you were still suffering, and though I believe you won't turn your own blade against yourself again, I know you're not certain of yourself yet. I won't break my word.'

Gora stood to the side, feeling like an onlooker while the mentor and student locked gazes and discussed old promises. He looked away awkwardly, staring around him at the castle grounds and the buildings, noticing the spiralling shape in the roof tiling edging. He saw something new every time he came here. When he felt there'd never be a decision, he turned back to the pair and interrupted their discussion.

'Look, as much as I'd rather you were both here to watch over Yoshiko, I can understand what you're both sayin'. If the lad wants to honour his word, there ain't anything wrong with that. Promises are promises, and right now, I need all the help I can get. We've not got many fighters, and the lad's got skills we could use.' He looked now at Ikeda, whose eyes had widened. 'You don't have to make a permanent decision now. If you want to start with us, I'll agree to that. If on our next visit back here you want to stay, that's fine, too. No need to make hard choices. Do what feels right at the time.'

The young man's face softened, and Gora could tell it was like a weight had been lifted from the young man's face. He looked again at his mentor, and Daiki shrugged.

'I only want what's best for you. If that's what you want to do, of course it's fine.'

Ikeda nodded, and Gora clapped them both on the shoulders and led them back towards the group at the main entrance. Yoshiko was watching them, and he knew she'd have heard everything they said with her cursed hearing. And though she'd be embarrassed to admit she'd listened, Gora felt it would make explaining to her so much easier. 'Let's just get the official permission from the daimyō, first,' he told them, knowing she'd already reached her decision. When he caught her gaze, she smiled and gave a short, single nod.

* * *

On the grand day of the launch of Hié's first navy ship—a huge Acrein warship that was left and had been fixed up, lacquered, and decorated with Hién mastercraft—Gora stood on the deck and watched as the final preparations were made. He looked down at the port to see Yoshiko standing on the docks under a paper parasol to watch Gora and his new crew leave, Suki stood at her side. Suki had been given the new position as Yoshiko's primary maid now that her friend, Haruki, would never return, and Gora felt happy knowing Yoshiko would have someone close to her. Since her role in guiding Yoshiko and the samurai woman Masa into the castle to take it back, Suki had been a kind person at Yoshiko's side, helping take care of Yoshiko's wounds and bring her back to health and get used to castle life once again. She stood now with Yoshiko, eyes carefully flicking from the people around them to her charge. Around the two women was the festival of merriment of the first Hién navy ship launch, and Yoshiko was expected to play her part as the daimyō—to launch and bid his crew fair sailing on their mission to make the seas safer. Gora stomped to Yoshiko's side for a final farewell to the woman who'd become his family.

'Ye'll be alright, lass. No worries. And we'll be back.' He smiled and rested a hand on her head. She looked at him with wide, dark eyes, no doubt worrying about him being so informal in public. But, the softer side of her won, and she smiled.

'And I know you'll be alright. You have two of my best guards with you.' She looked past him at Daiki and Ikeda standing beside the gangway, katanas at their sides, waiting for Gora. 'I'm glad you'll have them with you, though I'll miss all three of you. I'll have to make new friends.'

Gora grinned, telling her he had no doubts that she'd be able to make plenty of new friends. Then, with one final farewell, he bowed to her for the sake of formality and turned on his heels, boots thudding up the gangway. Daiki and Ikeda turned to follow him, and as they reached the deck, Gora saw Ikeda giving the young daimyō one last glance before stepping fully onto the deck and turning away. Gora chuckled to himself, meeting a knowing glance at Daiki and both men shrugging in agreement before Gora called out for his crew to raise the anchor and pull in the gangway. Port workers released the ropes and the great ship pushed gently away, the official start of their new quest.

Standing at the banister, Gora looked out over Hié, taking in the buildings of the main town on the hill, the castle at the centre, and the forest and mountain behind that. His home village, Yamamoto, was out there somewhere, and though he'd already said fond goodbyes to his neighbours, he knew he'd miss them. Then, he looked down at those who'd come to the port to say goodbye. Gora knew he'd make it back here. With a strong crew there to help him—Hién fishingfolk and ex-slaves who wanted to join him on his mission, and a couple of Qeclans who felt unable to return home, knowing they'd have no family to return home to—there would be no way he'd fail to come back.

He watched the dock slip further away and hummed to himself happily as the crew rushed about him to begin their first mission on the open sea. Watching Yoshiko stand on the docks, he heard her head cock as her insanely good hearing picked up his song. She smiled, and to Gora's surprise, Yoshiko tossed her parasol to the ground and ran across the docks and towards the sea, Suki's shock easy to read as she chased after the daimyō, just like the first day they'd met, he'd heard, hand outreaching.

What's she doing? He watched in disbelief as the young daimyō dived into the sea, Suki and her guards running after her and crying out in protest, watching the waters and unable to find her.

But a golden glow in the water told them all where she was, shortly before a navy dragon broke the surface of the water, throwing water droplets all about her, and snaked into the air. Gora laughed and watched the dragon fly towards his ship, diving back into the sea just as she got close. He ran to the other side of the deck, along with many others of his crew, to watch where the dragon might resurface. He saw Ikeda standing not far from him, eyes wide with concern as he leant over the banister to look for her, hand keeping his fringe from his eyes to help him see better. Gora followed the young man's gaze, unable to see where she'd be. Then, a crashing of water came from the bow of the ship, and the dragon leapt back into the air. Gora stared as the blue dragon rose into the sky among the silvery droplets of water, spiralling in the sky above them in a storm of jewels in the evening light. The droplets fell among the crew, sending icy shivers down Gora's back. The crew squealed at the cold, and Yoshiko roared in the skies above them. Gora bellowed with laughter, urging his crew on towards the west, out into the Taiheiyō Ocean and beyond, and Yoshiko returned to the shore.

Sneak Peek of Book 2— Dynasty Codes: Dark Tides

The boy was young when he was stolen from his home. He could never remember how old he'd been, just that he wasn't old enough to have become an apprentice. Where the boy came from, all children became an apprentice in a trade when they turned eleven. He never made it.

He grew up by the sea, in a land known as Eire to the world of trade. He just called it home. Back then, the boy never cared what his country or even his village was called. Had he known back then he would one day be taken from it, he may have paid closer attention. After all, how could the lad have known then how big the world was? Or how he'd never be able to find his way back.

The boy was taken in the dead of night. Boots thudded over the straw-covered mud that made the floor of the stone house more bearable to walk on. Before he'd fully woken, rough hands grabbed at his head and forced his mouth shut. A sack covered his head, blinding him, and he was pulled from the house before he could make a sound. He stumbled along at the fast pace of his captors, tripping over something beneath his bare feet. He heard the rush of the wind and the crash of the ocean against the cliffs, he smelt the sea-air, he stumbled in the sand. Then he heard footsteps thudding on wood, feeling his soles scrape against it. When they finally uncovered the boy's face, he saw the inside of a ship. That's all he saw for a couple of days, other than two other children stowed away with him. Not from his village, but he thought he recognised the boy from the next village along the cliffs. The girl, he'd never seen before.

The children weren't allowed on deck until the ship was long out at sea. There was no hope to squint into the distance and try to recognise the shape of the land to one day identify it as their long-lost home.

Only a few days after they'd been taken, the girl was pulled from their stowing place and taken elsewhere on the ship. She died, screaming. She screamed a lot that night. Sometimes it was muffled, sometimes not. The boy didn't know how or why or where at the time. He could just hear the screams. It would scar him forever. When the screaming stopped suddenly, the lad held his breath and waited. A splash. He knew her body had been thrown overboard.

A soul for the great sea witch.

The other boy died days afterwards. He went pale and grey and thin and looked like the ghouls from the scary folk tales the people from the lad's village tried to scare children with to get them to behave. He tried not to think about those scary stories. Instead, he guessed the other boy hadn't taken to the conditions of life on the ship or had eaten bad food. He knew some folks didn't handle change well, especially when the change had been that forced. Years later, he'd learn the other boy's condition had been more like the scary folk tales.

Another soul for the great sea witch.

He didn't ask what had happened to either of the other kids. He learned early on that if you ask questions, you get beaten. He'd learned that the hard way—the same way he learned scars never faded and acted as lessons for the future.

The young boy slaved on the pirate ship for so long that he lost track of how much time had passed. The days were strange out at sea, and sometimes he didn't even go up into the light or into the dark, depending on shifts. Like that, a long time passed. His body grew less frail and weak. It became less easy to man-handle and the pirates knew that. It was time to move him on—to sell him, get the money, and start again.

The boy, likely well in his teen years then, was moved onto a different ship. One just as vile and from the same pirate group.

This one had room for a lad his age, and they were just as ready to beat submission into him and make sure the questions were kept beaten out of him. They'd killed the previous youngster this way—too fierce with a punishment. Someone died, you got them replaced. He knew it would be the same if he died. He'd just be another soul sent to the sea witch. So, he refused to die. The lad knew within days on that godforsaken ship that he wouldn't die on it, just like he knew he wouldn't die on the last one.

His soul was his.

Another soul for the great sea witch ...

Glossary

Akuma—A type of *yōkai*. Malevolent fire spirit, often translated to demon.

Daimyō—Powerful magnates and feudal lords who control regions of land. Subordinates/vassals to the shōgun.

Futon—Traditional bedding used on the floor. A complete set comes with a mattress and a duvet, both thin enough to fold away to allow space in the day and to hang out to air for regular cleaning.

Genkan—Entryway areas in traditional homes. By the front door, it is often at a lower level than the main house, used for the removing of outdoor shoes and swapping for indoor shoes before entering the main house.

Genmaicha—Roasted brown rice green tea.

Hakama—Loose, traditional trousers with pleats in the front, worn by the samurai class. Tied at the waist and fall to the ankles. Worn over the kimono.

Haori—Traditional loose-fit jacket, often hip- or thigh-length, worn over a kimono.

Harumatsuri—Translates to 'spring festival'.

Hyoutan—AKA gourd. Used as a drinking vessel. The gourd is left on the vine longer than should one want to eat it. It is then dried and ovened to become durable and waterproof.

Imo—Sweet potato.

Jikatabi—A traditional style of footwear with a divided toe. Similar to tabi socks, but are worn as boots.

Kanzashi—Traditional hair ornaments with folded paper flowers as decoration. In this case, the book refers to the hairpin style.

Karamété-mon—One of the castle ground gates. *Karamété-mon* gate is located at the back of the castle.

Katana—A long, single-edged sword with a curved edge used by the samurai. Used with two hands. Worn with the curved blade facing upwards. Paired with a *tanto*.

Kitsuné—A type of *yōkai* (animal type) from traditional folklore. Intelligent fox-like spirits with paranormal abilities. Can have up to nine tails.

Kiyohimé—A princess of old folklore who fell in love with a monk when he stayed at her house for a night while on pilgrimage, with the promise of marriage when he returned. When he returned, he snuck past her house, and Kiyohimé learned he had no intention of marrying her. Feeling betrayed, she transformed into a demonic dragon and incinerated him in her fury, killing herself in the river shortly afterwards.

Naginata—A traditional halberd-like weapon with a one- to two-foot curved blade at the end. Often used by *onna-bugeisha* (women warriors) of the noble sumarai class, footsoldiers, or sōhei (warrior monks).

Omatsuri/matsuri—Traditional festivals. Each has a meaning and are close to spiritual events. Popular are summer matsuri, various lantern matsuri, and a snow festival in the northern island.

Oni—A type of *yōkai*. Often the larger demon type—ogre or troll—with one or two horns coming out of their heads, known for fierce and evil natures.

Oté-mon—One of the castle ground gates. *Oté-mon* gate is located at the front of the castle.

Samurai—The hereditary nobility and warrior caste in the feudal era, serving under the daimyō and shōgun. Military retainers of the daimyō, practicing the conduct of Bushido (the way of the warrior).

Satsuma-imo—Japanese orange sweet potato.

Shōgun—The hereditary military ruler during the feudal era. Appointed by the emperor, a shōgun was a de facto ruler, often with more power than the emperors themselves due to the feudal period.

Tanto—A traditional T-shaped wrapped-front garment with square sleeves and a long, rectangular body. Ankle length. Worn daily.

Tatami—Woven straw mats used as flooring in traditional rooms.

Tenshu—The highest tower (main keep) within the castle grounds and symbolic of the castle.

Wabi-sabi—In traditional aesthetics, wabi-sabi describes the beauty of the imperfect, impermanent, or incomplete.

Yōkai—Supernatural creatures and spirits of traditional folklore. Encompasses monsters and pure supernatural beings, including fairies, demons, ghosts, animal creatures.

Youkan—Traditional jelly-like confection. Often made with *anko* (red bean paste) and solidified with *kanten* (agar).

Zori—Traditional flat, thonged sandal made of rice straw, cloth, lacquered wood, or leather.